The Great Fortune

Olivia Manning, OBE, was born in
Portsmouth, Hampshire, spent much of her
youth in Ireland and, as she put it, had 'the
usual Anglo–Irish sense of belonging
nowhere'. She married just before World
War II and went abroad with her husband,
R.D. Smith, a British Council lecturer in
Bucharest. Her experiences there formed
the basis of the work which makes up *The
Balkan Trilogy*. As the Germans
approached Athens, she and her husband
evacuated to Egypt and ended up in
Jerusalem, where her husband was put in
charge of the Palestine Broadcasting
Station. They returned to London in 1946
and lived there until her death in 1980.

D1343384

C015030235

Also by Olivia Manning

Novels
Artist Among the Missing
School for Love*
A Different Face
The Doves of Venus*
The Play Room
The Rain Forest*

*The Balkan Trilogy**
   The Great Fortune*
   The Spoilt City*
   Friends and Heroes*

The Levant Trilogy
   The Danger Tree
   The Battle Lost and Won
   The Sum of Things

Short Stories
Growing Up
A Romantic Hero

* *available from*
  Mandarin Paperbacks

OLIVIA MANNING

The
Great Fortune

Mandarin

A Mandarin Paperback
THE GREAT FORTUNE

First published in Great Britain 1960
This edition published 1994
by Mandarin Paperbacks
an imprint of Reed Consumer Books Ltd
Michelin House, 81 Fulham Road, London SW3 6RB
and Auckland, Melbourne, Singapore and Toronto

Copyright © the Estate of Olivia Manning 1960

A CIP catalogue record for this title
is available from the British Library
ISBN 0 7493 1762 0

Printed and bound by Firmin-Didot (France),
Group Herissey. No d'impression : 31141.

This book is sold subject to the condition
that it shall not, by way of trade or otherwise,
be lent, resold, hired out, or otherwise circulated
without the publisher's prior consent in any form
of binding or cover other than that in which
it is published and without a similar condition
including this condition being imposed
on the subsequent purchaser.

To
Johnny and Jerry Slattery

Contents

PART ONE

The Assassination

1

SOMEWHERE NEAR VENICE, Guy began talking with a heavy, elderly man, a refugee from Germany on his way to Trieste. Guy asked questions. The refugee eagerly replied. Neither seemed aware when the train stopped. In the confusion of a newly created war, the train was stopping every twenty minutes or so. Harriet looked out and saw girders, darker than the twilit darkness, holding an upper rail. Between the girders a couple fumbled and struggled, every now and then thrusting a foot or an elbow out into the light that fell from the carriage windows. Beyond the girders water glinted, reflecting the phosphorescent globes lighting the high rail.

When the train was suddenly shunted into the night, leaving behind the lovers and the glinting water, she thought: 'Anything can happen now.'

Guy and the refugee went on talking across the carriage, their eyes fixed upon each other. Guy's sympathy had drawn the German half out of his seat. He held out his hands, cupped, palms up, side by side, occasionally shaking them for emphasis, while Guy gave him an anxious attention that lightened into excitement as he nodded his head, indicating that all he heard was exactly what he had expected to hear.

"What is he saying?" asked Harriet, who did not speak German.

Guy put a hand on hers to keep her quiet.

A current, like affection, seemed to keep Guy's attention directed on the refugee, but the refugee several times stared about him at the other passengers, with an aggressive confidence, as though to say: 'I am talking? Well what about it? I am a free man.'

The train stopped again: a ticket collector came round. The refugee rose and felt in an inner pocket of his greatcoat that hung beside him. His hand lingered, he caught his breath: he withdrew his hand and looked in an outer pocket. This time he withdrew his hand quickly and looked in another pocket, then another and another. He began pulling things out of the pockets of the jacket he was wearing, then out of his trouser pockets. His breath came and went violently. He returned to the greatcoat and began his search all over again.

Guy and Harriet Pringle, watching him, were dismayed. His face had become ashen, his cheeks fallen like the cheeks of a very old man. As he grew hot with the effort of his search, a sticky dampness spread over his skin and his hands shook. When he started again on his jacket, his head was trembling and his eyes darting about.

"What is it?" Guy asked. "What have you lost?"

"Everything. Everything."

"Your ticket?"

"Yes," the man panted between words. "My pocket-book, my passport, my money, my identity card . . . My visa, my visa!" His voice broke on the last word. He stopped searching and tried to pull himself together. He clenched his hands, then shook one out in disbelief of his loss.

"What about the lining?" said Harriet. "The things may have fallen through into the lining."

Guy did his best to translate this.

The man turned on him, almost sobbing as he was beset by this suggestion. He understood at last and started feeling wildly over the coat lining. He found nothing.

The other passengers had been watching him with detached interest while the collector took their tickets. When everyone else had handed over a ticket, the collector turned to him as though the scene had conveyed nothing at all.

Guy explained to the man that the refugee had lost his ticket. Several other people in the carriage murmured confirmation. The collector looked dumbly back at some officials who stood in the corridor. They took over. One remained at the carriage door while the other went off for reinforcements.

"He's penniless, too," said Guy to his wife. "What can we give him?"

They were on their way to Bucharest. Not being permitted to take money into Rumania, they had very little with them. Harriet brought out a thousand-franc note. Guy had three English pound notes. When offered this money, the refugee could not give it his attention. He was absorbed again in looking through his pockets as though the pocket-book might in the interval have reappeared. He seemed unaware of the group of officials now arrived at the door. When one touched his arm, he turned impatiently. He was required to go with them.

He took down his coat and luggage. His colour was normal now, his face expressionless. When Guy held the money out to him, he accepted it blankly, without a word.

After he had been led away, Guy said: "What will become of him?" He looked worried and helpless, frowning like a good-tempered child whose toy has been stolen out of its hands.

Harriet shook her head. No one could answer him. No one tried.

The day before had been spent on familiar territory, even if the Orient Express had kept to no schedule. Harriet had watched the vineyards pass in the late summer sunlight. Balls of greasy sandwich paper had unscrewed themselves in the heat, empty Vichy bottles rolled about under seats. When the train stopped, there was no sign of a station-master, no porters came to the windows. On the deserted platform, loud-speakers gave out the numbers of reservists being called to their regiments. The monotony of the announcer's voice had the quality of silence. It was possible to hear through it the hum of bees, the chirrupings of birds. The little squeak of the guard's trumpet came from a great distance, like a noise from the waking world intruding upon sleep. The train, gathering itself together, moved on for a few more miles and stopped again to the voice of the same announcer giving the numbers without comment.

In France they were among friends. Italy, which they crossed next day, seemed the end of the known world. When they awoke next morning, they were on the Slovenian plain. All day its monotonous cultivation, its fawn-coloured grainland and fields with hay-cocks, passed under a heavy sky. Every half mile or so there was a peasant hut, the size of a tool shed, with a vegetable garden and beds of great, flat-faced sun-flowers. At each station the peasants stood like the blind. Harriet attempted a smile at one of them: there was no response. The lean face remained as before, weathered and withered into a fixed desolation.

Guy, who was doing this journey for the second time, gave his attention to his books. He was too short-sighted to make much of the passing landscape, and he had to prepare his lectures. He was employed in the English Department of the University of Bucharest, where he had already spent a year. He had met and married Harriet during his summer holiday.

With only enough money left to pay for one meal, Harriet had chosen that the meal should be supper. As the day passed without breakfast, luncheon or tea, hunger lay bleakly over the Slovenian plain. Twilight fell, then darkness, then, at last, the waiter came tinkling his little bell again. The Pringles were first in the dining-car. There everything was normal, the food good, but before the meal ended the head waiter began to behave like a man in a panic. Baskets of fruit had been placed on the tables. He brushed them aside to tot up the bills, for which he demanded immediate payment. The charge, which was high, included coffee. When someone demanded coffee, he said "Later", throwing down change and hurrying on. One diner said he would not pay until coffee was served. The head waiter replied that no coffee would be served until all had paid. He kept an eye on those who had still to pay as though fearing they might make off before he reached them.

In the end, all paid. The train stopped. It had reached the frontier. Coffee was served, too hot to drink, and at the same time an official appeared and ordered everyone out of the car, which was about to be detached from the train. One man gulped at his coffee, gave a howl and threw down his cup. Several wanted to know why the car was being detached. A waiter explained that the car belonged to the Yugoslav railways and no sane country would permit its rolling-stock to cross a frontier in these hazardous times. The passengers were thrust out, all raging together in half-a-dozen languages, the war forgotten.

The frontier officials made a leisurely trip down the corridor. When that was over, the train stood on the small station, where the air, pouring cold and autumnal through open windows, smelt of straw.

Guy, in their compartment, which had now been arranged as a sleeping compartment, was still writing in his notebook. Harriet, at a corridor window, was trying to see something of the frontier village. She could not even be sure there was a village. The darkness seemed as empty as outer space, yet, blazing like a sun in the midst of it, there was a fair-ground. Not a sound came from it. A wheel moved slowly, bearing up into the sky empty carriages shaped like boats.

Immediately outside the window there was a platform lit by three weak, yellow bulbs strung on a wire. Beneath the furthest of these was a group of people – a tall man, unusually thin, with a long coat trailing from one shoulder as from a door-knob, surrounded by five small men in uniform. They were persuading him along. He seemed, in their midst, bewildered like some long, timid animal harried by terriers. Every few yards he paused to remonstrate with them and they, circling about him and gesticulating, edged him on until he reached the carriage from which Harriet was watching. He was carrying in one hand a crocodile dressing-case, in the other a British passport. One of the five men was a porter who carried two large suitcases.

"Yakimov," the tall man kept repeating, "Prince Yakimov. *Gospodin*," he suddenly wailed, "*gospodin*."

At this they gathered round him, reassuring him with "*Da, da*," and "*Dobo, gospodin*". His long, odd face was sad and resigned as he let himself be impelled towards the front of the train. There he was urged into a carriage as though at any moment the express would move.

The uniformed men dispersed. The platform emptied. The train remained where it was another half-an-hour, then slowly puffed its way across the frontier.

When the Rumanian officials came on board there was a change of atmosphere in the corridors. The Rumanian passengers were now in the majority. Stout, little Rumanian women, not noticeable before, pushed their way through the *wagon-lit* chattering in French. There was a general air of congratulation that they were safely within their own country. They gave little squeals of excitement as they chatted to the officials and the officials smiled down on them indulgently. When Guy emerged with the passports, one of the women recognised him as the *professor* who taught her son English. He answered her in Rumanian and the women crowded about him admiring his fluency and his pronunciation.

"But you are perfect," said one woman.

Guy, flushed by the attention he was receiving, made a reply in Rumanian that set them all squealing again.

Harriet, not understanding what he had said, smiled at the fun, pretending to be part of it. She observed how, in his response, Guy looked a little drunk and put out his arms to these unknown women as though he would embrace them all.

The Pringles had been married less than a week. Though she would have claimed to know about him everything there was to be known, she was now beginning to wonder if she really knew anything.

When the train got under way, the women dispersed. Guy returned to his bunk. Harriet remained a while at the window, watching the mountains rise and grow, ebony against the dim and starless sky. A pine forest came down to the edge of the track: the light from the carriages rippled over the bordering trees. As she gazed out into the dark heart of the forest, she began to see small moving lights. For an instant a grey dog-shape skirted the rail, then returned to darkness. The lights, she realised, were the eyes of beasts. She drew her head in and closed the window.

Guy looked up as she joined him and said: "What's the matter?" He took her hands, saw they were shrunken with cold and rubbed them between his hands: "Little monkey's paws," he said. As his warmth passed into her, she said: "I love you," which was something she had not admitted before.

The moment seemed to her one that should expand into rapture, but Guy took it lightly. He said: "I know," and, giving her fingers a parting squeeze, he released them and returned his attention to his book.

2

ON REACHING THE MAIN STATION at Bucharest, Yakimov
carried his luggage to the luggage office. He held a suitcase in each
hand and his crocodile dressing-case hoisted up under his right
elbow. His sable-lined greatcoat hung from his left arm. The
porters – there were about a dozen to each passenger – followed
him aghast. He might have been mobbed had not his vague, gentle
gaze, ranging over their heads from his unusual height, given the
impression he was out of reach.

When the dressing-case slipped, one of the porters snatched at
it. Yakimov dodged him with a skilled sidestep, then wandered on,
his shoulders drooping, his coat sweeping the dirty platform, his
check suit and yellow cardigan sagging and fluttering as though
carried on a coat-hanger. His shirt, changed on the train, was
clean. His other clothes were not. His tie, bought for him years
before by Dollie, who had admired its 'angelic blue', was now so
blotched and be-yellowed by spilt food. it was no colour at all.
His head, with its thin, pale hair, its nose that, long and delicate,
widened suddenly at the nostrils, its thin clown's mouth, was remote and mild as the head of a giraffe. On top of it he wore a
shabby check cap. His whole sad aspect was made sadder by the
fact that he had not eaten for forty-eight hours.

He deposited the two suitcases. The crocodile case, that held,
among his unwashed nightwear, a British passport and a receipt
for his Hispano-Suiza, he kept with him. When the car had been
impounded for debt by the Yugoslav officials at the frontier, he
had had on him just enough to buy a third class ticket to Bucharest.
This purchase left him with a few pieces of small change.

He emerged from the station into the confusion of a street
market where flares were being lit in the first fall of twilight. He
had shaken off the porters. Beggars now crowded about him.
Feeling in the air the first freshness of autumn, he decided to wear
rather than carry his coat. Holding his case out of reach of the
ragged children round his knees, he managed to shuffle first one
arm and then the other into the coat.

He looked about him. Hounded (his own word) out of one capital after another, he had now reached the edge of Europe, a region in which he already smelt the Orient. Each time he arrived at a new capital, he made for the British Legation, where he usually found some figure from his past. Here, he had heard, the Cultural Attaché was known to him; was, indeed, indebted, having come to one of those opulent parties Dollie and he had given in the old days. It occurred to him that if he drove to the Legation in a taxi, Dobson might pay for it. But if Dobson had been posted and there was no one willing to pay, he would be at the mercy of the taxi-driver. For the first time in his life he hesitated to take a risk. Standing amid the babble of beggars, his coat hanging like a bell-tent from the apex of his neck, he sighed to himself and thought: 'Your poor old Yaki's not the boy he was.'

Seeing him there, one driver threw open the door of his cab. Yakimov shook his head. In Italian, a language he had been told was the same as Rumanian, he asked to be directed to the British Legation. The driver waved him to get in. When Yakimov shook his head a second time, the man gave a snarl of disgust and began to pick his teeth.

Yakimov persisted: "*La legazione britannica, per piacere?*"

To get rid of him, the man flicked a hand over his shoulder.

"*Grazie tanto*, dear boy." Gathering his coat about him, Yakimov turned and followed a street that seemed a tunnel into desolation.

The light was failing. He was beginning to doubt his direction when, at a junction of roads, it seemed confirmed by a statue, in boyar's robes, wearing a turban the size of a pumpkin, that pointed him dramatically to the right.

Here the city had come to life again. The pavements were crowded with small men, all much alike in shabby city clothes, each carrying a brief-case. Yakimov recognised them for what they were; minor government officials and poor clerks, a generation struggling out of the peasantry, at work from eight in the morning until eight at night, now hurrying home to supper. In his hunger, he envied them. A tramway car stopped at the kerb. As the crowd pressed past him, he was buffeted mercilessly from side to side, but maintained his course, his head and shoulders rising above the surge with an appearance of unconcern.

He stopped at a window displaying jars of a jam-like substance that held in suspension transparent peaches and apricots. The light shone through them. This golden, sugared fruit, glowing through the chill blue twilight, brought a tear to his eye. He was pushed on roughly by a woman using a shopping basket as a weapon.

He crossed the road junction. Tramway cars, hung with passengers like swarming bees, clanged and shrilled upon him. He reached the other side. Here as he followed a down-sloping road, the crowd thinned and changed. He passed peasants in their country dress of whitish frieze, thin men, lethargic, down-staring, beneath pointed astrakhan caps, and Orthodox Jews with ringlets hanging on either side of greenish, indoor faces.

A wind, blowing up towards Yakimov, brought a rancid odour that settled in his throat like the first intimations of sea-sickness. He began to feel worried. These small shops did not promise the approach of the British Legation.

The street divided into smaller streets. Keeping to the widest of them, Yakimov saw in every window the minutiae of the tailoring trade – horse-hair, buckram, braid, ready-made pockets, clips, waistcoat buckles, cards of buttons, reels of cotton, rolls of lining. Who on earth wanted all this stuff? In search of even the sight of food, he turned into a passage-way where the stench of the district was muffled for a space by the odour of steam-heated cloth. Here, in gas-lit rooms no bigger than cupboards, moving behind bleared windows like sea creatures in tanks, coatless men thumped their irons and filled the air with hissing fog. The passage ended in a little box of a square so congested with basket-work that the creepers swathed about the balconies seemed to sprout from the wicker jungle below. A man leaning against the single lamp-post straightened himself, threw away his cigarette and began talking to Yakimov, pointing to bassinets, dress-baskets and bird-cages.

Yakimov enquired for the British Legation. For reply the man hauled out a dozen shopping-baskets tied with string and started to untie them. Yakimov slipped away down another passage that brought him, abruptly, to the quayside of a river. This was more hopeful. A river usually indicated a city's centre, but when he went to the single rusted rail that edged the quay, he looked down on a wretched soapy-coloured stream trickling between steep, raw banks of clay. On either bank stood houses of a dilapidated elegance. Here and there he saw windows masked with the harem grilles of the receded Ottoman Empire. A little paint still clung to the plaster, showing, where touched by the street lights, pallid grey or a red the colour of dried blood.

On Yakimov's side of the river, the ground floors had been converted into shops and cafés. China lettering on windows said 'Restaurantul' and 'Cafea'. At the first doorway, where the bead curtain was looped up to invite entry, he endured the sight of a man sucking-in soup from a bowl – onion soup. Strings of melted cheese hung from the spoon, a pollen of cheese and broken toast lay on the soup's surface.

He moved on. The interiors were full of speckled mirrors, rough chairs, and tables with dirty paper covers. An oily smell of cooking came from them. Again he was conscious that he had changed. In the past, often enough, he had eaten his fill, then somehow explained away his inability to pay. In different parts of the town, he might still attempt it: here he was afraid.

As he sidled from doorway to doorway, there suddenly came to him the rich scent of roasting meat. Saliva sprang into his mouth. He was drawn towards the scent, which came from a brazier where a peasant was cooking small pads of meat. The peasant customers, lit by a single flare, stood at a respectful distance, staring at the meat or occasionally turning to look at each other in a nervous, unsmiling intensity of anticipation. The cook seemed conscious of his superior position. He offered the meat with an air of bestowing it. He whose turn it was glanced about uncertainly before taking it and, when he had paid with a small coin, slipped away to eat in the shadows, alone.

After Yakimov had watched this exchange take place half a dozen times, he took the coins from his pocket and spread them on his palm. They comprised of a few *lire*, *filler* and *para*. The cook, to whom he presented them, examined them closely then picked out the largest of the Hungarian coins. He handed Yakimov a piece of meat. Like the others, Yakimov went aside to eat. The savour unbalanced him. He swallowed too quickly. For an ecstatic moment the meat was there, then it was gone. Nothing remained but a taste lingering about his neglected teeth, so honeysweet it gave him heart to ask his way again.

He returned to the brazier and spoke to a peasant who looked a little more alert than the others. The man did not answer or meet his eyes but, hanging his head, glanced from side to side as though at a loss to account for the noise he heard. A little dark gypsy of a fellow came bustling up and, pushing the peasant contemptuously aside, asked in English: "What is it you are wanting?"

"I am looking for the British Legation."

"Not here. Not anywhere here."

"But where?"

"A long way. It is necessary to find a conveyance."

"Tell me the way. I can walk."

"No, no. Too far. Too difficult." Dropping Yakimov abruptly, the gypsy went across to the other side of the brazier, where he stood looking resentfully across at him.

Yakimov was growing tired. His coat hung hot and heavy on his shoulders. He wondered if he could find some sort of lodging for the night, making his usual promise to pay next day.

As he went on, the quayside widened into an open cobbled space where a gritty wind sprang up and blew feathers into his face. On the further side, near a main road, stood several crates packed with live fowl. This, he realised, was a chicken market, the source of the pervading stench.

He crossed to the crates and took down one so that the others formed a seat. He sat protected by the crates behind him. The hens, stringy Balkan birds, stirred and cackled a while, then slept again. From somewhere in the market a clock struck nine. He had been wandering about for two hours or more. He sighed. His fragile body had become too heavy to move. Wedging his case out of sight between the crates, he drew up his feet, put down his head and slept.

When awakened by the long scream of a braking car, he murmured: "Unholy hour, dear boy", and tried to turn round. His knees struck the wire of the coop behind him. The cramp in his limbs forced him to full consciousness. He scrambled up to see what vehicles could be passing, so erratically and in such profusion when it was barely daylight. He saw a procession of mud-caked lorries swerving and swaying on the crown of the road. One lorry dipped towards the kerb, causing him to jump back in alarm. As it straightened and went on, he gazed after it, shocked, the more so because he himself drove with inspired skill.

Behind the lorries came a string of private cars – a seemingly endless string: all the same mud-grey, all oddly swollen in shape, the result, Yakimov realised, of their being padded top and sides with mattresses. The windscreens were cracked. The bonnets and wings were pockmarked. Inside the cars, the passengers – men, women and children – lay about, abandoned in sleep. The drivers nodded over the steering-wheels.

Who could they be? Where had they come from? Aching, famished, racked by the light of this unfamiliar hour, Yakimov did not try to answer his questions. But the destination of the cars? Looking where they were heading, he saw tall, concrete buildings evolving pearly out of the pinks and blues of dawn. Beacons of civilisation. He followed the road towards them.

After walking a couple of miles, he reached the main square as the sun, rising above the roof-tops, flecked the cobblestones. A statue, heavily planted on a horse too big for it, saluted the long, grey front of what must be the royal palace. At either end of the palace workmen had started screwing pieces of pre-fabricated classical façade on to scaffolding. The rest of the square was, apparently, being demolished. He crossed to the sunlit side where a white, modern building proclaimed itself the Athénée Palace Hotel. Here the leading cars had come to rest. Only a few of the occupants had roused themselves. The rest slept on, their faces ashen and grim. Some of them had roughly bandaged wounds. In one car, Yakimov noticed, the grey upholstery was soaked with blood.

He pushed through the hotel's revolving door into a marble hall lit brilliantly with glass chandeliers. As he entered, his name was called aloud: "*Yakimov!*"

He started back. He had not received this sort of welcome for many a day. He was the more suspicious when he saw it came from a journalist called McCann, who when they met in the bars of Budapest had usually turned his back. McCann was propped up on a long sofa just inside the vestibule, while a man in a black suit was cutting away the blood-soaked shirt-sleeve which stuck to his right arm. Yakimov felt enough concern to approach the sofa and ask: "What has happened, dear boy? Can I do anything to help?"

"You certainly can. For the last half-hour I've been telling these dumb clucks to find me a bloke who can speak English."

Yakimov would have been glad to sink down beside McCann, feeling himself as weak as any wounded man, but the other end of the sofa was occupied by a girl, a dark beauty, haggard and very dirty, who sprawled there asleep.

Leaning forward in an attitude of sympathetic enquiry, he hoped McCann would not want much of him.

"It's this!" McCann's left hand dug clumsily about in the jacket that lay behind him. "Here!" – he produced some sheets torn from a notebook – "Get this out for me. It's the whole story."

"Really, dear boy! What story?"

"Why, the break-up of Poland; surrender of Gdynia; flight of the Government; the German advance on Warsaw; the refugees streaming out, me with them. Cars machine-gunned from the air; men, women and children wounded and killed; the dead buried by the roadside. Magnificent stuff; first hand; must get it out while it's hot. Here, take it."

"But how do I get it out?" Yakimov was almost put to flight by the prospect of such an arduous employment.

"Ring our agency in Geneva, dictate it over the line. A child could do it."

"Impossible, dear boy. Haven't a bean."

"Reverse the charges."

"Oh, they'd never let me" – Yakimov backed away – "I'm not known here. I don't speak the language. I'm a refugee like yourself."

"Where from?"

Before Yakimov had time to answer his question, a man thrust in through the doors, moving all his limbs with the unnatural fervour of exhaustion. He rushed at McCann. "Where, please," he asked, "is the man with red hairs in your car?"

"Dead," said McCann.

"Where, please, then, is the scarf I lent to him? The big, blue scarf?"

"God knows. I'd guess it's underground. We buried him the other side of Lublin, if you want to go back and look."

"You buried the scarf? Are you mad that you buried the scarf?"

"Oh, go away!" shouted McCann, at which the man ran to the wall opposite and beat on it with his fists.

Taking advantage of this diversion, Yakimov began to move off. McCann seized a fold of his coat and gave a howl of rage: "For God's sake! Come back, you bastard. Here I am with this arm gone, a bullet in my ribs, not allowed to move – and here's this story! You've got to send it, d'you hear me? You've got to."

Yakimov moaned: "Haven't had a bite for three days. Your poor old Yaki's faint. His feet are killing him."

"Wait!" Pushing impatiently about in his coat again, McCann brought out his journalist's card. "Take this. You can eat here. Get yourself a drink. Get yourself a bed. Get what you damned well like – but first, 'phone this stuff through."

Taking the card and seeing on it the picture of McCann's lined and crumpled face, Yakimov was slowly revivified by the possibilities of the situation. "You mean they'll give me credit?"

"Infinite credit. The paper says. Work for me, you dopey duck, and you can booze and stuff to your heart's content."

"Dear boy!" breathed Yakimov; he smiled with docile sweetness. "Explain again, *rather* slowly, just what you want poor Yaki to do."

3

The Pringles settled into a small hotel in the square, on the side opposite the Athénée Palace. Their window looked out on to ruins. That day, the day after their arrival, they had been awakened at sunrise by the fall of masonry. At evening, as Harriet watched for Guy's return, she saw the figures of workmen, black and imp-small in the dusk, carrying flares about the broken buildings.

These buildings had been almost the last of the Biedermeier prettiness bestowed on Bucharest by Austria. The King, who planned a square where, dared he ever venture out so openly, he might review a regiment, had ordered that the demolitions be completed before winter.

Harriet had spent most of her day watching from the window. Though the university term had not started, Guy had set out that morning to see if there were any students in the common-room. He had promised to take Harriet out after luncheon but had returned late, his face aglow, and said he must eat quickly and hurry back. The students had been crowding in all morning eager for news of their English teachers and the term's work.

"But, darling" – Harriet, still filled with the faith and forbearance of the newly married, spoke only with regret – "couldn't you wait until Professor Inchcape arrives?"

"One must never discourage students," said Guy and he hurried off, promising to take her that evening to dine "up the Chaussée".

During the afternoon the receptionist rang through three times to say a lady wished to speak to Domnul Pringle. "The same lady?" Harriet asked the third time. Yes, the same lady.

When, at sunset, Guy's figure appeared in the square, Harriet's forbearance was not what it had been. She watched him emerge out of a blur of dust – a large, untidy man clutching an armful of books and papers with the awkwardness of a bear. A piece of pediment crashed before him. He paused, blinded; peered about through his glasses and started off in the wrong direction. She felt an appalled compassion for him. Where he had been a moment before, a wall came down. Its fall revealed the interior of a vast white room, fretted with baroque scrolls and set with a mirror that glimmered like a lake. Nearby could be seen the red wallpaper of a café – the famous Café Napoleon that had been the meeting-place of artists, musicians, poets and other natural non-conformists. Guy had said that all this destruction had been planned simply to wipe out this one centre of revolt.

Entering the hotel room, Guy threw down his armful of papers. With a casualness that denoted drama, he announced: "The Russians have occupied Vilna." He set about changing his shirt.

"You mean, they're inside Poland?" asked Harriet.

"A good move." Her tone had set him on the defensive. "A move to protect Poland."

"A good excuse, anyway."

The telephone rang and Guy jumped at it before anything more could be said: "Inchcape!" he called delightedly and without consulting Harriet added: "We're dining up the Chaussée. Pavel's. Come and join us." He put down the receiver and, pulling a shirt over his head without undoing the buttons, he said: "You'll like Inchcape. All you need do with him is encourage him to talk."

Harriet, who never believed she would like anyone she did not know, said: "Someone rang you three times this afternoon. A woman."

"Really!" The information did not disconcert him. He merely said: "People here are crazy about the telephone. It hasn't been installed long. Women with nothing better to do ring up complete strangers and say: 'Allo! Who are you? Let us have a nice little flirt.' I'm always getting them."

"I don't think a stranger would ring three times."

"Perhaps not. Whoever it was, she'll ring again."

As they left the room, the telephone did ring again. Guy hurried back to it. Harriet, on the stairs, heard him say: "Why, Sophie!" and she went down. Turning a corner, she saw the hall below crowded with people. All the hotel guests and servants were gathered there, moving about talking excitedly. Behind the reception desk the wireless, like a mechanical bird, was whirring in the persistent, nerve-racking music of the Rumanian *hora*. Harriet came to a stop, feeling in the air the twang of anxiety. When Guy caught her up, she said: "I think something has happened."

Guy went to the manager, who attended him with deference. The English were important in Bucharest. England had guaranteed Rumanian safety. Guy was told that foreign troops were massing on the frontier.

"What part of the frontier?" he asked.

That was not known: nor was it known whether the troops were German or Russian. The King was about to broadcast from his apartments and it was believed that at any moment general mobilisation would be ordered.

Moved by the stress of the occasion, the Pringles waited to hear the King. The mechanical bird stopped. In the abrupt silence, voices that had been bawling to be heard above the din now trickled self-consciously away. The wireless announced that the King would address his subjects in Rumanian.

At that. a man in a cape, too stout to turn only his head, turned his whole body and surveyed the gathering with an air of enquiring innocence. "*Sans doute l'émission est en retard parce que sa Majesté s'instruit dans la langue.*"

There was a laugh, but a brief one, an instant extracted from fear, then the faces were taut again. The group waited; a collection of drawn yellow-skinned men and heavily powdered women with dark eyes fixed on the wireless set, from which the King's voice came suddenly out of long silence. The audience bent expectantly forward, then began shifting and complaining that it could not understand his broken Rumanian. Guy did his best to translate the speech for Harriet:

"If we are attacked, we will defend our country to the last man. We will defend it to the last foot of soil. We have learned from Poland's mistakes. Rumania will never suffer defeat. Her strength will be formidable."

A few people nodded their heads and one repeated: "*Formidabil, eh! Formidabil!*", but several of the others looked furtively about fearing an enemy might mistake these words for provocation. The man in the cape turned again, screwing up his large, flexible, putty-coloured face and spreading his hands as though to say 'And now you know!' but the others were not so responsive. This was no time for humour. Giving Guy the smile of a fellow conspirator he strode away and Guy, flushed like a schoolboy, whispered that that had been an actor from the National Theatre.

The Pringles left by a side door that opened on to the Calea

Victoriei, the main shopping street, where the blocks of flats rose to such a height they caught the last rose-violet glow of the sun. A glimmer of this, reflected down into the dusty valley of the street, lit with violet-grey the crowds that clotted either pavement.

This was the time of the evening promenade. Guy suggested they should walk a little way; but first, they had to pass through the purgatory of the hotel's attendant beggars. These were professional beggars, blinded or maimed by beggar parents in infancy. Guy, during his apprentice year, had grown accustomed, if not inured, to the sight of white eyeballs and running sores, to have stumps and withered arms and the breasts of nursing mothers thrust into his face. The Rumanians accepted all this as part of life and donated coins so small that a beggar might spend his day collecting the price of a meal.

However, when Guy tried to do the same thing, a howl went up. Foreigners were not let off so lightly. All the beggars set upon the Pringles together. One hid half a loaf behind his back to join in the age old cry of: "*Mi-e foame, foame, foame.*" They were hemmed in by a stench of sweat, garlic and putrid wounds. The beggars took what Guy distributed among them, then whined for more. Harriet, looking at a child that trembled violently at her elbow, thought she saw in its face glee at its own persistence. A man on the ground, attempting to bar their way, stretched out a naked leg bone-thin, on which the skin was mottled purple and rosetted with yellow scabs. As she stepped over it, the leg slapped the ground in rage that she should escape it.

"Do they want to annoy one?" she asked, and realised there might be revenge for all this abasement in provoking some stranger like herself to the break-down of pure hatred.

At last they were free to join the promenade. The crowd was a sombre crowd, comprising more men than women. Women of the older generation did not walk abroad alone. There were a few groups of girls, their eyes only for each other, seeming unaware of the savage stares of solitary men. Mostly there were couples; tailored, padded, close-buttoned, self-consciously correct: for this, Guy explained, was an hour when only the employing class was free to walk abroad, Harriet might now observe the new bourgeoisie, risen from the peasantry and pretty pleased with itself for having done so.

Because the peasants themselves were given to holiday colours of great brilliance, their male descendants dressed in grey, the women in Parisian black with such pearls, diamonds and silver fox furs as they could afford.

Harriet, meeting glances that became critical, even slightly derisive, of the fact the Pringles were hatless and rather oddly dressed, became censorious herself. "They have," she said, "the uniformity of their insecurity."

"They're not all Rumanians," said Guy. "There are a great many stateless Jews; and there are, of course, Hungarians, Germans and Slavs. The percentages are . . ." Guy, his head lifted above the trivialities of conduct, brought out statistics, but Harriet was not listening. She was absorbed in warfare with the crowd.

The promenade was for her a trial of physical strength. Though leisurely, the Rumanians were ruthless in their determination to keep on the pavement. Only peasants or servants could be seen walking in the road. The men might, under pressure, yield an inch or two, but the women were as implacable as steam-rollers. Short and strong, they remained bland-faced while wielding buttocks and breasts as heavy as bladders of lard.

The position most fiercely held was the inner pavement beside the shop windows. Guy, too temperate, and Harriet, too light-boned, for the fray, were easily thrust out to the kerb, where Guy gripped Harriet's elbow to keep her from slipping into the gutter. She broke from him, saying: "I'll walk in the road. I'm not a Rumanian. I can do what I like."

Following her, Guy caught her hand and squeezed it, trying to induce in her his own imperturbable good humour. Harriet, looking back at the crowd, more tolerant now she was released from it, realised that behind its apparent complacency there was a nervous air of enquiry, an alert unease. Were someone to shout: 'The invasion has begun,' the whole smug façade would collapse.

This unease unmasked itself at the end of the Calea Victoriei where the road widened in a no-man's-land of public buildings. Here were parked a dozen or so of the Polish refugee cars that were still streaming down from the north. Some of the cars had been abandoned. From the others women and children, left while the men sought shelter, gazed out blankly. The well-dressed Rumanians, out to appreciate and be appreciated, looked affronted by these ruined faces that were too tired to care.

Harriet wondered what would be done with the Poles. Guy said the Rumanians, once stirred, were kindly enough. Some who owned summer villas were offering them to Polish families, but stories were already going round about the refugees; old anti-Polish stories remembered from the last war.

Near the end of the road, near the cross roads where the turbaned boyar, Cantacuzino, pointed the way to the Chicken Market, a row of open *trăsurăs* waited to be hired. Guy suggested they drive up the Chaussée. Harriet peered at the horses, whose true condition was hidden by the failing of the light.

"They look wretchedly thin," she said.

"They're very old."

"I don't think we should employ them."

"If no one employed them, they would starve to death."

Choosing the least decrepit of the horses, the Pringles climbed into the carriage, which was about to start when commanded to a halt. A tall, elderly man was holding out his walking-stick with an imperious air.

Guy recognised the man with surprise. "It's Woolley," he said. "He usually ignores 'the culture boys'." Then his face lit with pleasure: "I expect he wants to meet you." Before Woolley could state his business, Guy introduced him to Harriet: "The leading English businessman, the chairman of the Golf Club", enhancing from sheer liberality of spirit such importance as Woolley had; then, turning with tender pride towards Harriet, he said: "My wife."

Woolley's cold nod indicated that duty not frivolity had caused him to accost them. "The order is," he announced in a nasal twang, "the ladies must return to England."

"But," said Guy, "I called at the Legation this morning. No one said anything about it."

"Well, there it is," said Woolley in a tone that implied he was not arguing, he was telling them.

Harriet, exasperated by the mildness of Guy's protest asked: "Who has given this order? The Minister?"

Woolley started, surprised, it seemed, not only by the edge on her voice but by the fact she had a voice at all. His head, hairless, with toad-mottled skin, jerked round and hung towards her like a lantern tremulous on a bamboo: "No, it's a general order, like. I've sent me lady wife home as an example. That was enough for the other ladies."

"Not for me, I'm afraid. I never follow examples."

Woolley's throat moved several times before he said: "Oh, don't you? Well, young woman, I can tell you this: if trouble starts here, there'll be a proper schemozzle. The cars and petrol will be requisitioned by the army and the trains'll be packed with troops. I doubt if anyone'll get away, but if you do, you'll go empty-handed, and it won't be no Cook's tour. Don't say I haven't warned you. What I say is, it's the duty of the ladies to go back home and not to be a drag on the gents."

"You imagine they'll be safer in England? I can only say, you don't know much about modern warfare. I think, Mr. Woolley, it would be better if you set an example by not getting into a panic."

Harriet poked at the coachman and the *trăsură*, seeming about to break fore from aft, heaved itself to a start. As it went, Harriet looked back to give a regal nod and saw that Woolley's face, under a street lamp, had lost what colour it had. He shouted after them, his voice passing out of control: "You young people these days have no respect for authority. I'd have you know, the Minister described me as the leader of the English colony."

They were under way. Guy, his brows raised, gazed at Harriet, having seen an extra dimension added to the woman he had achieved. "I never dreamt you could be so grand," he said.

Pleased with herself, she said: "He's an impossible old ass. How could you let him bully you?"

Guy laughed. "Darling, he's pathetic."

"Pathetic? With all that self-importance?"

"The self-importance is pathetic. Can't you see?"

For a sudden moment she could see, and her triumph subsided. His hand slipped into hers and she raised to her lips his long, unpractical fingers. "You're right, of course. Still . . ." She gave his little finger a bite that made him yelp. "That," she said, "is in case you get too good to be true."

They had returned down the Calea Victoriei, crossed the square and had reached the broad avenue where the German Embassy stood among the mansions of the very rich. This led to the Chaussée, that stretched, wide and tree-lined, into open country. The trees, a row on either side of the pavements, were almost bare, what leaves that remained so scorched by the summer's heat that they hung like scraps blown from a bonfire.

It was almost dark. The stars grew brilliant in the sky. The

Pringles, sitting hand-in-hand in the old four-wheeler that smelt of horse, were more aware of each other than of anything else. Here they were, a long way from home, alone together in a warring world.

Made a little self-conscious by these thoughts, Guy pointed out an archway at the end of the vista. "The Arc de Triomphe," he said.

"The Paris of the East," Harriet said, somewhat in ridicule, for they had disagreed as to the attractions of Bucharest. Guy, who had spent here his first year of adult freedom, living on the first money earned by his own efforts, saw Bucharest with a pleasure she, a Londoner, rather jealous of his year alone here, was not inclined to share.

"What is it made of, the arch? Marble?" she asked.

"Concrete." It had been built previously by a fraudulent contractor who had used inferior cement. When it fell down, the contractor was put in prison and the arch re-erected to the glory of Greater Rumania – the Rumania that came into existence in 1919 when the Old Kingdom acquired, as a reward for entering the war on the side of the victors, parts of Russia, Austria and Hungary. "And so," said Guy, "like most people who did well out of the war, she is now a nice comfortable shape."

While Guy talked, young men howled past the *trăsură* in racing cars, each with a foot on his accelerator, a hand thumping up and down on the hooter. The horse – revealed by the street lights as a phantom horse, a skeleton in a battered hide – was not disturbed. Equally undisturbed was the coachman, a vast cottage loaf in a velvet robe.

Guy whispered: "A *Skopit*. One of the sights of the city. The *Skopits* belong to a Russian sect. They believe that to find grace we must all be completely flat in front, women as well as men. So, after they've reproduced themselves, the young people hold tremendous orgies, working themselves into frenzies in which they mutilate themselves."

"Oh!" said Harriet. She gazed in wonder at the vast velvet backside of the eunuch before her, then she gazed out at the dark reaches of the Muntenia plain, on which the city stood like a bride-cake on a plate. "A barbarous country," she said.

They had now passed the last of the houses. On either side of the road, adazzle beneath the dark, star-lighted violet of the sky, were the open areas owned by the restaurants that had no gardens in the town. Each spring, when the weather settled, they shut their winter premises and brought their chairs and tables up the Chaussée. Within these enclosures the limes and chestnuts, hose-drenched each morning, spread a ceiling of leaves.

When the *trăsură* stopped at Pavel's, one of the largest of the open-air restaurants, there could be heard above the traffic the shrill squeak of a gypsy violin. Within the shrub hedge of the garden, all was uproar.

The place was crowded. The silver-gilt glow from the globes set in the trees lit in detail the wrinkled tree-trunks, the pebbled ground, and the blanched faces of the diners that, damp with the excitement of food, gazed about them with deranged looks, demanding to be served. Some rapped with knives on wine-glasses, some clapped their hands, some made kissing noises at the waiters, while others clutched at every passing coat-tail, crying: '*Domnule, domnule!*' for in this country even the meanest was addressed as 'lord'.

The waiters, sweating and disarranged, snapped their civilities and made off before orders were complete. The diners shouted to the empty air, sometimes shaking their fists as they seethed in their seats, talking, gesturing, jerking their heads this way and that. It was an uproar in which there was little laughter.

"They all seem very cross," said Harriet, who, caught into the atmosphere, began to feel cross herself.

A waiter, flapping at the Pringles like an angry bird, conveyed to them the fact they were blocking the way to the kitchen building. They stood aside and watched him as he rushed to an open window and bawled into the kitchen's bang and clatter. The cooks, scowling in the heat from the giant grill, ignored him. The waiter brought his fists down on the sill, at which one of the cooks lunged at the window, flinging himself half from it as an enraged dog flings himself the length of his chain. He struck the waiter, who fell gibbering.

"It's all just Rumanian animation," said Guy as he led Harriet to an alcove where the foods were displayed beneath a canopy of vines.

The heart of the display was a rosy bouquet of roasts, chops, steaks and fillets frilled round with a froth of cauliflowers. Heaped extravagantly about the centre were aubergines as big as melons, baskets of artichokes, small coral carrots, mushrooms, mountain

raspberries, apricots, peaches, apples and grapes. On one side
there were French cheeses; on the other tins of caviare, grey river
fish in powdered ice, and lobsters and crayfish groping in dark
waters. The poultry and game lay unsorted on the ground.

"Choose," said Guy.

"What can we afford?"

"Oh, anything. The chicken is good here." He pointed in to the
grill, where spitted birds were changing from gold to deeper
gold.

As he spoke a woman standing nearby turned, looked accusingly
at him, and said in English: "You are English, yes? The English
professor?"

Guy agreed that he was.

"This war," she said, "it is a terrible thing for Rumania." Her
husband, who was standing apart, gazed away with an air of non-
participation. "England has guaranteed us," said the woman,
"England must protect us."

"Of course," said Guy as though offering her his own personal
guarantee of protection. He glanced over at the husband, smiling
to introduce himself, and at once the man started into ingratiating
life, bowing and beaming at the Pringles.

"Even if we are not attacked," said the woman, impatient of
this interruption, "there will be many scarcities," she looked down
at her high-heeled shoes, shoes that seemed too small for the legs
above them, and said: "In the last war there were many scarcities.
I remember my father paid for me two thousand *lei* for shoes of
felt. I wear them to school the one day only, and when I return,
no soles left. And food! How terrible if Rumania were short of
food!"

Guy turned, laughing, towards the alcove. "Could Rumania be
short of food?"

"No? You think not?" She paused and glanced at her husband.
"It is true," she said, "we have much food." The husband
shrugged and smiled again.

At last Guy was released. Harriet, who had been watching the
activity of the restaurant, said: "There are no free tables."

"Oh yes, there are." Firmly, short-sightedly, Guy led her to a
table marked '*Rezervat*'.

"*Nu nu, domnule*." The head waiter pointed them to a vacant
table beside the orchestra.

Harriet shook her head: "The noise would be intolerable." The man grumbled.

"He says," said Guy, "we are fortunate to find any table in a time of war."

"Tell him it's our war, not his. We must have a better table."

The head waiter flung out his hands in a distracted way and called to an assistant to take charge of the Pringles. The assistant, dodging like a rugger player through the hazards of the garden, led them to a platform where half-a-dozen privileged tables were raised above the rest. He whipped a 'reserved' notice from one and presented it like a conjurer completing a trick. Guy handed him a bundle of small notes.

Now, seated as on a headland, the Pringles gazed across the surge at a wrought-iron cage, lighted with 'fairy' lights and hung with green branches and gilded oranges, where the orchestra laboured to be heard above the general din. Squeaking and pompomming at an insane pitch, the instruments produced an effect not so much of high spirits as of tearing rage.

Guy tilted forward his glasses and tried to focus the spectacle before him. He was, Harriet knew, happy to be in this advantageous position even though he would not have demanded it for himself. In appreciation, he stretched his hand to her across the table. As she touched it, she saw they were being observed from the next table by a man who, meeting her glance, smiled and looked away.

"Who is that?" Harriet whispered. "Does he know us?"

"Everyone knows us. We are the English. We are at war."

"But who is he?"

"Ionescu, the Minister of Information. He's always here."

"How odd to live in such a small capital!"

"There are advantages. Whatever happens here, one is in the midst of it."

Ionescu was not alone at his table. He had with him five women of different ages, all plain, staid and subdued in appearance, from whom he sat apart. He gazed fixedly at the orchestra stand and picked his teeth with a golden pick.

"Who are the women?"

"His wife and her relatives. The wife is the one nearest him."

"She looks down-trodden."

"She probably is. Everyone knows he comes here only to see the singer Florica. He's her latest *affaire*."

Harriet watched a man below, who, newly served, guarded his plate with one hand against the waiters and passers-by while with the other he forked-in his food, eyes oblique, as though fearing to have it snatched from him. She was hungry herself.

"Will they ever bring the menu?" she asked.

Guy said: "Sooner or later someone will remember us. There's Inchcape." He pointed to a man in late middle-age, thickly built and very upright, who had paused with an ironically humorous courtesy while a group pushed fiercely past him searching for a table. As Guy rose and waved, Inchcape nodded up to him, then, when free to move, did so with the same air of amused irony, giving, for all his lack of height, the impression of towering over those about him. He had, Harriet remembered, once been head-master of a minor public school.

As he advanced, she noticed someone was following him – a taller, leaner man, no more than thirty years of age, who came sidling among the tables, effacing himself behind his companion.

"Why, Clarence!" Guy called on a rising note of delighted surprise, and the second man, smirking, cast down his eyes. "That," said Guy, "is my colleague Clarence Lawson. So we're all back together again!" He stretched out his hands as the two arrived at the table. They seemed both pleased and embarrassed by his enthusiasm.

Taking Guy's left hand, Inchcape gave it an admonitory tweak. "So you've got yourself married!" he said and turned with a mocking half-smile towards Harriet. She saw that beneath the smile his glance was critical and vulnerable. One of his men had brought back a wife – an unknown quantity, perhaps a threat to his authority. When Guy made the introductions, she greeted Inchcape gravely, making no attempt to charm.

His manner, when responding, admitted her to his grown-up world. It changed as he turned back to Guy. Guy, it seemed, was not a grown-up; he was a boy – a favoured boy, a senior prefect, perhaps, but still a boy.

"Where did you go this summer?" Guy asked Clarence, who was standing, a little aloof, from the table. "Did you do that bus journey from Beirut to Kashmir?"

"Well, no, I didn't." Clarence had an awkward, rather confused smile, that made the more surprising the firm and resonant richness of his voice. Catching Harriet's eyes on him, he looked quickly from her. "Actually, I just stuck in Beirut. I spent the summer bathing and lounging around the beach. Much as you might expect. I did think of flying home to see Brenda, but somehow I never got around to it."

Guy asked Inchcape what he had done.

"I was in Rome," he said, "I spent a lot of time in the Vatican Library." He looked at Harriet. "How was England when you left it?"

"Calm enough. Foreigners were leaving, of course. The official who examined our passports at Dover said: 'The first today'."

Inchcape took a seat. "Well" – he frowned at Clarence – "sit down, sit down," but there was nowhere for Clarence to sit.

A chair was brought from a neighbouring table but Clarence remained standing. "As a matter of fact," he said, "I only came to say 'Hallo'."

"*Sit down*." Inchcape impatiently slapped the chair seat and Clarence sat. When all the party was settled, Inchcape surveyed it, drawing down the corners of his lips in ridicule of the announcement he had to make. "I've just been put in charge of British propaganda in the Balkans," he said. "An official appointment."

"Why, splendid!" exclaimed Guy.

"Umph! It'll lead to a rearrangement of duties, of course. You," he nodded to Guy, "will take over the English Department – a much reduced department, needless to say. You can get some of the local teachers of English to give you a hand. I'll remain in charge; all you'll have to do my dear fellow is work." He pushed Guy's shoulder in humorous dismissal, then turned to Clarence: "We're opening a propaganda bureau in the Calea Victoriei opposite the rival establishment. You will be required to bring out a news sheet." He smiled at Clarence but did not attempt to touch him. Clarence, tilted back from the table, his hands in his pockets, his chin on his chest, was not responsive. He seemed to be rejecting patronage with an uneasy air of ease. "You'll have plenty of other jobs to do, of course."

Clarence said slowly: "I'm not at all sure I can take on this sort of work. I'm seconded from the British Council. The Council is purely cultural and Lord Lloyd . . ."

"I'll deal with Lloyd." Inchcape jerked upright and looked about him. "Where's the waiter? What about a drink?" He turned his neat Napoleonic face towards a waiter, who, conscious of having neglected the table, now sprang on to the platform with exaggerated alacrity.

When their order had been given, Harriet said to Inchcape: "So you think we shall stay here?"

"Why should we not?"

Guy said: "Woolley stopped us earlier this evening and tried to order Harriet home."

Inchcape, eyes and nostrils distended, looked from Guy to Harriet and back again: "Woolley took it upon himself to give you orders?"

Enjoying Inchcape's indignation, Harriet said: "He said that he is the leader of the English colony."

"He did, did he? The old fool's in his second childhood. He spends his days in the bar at the Golf Club getting sustenance out of a bottle, like a baby. In his dotage; his anecdotage, I'd say. Ha!" Inchcape gave a laugh, cheered by his own wit, then he fell to brooding and, after a pause, said: "Leader of the English colony forsooth! I'll show him who's leader if he tries to order my men about."

Guy and Clarence exchanged smiles.

Harriet asked Inchcape: "If there were an invasion, if we had to leave here in a hurry, where would we go?"

Inchcape, still annoyed, answered shortly: "Turkey, I suppose."

"And from there?"

"Oh!" His tone became milder. "Make our way through Syria to the Middle East." He assumed his old joking manner. "Or we might try a little trek across Persia and Afghanistan to India." But he still spoke grudgingly. He interrupted himself to say: "But there'll be no invasion. The Germans have better things to do with their troops than spread them out over Eastern Europe. They'll need all they've got to hold the Western front."

Clarence stuck out his lower lip. He 'hmmd' a bit before remarking in a casual tone: "Nevertheless, the situation is serious. I bumped into Foxy Leverett today and he advised me to keep my bags packed."

"Then you'll keep them packed a long time." Inchcape now

shrugged the matter off. He might have been dealing with a junior-school fracas of which he had had enough.

The piccolo arrived, a scrap of a boy, laden with bottles, glasses and plates. Breathing loudly, he set the table.

Glancing up, Harriet found Clarence's gaze fixed on her. He looked away at once but he had caught her attention. She noted his long, lean face with its long nose, and felt it unsatisfactory. Unsatisfactory and unsatisfied. As she assessed him, his eyes came, rather furtively, back to her and now he found her gazing at him. He flushed slightly and jerked his face away again.

She smiled to herself.

Guy said: "I asked Sophie to join us here."

"Why, I wonder?" Inchcape murmured.

"She's very depressed about the war."

"Imagining, no doubt, that it was declared with the sole object of depressing her."

Suddenly all the perturbation of the garden was gathered into an eruption of applause. The name of the singer Florica was passed from table to table.

Florica, in her long black and white skirts, was posed like a bird, a magpie, in the orchestra cage. When the applause died out, she jerked forward in a bow, then, opening her mouth, gave a high, violent gypsy howl. The audience stirred. Harriet felt the sound pass like a shock down her spine.

The first howl was followed by a second, sustained at a pitch that must within a few years (so Inchcape later assured the table) destroy her vocal chords. People sitting near Ionescu glanced at him and at his women. Sprawled sideways in his seat, he stared at the singer and went on picking his teeth. The women remained impassive as the dead.

Florica, working herself into a fury in the cage, seemed to be made of copper wire. She had the usual gypsy thinness and was as dark as an Indian. When she threw back her head, the sinews moved in her throat: the muscles moved as her lean arms swept the air. The light flashed over her hair, that was strained back, glossy, from her round, glossy brow. Singing there among the plump women of the audience, she was like a starved wild kitten spitting at cream-fed cats. The music sank and her voice dropped to a snarl. It rose and, twisting her body as in rage, clenching her fists and striking back her skirts, she finished on an elemental screech that was sustained above the tremendous outburst of applause.

When it was over, people blinked as though they had survived a tornado. Only Ionescu and his women continued, to all appearance, unmoved.

Inchcape, not himself applauding, pointed in amusement at Guy, who, crying "Bravo, bravo!" was leaning forward to bang his hands together. "What energy," smiled Inchcape. "How wonderful to be young!" When there was silence again, he turned to Harriet and said: "She was a failure when she toured abroad, but here she's just what they like. She expresses all the exasperation that's eating these people up." As he turned in his seat, he suddenly saw Ionescu's party. "Oh ho!" he said, "Ionescu complete with harem. I wonder how his wife enjoyed the performance."

"You think," Harriet asked him, "she knows about Florica and her husband?"

"Dear me, yes. She probably has on record everything they have ever said or done during every moment they have spent together."

To encourage him, Harriet made a murmur of artless interest. Inchcape settled down to instruct her. He said: "Rumanian convention requires her apparent unawareness. Morality here is based not on not doing, but on recognising what is being done."

They had been served with a rich goose-liver paté, dark with truffles and dressed with clarified butter. Inchcape swallowed this down in chunks, talking through it as though it were a flavourless impediment to self-expression.

"Take, for instance, the behaviour of these women in company. If anyone makes an improper joke, they simply pretend not to understand. While the men roar with laughter, the women sit poker faced. It's ridiculous to watch. This behaviour, that fools no one, saves the men having to restrict their conversation when women are present."

"But the young women, the students, don't they rebel against this sort of hypocrisy?"

"Dear me, no. They are the most conventional *jeunes filles* in the world, and the most knowing. 'Sly', Miss Austen would have called them. If, during a reading in class, we come on some slight indecency, the men roar their enjoyment, the girls sit blank. If they were shocked, they would not look shocked: if they were innocent, they would look bewildered. As it is, their very blankness betrays their understanding." Inchcape gave a snort of disgust, not, apparently, at the convention but at the absurdity of the sex on which it was imposed.

"How do they become so knowledgeable so young?" asked Harriet, half listening to the talk between Clarence and Guy, in which she caught more than once the name of Sophie. Clarence, half in the party and half out of it, was taking a bite or two of paté.

"Oh," Inchcape answered Harriet, "these Rumanian homes are hot-beds of scandal and gossip. It's all very Oriental. The pretence of innocence is to keep their price up. They develop early and they're married off early, usually to some rich old lecher whose only interest is in the girl's virginity. When that's over and done with, they divorce. The girl sets up her own establishment, and, having the status of divorcée, she is free to do what she chooses."

Harriet laughed. "How then is the race carried on?"

"There's a quota of normal marriages, of course. But surely you've heard the story of the Rumanian walking with his German friend down Calea Victoriei – the Rumanian naming the price of every woman they meet? 'Good heavens,' says the German, 'are there no honest women here?' 'Certainly,' replies the Rumanian, 'but – *very expensive!*' "

Harriet laughed, and Inchcape, with a satisfied smile, gazed over the restaurant and complained: "I've never before seen this place in such a hubbub."

"It's the war," said Clarence. "Eat, drink and be merry, for tomorrow we may be starving to death."

"Fiddlesticks!"

The second course arrived, a duck dressed with orange. As this was being carved, Inchcape said quietly to Harriet: "I see your friend Sophie Oresanu in the distance."

Not avoiding the underlying question, Harriet replied: "She is not my friend. I have never met her. What is she?"

"Rather an advanced young lady for these parts. Her circumstances are peculiar. Her parents divorced and Sophie lived with her mother. When the mother died, Sophie was left to live alone. That is unusual here. It gives her considerable freedom. She worked for a while on a student's magazine – one of those mildly anti-fascist, half-baked publications that appear from time to time. It lasted about six months. Now she thinks the Germans have marked her down. She's taking a law degree."

"Really!" Harriet was impressed by the law degree.

"It doesn't mean anything here," said Inchcape. "They all take law degrees. That qualifies them to become second assistant stamp-lickers in the civil service."

"Guy says the Rumanian girls are intelligent."

"They're quick. But all Rumanians are much of a muchness. They can absorb facts but can't do anything with them. A lot of stuffed geese, I call them. An uncreative people." While speaking, he kept his eye on a young woman who now mounted the platform and, stopping at the table and ignoring the others present, stared mournfully at Guy. He, talking, failed to notice her.

In a plaintive, little voice she said: " 'Allo!"

"Why, hello!" Guy leapt to his feet and kissed her on either cheek. Sophie suffered the embrace with a slight smile, taking in the company as she did so.

Guy turned cheerfully to Harriet: "Darling, you must meet Sophie. Sophie, my wife."

As Sophie looked at Harriet, her expression suggested she was at a loss to understand not only how he had acquired a wife, but how he had acquired such a wife. She eventually gave a nod and looked away. She was a pretty enough girl, dark like most Rumanians, too full in the cheeks. Her chief beauty was her figure. Looking at Sophie's well developed bosom, Harriet felt at a disadvantage. Perhaps Sophie's shape would not last, but it was enviable while it lasted.

Guy looked for another chair.

"Here," said Clarence, "take mine. I must go."

"No, no." Guy tried to hold him, but, after pausing uncertainly for a while, Clarence suddenly darted off.

"Now where's he gone?" Inchcape stared after Clarence, then gave Sophie a frown of annoyance, making it clear he thought her a poor exchange. Ignoring him, Sophie watched Guy reproachfully. It was some time before he noticed this, then he said:

"What's the matter?"

"Nothing," she said. "Nothing to be discussed in public." After a pause, she added: "Ah, this war! Such a terrible thing! It has made me so sad. When I go to bed at night, I am thinking of it: when I wake, I am thinking of it. Always I am thinking of it."

Inchcape filled a glass and put it in front of her. "Here," he said, "have a drink and cheer up." When Sophie ignored the wine, Inchcape turned his back on her and indicated the diners below.

"Down there," he said, "unless I'm much mistaken, there's a fellow who was at the Crillon when I stayed there some years ago. A Prince Yakimov. He used to be a very well known figure in Paris society."

While Inchcape spoke, Harriet heard Sophie's voice, uneven with tears: "How can he say to me 'Cheer up'? Is this a time to cheer up? It is very well, the 'stiff upper lip', if you are not sensitive. But me – I am very sensitive." Guy was trying to distract her with the menu. What would she eat? It was difficult to decide. She had just come from a party where she had eaten this and that; and was not hungry but perhaps she would have a little smoked salmon.

"Yakimov?" Harriet tried to sort that name out of her memory. "Which do you mean?"

"There, dining with Dobson. Haven't you met Dobson? Yakimov's the long, lean fellow, face like a camel. Not, I may say, that he's one for going long without a drink."

"I've seen him befqre. He came on our train."

This concentration of interest elsewhere was too much for Guy. Breaking through a new plaint from Sophie, he asked: "What are you talking about?"

"A man called Yakimov," said Inchcape. "Something of a *raconteur* and joker. There's a story about his painting the windows black."

Harriet asked: "Which windows? Why?"

"I've no idea. Being half Irish and half White Russian, he's said to have a peculiarly English sense of humour."

The three of them watched Yakimov, who, intent upon his food, was not recounting at that moment.

Petulantly Sophie broke in on them to ask: "What is a peculiarly English sense of humour?"

"A pleasant humour, I suppose," said Guy, "a good-humoured humour. Here a painful boot in the arse is called a Rumanian kick, and a dunt with the knee is called the English kick. That's the idea."

At the word 'arse' Sophie's face went blank, but only Harriet noticed it.

Guy said: "I'd like to meet Yakimov. Let's ask them over."

"Oh," Inchcape protested, "do we want Dobson here?"

Guy said: "I don't mind Dobson. He entered the diplomatic service so late in life, he is still reasonably human."

"An amateur diplomat, you might say. Drifted into the service after a rich and idle youth. I don't dislike him myself. If it costs him nothing, he'd as soon be pleasant as unpleasant."

Guy tore a sheet from a notebook and scribbled on it while Inchcape, having no part in the invitation, looked the other way. The note was taken by the waiter. Dobson wrote a line on it and sent it back.

"They're coming for coffee," said Guy.

"Ah!" Inchcape let his breath out and helped himself to wine.

Before retiring to bed that afternoon, Yakimov had sent to the station for his cases and handed most of his clothing over to the hotel valet.

Now, sauntering behind Dobson across the restaurant, his yellow waistcoat newly cleaned, the fine line of his check suit accentuated by skilful pressing, he had an air of elegance, even if rather eccentric elegance. When he reached the table to which he was being led, he smiled benignly upon it. After he had been introduced to the table, he picked up Harriet's hand, kissed it and said: "How delighful, when one has lived too long abroad, to meet an English beauty."

"I'm told you have a peculiarly English sense of humour," said Harriet.

"Dear me! Has poor Yaki's reputation preceded him?" Yakimov showed his gratification so simply, it dissipated Harriet's first suspicion of him – a suspicion based on nothing she could define. He repeated: "A peculiarly English sense of humour! I am flattered," and he looked to see if Dobson had overheard the tribute, but Dobson was talking to Guy. He said: "I was delighted to hear you chaps were back, but surprised they let you come." His nervous explosion of laughter softened his remark, but Inchcape's mouth turned down.

Dobson, who had walked trippingly, carrying himself so that his back line curved in at the waist and his front line curved out, was in young middle age, plump, dimpled, pink and white as a cupid. He was very bald but over his pate were pools of baby-soft fluff left by the receding hair.

Guy said: "I was ordered back here. The London office says we're in a reserved occupation."

"So you are," Dobson agreed, "but they don't think what a

worry it is for us chaps now having a lot of British nationals here without diplomatic protection." His laughter exploded again, joking and tolerant, but Inchcape was not amused.

He said: "I imagine that worry is part of your job."

Dobson jerked his head up, discomforted at being taken so seriously. He laughed again and Harriet understood why he seemed to Guy 'reasonably human'. This constant nervous laughter rippling over his occupational self-possession gave the impression he was more approachable than his kind. At the same time, she realised he was more than a little drunk. She decided he might be an easy acquaintance, but would not be easy to know.

Chairs were becoming scarce now. Guy had to tip the waiter before he would set out in search of more. When two arrived, Dobson lay on his as though about to slide off it, and stared at a slip of paper he held in his hand. It seemed so to bewilder him that Harriet looked over his shoulder. He was studying his dinner bill.

Yakimov placed his chair beside Harriet. To Sophie, on the other side of the table, the arrival of these newcomers was, apparently, an imposition scarcely to be borne.

Harriet said to Yakimov: "I saw you on the train at the frontier."

"Did you indeed!" Yakimov gave Harriet a wary look. "Not to tell a lie, dear girl, I was having a spot of bother. Over m'Hispano-Suiza. Papers not in order. Something to do with a permit. 'Fraid they impounded the poor old girl. Was just explaining to Dobbie here, that little frontier incident cleared me right out of the Ready."

"Where were you coming from?"

"Oh, here and there. Been touring around. Too far from base when trouble started, so came in to the nearest port. Times like these after all, a bloke can be useful anywhere. 'S'matter of fact, m'chance came this morning. *Ra*-ther an amusing story," he looked about him to gather in a larger audience and, seeing that Guy was ordering coffee for the party, he said: "How about a drop of brandy, dear boy?"

The waiter placed out some small brandy glasses. "Tell him to leave the bottle." Then, wriggling in his chair, trying to mould the seat more comfortably to his shape, he lifted his glass to Harriet, drained it and smacked his lips in an exaggerated play of appreciation. "Nourishment!" he said.

For a moment Harriet thought she saw in him an avidity, as though he would, if he could, absorb into his own person the substance of the earth; then he glanced at her. His eyes were guileless. Large, light green, drooping at the outer corners, they were flat-looking, seeming to have no more thickness than a lens and set, not in cavities, but on a flat area between brow and cheek.

He refilled his glass, obviously preparing to entertain the company. As Guy gazed expectantly at him, Sophie gazed at Guy. She plucked at his sleeve and whispered intimately: "There is so much I must tell you. I have many worries."

Guy, with a gesture, cut short these confidences, and Yakimov, unaware of the interruption, began: "This morning, coming down early, who should I see in the hall of the Athénée Palace but . . ."

Yakimov's normal voice was thin, sad and unvarying, the voice of a cultured Punchinello, but when he came to report McCann, it changed dramatically. As he reproduced McCann's gritty, demanding tones, he somehow imposed on his own delicate features the shield-shaped, monkey mug that must be McCann.

He told the whole story of his meeting with McCann, of the plight of the Poles outside the hotel, of the sleeping girl, the scarf that had been buried with the dead. Although he mentioned, apologetically, that he did not speak Polish, he produced the accent of the angry Pole.

Guy, in appreciation of this piece of theatre, murmured "Marvellous" and Yakimov gave him a pleased smile.

The others, though entertained, were disconcerted that such a story should be told like a funny anecdote, but when he opened his arms and said: "Think of it! Think of your poor old Yaki become an accredited war correspondent," his face expressed such comic humility at so unlikely a happening that they were suddenly won to him. Even Sophie's sullen mouth relaxed. He united them in the warmth of amusement and, at least for the time, they accepted him like a gift – their Yaki, their poor old Yaki. His height, his curious face, his thin body, his large, mild eyes, his voice and, above all, his humility – these were his components and they loved them.

Dobson had clearly heard the story before. Glancing up from the bill, he smiled at its effect. When the laughter had died down, Sophie, who had not laughed, took the floor with impressive seriousness: "It is not so difficult to be journalist, I think. I have been journalist. My paper was anti-fascist, so now things will be difficult for me. Perhaps the Nazis will come here. You understand?" As Yakimov blinked, appearing to understand nothing, she gave an aggravated little laugh: "You have heard of the Nazis, I suppose?"

"The Nasties, dear girl, that's what I call 'em," he giggled. "Don't know what went wrong with them. They seemed to start out all right, but they overdid it somehow. Nobody likes them now."

At this Inchcape gave a hoot of laughter. "The situation in a nut-shell," he said.

Sophie leant forward and gazed earnestly at Yakimov. "The Nazis are very bad men," she said. "Once I was in Berlin on holiday – you understand? – and a Nazi officer comes with big steps along the pavement. I think: 'I am a young lady, he will step aside for me', but no. Pouf! He brushes me as if I were not there and I am flung into the road with the traffic."

"Dear me!" said Yakimov.

As Sophie opened her mouth to talk on, Harriet broke in to ask Yakimov: "Are you the man who painted the windows black?"

"Why, yes, dear girl, that was poor Yaki."

"Won't you tell us the story?"

"Another time, perhaps. It's a trifle *outré* and happened long ago. Soon after m'schooldays, in fact."

Sophie, who had been watching Harriet sulkily, now smiled in triumph. Harriet realised, with surprise, that she saw this refusal as a point to her.

Harriet had failed to consider the possibility of a Sophie. Foolishly. There was always someone. There was also the fact that, whether Sophie had received encouragement or not, Guy's natural warmth towards everyone could easily be misinterpreted. She had herself taken it for granted that it was for her alone. (She had a sudden vivid memory of one of their early meetings when Guy had taken her claw of a hand and said: "You don't eat enough. You must come to Bucharest and let us feed you up.") They had slipped into marriage as though there could be no other possible resolution of such an encounter. Yet – supposing she had known him better? Supposing she had known him for a year and during that time observed him in all his other relationships? She would have hesitated, thinking the net of his affections too widely spread to hold the weighty accompaniment of marriage.

As it was, she had, in all innocence, been prepared to possess him and be possessed, to envelop and be enveloped, in a relationship that excluded the enemy world. She soon discovered that Guy was not playing his part. Through him, the world was not only admitted, it was welcomed; and, somehow, when he approached it, the enmity was no longer there.

"I imagine" – Inchcape was speaking to Yakimov, his ironical smile giving a grudging credit – "I imagine you were at Eton?"

"Alas, dear boy, no," said Yakimov. "M'poor old dad could not cough up. I went to one of those horrid schools where Marshall is beastly to Snelgrove, and Debenham *much* too fond of Freebody. But while we're on the subject, there's rather an amusing story about a croquet match played by the headmistress of a famous girls' school against the headmaster – an excessively corpulent man – of a very famous boys' school. Well . . ."

The story, vapid in itself, was made outrageously funny for his audience by the inflections of Yakimov's frail voice. Pausing on a word, speaking it slowly and with an accent of a slightly breathless disapproval, he started everyone, except Sophie, first into titters, then to a gradual crescendo of laughter. Sophie, her face glum, stared in turn at the reactions of the three male listeners – Guy saying "Oh dear!" and wiping his eyes, Inchcape with his head thrown back, and Dobson rocking in quiet enjoyment.

"But what sort of balls?" she asked when the story was over.

"Croquet balls," said Inchcape.

"Then I do not understand. Why is it funny?"

"Why," Inchcape blandly asked, "is anything funny?"

The answer did not satisfy Sophie. She said with some asperity: "That is an English joke, eh? Here in Rumania we have jokes, too. We ask 'What is the difference between a kitten and a bar of soap?' I think they are silly, such jokes."

"Well, what is the difference?" Guy asked.

Sophie gave him an irritated look and would not answer. He set about persuading her until at last she whispered in a petulant little voice: "If you put a kitten to the foot of a tree, it will climb up."

Her success surprised her. She looked around, suspicious at first, then, growing complacent, said: "I know many such jokes. We told them at school."

"Tell us some more," said Guy.

"Oh, they are so silly."

"No, they are very interesting." And after he had coaxed her to tell several more, all much alike, he began a dissertation on basic peasant humour, to which he related the riddles to be found in fairy-tales. He called on Yakimov to confirm his belief that Russian peasant tales were similar to all other peasant tales.

"I'm sure they are, dear boy," Yakimov murmured, his eyes vacant, his body inert, life extinct now, it seemed, except in the hand with which, every few minutes, he lifted the brandy bottle and topped up his glass.

Dobson, almost asleep, slid forward in his chair, then, half-waking, slid back again. Inchcape was listening to Guy, his smile fixed. It was late, but no one showed any inclination to move. The restaurant was still crowded, the orchestra played on, Florica was expected to sing again. Harriet, suddenly exhausted, wished she were in bed. Guy had told her that on hot summer nights the diners in these garden restaurants might linger on under the trees until dawn. This, however, was not a hot summer night. Gusts of autumnal chill came at intervals from outer darkness and hardened the summer air. Someone, earlier in the evening, had mentioned that the first snow had fallen on the peaks that rose north of the city. She hoped that discomfort, if nothing else, would soon set people moving.

She watched Yakimov drain the last of the bottle into the glass. He then began glancing about, his eyes regaining the luminous gleam of life. When a waiter approached, he made a minimal movement and closed his eyes at the bottle. It was whipped away and replaced at such speed, Harriet could only suppose Yakimov had over waiters the sort of magnetic power some people have over beast and birds. His glass newly filled, he sank back, prepared, Harriet feared, to stay here all night.

As for Guy, the evening's drinking had not touched on his energy. It had merely brought him to a garrulous euphoria in which discoveries were being made and flights taken into metaphysics and the moral sciences. Every few minutes, Sophie – happy and vivacious now – interrupted him possessively to explain what he was saying. Was it possible, Harriet wondered, that this talk was as fatuous as it seemed to her?

"One might say," Guy was saying, "that riddles are the most primitive form of humour: so primitive, they're scarcely humour at all, but a sort of magic."

Sophie burst in: "He means, like the sphinx and like the oracle. Oracles always spoke in riddles."

"Not the oracle at Delos," said Inchcape.

Sophie gave him a look of contempt. "The oracle was at Delphi," she said.

Inchcape shrugged and let it pass.

At midnight Florica came out to sing again. This time Guy was too absorbed in his own talk to notice her. Harriet looked towards Ionescu's table, but there was no one there. Florica, applauded with less vigour than before, departed and the orchestra strummed on.

Harriet yawned. Imagining she was accepting the situation indulgently, she watched Sophie and wondered: 'Is Guy really taken in by this feminine silliness? If I made all those grimaces and gestures as I talked, and interrupted and insisted on attention would he find it all attractive?' Almost in spite of herself, she said "I think we should go now."

Shocked by the suggestion, Guy said: "I'm sure no one wants to go yet."

"No, no," Sophie joined with him at once. "We do not go so soon."

Harriet said: "I'm tired."

"Tomorrow," said Sophie, "you have all day to sleep."

Inchcape stubbed his cigarette. "I would like an early night. I did not sleep much on the train."

"Well, let me finish this." Holding up his glass, which was full, Guy spoke in the tone of a child that begs to sit up ten minutes more.

Refilling his own glass, Yakimov said: "It's still very early, dear girl."

They sat another half-an-hour, Guy eking out his drink and trying to regain the rhythm of talk, but something was lost. An end-of-the-evening lameness was in the air. When, at last, they were agreed to go, there was still the business of finding the waiter.

Inchcape threw down a thousand-*lei* note and said: "That ought to cover me." Guy settled the rest.

They picked up a taxi in the Chaussée and started back. Sophie, whose flat was in the centre of the town, was dropped first. Guy descended with her and took her to her door where she talked at him urgently, holding to his arm. Leaving her, he called back to her: "We'll meet tomorrow."

Next Yakimov was taken to the Athénée Palace. Outside the hotel, he said: "Dear me, I'd almost forgotten. I'm bidden to a party in Princess Teodorescu's suite."

"Rather a late party," murmured Inchcape.

"An all-night party," Yakimov said.

Guy said: "When we find a flat, you must come to dinner with us."

"Delighted, dear boy," said Yakimov, who, as he struggled out of the taxi, was almost sitting on the step. Somehow he got down to the pavement and crossed it unsteadily. Pressing against the revolving doors, he waved back baby-fashion.

"I shall be interested," said Inchcape dryly, "to see what return you get for all this hospitality."

Reprovingly, Dobson spoke from his corner: "Yaki used to be famous for his parties."

"Oh, well," said Inchcape, "we'll see. Meanwhile, if you don't mind, I'd like to be dropped next."

The Pringles reached their room in silence, Harriet fearing complaint that she had broken up the party. A justified complaint. It was true she could sleep all day – and what did an hour or two matter in the face of eternity?

While she got into bed, Guy studied his face in the glass. He broke the silence to ask her: "Do you think I look like Oscar Wilde?"

"You do, a little."

He remained in front of the glass, distorting his face into the likeness of one famous film-star and another.

Harriet wondered if this was the moment to ask him about Sophie, and decided it was not. She said, instead:

"You're an incurable adolescent. Come to bed."

As he turned from the glass, he said with inebriated satisfaction: "Old Pringle's all right. Old Pringle's not a bad chap. Old Pringle's not a bad chap at all."

4

YAKIMOV FOUND HIS DRESS CLOTHES SPONGED, pressed and laid ready for him on his bed. When he changed, he put on one black shoe and one brown.

At the party someone would be sure to mention the fact that he was wearing odd shoes. He would then gaze down at his feet in surprise and say: "And do you know, dear boy, I have another pair at home exactly like these."

He believed this to be his most subtle party prank. He had not played it since dear old Dollie died, reserving it for those times when he was in the highest spirits. Now, so changed were his fortunes, he was ready for anything.

After he had dressed, he sat for a while re-reading a letter on which he was working. It was to his mother. In it he had already told her where he was to be found and had begged her to send his quarterly remittance as soon as possible. He was, he said, engaged on important voluntary war work, giving no details for fear she should be misled as to his need.

After a long reflective pause, he picked up his stub of pencil and added to please her: "Going tonight to Princess Teodorescu's bun-fight." Ordinarily the effort of one sentence would have brought him to a stop, but in his present mood his hand drove on. With some words written very large, some small, but all legible like the carefully written words of a child, he concluded: "All the best then, dear old girl, and keep your pecker up. Your Yaki is in the big times once again."

Filled with a sense of a task well done and pleasure ahead, he went down to meet Prince Hadjimoscos.

It had been for Yakimov a very satisfactory day. He was content, with a contentment he had ceased to experience since thrown penniless upon the world at Dollie's death. That afternoon, newly risen from his siesta, he had gone down to the hotel bar, the famous English Bar, where he had seen, as he hoped he might, someone he knew. This was an English journalist called Galpin.

Galpin, seeing Yakimov, had looked elsewhere. Unruffled, Yakimov had placed himself in view and said: "Why, hello, dear boy! We met last in Belgrade," then, before Galpin could reply, he added: "What are you drinking?" Whatever it was Galpin had been about to say, he now merely grunted and said: "Scotch."

Galpin was not alone. When Yakimov smiled around to ask what the others were drinking, they closed about him as an oyster closes about a pearl. He told the story of his encounter with Mc-Cann and received polite attention. "Think of it, dear boys," he said. "Your poor old Yaki become an accredited war correspondent!"

Galpin asked: "And did you get McCann's stuff out?"

"Naturally. Every word."

"Lucky for McCann," Galpin gazed glumly into his glass. It was empty.

Yakimov insisted on ordering a second round. The journalists accepted their drinks, then broke up to talk among themselves. They had been discussing the arrival in Bucharest of Mortimer Tufton, and now returned to the subject. Tufton, they said, had an instinct for coming events. When he arrived anywhere, the place became news. Yakimov was forgotten. He did not mind. He was happy that he could once again be a dispenser of hospitality. Having introduced himself as such, he might hope that in future no one would be actively rude to him.

Disgorged by the group, he came face to face with the local hangers-on of the bar that had been attracted over by the scent of Yakimov's largesse. They stared admiringly at him. He let them introduce themselves: Cici Palu, Count Ignotus Horvath and Prince Hadjimoscos. If there was in the smile with which he received them a trifle of condescension, it was very modest condescension. These, he knew, were his natural associates. He did not suppose they had any illusions about him, but it flattered him to be their patron. He ordered drinks for them. They all, as fashion required, took whisky, the most expensive drink in the bar. "After this," said Yakimov, "I must be on my way. I'm dining with my dear old friend Dobbie Dobson of the Legation."

At that the leader of the trio, Hadjimoscos, said: "I wonder, *mon cher Prince*, would you care to come to a little night party to be given by Princess Teodorescu in her hotel suite? There you will

meet the true Rumanian aristocracy, as distinct from the politicians and parvenus that pretend to the *beau monde* these days. We
are all so fond of the English."

"Dear boy," Yakimov beamed on him, "I would like nothing
better."

The bar closed at midnight. Yakimov was to meet Hadjimoscos
in the main room, where drinks were served while anyone remained to order them.

In the middle of the room, beneath the largest chandelier, were
laid out on a table copies of every English newspaper of repute.
Beside the table stood Hadjimoscos, drooping over a two-day-old
copy of *The Times*. He was, Yakimov had discovered from Dobson, a last descendant of one of the Greek Phanariot families that
had ruled and exploited Rumania under the Turks. He was small
and slight; and had an appearance of limp softness as though his
clothes contained not flesh and bone but cotton-wool. He wore
very delicately made black kid slippers, on which he now slid
soundlessly forward, putting out his small, white hands and placing
one on each of Yakimov's hands. There they lay inert. In a small
shallow voice he lisped: "How charming to see you again *cher
Prince*." His face, though fretted over with fine lines like the face
of an old woman, was still childish; his dark, small, mongoloid
eyes were bloodshot; his skull showed waxen through the fine
black strands of his hair.

The two men looked expectantly at one another, then Hadjimoscos turned his face aside, sighed and said: "I would so much
like to offer you hospitality, but I find I have come without my
wallet."

"Dear boy" – Yakimov suddenly remembered his position of
power – "it is I who should offer it. What will you take?"

"Oh, whisky, of course. I never touch anything else."

They sat themselves on one of the tapestry sofas and Yakimov
gave his order. Hadjimoscos, his head hanging as though he were
confiding some disgraceful secret, said: "It is most awkward, my
forgetting my money. The Princess is likely to start a table of
chemin or some such play. I am devoted to play. Could you, *mon
cher Prince*, lend me a few thousand?"

Yakimov fixed him with a concerned and regretful gaze:

"Would that I could, dear boy, but your poor old Yaki is living on tick at the moment. Currency regulations, y'know. Couldn't bring a *leu* with me. Waiting for m'remittance from m'poor old ma."

"Oh, la la!" Hadjimoscos shook his head and drained his glass. "In that case we may as well go up to the party."

The lift took them to the top floor of the hotel. A hotel servant stood on the landing to conduct the guests to Princess Teodorescu's drawing-room. On the way up, Hadjimoscos had remained silent: now, when Yakimov, bemused by the heat of the room and the reek of tuberoses, tried to take his arm, he eluded him. Yakimov came to a stop inside the doorway. The evening's drinking had blurred his vision. It seemed to him that the room, lit by black and gilded candles, stretched away in a funereal infinity. The floor looked a void, although it felt solid enough when tested with the foot. Realising that he trod a black carpet, that walls and ceilings were lost to view because painted black, he gained enough confidence to move forward. He saw Hadjimoscos in the centre of the room and, taking what looked like a short cut, he stumbled over a black velvet arm-chair. As he went down, several of the women guests drew attention to his fall by giving little artificial screams of alarm. He heard a voice cry ecstatically: "Hadji, *chéri*," and saw a head and neck floating in the air. The neck was strained forward, so that the sinews were visible. The face looked ravaged, not from age, but from a habit of unrelenting vivacity.

Hadjimoscos whispered savagely: "The Princess."

Yakimov picked himself up and was introduced.

"*Enchantée, enchantée*," cried the Princess. Something waved in front of Yakimov's face. Realising he was being offered a hand in a black velvet glove, he tried to seize and kiss it, but it was snatched away. Another guest had arrived.

Yakimov turned to speak, but Hadjimoscos was no longer there. Left un-anchored in the middle of the room, Yakimov peered about in search of a drink. As his eyes grew accustomed to the gloom he picked out small pieces of gilt furniture, but of the other guests he could see only faces and hands. He was reminded of Dollie's séances where ectoplasm had oozed out between the black curtains of the medium's cabinet.

He began to feel tired and befuddled. Cautiously he essayed out a little, feeling his way from one piece of furniture to another until he came upon a waiter carrying a tray. He sniffed at the glasses. He was about to take a whisky, when he was distracted by the larger glasses. "Ah, champers, dear boy," he said, "champers for me."

Smiling again, he moved cautiously about. Hadjimoscos was talking to two pretty girls. Approaching them, Yakimov heard Hadjimoscos say: "Think of it: one bläck shoe and one brown! I noticed them in the lift."

The younger girl gave a yelp. The other said: "*Les Anglais! Ils sont toujours sâouls.*"

Hadjimoscos's face, that had been agleam with mischief, straightened at the sight of Yakimov and assumed an enchanted smile. "Ah, there you are, *mon cher.*" He pressed Yakimov's arm. "Allow me to present you to my charming friends, Princess Mimi and Princess Lulie. Surnames do not matter."

Mimi, the younger girl, was very pretty in a babyish way. The other was sallow and drawn: her smile, that came reluctantly, was slight and did not linger long. They let him kiss their hands, then stood silent, examining him.

Hadjimoscos, still gripping Yakimov's arm, spoke effusively: "I was just saying, we must – a little later of course, when we are in the mood – play a delicious game called Snow White and the Seven Dwarfs. *Mon cher*, I *insist* that you be a dwarf."

"Not much good at games, dear boy."

"This is no ordinary game. We invented it ourselves. We choose an attractive girl – Mimi, say, or Lulie – and she is Snow White. Then we choose seven men to be the dwarfs. They leave the room and take off all their clothes. Inside the room, Snow White takes off hers. Then one at a time, the dwarfs enter and are confronted by Snow White. According to the reaction of each, so we name them – Happy, Sneezy, Grumpy and so on."

"And Dopey," Mimi cried, 'hen clapped her hand over her mouth.

"Now promise me" – Hadjimoscos gave Yakimov's arm another squeeze – "*promise* me you will be a dwarf!"

Yakimov stepped back nervously. "Not me, dear boy. I'm no good at that sort of thing."

"How sad for you." Hadjimoscos spoke gravely, then, releasing Yakimov and excusing himself, he trotted off on his soft shoes to where Princess Teodorescu sat on a sofa embracing a young man with a large red moustache. Above the other noises of the room, Yakimov heard Hadjimoscos's whisper: "He said: 'I'm no good at that sort of thing'." Yakimov was not disturbed. He was used to being quoted.

Suddenly Mimi, like a little clockwork doll that had been wound up, began chattering in French. Yakimov spoke French as well as he spoke English, but this Rumanian French confused him. He gathered she was speaking of a man who stood a few yards distant, a Baron Steinfeld, who was, it seemed, paying the rent of the apartment. Despite this, the Princess was devoting herself to a certain 'Foxy' Leverett, while the Baron was "*complètement* 'outsider'." As the girls bent together, Yakimov made off, thankful they were laughing at someone other than himself.

His move brought him to the Baron, who, showing all his large yellow teeth, greeted him courteously. Yakimov introduced himself.

"Ah, my dear Prince," said the Baron, "needless to say, I have heard of you. A great name. Was not your father equerry to the Czar?"

"Not to tell a lie, dear boy, *he was*." But even as Yakimov spoke he regretted what he said. The Baron had so eagerly awaited his reply, he feared it might be a trick question. He might be denounced to the party as an impostor. But the Baron, whose handsome high-coloured face was fixed in its eager smile, merely asked: "Are you an old friend of the Princess?"

"We met for the first time tonight. Hadjimoscos brought me."

"Ah!" Steinfeld nodded, then went on to speak, with relish and respect, of the Princess's ancient lineage: "She is descended from Dacian kings," he said. "She can trace a direct descent from Decebal, who defeated the Romans."

"Can she, indeed, dear boy?" Yakimov did his best to attend to Steinfeld while keeping his eye open for a waiter to refill his glass.

"The Teodorescu estates in Moldavia were once very fine, but now? Mortgaged and frittered away! Frittered away! These Princes, they think they can live in Paris or Rome and their lands will thrive without them. So feckless, yet so charming!" The Baron moved closer. "Now, my own little estate in Bessarabia is very well husbanded. We Germans, perhaps not so charming but, we understand to work. On my estate I make my own red wine, white wine, *ţuicǎ* and martini. The martini you can see in the shops. The King sells it in his own grocery store: Martini Steinfeld. It is excellent."

Yakimov, making an effort at approbation, said: "I suppose you make it from Italian recipes?"

"But naturally," said the Baron, "from raisins and recipes and herbs and all such things." As the Baron drew breath and started to talk again, Yakimov said: "Must get another, dear boy," and, ducking away, found himself in an ante-room where a buffet table stood laden with food.

The food was untouched, no invitation to eat having yet been given. Transfixed like one who has stumbled upon treasure, Yakimov murmured to himself: "*Dear boy!*" There was not even the presence of a waiter to curb his appetite.

He saw a row of roasted turkeys with breasts ready sliced, two gammons baked with brown sugar and pineapple, crayfish, salmon coated with mayonnaise, several sorts of paté, three sorts of caviare, many aspic dishes, candied fruits, elaborate puddings, bunches of hot-house grapes, pineapples and autumn raspberries, all set on silver plates and decorated with white cattleyas.

Trembling like a man in dire hunger, Yakimov darted forward. He stuck a table-spoon into the fresh caviare, brought it out full and licked it clean. He decided he preferred the saltier variety to which he was used, and of this he took three spoonfuls. While he held some turkey slices in one hand, eating them like bread, he piled up a plate with salmon mayonnaise, quails in aspic, paté and creamed chicken, putting into his mouth as he went along oddments of anchovies, olives and sweets. When the plate would hold no more, he ate ravenously. About to set upon the puddings, he was interrupted by a step – a very light step. He stared guiltily, Hadjimoscos was at his elbow.

"Felt a trifle peckish," said Yakimov.

"Please!" Hadjimoscos smiled, making a gesture towards the food, but Yakimov felt it seemly to say:

"Thanks, dear boy, had about enough." Regretfully he put aside his plate.

"Then come back to the party. We are going to play baccarat. Everyone will be playing. There will be two tables, at least. *Do* come. We would not have you feel neglected."

At the word 'baccarat' there came down on Yakimov memory of the boredom he had suffered in the casinos to which Dollie used to drag him. He said: "Don't worry about me, dear boy. I'm quite happy here." He noticed some tiny pies standing on a hot-plate and, unable to control his longing, snatched one up and swallowed it. A scalding interior of mushrooms in cheese sauce poured into his throat. His eyes streamed.

Hadjimoscos's laugh was a hiss, his lips widened to disclose his white, small, unconvincing teeth. For a second he looked as vicious as a little puma, but he was all persuasion as he said: "The Princess is mad about play. She would never forgive me if I failed to include you."

"As I told you, dear boy, your old Yaki hasn't a *leu*. Cleaned out till m'remittance arrives."

"No one," said Hadjimoscos, "would refuse your IOU."

"Scarcely know how to play," said Yakimov.

"To learn is the matter of a moment."

Sighing, Yakimov gave a farewell glance at the buffet and, for the first time, noticed it was overhung by a portrait of an old boyar – no doubt some member of the great Teodorescu family. The boyar wore a fur turban of enormous size and a brocaded tunic beneath a mantle of fur. A pair of hands, white and delicate, rested on an embroidered cummerband, one thumb curled round the hilt of a heavily bejewelled dagger.

Yakimov was abashed, not by these accoutrements of wealth but by the face they surrounded – the long, corpse-pale nose and cheeks, the lips with their tattered fringe of beard, the heavy eye-lids beneath which a thread of iris peered malevolently.

He let himself be led away.

The lights had been switched on over two oval tables. A servant was shuffling the packs. A dozen or so people sat at one table and a few others stood about behind the chairs. Yakimov could see no rush to join in the play. The Princess and the red-haired 'Foxy' Leverett remained in an embrace on the sofa. Other couples were lying about in shadowed corners. The Baron, still grinning, stood at the table, but at such a distance that it was clear he did not intend to be drawn in.

Hadjimoscos, who had made another trip over to the Princess, returned with a bundle of notes. Their hostess, he announced, had a headache, so he would take the bank on her behalf. The bank was for 200,000 *lei*. He gave Yakimov a smile: "You see, *mon cher*, our game is modest. You cannot lose much. How many counters will you take?"

Yakimov, knowing the croupier received five per cent on the bank, made a wild bid to escape: "You'll need a croupier, dear boy. Why not let your poor old Yaki . . ."

"I am croupier," said Hadjimoscos. "It is the tradition here. Come now, how many chips?"

Resignedly Yakimov replied: "Give me a couple of thou."

Hadjimoscos laughed: "Each piece is for five thousand. We do not play for less."

Yakimov accepted five counters and handed over his receipt for twenty-five thousand *lei*. Hadjimoscos took his place before the shoe. As soon as he had drawn the cards, he became serious and businesslike. At first the game went much as Yakimov had expected, with the bank increasing steadily and an occasional win for the player on the right. Yakimov, on the left, frequently let his right to play pass on his neighbour. Despite this, he had lost twenty thousand *lei* in ten minutes. He was resigned to losing all his chips, but with his last five thousand he turned over a seven and a two. At the next *coup*, Hadjimoscos said: "I give." The player on the right held a king and a queen: Yakimov held a six and a two. When his next hand proved to be a nine and a ten, the punters began to bet on the left and Yakimov began to regain himself. He was even winning at baccarat: something he had never done before. He used his winnings to increase his bets.

As Yakimov's pile of chips grew, Hadjimoscos's manner became increasingly sharp and cold. He dealt with great speed and he brushed Yakimov's gains towards him in a disapproving way. Hadjimoscos's face, that ordinarily was as round as the face of a Japanese doll, lengthened and thinned until it might have been the face of the boyar portrayed above the supper buffet. Suddenly, he lifted the shoe and slapped it down again. With no trace of his usual lisp, he announced the bank was broken.

"I'll have to see the Princess," he said and hurried away. He returned to say the Princess had refused to replenish the bank. He went to the Baron's elbow and said: "*Mon cher Baron*, I appeal to you."

With an affable flash of teeth, the Baron replied: "Surely you know I never lend money." 'No wonder,' thought Yakimov, the Baron was "*complètement* 'outsider'."

Hadjimoscos began to appeal elsewhere, while Yakimov, his chips on the table, wished only that he could change them and go. Having little hope of this, he sat on. A withered little man, whose hands had trembled so, he could scarcely pick up his cards, now moved stealthily round the table and murmured to Yakimov: "*Cher Prince*, surely you remember me? I am Ignotus Horvath. We met in the English Bar. I wonder ..." Horvath's hand, dark and dry as an old twig, hovered near Yakimov's chips. "A little loan. A mere ten thousand would do."

Yakimov passed them over, then heard a murmur at his other side. Turning warily, he met the black, astute gaze of a woman, lean with age, who leant towards him, attempting a charm that did not come easily to her. "I have had such misfortune ..." she was beginning, when Hadjimoscos caught Yakimov's arm and gave him excuse to turn away.

Hadjimoscos said: "I deeply regret, *mon cher*. I must appeal to you."

Yakimov was prepared for this. "I am willing to take the bank," he said.

"Impossible," Hadjimoscos looked shocked. "The Princess is always the banker."

Realising he would be as likely to lose them by playing as by lending them, Yakimov handed over his winnings. He said: "Think I'll take a breather," and no one hindered him.

A waiter was carrying round glasses of wine. Yakimov asked for whisky but there was none. The drink was running out. This, he knew, was the time to go, but he was now so weary he could scarcely face the descent to his room. He decided to revive himself with one more drink. He took his glass to a sofa, settled down comfortably, and when the glass was empty, fell asleep.

Some time in the middle of the night he was violently wakened. Half a dozen people, Hadjimoscos among them, were pulling at him. When he was on his feet, they began to rip off his clothes. Bewildered, frightened and still half-asleep, he saw – scarcely believing he saw – that all the guests were naked and shunting each other in a circle round the room. Handled in a frenzied fashion, he looked about for aid. Perhaps 'Foxy' Leverett, a fellow Englishman, would rescue him – but Leverett was nowhere to be seen.

When they had exposed and laughed at his long, fragile body, his assailants rejoined the circle and pulled him into it. With the woman behind thumping his buttocks and the woman in front complaining of his lack of enterprise, he spent the rest of the night trudging dismally round, dressed in nothing but his socks and one black shoe and one brown.

5

IN FRONT OF THE UNIVERSITY STEPS, where Harriet waited at noon next day, the gypsies were conducting their flower-market. The baskets were packed as high as hay-cocks with the stiff, tall flowers of the season. Among all this splendour of canna lilies, gladioli, chrysanthemums, dahlias and tuberoses, the gypsies, perched like tropical birds, screeched at the passers-by "*Hey, hey, hey, domnule! Frumosă. Foarte frumosă.* Two hundred *lei* . . . for you, for you, only one fifty! For you, only one hundred. For you, only fifty . . ." As the passers-by went on, unheeding, the cry followed, long-drawn, despairing as a train-whistle in the night: "*Domnule . . . domnule!*" to be plucked back with new vitality as a newcomer drew near. The bargaining, when it started, was shrill, fierce and dramatic. If a customer chose, as a last resort, to walk away, the gypsy would usually follow, looking, among the pigeon-shaped women on the pavement, long, lean and flashy, like a flamingo or a crane.

The gypsy women all trailed about in old evening dresses picked up from second-hand stalls down by the river. They loved flounced and floating chiffons. They loved colour. With their pinks and violets, purples and greens, their long, wild hair, and shameless laughter, they seemed to have formed themselves in defiant opposition to the ideals of the Rumanian middle class.

While watching the traffic of the gypsies, Harriet saw Sophie arrive among them and start bargaining sharply at one of the smaller baskets. When the deal was completed, she mounted the University steps, pinning one bunch of parma violets into the belt of her dress and another into her bosom. She started an animated waving, and Harriet, standing aside and unseen, looked and saw that Guy had appeared in the doorway. Sophie hurried to him, calling: "I say to myself I shall find you here, and I find you. Is it not like old times?" Her grievance, whatever it was, and the war – both were forgotten.

Guy, seeing Harriet, said: "Here's Harriet." It was a mere

statement of façt but Sophie chose to take it as a warning. She gasped, put a finger to her lip, looked for Harriet and, finding where she was, took on an air of elaborate unconcern. As Harriet joined them, Sophie gave Guy a consoling smile. He must not, said the smile, blame himself for the mishap of his wife's presence.

She said: "You go for luncheon, yes?"

"We were going to walk in the Cişmigiu," said Guy. "We might eat there."

"Oh, no," Sophie cried. "The Cişmigiu is not nice in this heat. And the café is too poor, too cheap."

Guy turned doubtfully to Harriet, looking to her to change their plans, but Harriet merely smiled. "I'm looking forward to seeing the park," she said.

"Won't you come with us?" Guy asked Sophie. When she complained that she could not, the sun was too much, she might get a headache, he took her hand consolingly and said: "Then let us meet for dinner tomorrow night. We'll go to Capşa's."

As they crossed the road to the park gates, Harriet said to Guy: "We cannot afford to go to expensive restaurants every night."

"We do so well on the black market," he said, "we can afford Capşa's once in a while."

Harriet wondered if he had any idea of what he could, or could not, afford on a salary of two hundred and fifty pounds a year.

A peasant had brought a handcart laden with melons into the town and tipped them out at the park gates. He lay among them, sleeping, his arms crossed over his eyes. The melons were of all sizes, the smallest no bigger than a tennis ball. Harriet said: "I've never seen so many before."

"That is Rumania," said Guy.

Repelled by their profusion, she had an odd fancy that, gathered there in a flashing mass of yellow and gold, the melons were not really inert, but hiding a pullulating craftiness that might, if unchecked, one day take over the world.

The peasant, hearing voices, roused himself and offered them the biggest melon for fifty *lei*. Guy was not willing to carry it about so they went on, passing out of the aura of melon scent into the earthy scent of the park. Guy led Harriet down a side-path that was overhung by a block of flats and pointing up to the first floor, that had a terrace before it, he said: "Inchcape lives there."

Enviously, Harriet saw on the terrace some wrought-iron chairs, a stone urn, a trail of pink ivy geranium, and asked: "Does he live alone?"

"Yes, except for his servant, Pauli."

"Will we be invited there?"

"Some time. He does not entertain much."

"He's an odd man," she said. "That edgy vanity! – what is behind it? What does he do with himself alone there? I feel there's something secret about him."

Guy said: "He leads his life, as we all do. What do you care what he does?"

"Naturally I'm interested."

"Why be interested in people's private lives? What they are pleased to let us know should be enough for us."

"Well, I just am. You're interested in ideas; I in people. If you were more interested in people, you might not like them so much."

Guy did not reply. Harriet supposed he was reflecting on the logic of her statement, but when he spoke she realised he had not given it a thought. He told her the Cişmigiu had once been the private garden of a Turkish water-inspector.

Brilliantly illuminated on spring and summer nights, it had a dramatic beauty. The peasants who came to town in search of justice or work saw the park as a refuge. They slept here through the siesta. They would stand about for hours gazing at the *tapis vert*, the fountain, the lake, the peacocks and the ancient trees. A rumour often went round that the King intended to take it all from them. It was discussed with bitterness.

"Will he take it?" Harriet asked.

"I don't think so. There's nothing in it for him. It is just that people have come to expect the worst from him."

In the last heat of the year, the greenery looked coarse and autumnal beneath a dust of light. The air was still. Noon weighed on everything. The great *tapis vert*, with its surround of leaf-hung poles and swags, its border of canna lilies and low bands of box, looked as unreal as some stage backdrop faded with age. A few groups of peasants stood about as Guy had described, but most of them had folded themselves into patches of shade and slept, faces hidden from the intolerable sun.

Everything seemed to give off heat. Harriet half expected the canna lilies, in great beds of sulphur, cadmium and red, to roar like a furnace. She stopped at the dahlias. Guy adjusted his glasses and examined the flowers, which were massive, spiked, furry, lion-faced, burgundy-coloured, purple and white, cinderous, heavy as velvet.

"Fine," he said at length.

She laughed at him and said: "They're like the invention of some ghastly interior decorator."

"Really!" Accepting the visible world because he so seldom looked at it, Guy was at first startled, then delighted, by this criticism of nature.

They followed a path that branched down to the lakeside. The water, glassy still, stretched out of sight beneath the heavy foliage of the lake-fed trees. The path ended beside a little thicket of chestnuts beneath which a small, derelict summer-house made a centre for commerce. Here the peasant who had any sort of stock-in-trade might begin a lifelong struggle up into the tradesman's class. One boy had covered a box with pink paper and laid out on it, like chessmen on a board, pieces of Turkish delight. There were not more than twenty pieces. If he sold them, he might be able to buy twenty-two. With each piece, the purchaser was given a glass of water.

"One eats," said Guy, "for the pleasure of drinking."

A man stood nearby with a weighing-machine. Another had a hooded camera where photographs could be obtained to stick on passports, or on the permits needed to work, to own a cart, to keep a stall, to sojourn in one town or journey to another.

At the appearance of the Pringles, some of the peasants lying on the ground picked themselves up and adjusted trays from which they sold sesame cakes, pretzels, matches and other oddments, and peanuts for the pigeons. Harriet bought some peanuts, and the pigeons, watching, came fluttering down from the trees to eat them. She was watched by some peasants standing near, whose eyes were shy and distrustful of the life about them. Newly arrived in the city, the men were still in tight frieze trousers, short jackets and pointed caps – a style of dress that dated back tc Roman times. The women wore embroidered blouses and fan-pleated skirts of colours that were richer and more subtle than those worn by the gypsies. As soon as they could afford it, they would throw off these tokens of their simplicity and rig themselves out in city drab.

Three girls, resplendent in sugar-pinks, plum-reds and the green of old bottle glass, were posing for a photograph. They might have been dressed for a fair or a festival, but they drooped together as though sold into slavery. Seeing the Pringles watching them, the girls looked uneasily away.

As they passed among the peasants, Guy and Harriet smiled to reassure them, but their smiles grew strained as they breathed-in the peasant stench. Harriet thought: 'The trouble with prejudice is, there's usually a reason for it,' but she now knew better than to say this to Guy.

The path through the thicket led to the lake café, which was situated on a pier built out into the water. On this flimsy, shabby structure stood rough chairs and tables with paper tablecloths. The boards creaked and flexed when anyone walked across them. Just below, visible between the boards, was the dark and dirty lake water.

The Pringles, seated in the sun, breathed air that was warm and heavy with the smell of water-weed. The trees on the distant banks were faded into the heat blur. An occasional rowing-boat ruffled the lake surface and sent the water clopping against the café piers. A waiter came running, producing from an inner pocket a greasy, food-splashed card. The menu was short. Few people ate here. This was a place where the city workers came in the cool of evening to drink wine or *ţuică*. Guy ordered omelettes. When the waiter went to the hut that served as a kitchen, he switched on the wireless in honour of the foreigners. A loud-speaker over the door gave out waltz music.

The café was, as Sophie had said, poor enough, but it had its pretensions. A notice said that persons wearing peasant dress would not be served. The peasants outside, whether they could read or not, made no attempt to cross on to the pier. With the humility of dogs, they knew it was no place for them.

There were a few other customers, all men. Stout and hot-looking in their dark town suits, they sat near the kitchen where there was shade from the chestnut trees.

Guy, exposed out in the strong sunlight, took off his jacket, rolled up his shirt-sleeves and stretched his brown arms on the table so that they might get browner. He stretched his legs out lazily and gazed round him at the tranquil water, the tranquil sky, the non-belligerent world. For some time they sat silent listening to the music, the lap from the rowing-boats and the ping of chestnuts dropping on to the kitchen's iron roof.

"Where is the war now?" Harriet asked.

"As the crow flies, about three hundred miles away. When we go home at Christmas . . ."

"Do you really think we will?" She could not believe it. Christmas brought to her mind a scene, tiny and far away like a snowstorm in a globe. Somewhere within it was 'home' – anyway, England. Home for her was no more defined than that. The aunt who had brought her up was dead.

"If we could save enough, we could go by air."

She said: "We shall certainly have to save if we're ever to have a home of our own."

"I suppose so."

"And we can't save if we're going to eat all the time at expensive restaurants."

Guy looked away at this unwelcome conclusion and asked if she knew the name of the piece they were playing on the wireless.

"A waltz. Darling, we'll . . ."

He caught her hand and pinned it down. "No, listen," he insisted as though she were trying to deflect him from an enquiry of importance. "Where have I heard it before?"

"All over the place. I want to know about Sophie."

Guy said nothing, but looked resigned.

Harriet said: "Last night she said she was depressed because of the war. Was it only because of the war?"

"I suppose so."

"Nothing to do with your getting married?"

"Oh, no. *No*. She'd given up that idea ages ago."

"She once had that idea, then?"

"Well," Guy spoke in an off-hand way, perhaps to hide discomfort. "Her mother was Jewish, and she worked on this anti-fascist magazine . . ."

"You mean she wanted a British passport."

"It was understandable. I felt sorry for her. And, don't forget, I didn't know you then. Two or three of my friends married German anti-fascists to get them out of Germany and . . ."

"But they were homosexual. It was just an arrangement. The couples separated outside the registry office. You would have been landed with Sophie for life."

"She said we could get divorced straight away."

"And you believed her? You must be mad."

Guy gave a discomforted laugh: "As a matter of fact, I didn't really believe her."

"But you let her try and persuade you. You might have given in if you hadn't met me? Isn't that it?" She watched him as though he had changed before her eyes into a different person. "If anyone had asked me before I married, I would have said I was marrying the rock of ages. Now I realise you are capable of absolute lunacy."

"Oh, come, darling," Guy protested, "I didn't want to marry Sophie, but one has to be polite. What would you have done under the circumstances?"

"Said 'No' straight away. One doesn't complicate one's life unnecessarily. But she would never have tried it on with me. Knowing I was not susceptible, she disliked me on sight. With you, of course, she thinks she can get away with anything."

"Darling, don't be so harsh. She's an intelligent girl. She can speak half a dozen languages . . ."

"Did you lend her any money?"

"Well, yes. A few thousand."

"Did she pay it back?"

"Well – she didn't regard it as a loan."

Harriet enquired no further but said only: "I don't want to see her every night."

Guy stretched across the table and squeezed Harriet's arm. "Darling," he said, "she's sad and lonely. You can afford to be kind to her."

Half-heartedly, Harriet said: "I suppose I can," and let the matter drop.

They had eaten their omelettes and were waiting for coffee, when Harriet noticed two beggar children who had climbed up on the pier from the lake and were keeping out of the waiter's sight. The older child came crawling under the tables until it reached the Pringles, then it stood up, ragged, wet and dirty, thin as a gnat, and clutching the edge of the table with its bird-small hand, began the chant of "*Mi-e foame*".

Guy handed over his small coins. The child scuttled off and at once its place was taken by the younger child, who, hopping from one foot to the other, eyes on a level with the table-top, kept up, in a sing-song, what seemed to be a long, unintelligible story.

Having no more change, Guy waved it away. It flinched from his movement as from a blow, but, recovering at once, went on with its rigmarole. Harriet offered it a piece of bread, then an olive, then a piece of cheese. These offerings were ignored, but the whine went on.

After some minutes of this, Harriet, irritated, hunted through her bag and found an English sixpence. The child snatched it and ran. They had returned to the quiet that came of being surrounded not by land but water, when the music stopped abruptly. The silence was suddenly so dense that Harriet looked round, expecting something. At that moment a voice broke shrilly from the loud-speaker.

The men near the kitchen sat up. One jumped to his feet. A chair fell. The voice spoke again. The waiter came from the kitchen. Behind him, in singlet and trousers, very dirty, came the cook. The man who had jumped up started shouting. The waiter shouted back.

"Is it the invasion?" asked Harriet.

Guy shook his head. "It was something to do with Călinescu."

"Who is Călinescu?"

"The Prime Minister."

"Why is everyone so excited? What did the announcer say?"

"I don't know."

Taking advantage of the distraction, the elder beggar boy had come up under the very nose of the waiter and was now begging urgently, time being short. The waiter went to the rail and shouted down to a man who hired rowing-boats. The man shouted back.

"He says," said Guy, "that Călinescu has been shot. They announced that he is either dead or dying. We must go to the English Bar. That's where you get all the news."

They left the park by a side gate where a statue of a disgraced politician stood with its head hidden in a linen bag. Hurrying through the back streets, they came into the main square as the newsboys were calling a special edition of the papers. People were thrusting each other aside to seize them, and when they had read a line were throwing the papers away. The square was already littered with sheets that stirred slightly in the hot breeze.

Guy, pushing his paper under his arm, told Harriet: "He was assassinated in the Chicken Market."

As he spoke, a man standing nearby turned sharply and said in

English: "They say the Iron Guard is wiped out. Now such a thing happens! It can mean anything. You understand that? It can mean anything."

"What can it mean?" Harriet asked as Guy hurried her across the square.

"That the Germans are up to something, I suppose. We'll hear everything in the bar."

But the English Bar, with its dark panelling and palms in brass pots, was dismally empty. The hard shafts of sunlight falling in from high-set windows made the place look like cardboard. There must have been a crowd in recently because the air was heavy with cigarette smoke.

Guy spoke to the barman, Albu, a despondent, sober fellow regarded in Bucharest as a perfect imitation of an English barman. Where was everyone? Guy asked.

Albu said: "Gone to send news."

Guy, frowning with frustration, asked Harriet what she would drink. "We'll wait," he said. "They're sure to come back. This is the centre of information."

6

In an upper room of the hotel, Yakimov was roused to reluctant consciousness by the squawks of the newsboys in the square.

The day before, when he handed his British passport to the clerk, he had been asked if he wished to be awakened in the 'English manner' with a cup of tea. He had replied that he did not wish to be awakened at all but would like a half-bottle of Veuve Clicquot placed beside his bed each morning. Now, getting his eyes open, he saw the bucket and was thankful for it.

An hour or so later, having bathed, dressed and been served with a little cold chicken in his room, he made his way down to the bar. The bar was now crowded. Yakimov ordered a whisky, swallowed it and ordered another. When the drinks had steadied him a little, he turned slowly and looked at the group behind him.

The journalists were standing around Mortimer Tufton, who sat on the edge of a stool, his old, brown spotted hands clenched on the handle of his stick.

Galpin, noticing Yakimov, asked: "Any news?"

"Well, dear boy, it was quite a party."

"I'll say it was," said Galpin. "One hell of a party. And the old formula, of course: someone inside creates a disturbance and the bastards march in to keep order."

Yakimov stared at Galpin some moments before comment came to him, then he said: "Quite, dear boy, quite."

"I give them twenty-four hours." Galpin, sprawled with his back against the bar, was a string of a man in a suit that seemed too small for him. He had a peevish, nasal voice and, as he talked, he rubbed at his peevish yellow, whisky-drinker's face. Over his caved-in belly, his waistcoat was wrinkled, dirty and ash-spattered. There was a black edging of grease round his cuffs; his collar was corrugated round his neck. He sucked the wet stub of a cigarette. When he talked the stub stuck to his full, loose lower lip and quivered there. His eyes, that he now kept fixed on Yakimov, were chocolate-coloured, the whites as yellow as limes. He repeated: "Twenty-four hours. You wait and see," his tone aggressive.

Yakimov did not contradict him.

He was bewildered, not only by Galpin's remarks, but by the atmosphere in the bar. It was an atmosphere of acute discontent.

In a high, indignant voice, Galpin suddenly said to Yakimov: "You heard about Miller of the *Echo*, I suppose?"

Yakimov shook his head.

"As soon as it happened, he got into his car and drove straight to Giurgiu. He may have got across, and he may not, but he's not stuck here like a rat in a trap."

Galpin was clearly speaking not for Yakimov's enlightenment but from a heart full of bitterness. Letting his eyes stray about, Yakimov noticed the young couple called Pringle whom he had met the night before. There was something reassuring about Guy Pringle's size and the mildness of his bespectacled face. Yakimov edged nearer to him and heard him say: "I still don't see how the Germans will get here. The Russians have moved into Eastern Poland. They've reached the Hungarian frontier."

"My good chappie" – Galpin turned, expressing his bitterness in contempt – "the Nazis will go through the Russkies like a hot knife through butter."

Guy put an arm round his wife's shoulder and looked into her strained, peaky face. "Don't worry," he said to her, "I think we're safe."

A small man, grey-haired, grey-faced, grey-clad, more shadow than substance, entered the bar and, skirting apologetically round the journalists, handed Galpin a telegram and whispered to him. When the man had gone, Galpin said: "My stringman reports: German Embassy claims to have proof the murder was organised by the British Minister in order to undermine Rumania's neutrality. That gets a laugh." He opened and read the telegram and said: "So does this: '*Echo* reports assassination stop why unnews stop asleep query.' So Miller made it! Nice scoop for Miller! And a raspberry for the rest of us."

Tufton said: "There's safety in numbers. We couldn't all be flogging the dog."

Under cover of this talk, Yakimov whispered to Guy: "Dear boy, what *has* happened? Who's been assassinated?"

It so happened this whisper came out during a moment of silence and Galpin caught it. He turned to Yakimov, demanding in scandalised tones: "You mean to say, you didn't know what I was talking about?"

Yakimov shook his head.

"You hadn't heard of the assassination? You didn't know the frontier's closed, the international line is dead, they won't let us send cables, and no one's allowed to leave Bucharest? You don't know, my good chappie, that you're in mortal danger?"

"You don't say!" said Yakimov. Stealthily he glanced around for sympathy but was offered none. Trying to show interest, he asked: "Who assassinated who?"

The journalists made no attempt to reply. It was Guy who told him that the Prime Minister had been assassinated in the Chicken Market. "Some young men drove in front of his car, forcing him to stop. When he got out to see what was wrong, they shot him down. He was killed instantly. Then the assassins rushed to the broadcasting studios, held up the staff and announced he was dead, or dying. They didn't know which."

"Filled him full of lead," Galpin broke in. "He clung to the car door – little pink hands, striped trousers, little new patent-leather shoes. Then he slid down. Patches of dust on the side of his shoes . . ."

"You saw it?" Yakimov opened his eyes in admiration, but Galpin remained disapproving.

"It was seen," he added: "What the heck were you up to? Were you drunk?"

"Did have rather a heavy night," Yakimov admitted. "Your poor old Yaki's just levered head from pillow."

Tufton shifted impatiently on his stool. "Fortune favours fools," he said. "We were forced to tarry while he slumbered."

The hotel clerk entered the bar and announced that cables could now be sent from the Central Post Office. As the journalists jostled their way out, Yakimov imagined his ordeal was over. He was about to order himself another drink, when Galpin gripped his arm.

"I'll give you a lift," said Galpin.

"Oh, dear boy, I don't think I'd better go out today. Don't feel at all well."

"Are you doing McCann's job or aren't you? Come on."

Looking into Galpin's crabbed, uncharitable face, Yakimov dared not refuse to go.

At the post office he wrote on his form: "Very sorry to tell you the Prime Minister was . . ." then hesitated so long over the spelling of the word 'assassinated' that the office emptied and he was alone with Galpin. Galpin, his face solemn, said: "You've got the story, of course? Who's at the bottom of this? And so on?"

Yakimov shook his head: "Haven't a clue, dear boy."

Galpin tut-tutted at Yakimov's ignorance. "Come on," he said more kindly, "I'll give you a hand."

Taking out his fountain-pen, Galpin concocted a lengthy piece which he signed: 'McCann'.

"That'll cost you about three thousand," he said.

Yakimov gasped, dismayed. "But I haven't a *leu*," he said.

"Well, this once," said Galpin, "I'll lend you the cash, but you must have money for cables. The international line may be closed down for weeks. Trot along now and see McCann."

Next morning, as he went to the breakfast room, Yakimov saw Galpin and a Canadian called Screwby coming purposefully from the bar. Suspecting they were on the track of news, he tried to avoid them, but it was too late. Galpin had already seen him.

"There's a spectacle in the Chicken Market," said Galpin as though Yakimov would be delighted to hear it. "We'll take you in the old Ford."

Yakimov shied away: "Join you later, dear boy. Trifle peckish. Must get a spot of brekker."

"For Christ's sake, Yakimov," said Galpin unpleasantly, "I'm McCann's friend. I'll see him served right. You do your job." And, taking Yakimov's arm, he led him out to the car.

They drove through the Calea Victoriei towards the river Dâmbovita. Yakimov had been put into the uncomfortable back seat. Galpin, apparently satisfied by his submission, talked over his shoulder: "You've heard, of course, they got the chappies who did it?"

"Have they, dear boy?"

"Yah. Iron Guardists, just as I said. A German plot, all right: an excuse to march in and keep order, but they reckoned without the old Russkies. The old Russkies got in their way. The Germans couldn't march through them. But these Guardist chappies didn't realise. They thought, when the Germans got here, they'd be the heroes of the new order. No one'd dare touch them. They didn't even go into hiding. They were picked up before the victim was cold and executed during the night."

"But what about the King, dear boy?"

"What about him?"

"You said he said he'd get Călinescu."

"Oh, that! It's a complicated story. You know what these Balkan countries are like." Galpin broke off to nod out of the car window. "Tension's relaxed," he said.

Screwby gave the passers-by a knowing look and agreed that tension was relaxed.

"Not that most of them wouldn't rather have the Germans here than the Russians up on the frontier." Galpin nodded again. "Look at that fat bastard. Got pro-German written all over him."

Yakimov looked, half expecting to see a duplicate of Goëring, but he saw only the mid-morning Rumanian crowd out for its refection of chocolate and cream cakes. He sighed and murmured: "Don't feel so well. Hollow with hunger," but he was ignored.

They crossed the tram-lines and entered the road that sloped down to the river. Galpin parked the car on the quayside and Yakimov saw the enormous winding queue, compacted like gut, that filled the market area. It gave him hope. Even Galpin must think twice of joining it.

"Dear boy," he said, "we might wait all day."

Galpin sharply asked: "You've got your card, haven't you? Then follow me." He strode authoritatively into the multitude, holding up his card to proclaim his privileged position. No one questioned him. The peasants and workpeople gave way at the sight of him and Screwby and Yakimov followed in his wake.

A square had been cordoned off in the centre of the market place. It was guarded by a dozen or so police lolling about in their dirty sky-blue uniforms. They stood upright at the sight of Galpin. One of them examined his card, pretended to understand it, then began, importantly, to clear a viewpoint. The assassins were revealed.

Yakimov, who disliked not only violence but the effects of violence, hung back till ordered forward by Galpin. With distaste, fearing a loss of appetite, he looked at the bodies.

"Just been tumbled out of a lorry," said Screwby. "How many are there? I can see four . . . five, six, I'd guess."

They looked like a heap of ragged clothes. The sightseers, kicking at them under the rail, had brought to view a head and a hand. On the head there was a bald spot, like a tonsure. One side of the face was pressed into the ground. The visible eye and nostril were clotted with blood; blood caked the lips together. The hand, growing dark and dry in the hot sun, was stretched out stiffly as though in search of aid. Blood, running down from beneath the sleeve, had stained the cobbles.

Galpin said: "That one wasn't dead when they pitched him out."

"How do you know, dear boy?" Yakimov asked, but received no reply.

Galpin put his foot under the rail and, stirring the heap about, uncovered another face. This one had a deep cut across the left cheek. The mouth was open, black with a vomit of blood.

Galpin and Screwby began scribbling in notebooks. Yakimov had no notebook, but it did not matter. His mind was blank.

Back in the car, he said to Galpin: "Dear boy, I'm faint. Wonder if you've a hip-flask on you?"

For answer Galpin started up the car and drove at speed to the Post Office. There they were given forms, but when Galpin presented his story he discovered that once again the stop was down. Nothing could be sent out. This was a relief for Yakimov, who had created five words ('They caught the assassins and . . .'). His eyes glazed with effort, he moaned: "Not used to this sort of thing. Simply must wet m'whistle."

"We're due at the press luncheon," said Galpin. "You'll get all you want there."

"But I'm not invited," said Yakimov, near tears.

"You've got your card, haven't you?" Galpin, his patience exhausted, said. "Then, for heaven's sake, come along."

With the quivering expectancy of an old horse headed for the stables, Yakimov followed the others into the desolate building which had been recently refurbished as a Ministry. They passed through a tunnelling of china-tiled passages to a room too high for its width, where, sure enough, food was lavishly displayed on a buffet table. The buffet was roped off. Before it stood several rows of hard chairs. It was to these the journalists were conducted.

Most of those present, being in Bucharest temporarily, to cover the assassination, had seated themselves unobtrusively at the back. Only Mortimer Tufton and Inchcape, now British Information officer, were in front. Tufton had placed his stick across the three chairs that separated them. He lifted it and motioned Galpin to sit beside him.

Inchcape sat askew, his legs crossed at the knee, an arm over his chairback and his cheek pressed back by his finger-tips. He looked sourly at Yakimov, who took the chair beside him, and said: "Something fishy about all this."

Yakimov, seeing nothing wrong but fearing to betray again his inexperience in the cunning world of journalism, murmured: "Quite, dear boy, quite!" His tone lacked conviction and caused Inchcape to wave an irritable hand at the buffet.

"Roped off!" he said. "Why? Never saw such a thing before at a public function. These people are nothing if not hospitable. And what are all these damned insolent flunkeys doing here? Are they on guard? Or what?" In an access of indignation, he jerked round his head and stared at the back rows.

There were, Yakimov now observed, a remarkable number of waiters; and these were smirking together as though involved in a hoax. Yet the food looked real enough. A side table was crowded with bottles of wines and spirits. Thinking he might get himself an apéritif, he motioned the nearest waiter and made a sign that seldom failed. It failed this time. The man, his lips twitching, lifted his face and appeared entranced by the fretted wooden ceiling.

Yakimov shuffled unhappily in his seat. Others shuffled and talked behind him. There were no new arrivals; time was passing; there was no sign of the Minister of Information. Inchcape's suspicion was extending itself through the room.

Suddenly Galpin said: "What's going on? Not a Boche or a Wop at the party. Nobody here but the friends of plucky little Rumania. And why are we being kept waiting like this?"

Tufton rapped with his stick on the floor. As the waiter looked up, he commanded: "Whisky."

One of the waiters, giving his fellows a sly, sidelong glance, replied in Rumanian.

"What the devil did he say?" asked Tufton.

Inchcape translated: "We must await the arrival of His Excellency Domnul Ionescu."

Tufton looked at his watch: "If His Excellency doesn't come within the next five minutes, I'm off."

The servants, expecting uproar, watched this exchange with interest and looked disappointed when nothing more resulted. The five minutes passed. Ionescu did not arrive, but Tufton remained in his seat. After a long pause, he said: "I suspect this is leading up to a reprimand."

"They'd never dare," said Galpin.

Yakimov's spine drooped. His hands hung, long, delicate and dejected, between his knees. He sighed repeatedly, like a dog kept too long on trust, and at one point told the world: "Haven't had a bite today." Placing his elbows on his knees, he buried his face in his hands and his thoughts wandered. There had been a time when he could dress up into an anecdote every incident of his life. Every situation became a comic situation. He had, he supposed, a gift for it. In those days he had entertained for the sake of entertaining. It delighted him to be the centre of attention. When times changed, he had entertained for any reward he could get. He told himself: 'Poor old Yaki has to sing for his supper.' Now he had lost interest in anecdotes. He felt no great inclination to entertain anyone. This working for food and drink was exhausting him. He only wanted sustenance and peace.

An electric bell rang in the room. The servants hurried to open the double doors. Yakimov roused himself hopefully. The journalists fell silent.

There was a further interval, then Ionescu entered, almost at a run. He stared, wide-eyed, at his guests and flapped his hands in humorous consternation that he should have kept them waiting so long. "*Comment faire mes excuses? D'être tellement en retard est inexcusable*," he said, but he was grinning, and when he came to a stop in the middle of the room he appeared to be expecting applause. Being met with nothing but silence, he raised his brows; his eyes, black and small as currants, darted from face to face; his moustache twitched; he bit his lower lip as though he could scarcely keep from laughing outright.

He exuded a comic bewilderment that seemed to ask what could be the matter with them all. Hadn't he apologised? Suddenly sobering, he started to address the gathering in English:

"Gentlemen – and, ah yes, ladies! How charming!" He bowed at the two women present, one of whom was American, the other French. "Ladies and gentlemen, I should say, then, should I not?" He started to smile again, but, receiving no response, he shook his head to show bewilderment, and went on: "Yesterday afternoon, ladies and gentlemen, you were privileged to send your papers – cables. Was that not so?" He looked round in enquiry, moving his head with bird-like pertness. When no one replied, he answered himself: "Yes, it was so. And what cables! I may here and now tell you that in place of the fantasies handed in at the Central Post Office, the following announcement was sent to all papers . . ." He brought out a pair of heavily rimmed glasses and, placing them half-way down his nose, slowly searched his pockets. "Ah!" he said. He sobered again, produced a paper and, after gazing at it for some moments, read out unctuously: " 'Today Rumania with broken heart announces the tragic loss of her much loved son and Premier A. Călinescu, assassinated by six students who failed to pass their baccalaureate. While attempting to forgive this mad act of disappointed youth, the nation is prostrate with grief.' "

He stepped forward, bowed and handed the paper to Inchcape.

"I take it," said Galpin, "we'll get our money back?"

Ionescu gave his head a sharp shake: "No money back." He wagged a finger before his nose. "This is, as the English say, a little lesson. You have all been very naughty, you know." He moved back to the rope and, catching it with either hand, swung on it.

"Like a bloody parrot on a perch," whispered Galpin.

Ionescu's smile widened. "You must remember," he said, "you are guests of a neutral kingdom. Here we are peaceful. We wish no quarrel with our neighbours. While living here, you must behave like good children. Isn't it so?"

Turning in his chair, Tufton asked his neighbours: "How long's this nonsense going on?"

A voice from the back asked. "What fantasies? What's biting him?"

"Ah, dear friends," said Ionescu, "am I perhaps mistaken? Did no one here invent the story that the assassins were Guardists in German pay? That the Germans had planned an invasion? That a certain foreign diplomat was under house arrest, having been found in possession of a cheque with which to reward the assassins?"

"Is von Steibel under house arrest, or isn't he?" asked Tufton.

Smiling, Ionescu said: "He is in bed with influenza."

"He's been ordered to leave the country, hasn't he?"

"Tomorrow he returns to Germany for a cure."

Questions now followed one another rapidly. In the confusion Ionescu straightened himself, raised his hands in alarm and waved for quiet: "A little moment, ladies and gentlemen. There is a more serious matter of which I am compelled to speak." His face grew grave and his voice became portentous. "This," he said, "is scarcely to be believed. Had I not seen with my own eyes the cable, I would have said such an invention was not possible."

Having made this statement, he paused so long that Galpin said: "All right. Let's have it."

Ionescu said: "A reputable journalist, representative of a famous paper, invented a story so scandalous I hesitate to speak of it. In short, he accused our great and glorious King, father of culture, father of his people, of being behind this fiendish murder. This journalist, we learn, is a sick man. He was wounded while driving out of Poland. He suffers, no doubt, a fever and we tell ourselves this story comes of delirium. No other explanation is possible. Nevertheless, as soon as he is capable, he will be ordered to leave."

Several present looked at Yakimov but Yakimov showed neither by expression or movement that he connected this reproof with anything he had permitted to be sent in McCann's name. Having administered this reproof, Ionescu relaxed and smiled again.

"Nearly three o'clock," said Tufton.

"One more little moment," said Ionescu. "We will now answer questions."

The American woman asked: "*M. le Ministre*, you have said the assassins were students. Isn't it possible they were Guardists, too?"

Ionescu smiled on her in pity: "*Chère madame*, was it not announced by His Glorious Majesty himself that not a single Guardist remains alive in this country?"

The French woman journalist now said: "It is widely rumoured that the assassins were in the pay of Germany."

Said Ionescu: "It is being widely rumoured that the assassins were in the pay of the Allied Powers. You must not believe café gossip, *madame*."

"I never go to cafés," said the Frenchwoman.

Ionescu bowed to her: "Then you must permit me to take you to one."

Tufton broke in on this exchange to ask with ponderous slowness: "And may we enquire who executed the assassins – no doubt without trial?"

Ionescu grew grave again. He recited quickly: "The military, mad with grief and indignation at the murder of a beloved Prime Minister, seized the young men and, unknown to the civil authorities, shot them out of hand."

"Is that official?"

"Certainly."

Someone asked: "Are you aware the bodies are being displayed at this moment down in the market-place? Do you approve of that sort of thing?"

Ionescu shrugged: "The military here is powerful. We dare not interfere."

"I saw the bodies," said Galpin. "They looked to me pretty old for students."

"In this country we have students of all ages. Some remain at the university all their lives."

Galpin grunted and looked at Tufton. Tufton said: "We're wasting our time."

Galpin rose, and the rest, needing no further encouragement, began to leave their seats. Roused by the squeak of chairs, Yakimov started up in wild hope. He blundered forward into Ionescu.

"Permit me," said the Minister, unable to hold back the surge, and, unhooking the cord where it joined in the middle, he admitted his guests to the buffet.

With a restraint that was painful to him, Yakimov awaited his associates. Tufton was slow in getting to his feet. "A slap for Rumania's kind friends," he said to Galpin. "A playful slap, but a significant one. Something has reminded them that Hitler is uncomfortably close."

Galpin said: "Those bastards accepted our guarantee *after* the Germans occupied Slovakia."

Tufton was up now. As he began to limp towards the buffet, he said: "So did the Poles."

That evening the autumn set in. The Pringles, leaving their hotel restaurant, where the air was hot and heavy with smoke, came out into an unexpected freshness. Rain had fallen. In the distance, wetly agleam, were the cupolas of the Opera House, where the Prime Minister lay in state.

Guy was in an exuberant mood. He had been exuberant all evening. It was now accepted – in most cases unwillingly accepted – that only the Russian occupation of Eastern Poland had kept the Germans out of Rumania. It was also believed that the Russian move had been the result of foreknowledge of the German plot. All this seemed to Guy a triumph for his political ideals. He said to Harriet: "Even the Legation must realise now that the Russians know what they're doing." To hearten Harriet he drew in his notebook a map that proved that the Germans could reach Rumanian soil only by violating Hungarian neutrality.

"And they won't do that," he said. "Not yet awhile."

"Why not?"

"Because they've got enough on their plate already."

Harriet smiled, this new sense of security coming to her like a gift. As they reached the street, they took hands, electrified by the changed air, and ran towards the Opera House, from which light fell through open doors. A queue had been moving all day. Now there was no queue. They took the opportunity to enter.

Inside the vestibule, where grey stone figures flew and gestured, there was a smell of wet rubber from the soldiers' capes. The floor shone with footprints. Within the auditorium, that had been cleared of seats, the bier, lit by candles, hung with purple and silver, stood islanded in spacious gloom. At its head and foot stood priests, black-bearded, black-robed, veils falling from their high head-gear. They were muttering prayers.

When he came within sound of them, Guy whispered "Mumbo-jumbo", and would have turned on his heel had not Harriet held to his arm and led him to the coffin. There was nothing to be seen but the Premier's nose, grey-white, with a sheen like putty.

The Pringles paused for a moment, then went to look at the wreaths. These, of immense size, were propped in a wide circle round the bier. The two largest, gigantic, towering like idols in the gloom, stood side by side behind the coffin's head. They were shield-shaped, formed of red carnations, one swathed with red, white and blue ribbon; the other with black and red. The black and red ribbon carried a swastika.

Galpin was gazing at these rival expressions of grief, a grin on his face. At the sight of him, Guy hurried forward to ask: "What price the old Russkies now?"

Galpin's mouth bunched itself in self-congratulation. He stared up at the ceiling, that was as obscure as the roof of a cave, and said: "It all happened more or less as I said. Thanks to the Russkies, we're not in Gestapo hands at this moment."

"You think we're safe, then?" said Harriet.

"Safe?" Galpin's mouth collapsed again. He eyed Harriet in bleak ridicule. "Safe? – with the Russian army massing on the frontier? Believe me, they'll be here before the winter sets in."

Guy said: "We needn't worry. We're not at war with Russia."

"I hope they give you time to tell them that."

Out in the street again, Harriet attempted philosophy: "Wherever one is," she said, "the only thing certain is that nothing is certain."

Guy looked surprised. "There are several things of which I am completely certain," he said.

"What for instance?"

"Well." He considered the question a moment, then said: "Among other things: that freedom is the knowledge of necessity and there is no wealth but life. When you understand that, you understand everything."

"Even the universe? Even eternity?"

"They're unimportant."

"I think they're important." Rather resentfully, Harriet took her hand from his. "Imagine the possibilities of eternity. This life is limited, whatever you do with it. It can only end in death."

"All these religious concepts," said Guy, "are only a means of keeping the poor poor; and the rich rich. Pie in the sky. Accept the condition it has pleased God to put you in. I am not interested in eternity. Our responsibilities are here and now."

They walked a little apart, divided by the statements of their differences. Before them there shone on a street corner the glass prow of the café they had set out to visit. This was the Doi Trandafiri, said now to be the meeting place of those turned out of the demolished Napoleon. Guy imagined he would find there all sorts of old friends. Harriet feared that he would. Imagining him disappearing into their embrace, she felt eternity to be doubtful and the universe black in its inhuman chill. She slid her hand back into his.

She said: "We're together. We're alive – anyway, for the moment."

Squeezing her hand, he asked: "When shall we be more than that?"

He pushed through the doorway into brilliance and she left the question unanswered.

7

INCHCAPE HAD RENTED AN EMPTY SHOP, which he was fitting out as the British Information Bureau. The shop stood in the Calea Victoriei, immediately opposite the German Information Bureau. This, that he described as 'the rival establishment', displayed pictures of the Siegfried Line and troops on the march. Inchcape said that so far he had been sent only a bundle of posters proclaiming 'Britain Beautiful' and advising tourists to 'See Britain First'. He told the Pringles they might view Călinescu's funeral from one of the upper windows of this office, and invited them to come beforehand to his flat for a drink.

Inchcape, when the Pringles arrived, made a grimace of disappointment. He had hoped they could take their drinks out to the terrace. "But today," he said, "even the sky mourns."

He had switched on two yellow-shaded reading lamps in his sitting-room: now he went round switching on three more. While the Pringles watched him, he studied the effect of this imitation sunlight on the white walls, the delicate gold and white furniture, the white pianoforte, and the books on their white shelves, then he smiled to himself. He insisted, he said, that Harriet come out for just a moment and view the park. She went out with him to the terrace and from there he turned and smiled back at the radiant room.

In the wintry, out-of-doors light, the concrete face of the flats, designed to reflect the sun, looked blotched and gimcrack. The geraniums were shedding their flowers, but Harriet, feeling that admiration was important to her host, admired everything. He touched one of his collection of large-leafed, fleshy plants and said: "Soon they must all come indoors. And that, in a way, is a good thing." When she looked at him in enquiry, he explained: "The snow will come soon and here we shall be, tucked away safe and sound."

She still did not understand.

He gave an exasperated little laugh: "Surely, my dear child, you know that no one invades in the winter! The time to invade is the autumn – after the harvest and before the snow blocks the passes."

"Why not this autumn?"

"Invasions take time to prepare, and there are no preparations. The patrol 'planes report all quiet on all fronts."

"That is something to be thankful for."

Rather to her surprise, he touched her arm. "Didn't I tell you there was no cause for alarm? I do not for a moment believe that anyone wants to invade this country. If they do, it won't be for six or seven months. A lot can happen in that time."

He smiled, very amiably. He was, she felt, being more than necessarily pleasant to her, not because he liked women, but because he did not. She suspected, also, that he was relieved to find they could get on so well. She was relieved herself: but she imagined it would always be a relationship that called for careful handling.

While Inchcape leant over the rail and pointed down through the trees to his glimpse of the lake, Harriet heard someone talking quickly and excitedly in the room behind them.

"Who is with Guy?" Harriet asked.

"It's Pauli, my Hungarian. All the best servants here are Hungarian. The Saxons are also good, but dour. Mean people, the Saxons; not much liked; no fun."

Pauli came out to them, putting his hands over his face then dropping them to express his delight at the story he had to tell. He was young and very good-looking. He bowed to Harriet, then shot out a hand at her, almost touching her as he begged her to listen. Speaking rapidly in Rumanian, he told all over again the story he had been telling Guy.

Watching him, Inchcape's smile softened indulgently. When the story was finished, he gave Pauli's shoulder a small push, dismissive and affectionate. As he made off, Pauli turned several times to comment excitedly on his own story.

Pretending impatience, Inchcape called after him: "Where are the drinks?"

"Ah, ah, I go now and get," cried Pauli, shaking repentant hands in the air.

"That," said Inchcape, "is the latest story going round about the King. A drunk in a café was reviling the King – calling him lecher, swindler, tyrant; all the usual things – when a member of the secret police, overhearing him, said: 'How dare you speak in this manner of our great and glorious Majesty, your King and mine?' 'But, but,' stammered the drunk, 'I was not speaking of *our* King. Far from it. I was speaking of another King. In fact – the King of Sweden.' 'Liar,' roared the policeman, 'everyone knows the King of Sweden is a good man.' "

They returned to the room where Pauli was putting out bottles and glasses. Realising his story was being retold, he stood grinning appreciatively until called away by a ring at the front door.

Clarence had arrived. He entered rather stiffly, greeting Guy and Inchcape, but keeping his glance averted from Harriet.

"Ah," said Inchcape, now both his men were present, "I have something to tell you: I shan't be able to view the funeral with you." He rubbed his brow into his hand and laughed at the absurdity of it all. "The fact is, your humble servant has been invited to attend the funeral. I shall be in one of the processional cars."

Guy, too startled to restrain himself, said: "Good heavens, why?"

"Why?" Inchcape was suddenly serious. "Because I am now in an official position."

"So you are!" said Guy.

Clarence, staring down at the carpet, grunted once or twice. This noise seemed to sting Inchcape, who said, off-handedly: "It's a bore, but quite an honour for the organisation. The only other members of the English colony invited are the Minister and Woolley."

Clarence grunted again, then said with sudden force: "Talking of honours, I hope you won't object to my accepting a little job that's just been offered me by the Legation?"

"Oh! What would that be?"

"The administration of Polish Relief. A large sum has been allocated by the Relief Committee at home and I've been recommended as a possible organiser. No salary. Just expenses and use of car. What about it?"

"Why you?"

"I did relief work in Spain. I was with the Council in Warsaw. I speak Polish."

"Humph!" Inchcape locked his fingers tightly together, examined them, then snapped them apart. "Let's have a drink," he said.

"So you don't object?" Clarence persisted.

"I *do* object." Inchcape swung round on him. "No one can do two jobs properly. You've been seconded by the British Council to our organisation. Now you're recommended for this work."

"It's war work. Someone must do it. I'll see the two jobs don't clash."

"They'd better not. Weil, help yourselves. I must go." He went from the room, and a little later they heard him slam the front door as he left the flat.

At the sound, Clarence jerked his head up and accidentally caught Harriet's eye. He coloured slightly but seemed relieved that he had acknowledged her presence at last. His manner eased. As he poured out the drinks, he laughed and said: "When we were merely outcast purveyors of British culture, Inchcape outdid us all in contempt for officialdom. Now, what a change is here! The next thing, he'll be dining with Woolley."

Clarence was wearing a tie decorated with the small insignia of his college and a blazer with the badge of his old school. Before they left the flat, he wrapped himself up in a long scarf knitted in the colours of a famous rowing club.

Harriet could not refrain from laughing at him. "Are you afraid," she asked, "that people will think you do not belong anywhere?"

Clarence paused, challenged, then looked gratified as though it had occurred to him this might be not so much criticism as coquetry. Opening the front door, he said: "I have a weak chest. I have to take care of myself."

There was a gleam in his eye. Harriet was aware she had been, as she too often was, misunderstood.

The rain had started. To cross the road, they pushed their way through several rows of spectators waiting under umbrellas. The British Information Bureau, a small building, had its windows whitewashed. The painters were at work inside. Above, in Inchcape's office, the walls had been stripped and given a first coat of white distemper. In one corner there was a stack of new wood cut for shelves. Clarence took the Pringles into the small back room that had been allotted to him. Nothing had been done there. The walls were still covered with a dirty beige paper of cubist design. A table had been put in to serve as a desk. There was nothing on it but a blotting-pad and a photograph in a frame.

Guy picked up the photograph: "Is this your fiancée?"

"Yep. Brenda."

"A nice, good face."

"Um." Clarence seemed to imply he could offer no excuse for it. They said no more about Brenda. Harriet went to the window and looked out at a large site being cleared in the parallel road, the new Boulevard Breteanu, that was being developed to draw the crowds off the Calea Victoriei. On either side of the site had been built wafer-thin blocks of flats, against which stood wooden lean-to sheds for the sale of vegetables and cigarettes. These had been put up by the peasants from the bug-ridden wood thrown out of the demolished houses. Other hovels stood about on the site, braced with flattened petrol cans, their vents protected with rags.

Clarence pointed out the skeleton of a new Ministry building that stood on the other side of the boulevard. Work on it had now come to a stop. The Minister had decamped to Switzerland with the Ministry funds. Meanwhile the workmen, left stranded, were camping in sheltered corners. Harriet could see them now, standing on the girders, gazing down into the street.

"Now it's growing cold," said Clarence, "they light bonfires and sit around them at night. Dear knows what they'll do when the winter comes."

Among the confusion below was a single rococo house, its stucco cracked and grey, its front door of engraved glass opening on to a pretty curve of broken steps, its garden a wasteland. Some-one was still living in it. At the windows hung thick lace curtains, as grimy as the stucco.

"Do you think we could find a house like that?" Harriet said.

As she spoke, some check in Clarence – a defensive prejudice against her, or perhaps mere shyness – broke suddenly, and he leant forward, smiling. "I'm fond of those old houses, too," he said, "but you can't live in them. They're alive with bugs. We're seeing the last of them, I'm afraid." He kept glancing sideways at her, awkwardly, half-smiling. "If Rumania had been as long under the Austrians as she was under the Turks, she might be civilised by now."

She noticed among his features, which before had had no special appeal to her, his sensitive and beautiful mouth. An occasional intentness in his glance made it clear to her that somehow there had been inaugurated an understanding, a basis for a relationship. It was an understanding in which she had no faith, a relationship she had no wish to pursue.

Their talk was interrupted by the distant thud-thud of a funeral march. The three hurried into the front room and, opening the windows leant out. The procession was appearing on the left and heading for the square. From there it would take a roundabout route to the station. Călinescu was to be buried on his own estate.

People were crowding out on to balconies, calling and waving to friends on other balconies. Despite the weather, there was an atmosphere of holiday. As the band drew near, the umbrellas, quilted below, moved towards the kerb: the police, wearing mourning bands on their arms, rushed wildly along in the gutter pushing them back again. A news-man on a lorry started turning his camera handle. The monstrous catafalque appeared, black and blackly ornamented with fringed draperies, ostrich feathers and angels holding black candles. It was drawn by eight black horses, weighted with trappings, the whites of their eyes flashing behind black masks. They slipped about on the wet road so that the whole vast structure seemed to topple.

The Prince walked behind it.

Ah! people shouted from balcony to balcony, this was just what they had expected. The King had been afraid to attend even in his bullet-proof car: yet there was the young Prince, walking alone and unprotected. It was felt that the crowd would give a cheer, were it an occasion for cheering.

Behind the Prince came the canopy of the Metropolitan. On either side the priests swept the watery streets with their skirts. The old Metropolitan with his great white beard, seeing the camera, plucked at his vestments, straightened his jewelled cross and lifted his face with mournful dignity.

The massed military bands, having changed from Chopin to Beethoven, went past uproariously. Then came the cars. Clarence and the Pringles looked out for Inchcape, but he could not be recognised among the anonymous, dark-clad figures within.

The tail of the procession crept past and hard upon it came the press of traffic released from the side streets. All in a moment, it seemed, even while the funeral was still thumping and wailing its way to the square, the Calea Victoriei was aswarm with cars hooting, dodging, cutting in upon each other, eager for life to return to normal.

The ranks of spectators broke up and people began crowding into bars and cafés. They swept past the neon-lit window of the German Information Bureau, which displayed a map of Poland partitioned between Germany and Russia. A swastika obliterated Warsaw. No one paused to give it a glance.

Confidence was growing again. The black market rate had dropped, so even Guy was inclined to agree they could not entertain Sophie every night. One Bucharest paper had expressed in a leader regret that Greater Rumania had not been given the chance to pit her strength against a mighty enemy. She would show the world how a war could be fought. Readers were reminded that in 1914 Rumania's gold had been sent for safety to Moscow. It had never come back again. Rumanian manhood was eager to redress this wrong – but would the opportunity ever come?

Clarence, drawing in his head and closing his window, said: "Now we've heard the last of Călinescu, let's go and get a meal."

But Călinescu was not to be so easily put out of mind. Three days of official mourning were proclaimed, during which the cinemas were to remain shut. When they opened, they showed a news-film of the funeral. For a week the giant coffin was carried by peasants through rain, to the family tomb, then, at last, the late Premier was replaced and forgotten. Forgotten also was the Iron Guard. Its members, declared Ionescu, had been wiped out to a man.

PART TWO

The Centre of Things

8

HARRIET PRINGLE, NO LONGER FEARING that she and her husband would have to flee at any moment, began to look for a flat, buy clothes and take an interest in the invitations that were arriving now that the university term had started. Among those invitations was one from Emanuel Drucker, the banker, whose son was Guy's pupil.

The rain came and went. At night the wind blew cold and the Chaussée restaurants moved their chairs and tables back to their winter premises. After a week of grey weather the sun shone again, but it was possible to sit out of doors only at mid-day.

To the north of the city, where before there had only been the sheen of sun and mist, mountains appeared, crevassed and veined with glaciers that looked like threads of cotton. One morning the highest peak was veiled with snow. Each day the snow grew a little whiter and spread further down the mountain-side. Although Guy laughed at Inchcape's theory of invasion, saying the Russians could come by the coastal plain any time they liked, Harriet was comforted by the thought of the high passes silting up with snow.

The day they were invited to luncheon with the Druckers was one of the last warm days of October. Harriet had arranged to meet Guy in the English Bar, but when she looked for him in the bar, he had not arrived. This did not surprise her, for she was beginning to realise that however late she might be for an appointment Guy could always be later.

The bar was not quite empty. Galpin sat at a table with a girl of dark domestic beauty, while Yakimov stood alone, disconsolately looking at them. Tufton and most of the visiting journalists had returned to their bases.

"Dear girl," Yakimov called when he noticed Harriet, "come and join poor Yaki in a whisky," his plaintive voice suggesting not the intimidating social background described by Inchcape, but a need for comfort.

She entered. The air was smoky and stifling, and she said: "Do you really like this bar? Hasn't the hotel a garden where we could sit?"

"A garden, dear girl?" He glanced around as though there might be a garden at his elbow. "I've seen one somewhere."

"Then let's look for it." Harriet left a message for Guy with Albu, and led Yakimov away.

The garden proved to be small, high-walled and accessible only through the French-windows of the breakfast room. Weatherworn tables and chairs stood under heavy trees. A few couples were sitting in secluded corners. The men glanced up at the newcomers in disconcerted surprise: the women, each of whom wore dark glasses, turned away. They all looked like people tracked down to a hide-out.

There were no flowers in the garden and no ornaments except, in the centre of the pebbled floor, a stone boy pouring an ewer of water into a stone basin. Sitting down beside the fountain, Harriet said: "This is better, isn't it?"

Yakimov murmured doubtful agreement and sat beside her.

There was a sense of pause in the air. The couples remained silent until Harriet and Yakimov began to speak. Harriet asked: "Who was that girl with Galpin?"

"Polish girl," said Yakimov, "Wanda Something. Came down here with McCann. Thought she was McCann's girl; now, apparently, she's Galpin's. I don't know!" Yakimov sighed. "Wanted to have a talk with Galpin about this mobilisation order. Y'know, I'm a journalist. Have to send stuff home. Important to discuss it, get it straight. Went up to them in the bar just now, said 'Have a drink', and got the nose bitten right off m'face."

He turned to stare at Harriet and she was surprised to see his eyes, set within the bewildered sadness of his face, become hard with grievance. He looked for the moment like an embittered child. Before she could speak, the waiter came to the table and she ordered lemonade. She said:

"Do you think it significant, the mobilisation order? Are they expecting trouble?"

"Oh no." Yakimov swept the thought aside with a movement of the hand. Galpin was forgotten now. Yakimov smiled with the delight of the entertainer. "You've heard about this frontier line the King plans to build round Rumania? Twice as strong as the Maginot and the Siegfried rolled into one? To cost a million million *lei*? The Imaginot Line, I call it, dear girl. *The Imaginot Line!*"

When Harriet laughed, he leant a little nearer to her and became gravely confiding. In the manner of an informed man, he said: "What I did think important was Hitler's peace plan. Said he had no more territorial ambitions. *Amazed* me when I heard they'd turned it down. Don't want to be critical, but I think Chamberlain slipped up there. No one wants this silly war, now *do* they?"

"But Hitler so often said he had no territorial ambitions. We couldn't possibly trust him."

"But we *must* trust him, dear girl." Yakimov's great eyes seemed to swim with trust. "In this life we have to trust people. It's the right thing to do."

Unable to think of a reply, Harriet drank her lemonade. Yakimov, his face relaxing after his effort at earnestness, said easily: "I wonder, dear girl, could you lend me a couple of thou?"

"What are 'thou'?"

"Why, mun, dear girl. Cash. Ready. Your poor old Yaki is broke until his remittance turns up."

She was so startled, her cheeks grew pale. She opened her bag and searching through it with flustered movements, found a thousand-*lei* note. "It is all I have," she said.

"Dear girl!" – he pocketed the note in an instant – "how can poor Yaki express his gratitude?" But Harriet did not wait to hear. As she rose and hurried from the garden, he called after her in hurt dismay: "*Dear girl!*"

She met Guy as he entered through the revolving door. He said: "What's the matter?"

She was too abashed to tell him, but after they had crossed the square, she had regained herself enough to laugh and say: "Prince Yakimov invited me to have a drink. I thought he was being kind, but all he wanted was to borrow some money."

Unperturbed, Guy asked: "Did you lend him any?"

"A thousand *lei*."

Now that Guy was treating the matter as unimportant, Harriet regretted her thousand *lei*. She said: "I hate lending money."

"Darling, don't worry about it. You take money too seriously."

She would have said that that was because she had never had any, but she remembered Guy had never had any, either. She said instead: "Yakimov is a fool. He was telling me we must trust Hitler."

Guy laughed. "He's a political innocent, but no fool."

They were approaching the back entrance to the park where the disgraced politician stood with his head in a bag. The Drucker family lived nearby in a large block of mansion flats owned by the Drucker bank.

Within the doorway of the block were two life-sized bronze figures holding up bunches of electric-light bulbs. There was an impressive stairway, heavily carpeted. The hall had an atmosphere of France, but smelt of Rumania. The porter, who, in hope of a tip, pushed his way into the lift with them, reeked powerfully of garlic, so that the air seemed filled with acetylene gas.

They were taken to the top floor. When the Pringles stood outside the great mahogany doors of the Druckers' flat, Harriet said: "I cannot believe that anything human exists behind these doors," but they opened even as Guy touched the bell and behind them stood Drucker and his sister and daughters. The actual opening of the door had been accomplished by a manservant, but Drucker's impulsive movement forward suggested that, had convention permitted a gentleman to open his own front door, he would have done it for Guy's sake.

At the sight of Drucker, Guy gave a cry of pleasure. Drucker shot out his arms and at once Guy threw wide his own arms. A tremendous babble of greetings, questions and laughter broke out while Guy, breathlessly trying to answer all that was asked of him, bent about him, kissing the women and girls.

Harriet stood back, watching, as she had watched the similar excitement in the *wagon-lit*.

It was Drucker himself – a tall, slow-moving man, stooping, heavy, elegant in silvery English tweeds – who came with outstretched hands to include her: "Ah, so charming a wife for Guy! *Si jolie et si petite!*" He gazed down on her with a long look of ardent admiration. He took her hands with confidence, a man who knew all about women. Added to the sensual awareness of his touch was a rarer quality of tenderness. It was impossible not to respond to him, and as Harriet smiled he nodded slightly in acknowledgement of response. He then called to his eldest sister, Doamna Hassolel.

Doamna Hassolel detached herself from Guy, giving a slight "Ah!" of regret. The animation of her face became restrained and critical as she was called to give attention to Harriet.

She was a small, stout, worn-faced woman with a decided manner. She took charge of the guests, apologising for the absence of the hostess, Drucker's wife, who was still at her toilette. Harriet was introduced to the younger sisters, Doamna Teitelbaum and Doamna Flöhr. The first had a worried thinness. Doamna Flöhr, the beauty of the family, was plump and would, in time, be as stout as the eldest sister. She examined Harriet with bright, empty eyes.

They moved into the living room. As soon as they had sat down, a servant wheeled in a trolley laden with hors-d'œuvres and the little grilled garlic sausages made only in Rumania. Harriet, having learnt by now that luncheon might be served any time between two o'clock and three, settled down to drink *ţuică* and eat what was offered her.

The room was very large. Despite its size, it appeared over-full of massive mahogany furniture and hemmed in by walls of so dark a red they were almost black. Hung on the walls, darker than the paper, were portraits heavily framed in gold. A vast red and blue Turkey carpet covered the floor. In the bow of the window, that overlooked the park, stood a grand pianoforte. Drucker's eldest daughter, a school-girl, sat on the stool, occasionally revolving on it and touching a note whenever she stopped before the keyboard. The younger girl, a child of nine, dressed in the uniform of the Prince's youth movement, stood very close to her father. When he had filled the glasses, he whispered to her. Shyly, she drew herself from his side to hand the glasses round.

The women talking in French and English, questioned Guy about his holiday in England – a journey that now seemed to Harriet to have happened long before – and all he and his wife had done since their arrival. Across the boisterous talk, Drucker smiled at Harriet but he was too far from her to draw her into the conversation. When she answered the questions that Guy referred to her, her voice sounded to her discouraging and remote. She had the sense of being isolated in this tumult of vivacious enquiry. Guy, flushed and excited, seemed as far from her as they were. The first time he had visited here, he had been a stranger like herself but he had been taken immediately into the family's heart. She, she felt, was not what they expected; not what they felt she ought to be. She would be a stranger here for ever.

They began to talk of the war. "Ah, the war!" The word flashed from one to the other side of the little, quick-speaking women with intonations of regret. Now they had touched upon this serious subject, they turned to Drucker for comment.

He said: "Because of the war, we make much business: but still, it is a bad thing."

Harriet glanced at Guy, wondering what he would think of this, but whatever he thought, he was distracted from it by the entry of Drucker's parents. They came in slowly, with an air of formal purpose, the wife leaning on her husband's arm. Both were small and very frail. Drucker hurried to them and led them carefully in to greet Guy and meet Harriet. They had been born in the Ukraine and spoke only Russian. The old man, slowly shaking Guy by the hand, made a little speech in a voice so quiet it could scarcely be heard.

Guy, delighted, brought out his four words of Russian – an enquiry as to their health. This gave rise to wonder and congratulations, during which the old couple, smiling their ghostly smiles, excused themselves and made their way out again.

Drucker said: "They tire very easily and prefer to eat in their own drawing-room."

The flat, Harriet thought, must be very large. She later learnt that the Drucker family occupied the whole of the block's top floor.

Before the conversation could start again, Drucker's brothers-in-law began to arrive from their offices. Hassolel, dry-faced and subdued, dressed in silver-grey with white spats, arrived first but had scarcely spoken before the two younger men came in together. Teitelbaum wore several gem rings, a gold watch bracelet, diamond cuff-links, a diamond tie-pin and a broad gold clip to hold down his tie. His elderly, humourless manner made this jewellery seem less an ornament than a weariness of the flesh. The two older men, dispirited though they seemed, did their best to be affable, but Flöhr made no effort at all. Though still in his thirties, he was bald. His fringe of red hair and his striped chocolate-brown suit gave him a flamboyance that did not seem to be part of his personality.

He took a seat outside the circle, apparently resenting the fact there were visitors in the room.

Guy had told Harriet that the brothers-in-law were all of different nationalities. Only Drucker held a Rumanian passport. It was evidence of Drucker's power in the country that the others – one German, one Austrian and one Polish – had been granted *permis-de-séjour*. They existed in his shadow.

The large skeleton clock over the fireplace struck two. Drucker's wife had not yet appeared. The door opened and the new arrival was the son Sasha, Guy's pupil. Doamna Hassolel explained that he was late because he had gone from the University to his saxophone lesson. When introduced to Harriet, he crossed the room to kiss her hand. He was a tall boy, as tall as his father, but thin and narrow-shouldered. As he bent over Harriet, the light slid across the black hair, which he wore brushed back from a low and narrow brow. Like his sisters, he resembled his father without being handsome. His eyes were too close together, his nose too big for his face, but because of his extraordinary gentleness of manner Harriet felt drawn to him. There was in him no hint of the family's energy and drive. He was like some nervous animal grown meek in captivity.

He left Harriet and went to shake hands with Guy, then he stood against the wall, his eyes half-shut.

Watching the boy, Harriet thought that were one to meet him in any capital in the world, one would think not 'Here is a foreigner' but 'Here is a Jew'. Though he would be recognisable anywhere, he would be at home nowhere except here, in the midst of his family. Despite the fact he did undoubtedly belong – as though to prove it his aunts had each as he passed given him a pat of welcome – there was about him something so vulnerable and unprotected that Harriet's sympathy went out to him.

After a while he whispered to Doamna Hassolel. She shook her head at him, then turned to the company: "He wants to play his gramophone but I say 'No, soon we must eat'." She reflected in her speech the family pride in the boy.

The rest of the family kept silent while Drucker and Guy discussed Sasha's progress at the University. He had been educated at an English public school and would be sent, when the war ended, to learn the family profession in the bank's New York branch.

The other men kept nodding approval of all Drucker said. There could be no doubt that it was he who gave them all status. Had a stranger asked: "Who is Hassolel? Who Teitelbaum? Who Flöhr?" there could be only one answer to each question: "He is the brother-in-law of Drucker, the banker."

When there was a pause, Teitelbaum said: "How fortunate a young man that can go to America. In this country, who can tell? Already there is general mobilisation and young men are taken from their studies."

"All the time now," said Doamna Hassolel, "we must pay, pay, pay that our Sasha may have exemption."

While the others spoke of Sasha, Drucker smiled at the little girl at his side so that she might know she was not forgotten. He gave her a squeeze, then said to Harriet: "This is my own little girl. She's so proud of her beautiful uniform." He fingered the silk badge on her pocket. "She is learning to march and shout 'Hurrah' in chorus for her handsome young Prince. Isn't she?" He gave her another squeeze and she blushed and pressed her face into his coat. As he smiled, there could be seen, behind the ravages of the years, the same sensitivity that on Sasha's face was unhidden and defenceless.

Feeling enough had been said about Sasha, Doamna Hassolel now questioned Guy about his friend David Boyd whom he had once brought to luncheon with them. Would David Boyd return to Rumania?

Guy said: "He planned to come back, but now I do not know. In war-time we have to do what we are told."

The sun, that had been for a while behind a cloud, burst through the window and lit the famous corn-coloured hair of Doamna Flöhr, who was said to have once been a mistress of the King. Peering short-sightedly at Guy, her head flashing unnatural fire, she cried: "Ah, that David Boyd! How he talked! He was a man who knew everything."

Guy agreed that his friend, an authority on the Balkans, was very knowledgeable.

"He was a man of the Left," said Teitelbaum. "What would he think, I wonder, of this German-Soviet Friendship Treaty?"

Everyone looked at Guy to see what he, another man of the Left, thought of it. He merely said: "I imagine Russia has a plan. She knows what she is doing."

Doamna Hassolel broke in quickly to say: "Never will I forget how David Boyd was talking of Vâlcov – how he rose at dawn and rowed out alone in the waterways and saw the thousands of birds, and how he saw a big bird called a Sea Eagle. It was so interesting. You would think he would be lonely and afraid in such places."

Guy said that David had travelled over all the Balkan countries and spoke the language of each.

"These Balkan countries are wild," said Doamna Hassolel. "They have dangerous wild beasts. I would not travel here. In Germany it was different. There Willi and I would take out walking sticks and . . ." She talked affectionately of life in Germany.

The clock had struck half past two before Doamna Drucker made her appearance. She had not met Guy before, having married Drucker only that summer, but she gave him her hand with barely a glance. She was a few years older than Sasha; not Jewish; a Rumanian beauty, moon-faced, black-haired, black-eyed, like other Rumanian beauties. She wore the fashionable dress of the moment, black, short, tight-fitting, with pearls, a large diamond brooch and several diamond rings. As she crossed to the chair, her body undulating with an Oriental languor, Drucker's gaze was fixed upon her. Settling like a feather settling, lolling there without giving a glance at the company, she expressed her boredom with the whole Drucker ménage. Her husband asked her if she would take *ţuică*. She replied: "*Oui, un petit peu.*"

When Drucker sat down again, the little girl patted his arm and whispered urgently to him, but now his attention was only for his wife. Unable to distract him, the child stood looking at her stepmother, her expression pained.

Luncheon was announced. Doamna Hassolel led the way to the dining-room. Drucker sat at one end of the table, but the other end was taken by Doamna Hassolel, who served from a great silver tureen a rich chicken soup made of sour cream. Doamna Drucker sat half-way down the table between Sasha and Flöhr.

Drucker, having Harriet at his hand, began to question her about her impression of Bucharest.

Looking admiringly at his wife, Guy said: "Apart from the Legation women, who have diplomatic immunity, Harriet is the only Englishwoman left here." Before he could say more, Doamna Hassolel interrupted rather sharply:

"Surely," she said, "Doamna Niculesco is here? She is an Englishwoman. You have met her?" She looked at Harriet, who said she had not. Harriet glanced at Guy, who dismissed Bella, saying: "Bella Niculesco is a tiresome woman. You would not have much in common."

At this Doamna Teitelbaum, whose cheeks hung like curtains on either side of the drooping arc of her mouth, said eagerly: "You do not like her? Me neither. Perhaps on you, too, she has tried the snub?"

The Drucker sisters, hoping for scandal, all turned to Guy, who innocently replied: "No, but I did upset her once – the only time I was taken to the Golf Club. Bella was supervising the hanging of a portrait of Chamberlain painted by some local artist. A ghastly thing. It was inscribed: 'To the Man who Gave us Peace in Our Time.' Chamberlain was holding the flower Safety and had the nettle Danger crushed beneath his foot. I said: 'What's that thing painted with? Treacle?' Bella Niculesco said: 'Mr. Pringle, you should have more respect for a great man.' "

This story did not meet with the acclaim it would have received in Guy's more immediate circle. Doamna Hassolel broke the silence by insisting that the Pringles must take more soup. Most of the members of the family had taken two or three plates. Doamna Flöhr had excused herself, saying she was slimming. Harriet tried to do the same.

"No, no," protested Doamna Hassolel, "it is not possible. If you grow more slim, you will disappear."

The soup was followed by sturgeon, then an entrée of braised steak with aubergine. The Pringles, supposing the entrée to be the main dish, took two helpings and were dashed by the sight of the enormous roast of beef that followed it.

"I went myself to Dragomir's," said Doamna Hassolel, "and ordered it to be cut 'sirloin' in the English fashion. We are told how you eat much roast beef. Now you must fill your plate, two, three times."

While the Pringles were silenced by food, the family grew relaxed and even more talkative. Doamna Flöhr said to Harriet: "You are looking for a flat?"

Harriet said she had started looking now it seemed they would stay.

"Ach," said Hassolel, "the Germans won't come here. The

Rumanians are clever in their way. Last war, they gained much territory. This time they will keep a foot in each camp and come out with even more."

Flöhr gave a snort of disgust. Speaking for the first time, he said: "Such a war! An unexploded squib of a war! What folly ever to start it. The great nations think only of power. They do not think of the ones who suffer for such a war."

In a conciliatory way, Guy said: "They say there will be financial collapse in Germany soon. That might shorten the war." He looked round for applause and met only shocked alarm.

Doamna Flöhr, moving anxiously in her seat, cried: "It would be terrible, such a collapse! It would ruin us."

Drucker, lifting his head tortoise-fashion out of his silence, said: "That is a rumour put around by the British. There will be no collapse." This firm assurance brought immediate calm. Harriet looked at Guy, but he, drowsy with food and wine, seemed unaware of the disturbance he had created. Or perhaps he preferred to seem unaware. It came into her mind that, where his friends were concerned, he was inclined to excuse anything.

Drucker, noticing her look, said quietly: "It is true our business is much dependent on German prosperity. But we made our connections long ago. We do not love the Germans any more than you, but we did not cause the war. We must live."

Doamna Hassolel broke in aggressively. "A banker," she said, "upholds the existing order. He is an important man. He has the country behind him."

"Supposing the order ceases to exist?" said Harriet. "Supposing the Nazis come here?"

"They would not interfere with us," Flöhr said with a swaggering air. "It would not be in their interests to do so. They do not want a financial débâcle. Already, if it were not for us, Rumania would be on her knees."

Teitelbaum added sombrely: "We could a dozen times buy and sell this country."

Drucker, the only member of the family who seemed aware that these remarks were not carrying Harriet where they felt she should go, lifted a hand to check them, but as he did so his youngest sister broke in excitedly to urge the pace:

"We work, we save," she said, "we bring here prosperity, and yet they persecute us." She leant across the table to fix Harriet with her reddish-brown eyes. "In Germany my husband was a clever lawyer. He had a big office. He comes here – and he is forbidden to practise. Why? Because he is a Jew. He must work for my brother. Why do they hate us? Even the *trăsură* driver when angry with his horse will shout: 'Go on, you Jew.' Why is it? Why is it so?"

The last query was followed by silence, intent and alert, as though, after some introductory circling over the area, one of the family had at last darted down upon the carcase of grievance that was the common meat of them all.

Drucker bent to his daughters and whispered something about "*grand-mère et grand-père*". They whispered back. He nodded. Each took an orange from the table, then, hand-in-hand, left the room.

The talk broke out again as the door closed after the children. Each member of the family gave some example of persecution. Drucker's long aquiline head drooped over his plate. He had heard it all before and knew it to be no more than truth. Guy, roused by the talk, listened to it with a crumpled look of distress. The only persons unaffected were Sasha and Doamna Drucker. Doamna Drucker looked profoundly bored. As for Sasha – the stories, it seemed, did not relate to him. His thoughts were elsewhere. He was the treasured fœtus in the womb that has no quarrel with the outside world.

"Yet you are not in danger here," said Harriet.

"It is not the danger," said Hassolel. "There is danger everywhere. It is the feeling, a very ancient feeling. In the Bukovina you will see the Jews wear fox-fur round their hats. So it was ordered hundreds of years ago to say they are as crafty like a fox. Today they laugh and wear it still. They are clever, it is true, but they live apart: they harm no one."

"Perhaps that is the trouble," said Harriet, "that they live apart. Your first loyalty is to your own race. And you all grow rich. The Rumanians may feel you take from the country and give nothing back."

Harriet had offered this merely as a basis for discussion and was startled by the tumult to which it gave rise. In the midst of it, Doamna Flöhr, near hysteria, shouted: "No, no, we are not to blame. It is the Rumanians. They shut their doors on us. They are selfish people. This country has everything but they do not want to share. They are greedy. They are lazy. They take everything."

Drucker, when he could be heard, said: "There is room for all here: there is food and work for all. The Rumanians are content to do nothing but eat, sleep and make love. Such is their nature. The Jews and the foreigners, they run the country. Those who do the work, make the money. Isn't it so? One might rather say of the Rumanians that they take and give nothing back."

This statement was greeted with nods and exclamations of agreement. Teitelbaum, his flat, depressed face looking newly awakened, said: "But we are generous, we Jews. We always give when we are asked. When the Iron Guard was powerful in 1937, the green-shirt boys came to the offices collecting for party funds. The Jewish firms gave twice, even three times, more than the Rumanians, and what was the gratitude? The Iron Guard made laws against us. Only last year there was a pogrom."

Hassolel was peeling an orange. Without looking up from this employment, he said heavily: "At the University our boy was thrown from a window. His spine was broken. Now he is in a sanatorium in Switzerland. Our daughter was medical student. In the laboratory the young men took off her clothing and beat her. She went to America. She is ashamed to come back. So, you see, we have lost both our children."

In the silence that followed, Hassolel went on peeling his orange. Harriet looked helplessly across at Guy, who had grown pale. He said suddenly: "When the Russians come here, there will be no more persecution. The Jews will be free to follow any profession they choose."

At these words, intended to comfort, the brothers-in-law turned on him faces so appalled that Harriet laughed in spite of herself. No one looked at her or spoke, then Doamna Hassolel began pressing people to take sweets and chocolates from the little trays round the table. Coffee was served. When he had drunk a cup, Teitelbaum declared slowly:

"The Communists are bad people. Russia has done great harm. Russia steals from Europe her trade."

At the appearance of this familiar argument, Guy recovered himself and laughed good-humouredly. "Nonsense," he said; "Europe suffers from an out-dated economy. Take this country where a million workers – that's one twentieth of the population – contribute half of the total yearly value of production. That means each worker carries on his back four adults – four male non-workers. And these workers are not only scandalously under-paid, they pay more than they should for everything they buy, except food. For food, of course, they pay too little."

"*Too little!*" The sisters were scandalised.

"Yes, too little. There is no country in the world where food is so cheap. At the same time, factory-made articles are priced out of all proportion to their value. So you get the wretched peasants labouring for a pittance and paying an absurd price for every article they buy."

"The peasants!" Doamna Drucker hissed in contempt and turned her head aside to suggest that when the conversation touched so low a level, it was time for her to depart.

"The peasants are primitive," said Guy, "and, under present conditions, they will remain primitive. For one thing, they receive almost no education: they cannot afford to buy agricultural machinery: they . . ."

Doamna Drucker, her face sullen with scorn, interrupted angrily: "They are beasts," she said. "What can one do for such creatures? They are hopeless."

"In one sense," Guy agreed, "they are hopeless. They have never been allowed to hope. Whatever has happened here, they have been the losers."

She rose from the table. "It is time for my siesta." She left the room.

There was an embarrassed pause, then Hassolel asked Guy if he had been that week to see Shirley Temple at the Cinema. Guy said he had not.

Hassolel sighed. "Such a sweet little girl! Always I go to see Shirley Temple."

"I also." Drucker nodded. "Always she reminds me of my own little Hannah."

When they returned to the sitting room, Sasha invited Guy to go with him into the small ante-room he used as a music-room. Drucker said to Harriet: "Excuse me a little moment," and went off, no doubt in search of his wife. Flöhr, muttering something about work, went too. From the music-room came the sound of a gramophone playing 'Basin Street Blues'.

Harriet, left ‑alone with the Hassolels, the Teitelbaums and Doamna Flöhr, hoped the party would soon be over. But it was not over yet. A maid brought in some cut Bohemian glasses, red, blue, green, violet and yellow, and Doamna Hassolel began pour· ing liqueurs.

Doamna Teitelbaum, feeling perhaps that there had been too much of complaint at the meal, smiled on Harriet and said: "Still, you will enjoy life here. It is pleasant. It is cheap. There is much food. It is, you understand, *comfortable*."

Before she could say more the manservant entered to say Dom- nul Drucker's car was waiting for him. He was sent to find Drucker, who, when he entered, said he would drop Guy and Sasha back at the University. Harriet rose, ready to go with them, but the women clamoured:

"Not Doamna Pringle. Doamna Pringle must stay with us. She must stay for the 'five-o'-clock'."

"Of course she will stay," said Guy. Harriet gave him an an- guished look but he did not see it. "She has nothing else to do. She would enjoy it."

Without more ado, he said his good-byes and was off with Drucker and Sasha, leaving her behind. There was a short pause, then Teitelbaum and Hassolel departed.

"You see," said Doamna Hassolel, "it is not yet half past four and they return to work. What Rumanian would work before five o'clock?"

The elder of the two Drucker girls came in to join her aunts. The women drew their chairs close together and sat with their plump, be-ringed hands smoothing their skirts over their plump, silk knees. Meanwhile they watched Harriet, somehow suggesting that even if she were formidable, she was outnumbered. They watched, she thought, with the purposeful caution of trappers.

The Drucker girl said: "She is pretty, is she not? Like a film star."

Now the men were all gone, Doamna Flöhr had taken a plati- num lorgnette from her bag. She examined Harriet through it. "What age are you?" she asked.

"Thirty-five," said Harriet.

The women gasped. The girl tittered behind her hand. "We thought you were twenty," she said.

Harriet wondered when they had joined in coming to this con- clusion. Doamna Flöhr looked puzzled and, pretending to fidget with the back of her dress, leant forward to take a closer look at Harriet.

Doamna Teitelbaum said in an extenuating tone: "Leah Blum, you remember, did not marry till she was thirty. Such happens, I am told, with Career Women."

The others laughed at the outlandishness of such women.

Doamna Hassolel said: "Here we say: at twenty, you marry yourself; at twenty-five, you must get the old woman to marry you; at thirty, the devil himself can't do it."

Harriet turned to Doamna Flöhr, because she was the youngest sister, and said: "What age are you?"

Doamna Flöhr started. "Here," she said, "women do not tell their ages."

"In England," said Harriet, "they are not asked to tell."

Doamna Hassolel now said: "How many children do you wish to have?"

"We shall probably wait until after the war."

"Then it will be too late."

"Surely not."

"But how many? Haven't you considered?"

"Oh, nine or ten."

"So many? Then you must start soon."

Harriet laughed and Doamna Teitelbaum, whose manner was more kindly than that of the others, said: "You are surely joking? You cannot be so old."

"I am twenty-two," said Harriet. "A year younger than Guy."

"Ah!" The others relaxed, disappointed.

Doamna Hassolel rang for the maid and gave an order. The maid brought in some jars of a sort of jam made of whole fruits.

Doamna Teitelbaum murmured her pleasure. "A little spoonful," she said, "I like so much gooseberry."

Harriet said: "I really must go." She started to rise, but the circle of women sat firm about her.

"No, no," said Doamna Hassolel, "you cannot go. Here already is the 'five-o'clock'."

A trolley was wheeled in laden with sandwiches, iced cakes, cream buns and several large flans made of sliced apples, pears and plums.

Harriet looked from the window. Rain was falling again. The wind was blowing it in sheets from the soaked trees. Doamna Hassolel watched her calmly as she returned to her chair.

9

With late November came the *crivaţ*, a frost-hard wind that blew from Siberia straight into the open mouth of the Moldavian plain. Later it would bring the snow, but for the moment it was merely a threat and a discomfort that each day grew a little sharper.

Fewer people appeared in the streets. Already there were those who faced the outdoor air only for as long as it took them to hurry between home and car. In the evening, in the early dark, there were only the workers hurrying to escape the cold. Taxis were much in demand. Run cheaply on cheap fuel from the oilfields that were only thirty miles distant, they charged little more than the buses of other capitals.

At the end of November there came, too, a renewal of fear as Russia invaded Finland. Although his friends were inclined to hold him responsible for the Soviet defection, Guy's faith did not waver. He and Harriet heard the news one night at the Athénée Palace, where Clarence had taken them to dine. They found as they left the dining-room that the main room had been prepared for a reception. The chandeliers were fully lit, the tables banked with flowers and a red carpet had been unrolled throughout the hall.

"Germans," said Guy when he saw the first of the guests. The Germans and the British in Bucharest knew each other very well by sight. This was Harriet's first real encounter with the enemy. Guy and Clarence pointed out to her several important members of the German Embassy, all in full evening dress, among them Gerda Hoffman, a stocky woman whose straw-coloured hair was bound like a scarf round her head. No one knew what her true function was, but a whispering campaign had given her the reputation of being the cleverest agent to come out of Germany.

A group of these Germans stood in the hall. Seeing the three young English people advance on them, they closed together on the red carpet so that the three had to divide and skirt them. As this happened, the Germans laughed exultantly among themselves. Harriet was surprised that people of importance should behave so crassly. Guy and Clarence were not surprised. This behaviour seemed to them typical of the sort of Germans sent out under the New Order.

"But they're certainly crowing over something," said Clarence. "I wonder what's happened. Let's ask in the bar."

In the bar they learnt of the invasion of Finland from Galpin, who said: "That's the beginning. The next thing, Russia'll declare war on us. Then the Huns and the Russkies will carve up Europe between them. What's to stop them?"

"A lot of things," said Guy, "I'm pretty sure the Russians won't commit themselves before they're ready."

Galpin looked him over with bleak amusement: "You think you know about Russia, the way the Pope knows about God. You wait and see. We'll have one or the other of the bastards here before you can say 'Eastern Poland'."

Guy laughed, but he laughed alone. The others were subdued by a sense of disaster.

The next morning, walking in the Cişmigiu, Harriet suffered again from uncertainty. She had made an appointment to see a flat, that mid-day. If they took it, they would be required to pay three months' rent in advance. She was unwilling to risk the money.

Guy said: "Don't worry. We'll be here at least a year."

They had the wintry park to themselves. When they reached the bridge, the wind came howling across the lake, carrying to them the icy spray from the fountain. They retreated and turned in among the flower-beds that displayed the last brown tattered silks of the chrysanthemums. A white peacock was trailing a few tail-feathers in the mud. Pigeon-down and some scraps of leaf spun along the path. The path curved and brought them to the chestnut thicket that led to the restaurant. Guy put his hand through Harriet's arm, but she was not responsive. He had promised to go with her and view the flat, but, having forgotten this promise, he had later arranged to give some special coaching to a student. The student's need seemed to him the greater.

"And I must see the landlord alone?" said Harriet.

"Oh no." Guy was delighted by his own resource. "I've rung up

Sophie and she has agreed to go with you." This he thought an altogether better arrangement, it being known that no English person could grapple unaided with the cunning of a Rumanian landlord.

It was an arrangement that did not please Harriet at all. Guy, as they walked, had been lecturing her on her unwisdom in not making better use of Sophie, who would, he knew, be only too delighted to help Harriet, if only Harriet would ask for help. Sophie had been very helpful to him when he was alone here. He was sure she was, fundamentally, a good-hearted girl. She had had a difficult life. All she needed was a little flattery, a little management....

Harriet, whom he seemed to imagine was absorbing this advice, said at the end of it no more than: "I'm *sick* of Sophie." After a pause, she added: "And we can't afford to go on feeding her."

Guy said: "Things will be easier when we have our own flat. Then we can entertain at home."

They had now strolled out of the trees and could see the café's wooden peninsula with the chairs and tables stacked up under tarpaulins. The kitchen was shuttered. A lock hung quivering in the wind. Guy asked Harriet if she remembered hearing here the announcement of Călinescu's assassination. Did she remember the heat, the quiet, the chestnuts falling on the tin roof? Rather sulkily, she replied that she did. Taking her hand, Guy said:

"I wish, darling, you liked Sophie better. She is lonely and needs a friend. You ought to get on well with her. She is an intelligent girl."

"She lets her intelligence trickle away in complaints, self-pity and self-indulgence."

"You are rather intolerant."

Before Harriet could reply to this, they heard a step behind them and glancing round saw a figure that was familiar but, so unlikely was the setting, unfamiliar.

"Good heavens," said Guy, glad of diversion. "It's Yakimov." Harriet said: "Don't let's talk to him."

"Oh, we must have a word." And Guy hurried out of reach of her restraint.

Yakimov, in his long full-skirted greatcoat, an astrakhan cap on top of his head, his reed of a body almost overblown by the wind, looked like a phantom from the First World War – a member of some seedy royal family put into military uniform for the purposes of a parade. As he tottered unhappily forward, his gaze on the ground, he did not see the Pringles. When stopped by Guy's exuberant "Hello, there!" his mouth fell open. He did his best to smile.

"Hello, dear boy!"

"I've never seen you in the park before."

"I've never been before."

"What a magnificent coat!"

"Yes, isn't it!" Yakimov's face brightened a little as he turned a corner of the coat to show the worn sable lining. "The Czar gave it to m'poor old dad. Fine coat. Never wears out."

"It's splendid." Guy stood back to admire the theatrical effect of the coat, his appreciation such that Yakimov's gaze went to Guy's coat in the hope of being able to return these compliments, but no return was possible.

Guy said: "It makes you look like a White Army officer. You should have a peaked cap. A sort of yachting cap."

"M'old dad had one; and a beard like Nicholas II." Yakimov sighed, but not, it seemed, over these glories of the past. His whole body drooped. Now he had come to a standstill, he seemed to lack energy to proceed.

Harriet, who had been watching him, felt forced to ask: "What is the matter?"

He looked up: "Not to tell a lie . . ." he paused, at a loss for a lie to tell. "*Not* to tell a lie, dear girl, I've been rather badly treated. Given the push. Literally." He laughed sadly.

"From the Athénée Palace?"

"No. At least, not yet. No, I . . . I . . ." he stared at the ground again, stammering as though his troubles were so compacted that they dammed the source of speech, then speech burst forth: "Given the push . . . flung out. Flung out of a taxi in a distant part of the town. Quite lost; not a *leu* on me: didn't know where to turn. Then someone directed me across this God-forsaken park."

"You mean, you couldn't pay the taxi?" Harriet asked.

"Wasn't my taxi, dear girl. McCann's taxi. McCann flung me out of it. After all I'd done for him." Yakimov's lips quivered.

Guy took his arm, and as they walked towards the main gate he persuaded Yakimov to describe exactly what had happened.

"McCann got me out of bed this morning at some unearthly

hour. Rang me up, and said he wanted to see me. Said he was in the hall, just leaving for Cairo. Well, dear boy, had to get m'clothes on. Couldn't go down in m'birthday suit, could I? Thought he was going to ask me to keep on the job. Didn't know whether to say 'yes' or 'no'. Hard work, being a war correspondent. Comes a bit rough on your poor old Yaki. Not used to it. Well, got myself titivated. 'Shall I accept the job, or shan't I?' kept asking m'self. Felt I ought to accept. War on, y'know. Man should do his bit. Thought I'd done a good job. If I couldn't get 'hot' news in the bar, always got a warmish version of it. Well, down I went – and there was McCann, fuming. But *fuming*! Said he'd be late for his 'plane. Bundled me into the taxi with him before I knew what was happening, and then started on me. And what do you think he said? He said: 'Might have known you hadn't a clue. All you could do was collect rumours and scandal'. "

"Really!" said Harriet with interest. "What scandal?"

"Search me, dear girl. I never was one for scandal. 'And you did yourself damned well,' he said. 'Two hundred thousand *lei* for a month's kip. What's my agency going to say when they have to pay that for the balderdash you've been sending home?' Then he stopped the cab, put his foot on m'backside and shoved me out." Yakimov gazed from one to the other of his companions, his green eyes astounded by reality. "And I've had to find m'way back here on m'poor old feet. Can you imagine it?"

"And he didn't pay you for the work you did?" Guy asked.

"Not a nicker."

"I suppose he paid the hotel bill?"

"Yes, but what has he said to the blokes there? That's what I'm asking m'self. Very worried, I am. Perhaps, when I get back, I'll find m'traps in the hall. It's happened before. I'd have to move to the Minerva."

"But that's a German hotel."

"Don't mind, dear boy. Poor Yaki's not particular."

They had reached the Calea Victoriei and there Yakimov looked vaguely about him. Recognising his whereabouts, he smiled with great sweetness and said: "Ah, well, we mustn't worry. We're in a nice little backwater here. We should get through the war here very comfortably." On this cheerful note, he set out to face the staff of the Athénée Palace.

Turning in the opposite direction, Harriet walked with Guy as far as the University gate. There he gave her two thousand-*lei* notes. "For lunch," he said. "Take Sophie. Go somewhere nice," and he went off with what seemed to her the speed of guilt.

Sophie opened the door in her dressing gown. Her face shone sallow for lack of make-up: her hair was pinched over with metal setting-grips.

In a high, vivacious voice she cried: "Come in. I have been washing my hair. Most times I go to the Athénée Palace salon, but sometimes – for an economy, you understand? – I do it myself. You have not been before in my *garçonnière*. It is not big, but it is convenient."

She talked them up the stairs. In the bed-sitting-room – an oblong modern room with an unmade bed and an overnight smell – she pushed some clothes off a chair and said: "Please to be seated. I am unpacking my laundry. See!" She lifted a bundle in tissue paper and gazed into it. "So nice! My pretty lingerie. I love all such nice things."

Looking round for a clock, Harriet noticed a photograph frame placed face downwards beside the bed. There was no clock, but Sophie wore a watch. Harriet asked the time. It was a quarter to twelve.

"The appointment with the landlord is at twelve o'clock," said Harriet.

"Ah!" Sophie, who was now unpacking her laundry, seemed not to hear. She lifted her underwear, piece by piece, with a sort of sensual appreciation. Smoothing down little bows, straightening borders of lace, she opened drawers and slowly put each piece away. When this task was completed, she threw herself on the bed. "Last night," she said, "I was out with friends, so this morning I am lazy."

"Do you think we could go soon?"

"Go? But where should we go?"

"Guy said you would come with me to see the landlord."

"But what landlord?"

Harriet explained her visit and Sophie, lying propped on one elbow, looked troubled: "He said you would call to see me. A friendly call, you understand, but he did not speak of a landlord." Sophie looked at her fingernails, then added as one who understood Guy better than Harriet did: "He arranges so many things, he forgets to explain, you know."

"Well, can you come?"

"But how can I? I must first have my bath. Then I must dress. It will take a long time because I meet a friend for lunch. And my fingernails. I must put on more varnish." Sophie spoke as though these activities might be a little selfish but were all the more endearing for that. She gave a laugh at Harriet's blank face and rallied her: "You can see the landlord by yourself. You are not afraid?"

"No." With a sense of giving Sophie a last chance, Harriet said: "The trouble is, I do not speak Rumanian."

"But the landlord will speak French. I am sure you speak very well French?"

"I hardly speak it at all."

"That is extraordinary, sure-ly?" Sophie's voice soared in amazement. "A girl of good family who cannot speak very well French!"

"Not in England." Harriet stood up.

Sophie encouraged her on the way out: "The landlord will not eat you. He will be nice to a young lady alone." She laughed, apparently delighted at the thought of it.

Harriet did not see Guy again until the evening. She told him she had come to an agreement with the landlord. She had taken the flat for six months.

"And what did Sophie think of it?"

"She did not see it."

"She dealt with the landlord, of course?"

"No, she could not come. She wasn't dressed when I called."

"But she promised to go with you."

"She said she hadn't understood."

Guy's expression left Harriet in no doubt but that Sophie had understood perfectly. He routed his dissatisfaction with a burst of admiration for Harriet: "So you did it all alone? Why you're wonderful, darling. And we have a flat! We must have a drink to celebrate." And Harriet hoped that for a few days, at least, she would hear no more of Sophie.

10

WHEN THEY MOVED INTO THE FLAT, the Pringles discovered that in negotiating with the landlord Harriet had not been as clever as they thought. Some of the furniture was missing. The bedside rug had been taken away. There were only two saucepans left in the kitchen. When telephoned, the landlord, with whom she had dealt in a mixture of English, French, Rumanian and German, told Guy he had explained to Doamna Pringle that these things would be removed from the flat.

They also discovered that if they wanted electricity, gas, water and telephone, they must settle the bills of the previous tenant, an English journalist who had disappeared without trace.

The flat was on the top floor of a block in the square. From the sitting-room, which was roughly coffin shaped, five doors opened. These led to the kitchen, the main bedroom, the balcony, the spare-room and the hall. The building was flimsy. What furniture remained was shabby, but the rent was reasonable.

When they took possession, on a day of exceptional cold, the hall-porter who brought up their luggage put a hand on the main radiator and grinned slyly. Noticing this, Harriet felt the radiator and found it barely warm. She told Guy to ask the man if it was always like this.

Yes, the flat was hard to let because it was cold. So the rent was low. The boiler, explained the porter, was not big enough to force the heat up to the top floor. Having made this revelation, he became nervous and insisted that the flats were of the highest class, each having attached to it not one servant's bedroom but two. He held up two fingers, pulling first one, then the other. *Two*. One was behind the kitchen, the other on the roof. Harriet said she had not noticed a bedroom behind the kitchen. The porter beckoned her to follow him and showed her a room some six feet long and three feet wide, which she had mistaken for a store cupboard. Guy surprised her by showing no surprise. He said most Rumanian servants slept on the kitchen floor.

When they had unpacked, they went out on to the balcony and surveyed the view that was their own. They faced the royal palace. Immediately below them, intact among the disorder left by the demolishers, was a church with gilded domes and crosses looped with beads. Apart from the Byzantine prettiness of this little church, and the palace façade, which had a certain grandeur, the buildings were a jumble of commonplaces, the skyline mediocre: and much was in ruins.

It was late afternoon. A little snow was falling from a sky watered over with the citrous gleams of sunset. Already, as the Pringles watched, the buildings were dissolving into dusk. The street-lamps came on one by one. At the entrance to the Calea Victoriei could be seen the first windows of the lighted shops.

A trumpet sounded from the palace yard. "Do you know what that says?" Guy asked. "It says: Come, water your horses, all you that are able. Come, water your horses and give them some corn. And he that won't do it, the sergeant shall know it: he will be whipped and put in a dark hole."

Harriet, who had not heard this jingle before, made him repeat it. As he did so, they heard a creak of wood below. The church door was opening and a light falling on to the snow-feathered cobbles. A closed *trăsură* drew up. Two women, like little sturdy bears in their fur coats and fur-trimmed snow-boots, descended. As they entered the church, they drew veils over their heads.

This incident, occurring there at their feet, beneath the balcony of their home, touched Harriet oddly. For the first time she felt her life becoming involved with the permanent life of the place. They might be here for six months. They might even be allowed a year of settled existence – perhaps longer. With so much time, one ceased to be a visitor. People took on the aspect of neighbours. There was a need to adjust oneself.

She said: "We could have done worse. Here we are at the centre of things," and she felt that, like herself, he was more impressed by that position than he cared to admit.

"We should buy things for the flat," she said. "Couldn't we go to the Dâmboviţa?"

"Why not?" The term had ended. Guy was on holiday. With the high spirits of a move accomplished and refreshment due, he said: "First, though, we will go and have tea at Mavrodaphne's."

This was the newest, the most expensive, and so, for the

moment, the most fashionable of Bucharest cafés. The Pringles had visited it before, but this visit was a gesture of belonging. They were going where everyone went.

The café was situated in a turning off the Calea Victoriei. This was an old street that had been renovated with black glass, chromium and marble composites so that the buildings gleamed in the street lights. Within the brilliant windows were French gloves and trinkets, English cashmere garments and Italian leatherwork, tagged with exotic words like 'pulloverul', 'chic', 'golful' and 'five-o'clockul'. These shops stayed open until late at night.

The enormous windows of Mavrodaphne's were steamed over by inner heat and outer cold. A colony of beggars had already established rights in the shelter of the doorway. They lay heaped together, supping off the smell of hot chocolate that came up through the basement grating. They roused themselves in a hub-bub when anyone passed inside. Within the door was a vestibule where a porter took the greatcoats of visitors and a piccolo, kneeling at their feet, removed their snowboots. This service was imposed. Customers were required to enter the better restaurants and cafés as they would enter a drawing room.

When the Pringles arrived, the whole vast area of the café, warm, scented, tricked out with black glass, chromium and red leather, was crowded for the 'five-o'clock', which for most people here meant coffee or chocolate, and cakes. Only a few had ac-quired the habit of drinking tea.

There seemed to be no vacant table. Wandering round in their search, Guy said: "We are sure to see someone we know," and almost at once they came upon Dobson, who invited them to join him. He had dashed out, he said, on some pretext, life in the Legation being now such that the girls had no time to make a decent cup of tea.

When the Pringles were seated, he asked: "You've heard about Drucker, of course?"

They, having spent their day packing and unpacking, had heard nothing. Dobson told them: "He has been arrested."

For some moments Guy looked blank with shock, then asked: "On what charge?"

"Buying money on the black market. Too silly. We all either buy or sell. They might have thought up a more substantial charge."

"What is the real reason for the arrest?"

"No one seems to know. I imagine it has something to do with his affiliations with Germany."

While they were talking, Guy was shifting to the edge of his seat, preparing, Harriet feared, to take some action. Not noticing this, Dobson chatted on, smiling as he did so: "I've heard for some time that Carol's been plotting to get his hands on the Drucker fortune. He can't do much because the bulk of it's in Switzerland. The Government could claim that the money had been deposited abroad contrary to Rumanian regulations, but that wouldn't cut much ice with the Swiss. No power on earth will get money out of a Swiss bank without the depositor's consent."

"So they may force Drucker to give his consent?" said Harriet.

"They may certainly try. Pressure *could* be brought to bear." Dobson gave a laugh at the thought. "Dear me, yes. We've felt for some time that Drucker was sailing too near the wind. His system of exchange was all in Germany's favour. The Minister of Finance told H.E. that the bank was ruining the country. Drucker claimed to be pro-British. You know what they said about him: that his heart was in England but his pocket was in Berlin . . ."

"The point was," Guy broke in, "he had a heart." Like Dobson, he spoke of Drucker in the past tense. He asked when the arrest had been made and was told "Early this morning."

"What about the other members of the family?"

Dobson had heard nothing about them.

As the waiter arrived to take their order, Guy rose. "I must go and see them," he said. "Sasha will be in a terrible state."

Harriet pleaded "Why not go after tea?", but Guy, looking like one on whom a heavy duty lay, shook his head and was gone. Harriet felt herself abandoned.

Dobson, startled by Guy's abrupt departure, turned and smiled on Harriet saying: "You will stay, won't you?" apparently so eager to retain her company that her composure was somewhat restored.

Feeling she might excuse Guy by echoing his concern for the Druckers, she said: "This is terrible news, isn't it?"

Dobson continued to smile: "Terrible for Drucker, of course, but you must remember his bank was serving the German cause."

Harriet said: "I suppose he'll soon buy his way out?"

"I don't know. This is a contingency against which he failed to provide. His wealth is outside the country. He could go to it, but it can't come to him."

The waiter brought tea and toast for Harriet, then, unasked, put on the table a plate of ball-shaped chocolate cakes pimpled over like naval mines. "Siegfrieds," he announced.

"Not our line," said Dobson, imperturbably, in English.

At once the waiter whipped away the plate, retreated a few steps, returned and put it down again. "Maginots," he said, and went off well satisfied by Dobson's amusement.

Beaming on Harriet, Dobson said: "I love these people. They have wit."

Harriet wondered if she would ever love them. She watched two girls, usually to be seen here, called, so Guy had said, Princess Mimi and Princess Lulie. They had just arrived and were making their way between the tables, faintly acknowledging their Rumanian friends. Keeping close together, their bodies seeming to melt and fuse, they had the air of lovers, too absorbed in each other to have other interests; but out of this confining intimacy, their glances strayed in search of someone to pay the bill. One of them saw Dobson. Somehow the fact of his presence was conveyed to the other. They moved towards him, all smiles now, then they noticed Harriet. The smiles vanished in an instant. They veered away.

Dobson glanced regretfully after them. "Charming girls!" he said.

"You prefer the Rumanians to other races?" Harriet asked.

"Oh no." Dobson talked quickly and willingly, used to doing his duty in important drawing-rooms. Harriet had heard people speak of his charm and she was grateful for it now she had been left on his hands, but she had noticed a curious thing about him. When he laughed – and he laughed very readily – his round, bright blue eyes remained as expressionless as the eyes of a bird. He was saying: "I love the French and the Austrians. And I simply *adore* the Italians. And," he added after a pause, "I've known some delightful Germans."

Harriet, feeling her conversation should be brighter, said: "Where do you think we met your friend Yakimov the other day?"

"Where? Do tell me?"

"Walking in the Cişmigiu."

"No, *never*! I can't believe it. Was he actually taking a walk?"

"Not voluntarily." She told the story of Yakimov's ejection from McCann's taxi and was gratified by Dobson's reception of it. His eyes grew damp and he shook all over his plump, soft body as he laughed to himself: "Ho-ho! Ho-ho-ho-ho-ho-*ho*!"

Her success was such, she felt she might safely question him about Yakimov, who had aroused her curiosity.

She asked: "Have you known Prince Yakimov long?"

"Oh *yes*. For years. He used to live in London, with Dollie Clay-Callard. They gave tremendous parties. Simply tremendous."

"I suppose you went to them?"

"Well, I went to one. It was fantastic. Out of doors in winter. The garden was floodlit and buried in artificial snow. We were told to wear furs, but, unfortunately, it was a muggy night and we were stifled. Yaki wore his sable-lined coat, I remember."

"The one the Czar gave his father?"

Dobson gave a burst of laughter: "The very one. And there was artificial ice. People skated and were pushed about in sleigh-chairs, carrying lanterns." He paused, reflected, and said: "Really, it was all rather charming. And there was a real Russian sleigh. At least Yaki said it was Russian. I wouldn't know. It was blue and gold and drawn by a pony with an artificial mane."

"Was everything artificial?"

"Everything that could be. The vodka was real enough. Dear me, I was younger then. I'd never seen anything quite like it. Soon afterwards Dollie and Yaki moved to Paris. Her money was running out. They couldn't live on that scale for ever."

"Where is Dollie now?"

"Dead, poor dear. She was much older than Yaki – twenty years or more. *And* looked it. But a wonderful old girl. We all loved her. We thought Yaki would inherit a fortune, but there wasn't a sou. Up to her eyes in debt. It must have been a shock to him."

"What did he do?"

"Travelled about. He never came back to England."

"So you never knew him really well?"

Dobson's eyes widened in surprise at this audacity, then he laughed again. "Oh, everybody knew Yaki." No one, it seemed, needed to know more than that.

She realised she was alarming him with this spate of questions, but there was one more she must ask: how did Yakimov live now? Perhaps suspecting what was coming, Dobson said quickly as she opened her mouth: "Here comes Bella Niculescu. *Such* a nice woman!"

Harriet let herself be distracted. She wanted to see Bella Niculescu.

Tall, broad-shouldered, her blonde hair knotted at the nape, Bella was a classical statue of a woman wearing a tailored suit. She was in the late twenties.

"She's very good-looking," said Harriet, thinking that Bella's over-stylish hat looked like a comic hat placed askew on the Venus de Milo. Behind her trotted a dark, moustached, little Rumanian Adonis. "Is that her husband?"

"Nikko? Yes. But surely you've met them?"

"No. She disapproves of Guy."

"Oh, nonsense," Dobson laughed, contradicting her with good-humoured confidence. "No one disapproves of Guy." He stood up to give his hand to Bella.

Bella's chief interest was in Harriet. When introduced, she said: "Someone told me that Guy had brought back a wife." Her tone and her use of Guy's Christian name seemed to Harriet an offer of friendship – one that Harriet felt inclined to accept.

Dobson, his admiring smiles now all for Bella, asked if the Niculescus would join him. But Bella refused. "We are meeting some Rumanian friends," she said, with a slight emphasis on the word Rumanian.

Dobson detained her with flattering interest: "Before you leave us, *do* tell us what lies behind Drucker's arrest. I'm *sure* you know."

"Well," – Bella straightened her shoulders, not displeased that the Legation came to her for information – "a certain lady – you can guess who! – discovered that Baron Steinfeld's holdings in Astro-Romano were in fact owned by Drucker. You know, of course, that all these rich Jews have foreign nominees so that they can avoid taxation. No need to tell you what those shares are worth at the moment! Well, the lady invited Drucker to supper and suggested he might care to make the holdings over to her as a Christmas present. He treated the suggestion as a joke. He had no holdings – in any case, Jews did not give each other Christmas presents, etcetera, etcetera. Then she tried other tactics. (I must say, I would have liked to have been a little mouse in the room, wouldn't you?) But Drucker, having a new young wife, was not susceptible. Then she became angry and said if he were not willing to hand over the shares, she would see they were confiscated. He thought, with his German connections, no one dared touch him – so he simply laughed at her. Twenty-four hours later he was arrested."

"I suppose," said Dobson, "the arrest could be something of an anti-German gesture."

"Oh, do you think so?" Bella's voice rose excitedly. "I must tell Nikko that. He'll be delighted. He's *so* pro-British." She waved to where Nikko had now joined his friends and said: "I must leave you. She gave her hand to Harriet. "I could never persuade Guy to come to my parties. Now you must bring him."

Harriet glanced after her as she went manoeuvring her broad and vigorous backside between the tables, and asked: "What does Nikko do?"

"Why nothing. He's married to Bella."

"You mean, she's rich?"

"Quite comfortably off."

Dobson had to return to the Legation. When he called the waiter, Harriet, knowing convention did not permit her to remain here alone, asked for her bill, which Dobson insisted on paying.

He had his car outside and offered her a lift, but she said she wanted to do some shopping.

As he was about to drive off, he said: "We don't get a moment to breathe these days, and now H.E. wants us to help with the decoding." He exploded with laughter at the thought of this humble employment.

Harriet remembered she had, when she first met him, decided he was difficult to know. She now thought she had been wrong. He was, she believed, as simply pleasant as he seemed.

She crossed over to a shop window in which she had seen an Italian tea-set of fine *sang-de-boeuf* china. She had suggested to Guy they might buy it with money given them as a wedding-present. Guy, who had no interest in possession, said: "Why waste money? When we leave here, we'll probably have to go empty handed." Now, in a mood to compensate herself, she looked defiantly at the tea-set, but, reflecting that she had been abandoned for the best possible motives by a husband made unreliable only by his abysmal kindness, she went instead to the Calea Victoriei and ordered an electric fire.

The wind had grown harder and there were occasional flurries of snow. The sky, black and unrelenting as iron, hung like a weight over the roof-tops. Not wishing to return to the empty flat, she took a taxi down to the Dâmboviţa. The market area around the river had a flavour more of the East than of the West. Guy had brought her here and shown her the houses, built in the style of Louis XIII, once the mansions of Turkish and Phanariot officials, now doss-houses where the poor slept twenty and thirty to a room. The windows were still barred against thieves and rebels. The Dâmboviţa River, that ran between them, had no beauty. Once navigable and the heart of the city, it was now dwindling from some failure at source, leaving high banks of clay. It was unused and in places covered to make a road.

When she left the taxi, she walked through the Calea Lipscani, searching for a stall that sold decorated Hungarian plates. The area was primitive, bug-ridden and brutal. Its streets, unlike the fashionable streets, were as crowded in winter as in summer. The gas-lit windows threw out a greenish glow. The stalls dripped with gas flares. Harriet pushed her way between men and women who, wrapped to the eyes in woollen scarves, were bulky with frieze, sheep-skin and greasy astrakhan. The beggars, on home ground, rummaging for food under the stalls, did not usually trouble to beg here, but the sight of Harriet was too much for them.

When she stopped at a meat stall to buy veal, she became conscious of a sickening smell of decay beside her. Turning, she saw an ancient female dwarf who was thrusting the stump of an arm up to her face. She searched hurriedly for a coin and could find nothing smaller than a hundred-*lei* note. She knew it was too much but handed it over. It led, as she feared, to trouble. The woman gave a shrill cry calling to her a troupe of children, who at once set upon Harriet, waving their deformities and begging with professional and remorseless piteousness.

She took the meat she had bought and tried to escape into the crowd. The children clung like lice. They caught hold of her arms, their faces screwed into the classical mask of misery while they whined and whimpered in chorus.

Guy had told her she must try and get used to the beggars. They could be discouraged by a show of amiable indifference. She had not yet learned the trick and perhaps never would. Their persistence roused her to fury.

She reached the stall where the Hungarian plates were displayed and paused. At once the children surrounded her, their eyes gleaming at her annoyance, seeming to be dancing in triumph. She made off again, almost running, only wanting now to get away from them. At the end of the road she saw a *trăsură* and shouted to it. It stopped. She jumped on board and the children followed her. They clung to the steps, wailing at her, until the driver struck them off with his whip. As they dropped down, one by one, her anger subsided. She looked back at them and saw them still staring after the dispenser of hundred-*lei* notes – a collection of wretched, ragged waifs with limbs as thin as sticks.

Heavens above, how did one settle down to life in this society that Doamna Teitelbaum had recommended for its comfort? The day before, she had seen a peasant slashing his horse across the eyes for some slip of the foot. Though she was so shaken she could have murdered the man, she had to recognise what deprivation lay behind his behaviour.

Before she left England, she had read books written by travellers in Rumania who had given a picture of a rollicking, openhearted, happy, healthy peasantry, full of music and generous hospitality. They were, it was true, mad about music. Music was their only outlet. They made themselves drunk on it. As for the rest, she had seen nothing of it. The peasants in this city were starved, frightened figures, scrawny with pellagra, wandering about in a search for work or making a half-hearted attempt to beg.

The situation would have been simplified for her could she, like Guy, have seen the peasants not only as victims, but as blameless victims. The truth was, the more she learnt about them, the more she was inclined to share Doamna Drucker's loathing of them; but she would not call them beasts. They had not the beauty or dignity of beasts. They treated their animals and their women with the simple brutality of savages.

Driving now down the long, deserted Calea Victoriei, it seemed to her she could smell in the wind those not so distant regions of mountain and fir-forest where wolves and bears, driven by hunger, haunted the villages in the winter snow-light. And the wind was harsher than any wind she had ever known. She shivered, feeling isolated in a country that was to her not only foreign but alien.

A few yards past the University, she saw Guy walking, rather quickly, and stopped the *trăsură*. His face was creased and troubled. He said he was returning to Mavrodaphne's to look for her.

"Surely you didn't suppose I should still be there?"

"I didn't know." He obviously had not supposed anything at all. His mind had been elsewhere.

As he took the seat beside her, she said: "Did you see Sasha?"

He shook his head. He had gone to the flat but no one opened the door. He found the porter, who told him that the whole family had left that morning with a great deal of luggage. The servants had gone soon after. The flat was deserted. Asked about Sasha, the man could not remember having seen him with the others. Guy had then gone to the University, where there were, as usual, students sitting about in the common-room for want of anything better to do. There he learnt that the Drucker sisters, their parents, their husbands and the two girls had been seen at the airport boarding a plane for Rome, but Sasha and his step-mother had not been with them. There was a rumour that Doamna Drucker had gone to her father's estate in Moldavia.

Guy said: "Perhaps Sasha has gone with her."

Harriet said nothing but she thought it unlikely that Doamna Drucker would burden herself with Sasha.

"Wherever he is," said Guy, "I shall hear from him. He knows I will help him if I can."

Harriet was thinking of the panic that must have filled the household after Drucker's arrest, the hasty packing, the hasty departure.

"How did they get extra visas so quickly?" she asked.

"They must have been prepared. Drucker after all had been warned. If the arrest had not been made so quickly, he might have got away."

Thinking of the household with its solid furniture, the family portraits in their huge frames, a setting designed as a background for generations of Druckers, she knew she had been envious of its permanence.

'And yet,' she thought, 'that enclosed family was no more secure than we are.'

The *trăsură* was crossing the cobbles of the square. The driver turned to ask for direction.

Guy said to Harriet: "Where are we going to eat? Shall we go back to the hotel?"

She replied: "Tonight we are going to eat at home."

11

WHEN YAKIMOV RETURNED to the Athénée Palace after his conflict with McCann, he went to the English Bar and ordered himself a double whisky.

"Chalk it up, Albu, dear boy," he said.

When Albu 'chalked it up', he knew that his credit was still good. His anxiety vanished. A problem that need not be faced straight away was no problem to him.

At the end of the week he was presented with a bill. He looked at it in pained astonishment and required the manager to come to him. The manager explained that, as Yakimov was no longer backed by McCann's agency, he must settle a weekly account in the usual way.

"Dear boy," he said, "m'remittance should be here in a week or two. Difficult time. Posts uncertain. War on, y'know."

His quarterly remittance had, in fact, come and gone. Bored by the menu of the hotel, he had spent it on some excellent meals at Capşa's, Cina's and Le Jardin.

The manager agreed to let the account run on and it ran un-questioned until Christmas visitors began to fill the hotel. This time it was the manager who sent for Yakimov.

"Any day now, dear boy," Yakimov earnestly assured him. "Any day."

"Any day will not do, *mon Prince*," said the manager. "If you cannot pay, I must now present this matter to the British Lega-tion."

Yakimov was alarmed. Galpin had told him: "These days you can be packed off under open arrest, third class and steerage, to Cairo, and there given the bum's rush into the ranks before you have time to say 'flat feet', 'conscientious objector' or 'incurable psychotic'."

Trembling slightly, Yakimov said to the manager: "Dear boy, no need to do that. I'll go there myself. M'dear old friend Dobbie

Dobson'll advance me the necessary. Just a question of asking. Didn't realise you were getting restless."

Yakimov was given another twenty-four hours. He did not go at once to Dobson, who was becoming less and less willing to lend him money, but first approached the hangers-on of the English Bar. Hadjimoscos, Horvath and Palu, as usual, together. He spoke first to Horvath:

"Dear boy, I have to settle a little bill. M'remittance is delayed. Never like to owe money. Wonder if you could manage to repay . . ."

Before he could finish, Horvath had spread hands so eloquently empty that Yakimov's words died in his throat. He turned to Hadjimoscos: "Do you think I could ask the Princess . . ."

Hadjimoscos laughed: "*Mon cher Prince*, rather ask the moon. You know the Princess. She is so irresponsible, one is made to smile. And it is the Rumanian habit never to repay a loan."

Yakimov moved his appealing eyes to Cici Palu, a handsome fellow who was said to do well out of women. Palu took a step back and glanced away with the air of one who sees and hears nothing that does not concern him. In desperation, Yakimov moaned: "Can no one lend me a *leu* or two?" To encourage them, he tried to order a round. Albu shook his head. The others smiled, deprecating this familiar refusal, but their contempt was evident. Yakimov was now no more than one of them.

He was forced in the end to return to Dobson, who agreed to settle the bill on condition that he moved to a cheaper lodging.

"I was thinking of trying the Minerva, dear boy."

Dobson would not hear of the Minerva, or, indeed, of any other hotel. Yakimov must find himself a bed-sitting-room.

So, on the morning of the following Saturday, having been permitted a last breakfast in the dining-room, Yakimov departed the Athénée Palace. When he carried his own luggage through the hall, the porters looked the other way. Even had they been willing to attend him, attention would have been distracted from him by a new arrival who caused even Yakimov, burdened as he was, to pause and stare.

This was a white-haired, dark-skinned little crow of a man in a striped blue suit. He moved with a rattle of chains. One of his eyes was covered with a patch; the other swivelled about in keen and critical survey of all it saw. His left arm, with hand too small in its skin-tight glove, lay crooked across his breast. He wore a gold chain in a loop from button-hole to trouser pocket. Another heavier chain, attaching a walking-stick to his right wrist, struck repeatedly against the stick's silver mounting. Clearly unimpressed by the hall and its occupants, he strode to the reception desk and rapped out: "Any letters for Commander Sheppy?"

Galpin, on his way to the bar, gawped, and Yakimov said: "Striking figure, that! Who can he be?"

"Arrived last night," said Galpin. "Probably secret service. Nothing so conspicuous as your old-time member of the British Secret Service." Noticing Yakimov's luggage, he added: "Not leaving us?"

Yakimov nodded sadly. "Found a nice little place of m'own," he said and went out to his *trăsură*.

That morning the early snow hung like swansdown in the air. It was forming a gauze over the tarmac. The cold was intense.

The *trăsură* took Yakimov in the direction of the station. The coachman was a lean and fierce-looking fellow, no Skopitz. The horse was a skeleton roughly patched over with hide. As it was spurred by the whip, its bones, stretching and heaving, seemed about to fall apart. Blood trickled down its flanks from several open sores.

As he watched the skittish jig of its pelvis, a tear came into Yakimov's eyes, but he was not weeping for the horse. He was weeping for himself. He was retreating, most unwillingly, from the heart of Bucharest life to its seedy, unprofitable purlieus. He felt injured by circumstances. The world had turned against him since Dollie died. Now he had not even the last relic of their life together, his Hispano-Suiza. He found himself longing for it as for a mother.

The appearance of the station reminded him of the evening of his penniless arrival. How short his period of fortune had been! His tears fell.

Hearing a gulp and a sniff, the coachman turned and gave Yakimov a stare of crude curiosity. Yakimov brushed his sleeve across his eyes.

Beyond the station the roads were unmade. The horse stumbled in pot-holes, the carriage shook. Puddles, thinly sheeted over with ice, cracked beneath the wheels. Here the houses were mostly wooden shacks, but among them were blocks of flats, recently built but already turning into slums. The paint was scratched from the doors; washing hung on the balconies and women bawled down into the streets.

It was in one of these flats that Yakimov had found a room. The room had been advertised on a notice-board as '*lux nebun*' – insane luxury. Insane luxury at a low rent seemed just the answer to his problem.

He had come upon the block after searching the back streets for an hour or more. The servant, who opened the door an inch, gabbled something about 'siesta'. He pretended not to understand. The stone staircase, ventilated with open spaces, seemed colder than the street. He pushed open the door and edged his way into the oily heat of the flat's interior. He would not be moved out. Defeated, the servant tapped with extreme trepidation on a door, entered and was met with uproar. At last a man and a woman, both in dressing-gowns, peered out at Yakimov with angry hauteur. The man said: "What does this person here in our house?"

The woman replied: "Tell him at once to go."

It was some moments before Yakimov realised that, beneath the clotted disguise of accent, the two were speaking English to each other. He bowed and smiled: "You speak English? As an Englishman, I am flattered. I have called to see the room you advertised."

"An Englishman!" The wife stepped forward with an expression of such avidity that Yakimov quickly amended his status.

"Of White Russian origin," he said. "A refugee, I fear, from the war zone."

"A refugee!" She turned to her husband with an expression that said: 'That's just the sort of Englishman we *would* get.'

"The name is Yakimov. Prince Yakimov."

"Ah, a Prince!"

The room offered was small, cluttered up with Rumanian carved furniture and embroidered hangings, but warm and comfortable enough. He agreed to take it.

"The rent a month is four thousand *lei*," said the woman, whose name was Doamna Protopopescu. When Yakimov did not haggle, she added: "In advance."

"Tomorrow, dear girl." He touched her fat, grimy little hand with his lips. "Tomorrow a large remittance arrives for me at the British Legation."

Doamna Protopopescu looked at her husband, who said: "The

Prince is an English Prince," and so the matter was left for the moment.

Doamna Protopopescu had advised Yakimov the correct *trăsură* fare from the city's centre. Now, his bags safely on the pavement, he handed up the fare and a ten *lei* tip. The driver looked dumbfounded, then gave an anguished howl. He demanded more. Firmly Yakimov shook his head and started to gather up his bags. The driver flung the coins upon the pavement. Ignoring this gesture, Yakimov began to climb the stairs.

Swinging his whip above his head and haranguing the passers-by right and left, the driver leapt down and followed. Bounding and bawling, he caught up with his fare at the first landing.

Yakimov did not know what the man was saying, but he was shaken by the fury with which it was being said. He tried to run. He stumbled, dropped a case, then shrank in fear against the wall. The man did not attack him, but instead, as Yakimov crept on, kept beside him, banging his jackboots on the stairs, slashing his whip and causing so much noise that people came to their doors to see what was happening. Doamna Protopopescu and her servant peered over the third landing.

"How much did you give him?" she asked.

Yakimov told her.

"That was more than enough." At once her face became a mask of fury. She threw up her fists and, rushing at the driver, she screamed out a virulent stream of Rumanian. The man stopped in his tracks. She waved him away, very slowly, turning every few moments to fix Yakimov with a stare of sullen loathing. At this show of defiance, the servant ran after him, echoing her mistress's rage, while the mistress herself conducted Yakimov indoors.

"Dear girl, you were magnificent," said Yakimov·as he sat panting on his bed.

"I said 'How dare you molest a nobleman' and he was afraid. So to deal with a filthy peasant." She flicked a hand, dismissing the matter, then said sharply: "And now, the money!"

"This evening," he promised her, "when the diplomatic post arrives, I'll stroll back to the Legation and pick up m'remittance."

Doamna Protopopescu's small black eyes bulged with suspicion. To greet her lodger, she had fitted herself into a short black dress that clung to the folds and wrinkles of her fat like a second skin. Her heavily whitened face sagged with annoyance like a flabby magnolia. She shouted through the door for her husband.

Protopopescu appeared, dressed in the uniform of an army officer of the lowest rank. He was a thin, drooping man with corseted waist, rouged cheeks and a moustache like that of a ringmaster, but he had nothing of his wife's fire. He said with a poor attempt at command: "Go this instant and get the money."

"Not now, dear boy." Yakimov settled down among the embroidered cushions. "Must have a bit of kip. Worn out with all this fuss." He closed his eyes.

"No, no!" cried Doamna Protopopescu and, pushing past her husband, she caught Yakimov by the arm and dragged him off the bed. "Go now. At once." She was extremely strong. She gave Yakimov a push that sent him headlong into the passage, then, closing the room door, she locked it and put the key in her handbag. "So! When you bring the money, I give the key."

Yakimov returned to the gnawing cold of the street. Where on earth could he find the money? He dared not approach Dobson who yesterday had lent him a last four thousand for the rent. Having no idea that Doamna Protopopescu could be so resolute, he had spent the money on a couple of excellent meals.

The pavements were freezing. He could feel the frost sticking to the broken soles of his shoes. He could not face the walk back to the main square and, realising he would have to learn to use public transport, he stood among the crowd waiting for a tramcar. When the tram came, there was an hysterical stampede in which Yakimov and an old woman were flung violently to the ground. The woman picked herself up and returned to the fray. Only Yakimov was left behind. When the next tram came along, he was prepared to fight. He was carried for a few *lei* to the city's centre. One could live here very cheaply, he realised, but who wanted to live cheaply? Not Yakimov.

He went straight to the English Bar and found it empty. Forced to search elsewhere, he crossed the square to Dragomir's food store, a refuge where a gentleman might sample cheese unchallenged and steal a biscuit or two.

The shop was decorated for Christmas. All about it peasants were selling fir trees from the Carpathians. Some trees were propped against the windows, some stood in barrels, some lay on the pavement among heaps of holly, bay and laurel. Great swags of snow-grizzled fir were tacked like mufflers about the shop front.

It was a large shop; one of the largest in Bucharest. Now it stood like a little castle embowered in Christmas greenery, its windows bright but burred with frost ferns.

A boar, on its feet, stood at the main entrance, its hide cured to a glossy blackness, its tusks yellow, snow feathers caught in its tough bristles. On either side of the door hung a deer, upside-down with antlers resting on the ground.

Yakimov sighed. These signs of festivity sent his thoughts back to Christmases at the Crillon, the Ritz, the Adlon and Geneva's Beau-Rivage. Where would he spend this Christmas? Not, alas, at the Athénée Palace.

As he entered the shop he found, crouched behind the boar, a heap of beggars, who set up a clamour at the sight of him that an assistant rushed out and kicked one, slapped another and attacked the rest with a wet towel. Yakimov slipped inside.

A little department at the door sold imports from England: Quaker Oats, tinned fruits, corned beef, Oxford marmalade – expensive luxuries eximious among luxury. These did not interest Yakimov, who made for the main hall, where turkeys, geese, ducks chickens, pheasant, partridge, grouse, snipe, pigeons, hares and rabbits were thrown unsorted together in a vast pyramid beneath a central light. He joined the fringe of male shoppers who went round with intent, serious faces examining these small corpses. This was not a shopping place for servants, nor even for wives. The men came here, as Yakimov did, to look at food, and to experience, as he might not, an ecstasy of anticipation.

He watched a stout man, galoshed, close-buttoned, Persian lamb on his collar, a cap in his hand, choose and order the preparation of a turkey still in its splendour of feathers. He swallowed hungrily as he watched.

This was not a good season for an onlooker. The counters that displayed shellfish, caviare and every sort of sausage were so hemmed in with customers he could see nothing of them. He wandered round with no more reward than the scent of honey-cured hams or the high citron fume of Greek oranges.

An assistant was sheering off the legs of live frogs, throwing the still palpitating trunks into a dustbin. Yakimov was upset by the sight, but forgot it at once as he peered into a basket of button mushrooms flown that morning from Paris. He put out a finger and brought it back tinged with the red dust of France.

In the cheese department, the sampling knife was in use. A little man in yellow peccary gloves, keeping an assistant at his heels, was darting about, nicking this cheese and that. As he waited, Yakimov eyed cheeses packed in pigs'-bladders, sheepskins, bark, plaited twigs, straw mats, grape pips, wooden bowls and barrels of brine. When he could bear it no longer, he broke off a piece of roquefort and would have put it into his mouth, but he realised he had been observed.

The observer was Guy Pringle.

"Hello, dear boy," said Yakimov, letting the cheese fall from his fingers into a bowl of soured cooking cream. "Difficult place to get served."

Guy, he saw, was not alone. Harriet Pringle had captured the assistant from the man in the peccary gloves. She seemed about to give an order, but at once the man, indignant at being deserted, began to demand attention. The assistant pushed past Harriet, almost bowling her over in his eagerness to assert his servility. "*Cochon*," said Harriet. The assistant looked back, pained.

Ever since the incident in the Athénée Palace garden, Yakimov had felt nervous of Harriet. Now, leaning towards Guy and whispering hurriedly, he said: "Your poor old Yaki's in a bit of a jam. If I can't lay m'hands on four thou, I'll have to spend the night on the streets."

Seeing Guy glance at Harriet, he added quickly: "Haven't forgotten. Owe the dear girl a thou. She'll get it soon's m'remittance turns up."

Guy took out the old note book in which he kept bank-notes and, leafing through it, found two thousand *lei*, which he handed to Yakimov. He said: "It's a pity you aren't a Polish refugee. I know the man who's administering relief."

"M'not exactly a Polish refugee, dear boy, but I'm a refugee from Poland. Got here through Yugoslavia, y'know."

Guy thought this fact might serve and gave him the address of the Polish Relief Centre, then mentioned that Yakimov had promised to visit them. Was he by any chance free on Christmas night?

"Curiously enough, I *am*, dear boy."

"Then come to dinner," Guy said.

Yakimov found the Relief Centre in a street of red, angular, half-built houses on which work had been abandoned for the winter. Builder's materials still lay about. Snow patched the yellow clay and the hillocks of sand and lime. Outside the one house that was nearly completed, a row of civilian Poles, in breeches and monkey-jackets, stood stamping their feet in the cold. Yakimov swept past them, wrapped in the Czar's greatcoat.

To the old peasant who opened the door, he said: "Prince Yakimov to see Mr. Lawson." He was shown straight into a room that smelt of damp plaster.

Clarence, seated behind a table, with an oil-stove at his feet and an army blanket round his shoulders, appeared to have a bad cold. When Yakimov introduced himself as a friend of Guy Pringle, Clarence looked shy, impressed apparently by the distinction of his visitor. Given confidence, Yakimov told how he had come down from Poland, where he had been staying on the estate of a relative. He had for a few weeks acted as McCann's deputy. When McCann left for Poland, Yakimov remained behind to collect a remittance which was being sent to him. The dislocations of war caused the delay of the remittance and so, he said: "Here I am on m'uppers, dear boy. Don't know where to look for a crust."

Strangely enough, Clarence did not respond as Yakimov had hoped to his story. He sat for some time looking at his fingernails, then said with sudden, startling firmness: "I cannot help you. You are not a Pole. You must apply to the British Legation."

Yakimov's face fell. "But, dear boy, I'm just as much in need as those blokes outside. Fact is, if I can't raise four thousand today, I'll have to sleep in the street."

Clarence said coldly: "The men outside are queuing for a living allowance of a hundred *lei* a day."

"You surely mean a thousand?"

"I mean a hundred."

Yakimov began to rise, then sank down again. "Never had to beg before," he said. "Good family. Not what I'm used to. Fact is, I'm desperate. The Legation won't help. They'll only send me to Cairo. 'S'no good to poor old Yaki. Delicate health. Been starving for days. Don't know where m'next meal's coming from." His voice broke, tears crowded into his eyes and Clarence, shaken by this emotion, put his hand into his pocket. He brought out a single note, but it was a note for ten thousand *lei*.

"Dear boy," said Yakimov, restored by the sight of it.

"Just a minute!" Clarence seemed rather agitated by what he

was doing. His cheeks reddened, he fumbled about looking for paper in a drawer. He took out a sheet and wrote an IOU. "I am lending you this," he said impressively, "because you are a friend of Guy Pringle. The money is from funds and must be paid back when your remittance arrives."

When the IOU was signed and the note had changed hands, Clarence, seemingly relieved by the generosity of his own action, smiled and said he was just going out to luncheon. Would Yakimov care to join him?

"Delighted, dear boy," said Yakimov. "*Delighted.*"

As they drove to Capşa's in the car which had been allotted to him, Clarence said: "I wonder if you know a Commander Sheppy? He's just invited me to a party. I don't know him from Adam."

"Oh yes, dear boy," said Yakimov. "Know him well. One eye, one arm – but keen as mustard."

"What is he doing here?"

"I'm told," Yakimov's voice dropped – "of course it's not the sort of thing one should pass round – but I'm *told*, he's an important member of the British Secret Service."

Clarence laughed his unbelief. "Who would tell you that?" he asked.

"Not in a position to say."

Capşa's was Yakimov's favourite among the Bucharest restaurants. As they passed from the knife-edge of the *crivat* into a lusciousness of rose-red carpeting, plush, crystal and gilt, he felt himself home again.

A table had been booked for Clarence beside the double windows that overlooked the snow-patched garden. To exclude any hint of draught, red silk cushions were placed between the two panes of glass. Clarence's guest, a thick-set man with an air of self-conscious pride, rose without smiling, and frowned when he saw Yakimov. Clarence introduced them: Count Steffaneski, Prince Yakimov.

"A Russian?" asked Steffaneski.

"White Russian, dear boy. British subject."

Steffaneski's grunt seemed to say 'A Russian is a Russian', and, sitting down heavily he stared at the table-cloth.

Defensively, Clarence said: "Prince Yakimov is a refugee from Poland."

"Indeed?" Steffaneski raised his head and fixed Yakimov distrustfully. "From where in Poland does he come?"

Yakimov, putting his face into the menu card, said: "I strongly recommend the crayfish cooked in paprika. And there is really a delicious pilaff of quails."

Steffaneski obstinately repeated his question. Clarence said: "Prince Yakimov tells me he stayed with relatives who have an estate there."

"Ah, I would be interested to learn their name. I am related to many landowners. Many others are my friends."

Seeing Steffaneski set in his deadly persistence, Yakimov attempted explanation: "Fact is, dear boy, there's been a bit of a misunderstanding. Left Poland before things started. Doing undercover work: saw trouble coming: was ordered to get away. White Russian, y'know. So, not to put too fine a point on it, your poor old Yaki had to take to his heels."

Watching him closely, Steffaneski was waiting for something to come of all this. When Yakimov paused, hoping he had given explanation enough, the Count said: "Yes?"

Yakimov said: "Got lost on the way down. Ended up in Hungary. Friend there, most generous fellow – Count Ignotus – invited me to stay on his estate. So, the fact was, the estate I spoke of was in Hungary."

"So you did not come down through Lvov and Jassy?" Steffaneski asked with apparent courtesy.

"No, just dropped straight down to Hungary."

"Through Czechoslovakia?"

"Naturally, dear boy."

"How then did you penetrate the German forces?"

"What German forces?"

"Can it be you did not encounter them?"

"Well." Yakimov looked appealingly at Clarence, who appeared embarrassed by these questions and answers. As Steffaneski began to harass Yakimov again, Clarence broke in to say: "He may have come through Ruthenia."

"Ruthenia?" Steffaneski jerked round to face Clarence. "Is Ruthenia not occupied, then?"

"I think not," said Clarence.

For some moments Clarence and the Count discussed, without reference to Yakimov, the possibility of his having passed unmolested through Ruthenia. Suddenly Steffaneski had another thought: "If he went through Ruthenia, he must have crossed the Carpathians." He returned to Yakimov. "You crossed the Carpathians?" he asked.

"How do I know?" Yakimov wailed. "It was terrible. You can have no idea what it was like."

"I can have no idea? I drive with refugees from Warsaw to Bucharest! I am machine-gunned and I am bombed! I see my friends die: I help bury them! And you tell me I can have no idea!" With a gesture that implied life was real but Yakimov was not, he turned to Clarence and began to question him about Polish Relief.

Thankful to be left in peace, Yakimov gave his thoughts to the pilaff of quails which was being served.

Despite Yakimov's recommendation of the Moselle '34 and '37 Burgundy, Clarence had ordered a single bottle of Rumanian red wine. The waiter arrived with three bottles which he put down beside Yakimov, who gave him a look of complete understanding.

Steffaneski was describing a visit he had paid the day before to a Polish internment camp in the mountains. When he arrived at the barbed-wire enclosure he had seen the wooden huts of the camp half buried in snow. A Rumanian sentry at the gate had refused to admit him without sanction of the officer on duty. The officer could not be disturbed because it was 'the time of the siesta'. Steffaneski had demanded that the sentry ring the officer and the sentry had replied: "But that is impossible. The officer does not sleep alone."

"And so outside the camp I sit for two hours while the officer on duty sleeps, not alone. Ah, how I despise this country! One and all, the Poles despise this country. Sometimes I say to myself: 'Better had we stayed in Poland and all died together.' "

"I couldn't agree more, dear boy," said Yakimov, eating and drinking heartily.

Steffaneski gave him a look of disgust. "I was under the impression," he said to Clarence, "that our talk was to be private."

A second course of spit-roasted beef arrived and with it the second bottle of wine was emptied. Clarence spent some time explaining to Steffaneski how he was arranging with a junior Minister for the Poles to be shipped over the frontier into Yugoslavia, whence they could travel to join the Allied armies in France.

For permitting these escapes, the Rumanian authorities were demanding a fee of one thousand *lei* a head.

The beef was excellent. Yakimov ate with gusto and was examining the tray of French cheese, when Clarence noticed that the waiter was serving them wine from a new bottle.

"I ordered only one bottle," he said. "Why have you brought a second?"

"This, *domnule*," said the waiter, giving the bottle an insolent flourish, "is the third."

"The *third*!" Clarence looked bewildered. "I did not ask for three bottles."

"Then why did you drink them?" the waiter asked as he made off.

Consolingly, Yakimov said: "All these Rumanian waiters are the same. Can't trust them, dear boy . . ."

"But did we drink three bottles? Is it possible?"

"The empties are here, dear boy."

Clarence looked at the bottles beside Yakimov, then looked at Yakimov as though he alone were responsible for their emptiness.

When the coffee was brought, Yakimov murmured to the waiter: "Cognac." Immediately a bottle and glasses were put upon the table.

"What is this?" Clarence demanded.

"Seems to be brandy, dear boy," said Yakimov.

Clarence called the waiter back: "Take it away. Bring me my bill."

The cheese tray still stood beside the table. With furtive haste, Yakimov cut himself a long slice of brie and folded it into his mouth. Clarence and Steffaneski watching with astonished distaste, he said in apology: "Trifle peckish, dear boy."

Neither made any comment.

When the bill was paid, Clarence took out a notebook and noted down his expenses. Yakimov, whose sight was long, read as it was written:

Luncheon to Count S. and Prince Y.:   *Lei* 5,500

Advance to Prince Y., British refugee from Poland: 10,000

For a moment Yakimov was discomforted at seeing his fantasy so baldly recorded, then he forgot the matter. As they left the restaurant, his well-fed glow was like an extra wrap against the cold. He said to Clarence: "Delightful meal! Delightful company!"

He carried his smile over to Steffaneski, who was standing apart.

Clarence barely responded.

Yakimov had expected the offer of a lift, but no offer was made. As Clarence and Steffaneski drove off without him, the glow began to seep from him. Then he remembered he had twelve thousand *lei*. He went into the *confiserie* attached to the restaurant and bought himself a little silver box full of raspberry pastilles. Holding this happily, he called a taxi and set out for his new lodgings, where he would sleep the afternoon away.

12

A FEW DAYS BEFORE CHRISTMAS, Bella Niculescu, meeting Harriet in the street, invited her to tea. Guy's only comment on this incipient friendship was: "She'll bore the arse off you."

Harriet said: "You scarcely know her."

"She's just a typical bourgeois reactionary."

"You mean, her prejudices are different from yours."

"You'll see for yourself," said Guy and, reminding her that they had been invited that evening to the Athénée Palace by a Commander Sheppy, he went to give a student private coaching. Harriet was left with doubts about her coming tea-party.

Bella's flat was in a new block on the Boulevard Brătianu. Walking there, Harriet felt the wind blow shrill across the desolate lots. Through the vents in the peasants' huts could be seen the flicker of lamps. The only crowds now were on the tramcars that clanked their way out of darkness into darkness. When she passed the vast black skeleton of the Ministry building, she saw a fire burning in a ground-floor corner. Beside it sat a huddle of workmen too old for the army and no use for anything else.

The blocks of flats rose out of the gloom like lighted towers. Their hallways, visible through glass doors, indicated the grandeur to which the designers of the boulevard had first aspired.

Harriet was shown into Bella's sitting-room. Low-ceilinged and very warm, it was carpeted in sky-blue and set about with walnut tables and blue upholstered arm-chairs. In the midst of this Bella, in a cashmere jersey and pearls, was seated before a silver tea-service.

Sinking into one of the chairs, Harriet said: "How comfortable!"

Bella replied: "It's cosy," as though Harriet had meant the reverse.

"This looks like English furniture."

"It *is* English furniture. Our wedding-present from daddy. He bought it for us from Maples. Everything came from Maples."

"And you brought it all this way? That must have been a business."

"It certainly was." Bella laughed, relaxing a little. "The amount it cost us in bribes, we might just as well have paid duty and have done with it."

While they were waiting for the tea to be brought in, Bella offered to show Harriet over the flat. They went first to Bella's bedroom, that contained a large double bed with highly polished walnut headboard and a pink counterpane braided, ruched, embroidered and embossed with satin tulips. Bella, touching out the collection of silver-backed brushes, silver-boxes and cut glass on her dressing table, said: "These peasant servants have no sense of anything."

She opened a door and disclosed a bathroom, as hot as a hothouse and closely packed with pink accoutrements.

"Delicious," said Harriet and Bella looked pleased.

"Now the dining-room!" she said and Harriet wished she had courage to tell her that she did not need to be impressed. She wanted to find herself in sympathy with Bella, who was, in a way, her own discovery – anyway, not a ready-made acquaintance imposed on her by Guy.

After luncheon with the Drucker family, she had said to Guy: "Your friends are disappointed in me. They expected you to marry someone exactly like yourself," but she had, she suspected, exceeded Bella's expectations.

In the dining-room, where Bella paused expectantly before a sideboard coruscant with silver and cut-glass, Harriet asked: "Do you use this stuff?"

"My dear, yes. Rumanians expect it. They look down on you if you can't make as big a show as they do." Bella smiled at the pretensions demanded of her, but her voice betrayed respect for them.

"The Pringle flat can provide nothing like this," said Harriet.

"Didn't you bring your wedding-presents?"

"We married in haste. We only got a cheque or two."

They had returned to the sitting-room, where tea awaited them. "Oh, I had a very big wedding," said Bella. "We came here with ten large packing-cases – *full*. Even the Rumanians were impressed. Still, you won't have to entertain them. The real Rumanians never mix with foreigners."

Harriet admitted they had been invited only to Jewish households and Bella, gratified, was about to say more when she noticed something amiss among the silver on the tray before her. She stopped and her lips tightened. With a purposeful movement, she pressed a bell in the wall and waited. Her silence was intent. When the servant appeared, Bella spoke two words. The girl gasped and fled, to return with a tea-strainer.

"These servants!" Bella shook her head with disgust. Becoming suddenly animated, she talked at length about the sort of servants to be found in Rumania. She placed them in two categories: the honest imbeciles and the intelligent delinquents, the words 'honest' and 'intelligent' being, of course, merely relative.

"Which have you got?" Bella asked Harriet.

Inchcape's man, Pauli, had acquired for Harriet his cousin Despina. "She seems to me," said Harriet, "not only intelligent and honest, but very good-natured."

Bella grudgingly agreed that Hungarians were 'a cut above the others' but she had no doubt Despina 'made a bit' on everything she was sent out to buy. Harriet described how Despina, on being shown the cupboard that passed for a servant's bedroom in the Pringles' flat, had sunk to her knees and, kissing Harriet's hand, had said that at last she would be able to have her husband to live with her.

Bella saw nothing astonishing in this story. "She's very fortunate to have a room of any sort," she said, and almost at once returned to the subject of the real Rumanians whom Harriet was never likely to meet. "They're terribly snobby," she kept saying as she gave examples of their exclusiveness.

Harriet was reminded of Doamna Flöhr's claim that the exclusiveness of the Jews was the exclusiveness of the excluded. What, she wanted to know, had the Rumanians to be so snobbish about? She said: "They must suffer from some profound sense of inferiority."

Such an idea was new and strange to Bella. She looked bewildered as she asked: "But what are they inferior to?"

"Why, to us, of course; to the foreigners and the Jews who run the country for them because they are too lazy to run it for themselves."

Bella, her mouth open, considered this point a moment, then she gave a gawp of laughter and said: "I don't know. Some of them still have a lot of money, but really, it's nothing compared with what people have in England and the States." A new vigour, roused by indignation, began to displace the careful refinement of her earlier speech: "And when you *do* get invited to their houses – the bother of it all! I can't tell you! Never a nice homey evening – always formality and everyone dressed up to the nines. All the time you have to think twice before you utter. And then this business of pretending you don't understand the men's jokes. Having to sit there like a dummy! My goodness, there's been times when I'd gladly go back to Roehampton. Anyone would think the women here were all bally virgins – and they're not, *believe me!*"

Exhilarated now by the daring of her own censure, Bella threw back her head, laughing and showing all her large, white, healthy teeth. Harriet laughed, too, feeling they had at last made contact.

"Here," said Bella, "have another cake. They're from Capşa's. I oughtn't to eat them; I'm putting on weight; but I do enjoy my food."

"Life here has its compensations," said Harriet.

"It certainly has. When I first arrived, the English wives were a bit snooty with me. They thought it a come-down to marry a Rumanian. But my Nikko could show them a thing or two. He's shown me that Englishwomen know nothing at all."

Harriet laughed. "I expect they know something."

"Not much. Anyway, not the lot we had here. And now they're all coming back. Old Mother Woolley wrote to me, and what do you think she said? She said: 'My Joe's just like other men. With me away, his health suffers.' *I ask you!*" Bella threw back her head again and her bosom shook with laughter. "My Nikko says those old boys only started the scare to get rid of their wives." She wiped a tear from her eye. "Oh dear, it's a relief to talk to a woman of my own age – an Englishwoman, I mean – especially now Nikko's away."

"He's away?"

"Recalled to his regiment. His papers came yesterday and off he had to go. This morning I went round to see his senior officer. That man's a crook if ever there was one. It was only October last I arranged for Nikko to be released from service for six months, and here he is called up again. 'Ah, Doamna Niculescu,' said the officer 'I, too, have a senior officer.' 'And what does your senior

officer want?' I asked. 'Oh, the usual! One hundred thousand *lei*.'
I told him straight: 'If this war goes on for long, you'll bankrupt
me.' He just roared with laughter."

"Your Rumanian must be very good?"

"I'm told it's perfect. I did languages, you know. I met Nikko
when I was at L.S.E. I speak French, German, Spanish and
Italian."

"So does Sophie Oresanu. I suppose you know her?"

Bella's face contracted significantly: "That little . . . um!"

"You really think she is . . . ?"

"I certainly do."

Harriet, confused by the liberal traditions of her generation,
had not been able to condemn Sophie so boldly, but now, hearing
Bella speak out without compromise – much, indeed, as Harriet's
aunt used to speak – Harriet was convinced by her certainty.

Bella said: "Nikko told me to say nothing, but really! The way
that girl runs after your husband! It's disgraceful. Quite frankly,
I don't think you should put up with it." She spoke rather breathlessly, in defiance of Nikko's ban. "It says a lot for Guy that there
hasn't been more gossip."

"Has there been gossip?"

"But of course there has. Can't you imagine it? In this place of
all places."

"I'm sure Guy doesn't realise . . ."

"I'm sure he doesn't. Still, he ought to have more sense. She's
the sort of girl who'd do anything for a British passport. If I were
you, I'd put a stop to it."

Harriet sat silent. Bella's statement that Guy should have 'more
sense' had struck her like a revealed truth.

When it was time for her to go, Bella came with her into the
hall, where the floor was tessellated in black and white. The white
walls were smooth as cream. Harriet said: "This is a very good
block. Ours is so flimsy, the wind seems to blow through
it."

Bella laughed. "You're in Blocşul Cazacul. That was built by
Horia Cazacu, whose motto is: *Santajul etajul*."

"What does that mean?"

"He's a financier but his income is chiefly from blackmail. It
more or less means 'Each blackmail builds a new floor'. Blocşul
Cazacul is bad even for Bucharest."

Feeling indebted to Bella for her friendly advances, Harriet asked her if she would be alone at Christmas.

"I'll be alone all right," said Bella. "Catch them asking me out without Nikko." The bitter amusement of Bella's tone disclosed her struggle to establish herself among the 'real' Rumanians.

Harriet squeezed her arm. "Then come and have supper with us," she said.

The public rooms of the Athénée Palace were crowded with visitors. On this, the first Christmas season of the war, war was forgotten. The threat of invasion had passed even from memory. Life here had always been uncertain and the people, like rabbits who have escaped the snare, recovered quickly. The Rumanian guests who sat drinking in the main room seemed to Harriet to exude confidence and self-sufficiency.

The new atmosphere had found expression in the Bucharest papers, which drew attention to the loss by Germany of the battle of the River Plate; and the fact that the Finns were making fools of the Russian invaders. Perhaps the threatening Powers were not, after all, so powerful! Perhaps the threat was all one great bluff! But, bluff or no bluff, Rumania had little to fear, being a richly provided country separated from the squabbles of others by a wall of snow-blocked mountains.

This attitude of self-congratulation did not persist into the breakfast room, where Dobson was introducing Commander Sheppy to those whom he had himself invited. There the air seemed edgy with uncertainties. Dobson, despite his charm, was a nervous host. When Harriet presented herself, he said: "You ought to meet Sheppy," but Sheppy was surrounded. "A little later, I think," said Dobson, dropping her and going to Woolley, who had entered behind her.

Guy, Inchcape and Clarence had not yet arrived. Among the other guests there was no one whom she knew well enough to approach. She took a drink and went to the French-window. Outside was the garden where she had sat in the sunlight with Yakimov only a short time before. Now the light from the room touched a bloom of snow on the north-east flanks of the trees. Somewhere outside in the darkness the boy was still emptying his urn. She thought she heard the tinkle of water, but could not be sure. Soon even moving water would be stilled to ice and the garden silent until spring.

A waiter, mistaking for a reprimand her interest in the world beyond the window, came fussily over and pulled the curtains. Then she had nothing to look at but the members of the business community gathered round the man who must be Commander Sheppy. She heard his voice come harsh and antagonising: "That, gentlemen, will be my problem." Then someone moved and she was able to see him.

Harriet noted the black eye-patch, the captive stick swinging and clattering beside him, the artificial hand held like an adornment, and smiled, thinking his manner that of someone who has taken a correspondence course in leadership. When she turned away she noticed Woolley at the bar and, crossing impulsively to him, said: " I hear your wife is returning. Now don't you think I was wise to remain in Bucharest?"

He stared at her, rebuking her with his long silence, then he said with decision: "No, I don't. If you want to know what I think of you staying here, after all it cost me to send my lady wife home – I think it wasn't playing the game." His brief nod underlined his opinion and he strode from her to join his associates round Sheppy.

At that moment Guy, Clarence and Inchcape arrived together. Guy and Clarence were at once seized upon by Dobson and taken to Sheppy. Inchcape was left, as Harriet had been, to find entertainment as best he might. He wandered over to Harriet, one eyebrow raised in a frown of bored enquiry.

"What've we been dragged here for?" he asked.

"No one seems to know."

"Which is Sheppy? I'm told he's an odd-looking cove."

Harriet pointed out Sheppy, who was now taking Guy, Clarence and some other young men to a corner of the room. When he had them to himself, he seemed to be lecturing them.

"What's he up to?" Inchcape stared over at the group. "And the chaps he has picked out – what have they in common?"

Harriet was about to say "Youth", but said instead: "They probably all speak Rumanian."

"So do I." Inchcape turned his back on Sheppy. "Well, I can't waste time here. I have people coming to dinner."

Sheppy did not keep the young men long. Clarence joined

Harriet and Inchcape, who at once asked him: "What's it all about?"

Clarence gave a provocative smile. "I'm not at liberty to say."

Inchcape put his glass to his lips and swallowed its contents. "I must be off," he said, and went with strides too long for his height.

Guy was still talking to the other young men. These were four junior engineers from the telephone company, an eccentric called Dubedat and an adolescent member of the English family Rettison that had lived in Bucharest for generations.

Harriet said: "Inchcape was wondering what you all had in common."

"The flower of the English colony," smirked Clarence.

"What *does* Sheppy want?" Harriet felt both pride and anxiety that Guy was among the chosen. "He really looks fantastic."

"Fact is, we don't know yet. He's calling us to a meeting after Christmas. I'd guess he's a 'cloak and dagger' boy – the lunatic fringe of security."

"What makes you think that?"

"He hinted he was here on a secret mission. But I shouldn't have told you that." Tilting back on his heels, displaying a diffident flirtatiousness, Clarence seemed to suggest she had wheedled a confidence out of him.

Harriet smiled it off but realised, whether she liked it or not, she had involved herself with Clarence. Nothing, she knew, would convince him she had not made a first move in his direction.

Impatiently she said: "What is Guy doing over there?" Guy was, in fact, talking enthusiastically to Dubedat.

Harriet had seen Dubedat about in the streets. He was a noticeable figure. He was said to have been an elementary-school teacher in England and had been 'thumbing' his way through Galicia when war broke out. He had walked over the frontier into Bessarabia. When the refugee cars came streaming down through Chernowitz, one of them gave him a lift. He called himself a 'simple lifer'. He had arrived in Bucharest in shorts and open-necked shirt, and for weeks wore nothing more. The *crivat* had eventually forced him into a sleeveless sheepskin jacket, but his legs and arms, remaining exposed, were whipped raw by the wind. When he walked in the street, his large, limp hands, mauve and swollen, swung about him like boxing-gloves on strings. Now, under Guy's regard, his face, hook-nosed, small-chinned, usually peevish, glowed with satisfaction.

Harriet asked Clarence: "Does Dubedat intend to stay in Bucharest?"

"He doesn't want to go home. He's a conscientious objector. Guy is taking him on as an English teacher."

At this piece of news, Harriet moved to take a closer look at Dubedat, saying: "I'll go and see what they're talking about."

Guy was including in his audience the engineers, who stood together with the bashful air of obscure men unexpectedly given prominence. He was on a favourite subject – the peasants. Describing how they danced in a circle, their arms about each other's shoulders while they stared at their feet and stamped, he put out his own arms to the engineers. As they drew nearer, Dubedat's expression changed to one of hostility.

Guy said: "The peasants just go round and round, stamping in time to that hysterical music, until they're completely crazy with it. They begin to believe they're stamping on their enemies – the King, the landowner, the village priest, the Jew who keeps the village shop . . . And when they're exhausted, they go back to work. Nothing's changed, but they're not angry any more."

Harriet, having reached Dubedat's side, noticed the sour smell that came from him. He had been watching Guy's performance with his lips open so that she could see his yellow and decaying teeth. The creases of his nostrils were greasy and pitted with blackheads: there were crusts of scurf caught in the roots of his hair and grime beneath his fingernails. As he lit a new cigarette from the stub of an old one, she noticed the first and second fingers of his right hand yellowed by nicotine.

The engineers, having moved into the aura of Dubedat, began edging away again. Guy, however, was not worried On the contrary he seemed like radium throwing off vitality to the outside world – not that he thought of it as the outside world. So spontaneous was his approach to it, he seemed unaware of any sort of frontier between himself and the rest of humanity.

Watching him, Harriet felt a wave of irritated love for him and heard this echoed by Clarence, who said behind her: "Let's get Guy away from here."

They had arranged to go that evening to see a French film at the main cinema and would have to leave soon. Harriet was about to speak to Guy, when young Rettison, on the fringe of the group, broke in in an accent that was peculiar to the Rettison family. He was a sleek, self-possessed and self-assertive young man who looked like a Rumanian. He said: "It has always been the same here. It was the same before the King became a dictator. It always will be the same. The English here criticise the King. They forget he is pro-British. We wouldn't have such a good time if he weren't here."

Guy said: "The King's pro-British because Britain is pro-King. That's the policy that's going to wreck us all."

The engineers glanced nervously towards Dobson, a representative of British policy, and Harriet said: "Darling, if you want to see the film, you must come now."

Guy wanted to see the film, but he also wanted to stay and talk. He looked like a baby offered too many toys.

"Come along," said Harriet and, to encourage him, she strolled on with Clarence out of the hotel. When Guy joined them he had brought Dubedat along too.

Clarence had his car with him. Harriet sat in the front seat beside him, while Guy sat with Dubedat in the back. As they drove across the square, Guy drew information from Dubedat. He asked him first where he came from.

Harsh and nasal, with a slight north country accent, Dubedat's voice came reluctantly from a corner. "I'm a scowse," he said. "From the dregs of the Liverpool soup."

He had won a scholarship to a grammar school, but at the school he had found not only the boys but the masters prejudiced against him. Everywhere he had gone, it seemed, he had met with prejudice.

"What sort of prejudice?"

"Social," said Dubedat.

"Ah!"

By the time they had reached the cinema, Guy was no longer interested in the film. "You go," he said to Harriet and Clarence. "I want to talk to Dubedat. We'll meet afterwards at the Doi Trandafiri."

Clarence protested, very annoyed, but Guy was too entranced to listen. Dubedat, looking smug, followed them across the road.

Clarence said: "It was Guy who wanted to see this film, not me."

"Would you rather go to the Doi Trandafiri?" Harriet asked.

"What! And listen to the confessions of Dubedat?"

The film was an involved and almost motionless domestic drama. Harriet's French was unequal to it and the Rumanian underlines did not help her much. It was preceded by a French news film that showed shots of the Maginot Line where trucks sped on rails through underground arsenals and barracks. There were vast stores of frozen meat and wine. A voice declared: "*Nous sommes imprenables.*"

"Let's hope so," said Clarence gloomily.

Behind the French lines soldiers filed through woods white with rime. They stood about, drinking from mugs and beating their arms for warmth while their breath clouded out on to the frozen air.

There was a little applause, but most of the time the audience shuffled and coughed, as bored by the war as were the idle men at arms.

Harriet and Clarence emerged, depressed, from the cinema. As they entered the Doi Trandafiri, an ancient beggar plucked at Clarence, repeating: "*Keine Mutter, kein Vater.*"

"*Ich auch nicht,*" replied Clarence and, cheered by his own wit, he turned smiling to Harriet: "I never give to beggars, on principle."

"On what principle?"

"They bring out the worst in me. They make me feel like a fascist."

Harriet laughed, but uneasily, recognising in Clarence something of herself. But because she loved Guy, she could feel safe. If she loved herself she would be lost indeed.

The interior of the Doi Trandafiri, with its yellow grained wood and horsehair sofas, the chess-sets and dominoes on the tables, the racks of newspapers mounted on batons, the faded photographs of writers, actors and painters, had a shabby, comfortable atmosphere of *Mitteleuropa*. It was a cheap café. In term-time it was crowded with students.

Guy and Dubedat were settled in the wide curve of the corner window. When the others sat down, Guy said delightfully: "Dubedat has been telling me he lives at the Dâmboviţa; actually in the Calea Plevna, with a family of poor Jews."

"The poorest of the poor," said Dubedat with glum satisfaction, "and the only decent folk in this dirty, depraved, God-forsaken capital." Fixing Clarence with a watery pink eye, he added, apparently in special reference to him: "A city of the plain."

"Oh, *really*!" Clarence, picking up a copy of the *Bukarester Tageblatt*, retired behind it in disgust.

Guy brushed aside the annoyance of the newcomers: "He doesn't mean any harm. You must hear about life at the Dâmboviţa." Guy swung round on Dubedat: "Tell them about the night the rats came in through the skylight."

Dubedat said nothing. Harriet was about to speak but Guy held up his hand. Gazing, aglow, at Dubedat, he coaxed: "Tell them about the mad beggar who drank silver polish."

Dubedat emptied his glass but remained silent. Clarence snorted behind his paper. When it became obvious that Dubedat was not to be persuaded, Guy, unaffected by rebuff, repeated his revelations for him while Dubedat, rather drunk, settled down into sleep.

They were as interesting as Guy promised, yet Harriet listened with impatience. At the same time she wondered whether she would have disliked Dubedat so much had his company not been forced upon her.

The difficulty of dealing with Guy, she thought, lay in the fact that he was so often right. She and Clarence could claim that their evening had been spoilt by the presence of Dubedat. She knew it had, in fact, been spoilt not by Guy's generosity but their own lack of it.

When it was time to go, Dubedat had to be roused and supported out to the car. They drove down through the Dâmboviţa area, which even at this hour was lively, with the brothels noisy and peasants and beggars wandering about in search of some night cover from the cold.

Wakened and questioned in the Calea Plevna, Dubedat managed to give his address. Guy said he would see Dubedat to his room on the top floor and wanted Clarence to come with him. Clarence insisted that they could not leave Harriet alone at such an hour, in this district.

When Guy and Dubedat had gone in, the other two sat for some time in silence. Suddenly, out of his thoughts, Clarence laughed and said in affectionate exasperation: "Guy is an extraordinary man with all this giving and expecting no return. Do you understand it?"

"It's partly pride," said Harriet, "and a habit of independence.

He wants to be the one to give because in the past he was always too poor to repay."

Upset by this rationalisation of Guy's virtue, Clarence sat up and said in reprimand: "He's a saint. In fact, a great saint. I often feel I'd like to give him something to show how much I admire him. But what can one give a saint?"

Considering this question in a practical way, Harriet said: "There are a great many things you could give him. Because he comes from a poor family, he has never had any of the presents that boys get as they're growing up. You could give him something useful – a set of hairbrushes or a fountain-pen or a shaving-brush . . ."

"Really!" Clarence interrupted with scorn. "Fancy giving Guy something like that! I thought of giving him a real present – two hundred pounds, say, so he would have something behind him if he needed it. But, of course, he wouldn't take it."

"I think he would. It would be wonderful."

"I couldn't offer it."

"Then why talk about it?"

Another long silence. Clarence sighed again. "I really want to do something for someone," he said, "but I let all my friends down in the end."

"Oh, well!" Realising that all this had merely been an exercise in self-mortification, Harriet left it at that.

When Guy returned to the car, he said: "We really must do something for Dubedat."

Harriet said: "What could we do? He's an exhibitionist. One should never separate an exhibitionist from his way of life."

"How else can he live?" Guy asked. "He has no money."

"Yet he smokes like a chimney."

"Oh, tobacco is necessary to him. From each according to his ability: to each according to his needs. We should offer him our spare room."

"I couldn't bear it," said Harriet, with such decision that Guy let the matter drop. She hoped she would hear no more of Dubedat, but next morning Guy mentioned him again: "We must ask him here on Christmas night."

"It's impossible, darling. The table only seats six. We've asked Inchcape and Clarence, and you asked Yakimov."

"That leaves room for one more."

"I've invited Bella."

"Bella Niculescu!"

"I suppose I can invite a friend?" said Harriet. "Nikko has been called to his regiment. Bella will be alone."

"All right." Guy could not fail to respond to Bella's situation, but he added: "What about Sophie?"

"Why should we ask Sophie?"

"She'll be alone, too."

"She's in her own country. She has friends. Bella's need is greater than Sophie's."

It was agreed at last that Sophie and Dubedat should be invited to come in after dinner. Both accepted when telephoned by Guy.

13

YAKIMOV WAS THE FIRST TO ARRIVE at the flat on Christmas night. He brought with him a thin, tall, narrow-shouldered, young man whom he introduced as Bernard Dugdale. Dugdale was a diplomat passing through Bucharest on his way to Ankara.

Barely touching Harriet's hand he sank into the only arm-chair and there he lay, seemingly lifeless except for his eyes, that roved around in critical appraisal of his surroundings.

Harriet hurried to Despina in the kitchen. When she explained there would be seven instead of six for dinner, Despina treated the emergency as a joke. She put a hand on Harriet's arm, squeezed it affectionately, then set off down the frosted fire-escape to borrow dishes from a neighbour's cook. When Harriet returned to the room, Inchcape and Clarence were entering from the hall. Yaki-mov, who had settled beside the electric fire with a glass of *ţuică*, appeared abashed by the sight of Clarence.

Clarence said when introduced: "We have met before."

"So we have, dear boy. *So* we have!"

Inchcape, looking in amusement from one to the other, noticed Dugdale and suddenly stiffened. When he learnt that this stranger was a diplomat, he asked: "You came by train?" set on edge by the possibility that this young man might have been granted a priority flight over Europe.

Dugdale, weary but tolerant in his manner, admitted he had come by train: "A somewhat hazardous journey at the moment."

"In what way hazardous?" Harriet asked.

"Oh, one thing and another, you know." Dugdale implied that he had passed through perils the others could not even guess at.

When the introductions were completed, both Inchcape and Clarence seemed to withdraw from the party. It was some moments before Harriet realised they were annoyed at finding other guests present. The original plan had been for a 'family' party within the organisation and no one had told them of the change.

While standing, each stared down at the floor. When invited to sit down, Clarence took himself to the fringe of the group and remained silent, his head back against the wall. Inchcape, his legs crossed at the knee, turned up his elegant toe and stared at it, disguising his exasperation with an appearance of amusement.

Before anyone could speak again, Despina sped through the room, banging doors after her, to admit Bella. Bella entered with Nikko behind her.

Her Nikko, she explained, had been restored to her only half an hour before. As she apologised for bringing him unexpectedly, she beamed about in pride of him. Nikko was less composed than his wife. He was, no doubt on Bella's advice, dressed informally. He kept his head lowered while he glanced anxiously at the dress of the other men, then, reassured, he turned on Harriet, bowed and presented her with a bouquet of pink carnations.

When they were seated again, Inchcape, his lips depressed, looked under his brows at Clarence. Clarence, eyes wide, looked back. They were surprised at seeing, of all people, the Niculescus, and were, of course, displeased. Harriet was interested to note how similarly the two men reacted. Critical as each was of the other, there they both were withdrawn, suspicious and hard to mollify – not that she had time to mollify anyone at that moment.

Despina, enjoying her own resource, collected the smaller chairs from under the guests and took them to the table, then she sang out: "*Poftiți la masă.*" On the table, among the Pringles' white china and napkins, were two yellow plates with pink napkins. Among the six chairs were the kitchen stool and the cork-topped linen box from the bathroom. This was the first dinner-party Harriet had ever given. She could have wept at its disruption.

When they were all seated, there was not much elbow room at the table. Nikko, pressed up against Yakimov, kept giving him oblique glances and at last blurted out: "I have heard of the famous English Prince who is so *spirituelle.*" Everyone looked at Yakimov, hoping for entertainment, but his eyes were fixed on Despina, who was carrying round the soup. When the bowl reached him, he filled his plate eagerly and emptied it before Guy had been served. He then watched for more.

Guy asked Nikko if there was any news of the Drucker family. Nikko, who had been for a short time an accountant in the Drucker bank, replied with satisfaction that there was none.

"And the boy?" Guy asked. "I have been hoping to hear from him."

"No one knows where he is," said Nikko. "He is not with Doamna Drucker, that is certain. He has disappeared. But of Emanuel Drucker I am told he is in a common cell with low criminals and perverts. Such must be very uncomfortable."

"Very indeed," murmured Inchcape with a sardonic smile.

"Who is this Drucker?" Dugdale asking, looking down with benign condescension upon Nikko.

Nikko swallowed and choked in his eagerness to reply: "This Drucker," he said, "is a big crook. A powerful lady – we do not name her – demanded of him certain holdings in Rumanian oil. He had been skinned before. Although he describes himself as pro-British, his business is with Germany – such a thing is not uncommon here – and he thinks Germany will protect him. So he refuses. He is arrested. He is jugged. Each minute a new charge is cooked for him – treason, forgery, plotting with Germany, plotting with Britain, black-market deals and so on. One would be enough. He is a Jew, so his possessions anyway are forfeit. His son has disappeared. His family has fled. His wife is demanding a divorce. The man himself? He will be in prison for life."

"Without trial?" Clarence asked, scandalised.

"Certainly not," said Nikko. "This is a democratic country. There will be a trial. A *great* trial. A trial that will squash him flat."

Dugdale gave a high neigh of a laugh. "Delicious!" he cried.

Clarence asked: "You are amused by a system of government that permits wrongful arrest, wrongful seizure of property and imprisonment for life on faked charges?"

Dugdale turned slowly to examine Clarence and smiled slightly at what he saw: "Aren't we in Ruritania?" he said. "What do you expect?"

Nikko, looking in consternation from Dugdale to Clarence, tried to reprove both at once: "This is not a bad country. Many people come here as guests. They make money, they live well, and still they criticise. One admires England. Another admires France. Another America. But who admires Rumania? No one. She is a cow to be milked."

The truth and vehemence of Nikko's statement brought the

table to a stop. After a silence, Harriet asked Dugdale if he thought he would enjoy Ankara.

"Things could be worse," he said. "My first appointment. I was offered Sofia – a deadly hole. However, I exerted a little pull and landed Ankara. It's an embassy. I'm not dissatisfied."

Yakimov, who had just filled his plate with turkey, taking most of the breast, said: "Let's face it, dear boy. An embassy is better than a legation." Having thus contributed to the conversation, he set about his food again.

Guy asked Dugdale what he imagined would be Germany's next move.

Dugdale answered in an authoritative tone: "In my opinion Germany has made her last move. Russia is the one we have to fear."

Yakimov, his mouth full, mumbled agreement.

"The next victim will be Sweden," said Dugdale, "then, of course, Norway and Denmark. After that the Balkans, the Mediterranean, North Africa – what's to stop them? The Allies and the Axis will watch helplessly, each unable to make a move for fear of bringing the other in on the side of Russia."

Guy began to say: "This is absurd. Russia has enough to do inside her own frontiers. What would she want . . ."

He was interrupted by Nikko, his brows raised in alarm. "But Rumania would fight," he said. "And the Turks, too. They would fight. At least I think so."

"The Turks!" Dugdale put a small potato into his mouth and swallowed it contemptuously. "We give them money to buy armaments, and what do they spend it on? *Education.*"

"Hopeless people!" Inchcape grinned at Clarence, who grinned back. Harriet was thankful they had, at last, decided to come down on the side of flippancy.

Despina had cut more turkey and was carrying the large serving dish round again. When she came to Yakimov, she held it so that the white meat was out of his reach.

"Just a *soupçon*, dear girl," he said with an air of wheedling intimacy and, stretching out his arms, he again took most of the breast. Only a few vegetables remained. He took them all. Despina, hissing through her teeth, attracted Harriet's attention and pointed to his plate. Harriet waved her on. Only Yakimov, intent on his food, remained unaware of Despina's indignation. He ate at speed, wiped his mouth with his napkin and looked around to see what was coming next.

Guy, having anticipated an evening of Yakimov's wit, now tried to encourage him to talk by telling stories himself. When his stories were exhausted, he started on limericks, occasionally pausing to ask Yakimov if he could not think of some himself. Yakimov shook his head. Despina having brought in a large mince pie, he could attend to nothing else.

Guy searched his mind for limericks and remembered one that he thought would seem particularly funny to the company. It concerned the morals of a British diplomat in the Balkans.

"That," said Dugdale coldly, "seems to me in rather bad taste."

"I couldn't agree more," said Yakimov heartily.

For some minutes there was no sound but that of Yakimov bolting down pie. He finished his helping before Despina had completed serving the others. "Hah!" he said with satisfaction and, unimpaired, looked to her for more.

As soon as was possible, Harriet motioned Bella to retire with her to the bedroom. There, not caring whether she was overheard or not, she raged: "How dare he snub Guy! The gross snob, wolfing down our food, and bringing that dyspeptic skeleton with him. When he gave his tremendous parties – if he ever gave them, which I doubt – he would not have dreamt of inviting us. Now he entertains his friends at our expense."

Bella was quick to echo this indignation: "If I were you, my dear, I wouldn't ask him here again."

"Certainly not," said Harriet, dramatic in anger; "this is the first and last time he sets foot in my house."

When the women returned to the room, the men were gathered round the electric fire. Guy was helping Yakimov to brandy. Dugdale, unperturbed, was sprawling in the arm-chair again. At the entry of the women, he lifted himself slightly and was about to drop back, when Harriet pushed the chair from him and offered it to Bella. He took himself to another chair with the expression of one overlooking a breach of good manners.

Inchcape smiled maliciously at Harriet, then turned to Yakimov and asked him: "Are you going on later to Princess Teodorescu's party?"

Yakimov lifted his nose from his glass. "I might," he said, "but those parties come a bit rough on your poor old Yaki."

To Harriet's annoyance, Guy was still trying to persuade Yakimov to talk. Yakimov seemed to be rousing himself, to be searching for jests through the fog of repletion, when there was a ring at the front door. Dubedat was admitted.

He made no concessions to the occasion. He had kept on his sheepskin jacket and to his personal smell was added the smell of badly cured skin. Looking, so Harriet thought, dirtier than ever, he surveyed the table grimly, aware the others had dined here and he had not.

At the sight of this new arrival, Dugdale rose and said he must go.

"Oh, no." Guy tried to detain him. "You have plenty of time to catch your train. You must have another brandy."

Guy began rapidly splashing brandy from glass to glass, but Dugdale stood firm. He had, he said, to collect his baggage from the cloak-room.

"Well, before you go," said Guy, "we must have 'Auld Lang Syne'."

Several people informed him that that was sung at New Year, but Guy said: "Never mind." His enthusiasm was such, the others rose and Dugdale let himself be drawn into the circle. When he had retrieved his hands, he said in a businesslike way: "Now, my overcoat."

While he was wrapping himself up, Yakimov sat down again and refilled his glass. Harriet, noticing this, said: "I imagine you will see your friend to the station."

"Oh, no, dear girl. Yaki isn't too well . . ."

"I think you should."

Even Yakimov recognised this as an invitation to go. Despondently, he gulped down the brandy and let himself be put into his coat.

When he and Dugdale had gone, Harriet and Bella freely expressed their indignation – an indignation that completely bewildered Guy.

"What are you two talking about?" he asked.

When they told him how he had been insulted, he burst out laughing. "I doubt whether Yaki even knew what he had said."

Harriet and Bella would have none of this, and Nikko backed them. While the other men sat complacently uninvolved in the situation, the two women insisted that he should never speak to Yakimov again.

Guy sat in silence, smiling slightly and letting the storm pass over his head. When at last it died down, Clarence said from the back of the room: "Yakimov came to the Relief Centre the other day presenting himself as a refugee from Poland. I lent him ten thousand."

"Oh," said Guy easily, "he'll pay it back."

Down in the street, Yakimov said: "Seems to me I was given the boot. Can't for the life of me think why."

Dugdale showed no interest. Calling a taxi, he said discouragingly: "I suppose you want to be dropped somewhere?"

"Athénée Palace, dear boy. Feel I ought to drop in on Princess T." As they drove across the square, he added: "I wonder, dear boy – end of the month and all that; bit short of the Ready – could you lend poor Yaki a *leu* or two?"

"No," said Dugdale, "my last five hundred went on tea."

"If you have any odd pennies or francs . . ."

Dugdale did not reply. When the taxi stopped, he opened the door and waited for Yakimov to descend.

Yakimov on the pavement said: "Delightful day. Thank you for everything. See you when you're back this way. Yaki's turn next."

Dugdale slammed the door on his speech and directed the taxi on. Yakimov pushed against the hotel door: the door revolved and he came out again. He stood for a moment looking after the taxi. Could he have brought himself to admit his address, he might have been driven all the way home.

He set out to walk. The Siberian wind, plunging and shrilling, stung his ears and tugged at the skirts of his coat. As he put up his collar and buried in it his long icicle of a nose, he murmured: "Poor Yaki's getting too old for his job."

Soon after the last of the Christmas guests had gone, the telephone rang in the Pringles' flat. Guy answered it. The caller was Sophie.

Sophie had not arrived, as expected, after dinner. Harriet went into the bedroom and left Guy to talk to her.

Sitting at her dressing-table, Harriet heard Guy's voice, concerned, solicitous, apparently pleading, and it renewed in her the anger Yakimov had aroused. Bella had said if she were Harriet, she would put a stop to that relationship. This, Harriet felt, was the moment to do it. She went into the sitting room and asked: "What is the matter?"

Guy was looking grave. He put his hand over the mouthpiece and said: "Sophie's in a state of depression. She wants me to go over and see her. Alone."

"At this time of night? Tell her it's out of the question."

"She's threatening to do something desperate."

"Such as?"

"Jump out of a window, or take an overdose of sleeping-tablets."

"Let me speak to her." Harriet took the receiver and said into it: "What is the matter, Sophie? You are being very silly. You know if you really intended to do anything like that, you would do it and not talk about it."

There was a long pause before Sophie's voice came, tearfully: "I will jump if Guy doesn't come. My mind is made up."

"Then go ahead and do it."

"Do what?"

"Why, jump, of course."

Sophie gulped with horror. She said: "I hate you. I hated you from the first. You are a cruel girl. A girl without heart." There came the thud of her receiver being thrown down.

"Now," said Guy severely, "I shall have to go. There's no knowing what she may do if I don't."

"If you go," said Harriet, "you won't find me here when you come back."

"You are being absurd," said Guy. "I expected more sense from you."

"Why?"

"Because I married you. You are part of myself. I expect from you what I expect from myself."

"You mean you are taking me for granted? Then you are a fool. I won't tolerate any more of this Sophie nonsense. If you go, I leave."

"Don't be a baby." He went into the hall and started to put on his coat, but his movements were uncertain. When he was ready, he stood irresolute, looking at her in worried enquiry. She felt a flicker of triumph that he realised he did not know her after all, then she choked in her throat. She turned away.

"Darling." He came back to the room and put his arms around her. "If it upsets you, of course I won't go."

At that, she said, "But you must go. I can't have you worrying about Sophie all night."

"Well!" He looked into the hall and then looked at Harriet. "I feel I ought to go."

"I know," she said, solving the problem as she had intended to solve it all along. "We'll go together."

The front door of Sophie's house was unlatched. The door into her flat was propped open with a book. When she heard Guy's step, she called in a sad little voice: "Come in, *chéri*." As he pushed wide the door, Harriet, behind him, could see Sophie sitting up in bed, a pink silk shawl round her shoulders. On the table beside her the picture that had been face downwards on Harriet's first visit now stood upright. It was a photograph of Guy.

Despite the smallness of her down-drooping smile, Sophie was much restored. She put her head on one side, sniffed and began to speak – then she noticed Harriet. Her expression changed. She turned on Guy.

"Your wife is a monster," she said.

Guy laughed at this statement, but it brought Harriet to a stop in the doorway. She said: "I'll wait for you downstairs."

She waited for about five minutes in the hallway of the house, then went out into the street. There she started to walk quickly, scarcely aware of the direction in which she went. For the first few hundred yards, feeling neither cold nor fear of the empty streets, she was carried on by a sense of injury that Guy should choose, after such a remark, to stay with Sophie: that he was, in fact, still with her.

Harriet was resolved not to go home. She found herself in the Calea Victoriei moving rapidly towards the Dâmboviţa, then she asked herself where she could go. In this country, where women went almost nowhere unescorted, her appearance, at this hour, luggageless, in an hotel would rouse the deepest suspicion. She might even be refused a room. She thought of the people she knew here – Bella, Inchcape, Clarence – and was disinclined to go to any of them with complaints about Guy. Inchcape might be sympathetic but would have no wish to be involved. Clarence would misunderstand the situation. Whever she went, she would take with her an accusation of failure against Guy's way of life. She reflected that for her, and for Clarence, life was an involute process: they reserved themselves – and for what? With Guy it was a matter to be lived.

Contemplating in Clarence her own willingness to escape from living, she felt a revulsion from it. She had, she knew, done her worst with Sophie. She had made no attempt to flatter, she had not admitted herself to be vulnerable, she had not wanted Sophie's assistance. She had made none of those emotional appeals to which Sophie, once put into a position of power, might have responded with emotion.

Had she, she wondered, lacked charity? Had Sophie had some justification in seeing her as a monster?

She had withheld herself. Now she could not defend herself. She turned and walked slowly back to Sophie's house. She arrived at the doorstep as Guy came out. He took her hand and tucked it under his arm.

"That was nice of you," he said.

"What happened?"

"I told her not to be ridiculous. She really is as big an ass as Bella, and she's a great deal more of a nuisance."

PART THREE

The Snow

14

THE NEW YEAR BROUGHT THE HEAVY SNOW. Day after day it clotted the air, gentle, silent, persistent as time. Those who walked abroad – and these now were only servants and peasants – were enclosed in flakes. The traffic crept about, feeling its way as in a fog. When the fall thinned, the distances, visible once more, were the colour of a bruise.

Those who stayed indoors were disturbed by the outer quiet. It was as though the city had ceased to breathe. After a few days of this, Harriet, hemmed in by her surroundings, ventured down the street, but her claustrophobia persisted outside in the twilit blanket of snow, and she lost her way. She returned to the flat and telephoned Bella, who suggested they go together to Mavrodaphne's. Bella called for her in a taxi.

The two women had met several times since Christmas and a relationship that neither would have contemplated in England was beginning to establish itself. Harriet was becoming used to the limitations of Bella's conversation and did not give it much attention. Bella was easy, if unstimulating, company, and Harriet was glad, in the prevailing strangeness, of a companion from a familiar world.

In the café, while Bella described the latest misdoings of her servants, Harriet gazed at the café window, through which there was nothing to be seen but the mazing, down-soft drift of snow. Occasionally a shadow passed through it, scarcely distinguishable as a cab, or a closed *trǎsurǎ*, or a peasant with a sack over his head. More often than not the cabs stopped at Mavrodaphne's. The occupants, having sped the pavements, escaped the clamour of the beggars in the porch and entered the heady warmth with the modish air of hauteur. Turning their backs on the barbarities of their city, they saw themselves in Rome or Paris or, best of all, New York.

Bella raised her voice against Harriet's inattention. "*And,*" she said, "I have to keep all the food locked up."

Recalled by Bella's aggravated tone, Harriet said: "Why bother? Food is so cheap here. It's less trouble to trust them." She regretted this remark as she made it. Tolerance, after all, should come of generosity, not expediency. Bella disapproved it for a different reason. She said:

"That attitude is unfair to other employers. Besides, one gets sick of their pilfering. If you'd had as much as I've had . . ."

When advising and informing the newcomer, Bella was as smug as an elder schoolgirl patronising a younger. Now she was in the presence of wealthy Rumanians, she reverted to refinement. Harriet could hear in her voice – especially in phrases like 'you daren't give them an inch', and 'the better you treat them the more they take advantage' – the exact inflections that had once made her aunt's dicta so irritating. For some moments it recalled an odd sense of helplessness, then she suddenly interrupted it.

"But what's the cause of all this?" she asked. "The poor aren't born dishonest any more than we are."

Bella looked startled. This was the first time Harriet had attempted to combat her. She tilted back her head and drew her fingers down her full, round throat. "I don't know." She spoke rather sulkily. "All I know is, that's what they're like." She bridled slightly and a flush spread down her neck.

In the uncomfortable pause that followed, Harriet saw Sophie enter. Hoping for diversion, she sat up, prepared to greet the girl, feeling she had come to terms with her; but when she raised a hand, she realised that only she had come to terms. Sophie had not. Sweeping past, with the sad averted smile of one who has been mortally wounded, Sophie joined some women friends on the other side of the room.

Rather out of countenance, Harriet turned back to Bella, who, given time to reflect, was saying defensively: "I know things aren't too good here. I noticed it myself when I first came, but you get used to it. You've got to, if you want to live here. You can't let things upset you all the time. There's nothing you can do about them. I mean, *is there*?"

Harriet shook her head. Bella was no reformer, but even if she had been prepared to beat out her brains against oppression, here she would not have changed anything. Having revealed her uncertainty in her situation, she looked rather shamefaced and for this reason Harriet warmed to her.

"No one can do much," said Harriet. "Nothing short of a revolution could force these people to change things. But why should you accept their absurd conventions? You are an English-woman. You can do what you like."

"You know," confided Bella, "when we talked that afternoon you came to tea, I remembered how free I was before I came here. And next day I wanted some things and I thought, 'Why shouldn't I go out and get them myself?' and I just took a shopping-basket from the kitchen and went out with it in my hand. I met Doamna Popp and *didn't she stare*!" Bella gave one of her vigorous laughs and Harriet liked her the more. Bella had felt satisfaction in instructing Harriet, and Harriet might find satisfaction in releasing Bella. To Harriet it seemed that to have found a sound basis for friendship with anyone as different from herself as Bella was a triumph over her own natural limitations.

When the snow stopped falling at last, the city was revealed white as a ghost city agleam beneath a pewter sky. The citizens crowded out again and the beggars emerged from their holes.

Beggars now were more plentiful than ever. Hundreds of destitute peasant families, their breadwinners conscripted, had been driven by winter into the capital, where, it was believed, a magical justice was dispensed. They would stand for hours in front of the palace, the law courts, the prefecture or any other large, likely-looking building. They dared not enter. When cold and hunger defeated them at last, they would wander off in groups to beg – women, children and ancient, creeping men. Lacking the persistence of professionals, they were easily discouraged. Many of them did no more than crouch crying in doorways. Some sought out the famous Cişmigiu, that stretched from its gates like a vast sheeted ballroom. Some slept there at night beneath the trees; others took themselves up to the Chaussée. Few of them survived long. Each morning a cart went round to collect the bodies dug from the snow. Many of these were found in bunches, frozen inseparable, so they were thrown as they were found, together, into the communal grave.

On the first morning that the air cleared, Guy and Clarence

were called by Sheppy to the Athénée Palace. At mid-day, when they were expected to leave the meeting, Harriet, anxious and curious, crossed the square to join them in the English Bar.

Wakening that morning she had seen the white light reflected on to the ceiling from the snowbound roofs. Emerging with a sense of adventure, she had been met by the *crivat*, blowing on a wire-fine note. In the centre of the square the snow was heaped like swansdown, its powdery surface lifting in the wind, but at the edge, where the traffic went, it was already as hard as cement. She walked round the statue of the old King, a giant snowman, shapeless and wild. The snow squeaked under her boots.

The cold hurt the flesh, yet even the most cosseted Rumanians had ventured out for the first sight of the city under snow. They trudged painfully, making for some café or restaurant, the men in fur-lined coats and galoshes, the women wrapped in Persian lamb, with fur snow-bonnets, gloves and muffs, and high-heeled snow boots of fur and rubber.

Outside the hotel the commissionaire stood, obese with wrappings, but the beggars were, as ever, half-naked, their bodies shaking fiercely in the bitter air.

As she passed the large window of the hair-dressing salon, Harriet saw inside, lolling on long chairs among the chromium and glass, Guy and Clarence having their hair cut. She went in to them and said: "Your meeting could not have lasted long."

"Not very long," Guy agreed.

"Well, what was it all about?"

He gave a warning glance towards the assistants and to deflect her interest said: "We are going to give you a treat."

"What sort of treat? When? Where?"

"Wait and see."

When they left the salon, Guy put on a grey knitted Balaclava helmet lent him, he said, by Clarence. It was part of an issue of Polish refugee clothing.

Clarence said: "Of course it must be returned."

"Really?" Harriet mocked him. "You imagine the Poles will miss it?"

"I am responsible for stores."

"It's a ridiculous garment," she said, dismissing it, and returned to the subject of Sheppy: "Who was he? What did he want? What was the meeting about?"

"We're not at liberty to say," said Guy.

Clarence said: "It's secret and confidential. I've refused to be in on it."

"But in on what?" Harriet persisted. She turned crossly on Guy. "What *did* Sheppy want with you?"

"It's just some mad scheme."

"Is it dangerous?" She looked at Clarence, who, self-consciously evasive, said: "No more than anything else these days. Nothing will come of it, anyway. I think the chap's crazy."

As they would tell her nothing, she decided she would somehow find out for herself. With this decision she changed the subject.

"Where are we going?"

"For a sleigh-ride," said Guy.

"No!" She was delighted. Forgetting Sheppy, she began hurrying the pace of the two men. They were approaching the Chaussée, that stretched broad and white into the remote distance. At the Chaussée kerb stood a row of the smartest *trăsurăs* in town. The owners had removed the wheels and fitted them with sleighs. The horses were hung with bells and tassels. Nets, decorated with pom-poms and bows, were stretched over the horses' hindquarters to protect the passengers from up-flung snow.

People were bargaining for sleigh-rides and about them were sightseers, and beggars battening on everyone.

"The important thing," said Harriet, "is to choose a well-kept horse." When they had found one rather less lean than the rest, she said: "Tell the driver we have chosen him because he is kind to his horse."

The driver replied that he was indeed a kind man and fed his horse nearly every day. Waving his rosetted whip in self-congratulation, he turned out of the uproar of the rank and sped away up the Chaussée to where the air was still and the wheels made no sound. In this crystalline world all was silent but the sleigh-bells.

On either side of the road the spangled skeletons of the trees flashed against a sky dark with unfallen snow. Across the snow-fields, that in summer were the *gradinas*, the wind leapt hard and bitter upon the sleigh. Its occupants shrank down among old blankets into a smell of straw and horse-dung, and peered out at the great plain of snow stretching to the lake and the Snagov woods.

They passed the Arc de Triomphe and came, at the furthest end of the Chaussée, upon an immense fountain that stood transfixed, like a glass chandelier, among mosaics of red, blue and gold.

As they reached the Golf Club, the driver shouted back at them. "He says," said Clarence, "he'll drive us across the lake. I doubt whether it's safe."

Excitedly, Harriet said: "We must cross the lake."

They slid down the bank to the lake, that was a plate of ice sunk into the billowing fields, and the wind howled over their heads.

"Lovely, lovely," Harriet tried to shout, but she was scarcely able to breathe. Her ears sang, her eyes streamed, her hands and feet ached. Her cheeks were turned to ice.

The ice creaked beneath the sleigh and they were relieved to mount the farther bank and find themselves safely on solid ground. They had reached one of the peasant suburbs. The houses were one-roomed wooden shacks, painted with pitch, patched with flattened petrol cans, the doorways curtained with rags. Despite the antiseptic cold the air here was heavy with the stench of refuse. Women stood cooking in the open air. They waved to the sleigh, but the driver, unwilling that foreigners should observe this squalor, pointed his passengers to the cloudy whiteness of the woods and said: "Snagov. *Frumosa.*"

They came out to the highway at the royal railway station, which stood by the roadside, painted white and gold, like a booth at an exhibition. The road turned back to the town, so now the wind was behind the sleigh. The singing died in their ears. The horse was allowed to relax and they returned at a slow trot to their starting point.

When they reached the rank, Harriet noticed a young man, too large for a Rumanian, standing head and shoulders above the crowd and observing with an amused air the excitement about him.

Guy cried: "It's David!" and, jumping down from the sleigh, made for the young man with outstretched arms. The young man did not move, but his small mouth stretched slightly more to one side as he smiled and said: "Oh, hello."

"When did you arrive?" Guy called to him.

"Last night."

Harriet asked Clarence who this new arrival was.

"It's David Boyd," said Clarence, rather grudgingly.

"But you know him, don't you?"

"Well, yes. But I expect he has forgotten me."

Guy swung round and commanded Clarence forward: "Clarence. You remember David?"

Clarence admitted that he did.

"He's been sent out by the Foreign Office," said Guy, "the best thing they've ever done. At least there's someone to counteract the imbecilities of the Legation."

Harriet had heard that Guy and David Boyd looked remarkably alike, but their difference was apparent to her at once. They were large young men, identical in build, short-nosed, bespectacled and curly-haired – but David's mouth was smaller than Guy's, his chin larger. He wore a pointed sheepskin hat that had settled down on to the rim of his glasses so that the upper half of his face was snuffed out while the lower looked larger than it probably was.

"Were you thinking of taking a sleigh-ride?" Harriet asked him.

"No." Looking at her from under his eyelids, he explained that Albu, the barman, had heard Domnul Pringle and Domnul Lawson enquiring if the sleighs were out. Guy was delighted by this intimation that his friend had actually been searching for him. He said: "Let's all go and have lunch somewhere."

"I've arranged to meet a man . . ." began David.

Guy interrupted gleefully: "We'll all go and meet him."

David looked doubtful and Clarence, taking this fact to himself, said: "Don't worry about me. I'm going to a party being given by the Polish officers."

Guy swept on ahead with David while Harriet followed behind with Clarence. As they crossed the square, the two men in front, looking over-large in their winter wrappings, talked with an intimate animation. Guy was wanting to know what David had been sent out to do.

"Anything I can to help." Now that this first shyness had passed, David was voluble. His voice, rich, elderly and precise, the voice of a much earlier generation, came back to Harriet and Clarence in the rear: "I saw Foxy Leverett this morning – that fellow with the big red moustache. I said: 'When's this war going to begin?' And what do you think he said? 'Oh, things'll hot up soon. We'll give the Huns a biff. We'll give 'em a bloody nose.' "

Guy was stopped in his tracks by his own laughter. Harriet and Clarence, who had to step aside to skirt him, now walked ahead.

When they reached the Calea Victoriei, the talk of the other two was lost in the noise of the traffic.

David was meeting his friend in an old eating-house in a back street. When they reached the corner of this street, Clarence said: "I go straight on," and paused with Harriet, waiting for the others.

A barrel-organ stood at the street corner. A white-bearded peasant, bundled up in a sheepskin, was turning the handle, producing a Rumanian popular tune of the past, haunting and sad. Harriet had heard the same organ playing this tune several times before and no one had been able to tell her what it was called. Now, as they stood in a doorway sheltering from the cold she asked Clarence if he knew.

He shook his head. "I'm tone deaf," he said.

Harriet said: "That's the last barrel-organ in Bucharest. When the old man dies and there's no one to play it, that tune will be lost for ever."

Clarence stood silent, apparently reflecting, as Guy would never reflect, on the passing of things. "Yes," he said and as he smiled down on her his rare and beautiful smile, they touched, it seemed, a moment of complete understanding.

David and Guy came up, both talking together, exuding an air of engrossment in larger issues. David's voice rose above Guy's voice as he firmly said: "Although Rumania is a maize-eating country, it grows only half as much maize as Hungary. So we have here the usual vicious circle – the peasants are indolent because they're half-fed: they're half-fed because they're indolent. If the Germans *do* get here, believe me, they'll make these people work as they've never worked before."

"Clarence is going a different way," said Harriet when she got a chance.

"*No!*" Guy protested, not having grasped that Clarence was bidden elsewhere. He caught Clarence's arm, unwilling to let any-one pass from his sphere of influence. When Clarence explained where he was going, Guy demanded: "How long will your party go on for? Where will you be afterwards? We must meet again this evening."

Clarence, not yet recovered from the defensive disapproval with which he faced each new situation, murmured: "Well, it's a luncheon party. I don't know . . . I can't say," but before he left them he agreed to come to the Pringles' flat that evening.

Now Harriet had joined Guy and David, their conversation halted and started again on a more personal plane. David began asking about the people he had known when he was last in Bucharest. He spoke of each with an uncritical, indulgent humour, as though all human beings were for him more or less of a joke. Guy, not given to gossip, had not much to tell. Harriet was silent, as she tended to be with strangers.

"And how's our old friend Inchcape?" David asked.

Guy said: "He's fine."

"I hear he's risen in the world. Gets invited to Legation parties."

Guy laughed and said he believed that was true.

"When I was last in Cambridge," said David, "I met a friend of Inchcape – Professor Lord Pinkrose. They were up together. He was asking me about him. He said that Inch had been a re- markable scholar: one of those chaps who are capable of so much, they don't know what to do first. In the end they usually do nothing at all."

The restaurant was housed in an early nineteenth-century villa, with a front garden where bushes like giant heads set their chins upon the snowy lawn.

David, without a glance about him, talked his way up the front steps and entered as though he had never been away. They passed from the icy outer air into a hallway over-heated and scented by grilled meat. A stream of waiters were clattering and grumbling in and out of the four rooms. One of them tried to direct the three to a back room, but David, without bothering to argue, led the way to the main front room. The tables and chairs were rough. On the walls, papered in faded stripes, hung a few old Russian oleo- graphs. From a dark ceiling hung a gilt chandelier laden with the grime of a decade. The place was noted for its excellent grilled veal.

When they were seated, David started at once to talk: "I saw Dobson, too, this morning – not a bad little chap. I always liked him, but the occupational disease is manifesting itself. I asked about the situation here. He said: 'Quite satisfactory. The Sover- eign is with us.' I said: 'What if the people are not with the Sovereign!' 'Oh, I don't think we need worry about that,' said Dobson. When I asked him a few more questions, he h'md and hawed, then said, 'The situation's a bit complex for a new- comer!' "

"He probably doubted your ability to understand it," Guy said, rousing David to a paroxysm of snuffling laughter.

When there was a pause in the talk, Harriet asked him where he was staying and learnt with surprise that he was at the Minerva. "But that is the German hotel!"

David said: "I like to practise my German." Turning to Guy, he said: "And one picks up useful odds and ends of information. In the bar there, where the German journalists congregate, you get the same stringmen that take the news to the English Bar. One version goes to the Athénée Palace another to the Minerva. In that way our Rumanian allies keep in with both sides at once."

Guy, proud of his friend, now mentioned to Harriet that David spoke all the Slav languages.

David smiled down modestly. "My Slovene is a little rusty," he said, "but I can manage in the rest. I got through the first volume of *Anna Karenina* in the train. Now I find I haven't brought the second volume. I'll have to fly to Sofia to get it from the Russian bookshop. I'd like to know how it ends."

"Haven't you read it in English?" Harriet asked.

"I scarcely need to brush up my English."

If this were a joke, David gave no indication of the fact, but, sitting four-square on his chair, he stared down solemnly at the menu. His cap, when taken off, had left some snow in his curled black hair. As this melted and trickled down his cheeks, he thrust out his lower lip and caught the drops. His brow, visible now, was as massive as his chin.

Putting the menu down he said: "This policy of backing the established order, whether right or wrong, is not only going to lose us this country. When the big break-up starts, it will lose us concessions all over the world. In short, it'll be the end of us."

When on his own subject, David's manner lost its diffidence. He tended, Harriet thought, to address his listeners less like a conversationalist than a lecturer – and a lecturer wholly confident in the magnitude of his knowledge. His self-sufficiency was now evident. She remembered that his hobby was bird-watching. He was saying:

"Those F.O. dummies can't see further than the ends of their noses. For them the position inside the country is of no importance. The Sovereign right or wrong – that's all they know and all they need to know."

While David talked – and he talked at length – a waiter came and stood by the table. David was not to be interrupted, but when the man decided to move away, David seized and held him by the coat-tails while saying:

"I learnt on the train that German agents have settled in all over the country. They're working through the Iron Guard, buying grain, secretly, at double the usual rate. They said: 'See how generous we Germans are! With Germany as an ally, Rumania would be rich.' But could I persuade H.E. of this? Not for a moment. The Sovereign says the Iron Guard has ceased to exist and the Sovereign *must* be right."

The waiter, his patience exhausted, began to tug at his coat-tails. Turning irritably on him and shouting: "*Stai, domnule, stai,*" David went on with his dissertation.

"Let us give our order," Harriet pleaded.

David jerked round on her and snapped: "Shut up."

"I won't shut up," she snapped back, and David, suddenly sniggering, looked down, all his diffidence returned. "We must order, of course," he said. "I suppose we'll have *Fleică de Braşov.*" They gave their order and the waiter was released.

"Tell us what is going to happen here," said Guy.

"Several things could happen." David shifted his chair closer to the table. "There could be a peasant revolt against Germany, but we, of course, will see that does not happen. The Peasant Party is in opposition to the Sovereign, so it gets no support from us. I'm the only Englishman in this country who has met the peasant leaders . . ."

Guy interrupted: "I met them with you."

"Well, we're the only two Englishmen who have bothered to meet them: yet those men are our allies. They are our true allies. They would lead a rising on our behalf, but they are ignored and snubbed. We have declared ourselves for Carol and his confederates."

"Why are the peasants so despised?" Harriet asked.

"They suffer from hunger, pellagra and sixteen hundred years of oppression – all enervating diseases."

"Sixteen hundred years?"

"Rather longer." David now set out upon a history of Rumania's oppression, beginning with the withdrawal of the Roman legions in the third century after Christ and the appearance of the

Visigoths. He passed from the ravaging Huns to Gepides, Lango-bards and Avars, to the Slavs and 'a race of Turkish nomads called Bulgars'. "Then in the ninth century," he said, "the Mag-yars swept over Eastern Europe."

"Isn't all this part of the migration of nations?" Harriet asked.

"Yes. Rumania is the part of Europe over which most of them migrated. There were, of course, intervals – for instance, a brief period of glory under Michael the Brave. That led to the most wretched and tragic period of Rumanian history – the rule of the Phanariots."

The waiter brought them soup. As David emptied his plate, he followed the further misfortunes of the Rumanian people until the peasant revolt of 1784. "Suppressed," he said, putting down his spoon, "in a manner I would not care to describe during a meal."

Harriet was about to speak. David raised a hand to silence her. "We come now," he said, "to the nineteenth century, when Turkish power was waning and Rumania was being shared out between Russia and Austria . . ."

They had ordered the veal grilled with herbs. It was brought to the table on a board and there chopped into small pieces with two choppers. Silenced by the noise, David frowned until it was over, then started at once to talk again. He was interrupted by the ar-rival of a short, round-bodied, round-faced man who entered quickly and came quickly to the table, smiling radiantly about him.

"Ah!" said David, rising, "here's Klein." Klein seized on both his hands and, talking rapidly in German, displayed an ecstatic pleasure in their reunion.

When introduced to the Pringles, Klein bowed from the waist, saying: "How nice . . . how pleased to meet you!" but he looked unsure of them until David said: "It's all right. They're friends."

The word 'friends' had, apparently, a special connotation. "Ah, so!" said Klein, relaxing into the chair that Guy had brought to the table for him. He had the fresh, snub, pink and white face of a child. Had it not been for the fact he was bald and what hair he had was grey, he might have passed for a very plump schoolboy – but a super-subtle boy who, despite his smile of good humour, was assessing everyone and everything about him. He accepted wine, which he poured into a tumbler and mixed with mineral water, but he would not eat. He had come, he said, from the first meeting of a newly formed committee.

"An important committee, you understand. It exists to discuss the big demand Germany now makes on Rumania for food. And what did we do on the committee? We ate, drank and made funny remarks. There was such a buffet – from here to here," he indicated some twenty foot of the wall, "with roasts and turkeys, lobsters and caviare. *Such food!* I can tell you, in Germany today they have forgotten such food ever existed."

He laughed aloud while David, watching him, curled his lip in appreciation of this picture of the Rumanians in committee.

Klein gave Guy a smile, confiding and affectionate, and said: "I am, you understand, economic adviser to the Cabinet. I am called to this committee because each day Germany asks for more – more meat, more coffee, more maize, more cooking oil. Where can it all come from? And now she says: 'Plant soya beans.' 'What are soya beans?' we ask one another. We do not know, but Germany must have them. Every day come these requests – and each time they are more like demands. The Cabinet is nervous. They say: 'Send for Klein, Klein must advise us.' I am a Jew. I am without status. But I understand economics."

"Klein was one of the best economists in Germany," said David.

Klein smiled and twitched a shoulder, but did not repudiate this claim. "Here it is very funny," he said. "They call me in to advise. I say: 'Produce more: spend less.' What do they reply? They laugh at me. 'Ach, Klein,' they say, 'you are only a Jew. What can you know of the soul of our great country? God has given us everything. We are rich. Our land all the time produces for us. It cannot be exhausted. You are a silly little Jew.' "

As Klein laughed, his face flushed with mischievous glee, Guy laughed with him, delighted by this new acquaintance. And no one, Harriet was beginning to realise, enjoyed a new acquaintance more than Guy did. Aglow with interest in Klein, he neglected his food and, leaning forward, questioned him about his unofficial position in the Cabinet, then about his departure from Germany and arrival in Rumania two years before.

Klein's story was much like that of other refugee Jews in Bucharest except that his reputation as an economist had enabled him to stay in Germany longer than most. He had been warned in the end by a German friend that his arrest was imminent. He had walked empty-handed out of his Berlin flat, taken a train to the Rumanian frontier and, having had no time to buy the usual entrance permit, had crossed the frontier on foot after dark. He had been caught and spent six months in the notorious Bistriţa prison, where Drucker was now held. Friends had bought his release.

"But still," he said, "I have no permit to work. Still I am illegal. If I am not useful, then back I go to Bistriţa." He laughed happily at the prospect.

David, watching Guy's eager questioning of Klein, twisted his mouth with a quizzical amusement, pleased that he had brought them so successfully together. Harriet felt less pleased. She had heard a great deal about David Boyd, whom Guy regarded as an especial friend, one whose knowledge and conversation offered considerably more than the limited, personal concerns of Inchcape and Clarence. Now here was David, whose interests were, like his own, impersonal, social, economic and historical. She sighed at the thought of so much talk. It was not, she told herself, that she was unappreciative, but the impersonal quickly tired her. She felt a little out of it, a little jealous.

Perhaps sensing this, Klein turned smiling to her to include her. He said: "So here we all are Left-side men, eh? And Doamna Preen-gel? She, too, is Left-side?"

"No," said Harriet, "I am fighting the solitary battle of the reactionary."

Guy laughed to prevent Klein taking this seriously, and squeezed her hand.

Klein said: "You like Rumania, Doamna Preen-gel? It is interesting here, is it not?"

"Yes, but . . ."

"But it is interesting," Klein insisted. "And wait! It will become more interesting. Do you think the Allies can safeguard this country? I think not. It will be necessary to buy off the Germans with more and more food – with so much food, there will be a famine. If you stay, you will see the break-up of a country. You will see revolution, ruin, occupation by the enemy . . ."

"I don't want to stay so long."

"But you will see so much," Klein reasoned with her, "and all so interesting." He looked round the table as though offering them all a joyous future. "I say to this committee: 'Listen! In this country it is necessary that we have 200,000 wagon-loads of wheat in one year. This year, with the land workers mobilised, we shall have perhaps 20,000, perhaps less. It is necessary,' I say, 'that you demobilise those peasants and at once send them back to the land. If you do not, the people will starve.' And they laugh at me and say: 'We know you, Klein, you are of the Left. You do not look to the glory of Greater Rumania, you look to the welfare of the stupid, dirty peasants. Rumania is rich. Rumania cannot starve. Here, one day you throw seed on the ground, the next day it is bread. If we are short of wheat, merely it is necessary to stop exports.' 'If you do that,' I say, 'how will you make up the money?' 'All that is necessary,' they say, 'is a new tax.' I say: 'What can we tax? What is not already taxed?' And they laugh at me: 'Ha, Klein, it is for you to answer! You are economist.' "

Shaking with laughter at the thought of the trouble ahead, Klein put a hand to Harriet's shoulder. "Listen, Doamna Preen-gel: Rumania is like a foolish person who has inherited a great fortune. It is all dissipated in vulgar nonsense. You know the story the Rumanians tell about themselves: that God, when He had given gifts to the nations, found He had given to Rumania everything – forests, rivers, mountains, minerals, oil and a fertile soil that yielded many crops. 'Hah,' said God. 'This is too much,' and so, to strike a balance, he put here the worst people he could find. The Rumanians laugh at this. It is a true, sad joke!" said Klein, but he told it without any sign of sadness.

The meal was finished. Most of the other diners had left the restaurant; David, Guy and Klein however seemed prepared to stay all afternoon. After a while, Klein passed to stories of his life in prison. He gave the impression it had all been uproariously funny.

"And it was so interesting," he said, "so *interesting*! With such a lot of people crowded in a common cell, there was such a life, such stories, such feuds, such scandals. Always something happening. I remember one day the warders came in to beat a prisoner who was a little mad – in prison many get a little mad – and as they beat him, he screamed and screamed. This the warders did not like, so they put over his head a pillow of feathers. It stopped the screaming but when they took it off – what a surprise! The man was dead. Smothered! The warders stood like this . . ." Klein's mouth fell open and his eyes protruded, then he laughed: "And the prisoners – oh, they laughed so much!"

Klein went on to describe the cells slimed with damp, the floors deep in filth, the raped boys who, once corrupted, sold themselves for a few *lei*, and all the new crimes that came into existence in this community of men packed together with the hatreds, angers and lusts of propinquity.

"How terrible!" said Harriet.

Klein laughed: "But so interesting!" He explained that he had never been officially released but had made a condoned escape. "And when they told me I might escape, almost I did not wish to leave, it was so interesting. Almost I wished I might stay to hear the end of so many scandals and feuds, and plots and plans. It was like leaving a world."

At last the head waiter came himself and slapped their bill down in the middle of the table. When they had no choice but to go, Guy invited Klein and David to come back to the flat for tea, but they were going to the Minerva for a private talk. David agreed to call in later and Harriet, rather thankfully, took Guy home alone.

When they were indoors, he handed her a sealed envelope on which was written 'Top Secret' and said: "Sheppy gave these out. He says they're to be kept under lock and key. I'm afraid of losing mine. Put it away for me, somewhere safe."

Most of the drawers of the flat had locks but not one lock a key. Harriet put the envelope into a small drawer inside the writing-desk, saying: "It should be safe there. After all, we're the only people in the flat."

15

CLARENCE, RETURNING FROM HIS PARTY with the Polish officers, made his appearance after tea. He entered unsteadily, tried to cross the room and fell, instead, into a chair. Despina, who had admitted him, went out exploding with laughter.

"I want to get drunk," said Clarence.

Harriet said: "You are drunk."

He waved an arm laxly in the air. "Tell Despina to go out and bring back lots of beer."

"All right, where's the money?"

"Ha, you spoil everything," Clarence grumbled. He shut his eyes.

Despina now made an excuse to return and take another look at him. He shouted at her: "Hey, Despina, buy beer," and handed her a hundred *lei*.

"You won't get drunk on a hundred *lei*," said Harriet.

"I don't want to get drunk. I *am* drunk. I only want to stay drunk."

Guy, who had been reading, put down his book, saying: "Stop wrangling, you two," and produced a five-hundred-*lei* note. He sent Despina for the beer. While she was out, David arrived, his cap and shoulders white with snow. When he had taken off his outdoor clothes and settled by the fire, he noticed Clarence sprawling, eyes shut, sulky and uncomfortable, and asked with derision:

"What's the matter with Clarence?"

"He's drunk," said Harriet.

"Not exactly drunk," Clarence's beautiful and gentle voice came as though from a great distance, "but I hope to be."

Harriet said: "Do you want to get drunk, too, David?"

"I don't mind." David looked round for a drink.

"It's coming."

Despina came back with a boy carrying a crate of beer. Excited by the sight of it, Guy jumped up, saying: "Let's have a party. Let's invite everyone we can think of."

"Oh, no." Clarence roused himself. "There won't be enough," but Guy was already at the telephone ringing Inchcape. Inchcape said the snow was falling heavily; and he was in no mood to come out. Guy then tried to contact Dubedat, whom he thought might, for some reason, be at the Doi Trandafiri. While a piccolo was searching the café for Dubedat, Guy, with nothing to do but hold the receiver, reaffirmed his belief that Dubedat should be invited to move into the spare room.

"A man is made by his circumstances," said Guy. "If you want to change him, you must change his circumstances."

Harriet was aggrieved by Guy's persistence, yet felt an irritated respect for it. She replied sharply: "He can change his own circumstances. He's earning money now. You should not deprive him of initiative."

Her tone caused in the other two a slightly embarrassed stir, so that she felt annoyed both with herself and with Guy.

Learning that Dubedat was not to be found in the Doi Trandafiri, Guy rang the English Bar to see whom he could find there. David, impatient with the disconnected conversation that resulted, began to talk of a visit he planned to make to the peasant leader, Maniu, who had a house at Cluj. Clarence sighed ostentatiously and said: "Oh Lord!" When David gazed at him in surprised enquiry, he giggled and said: "Why don't you learn to talk to yourself David?"

David's left eyebrow rose, his small mouth turned to one side. Surveying Clarence's abandoned figure with amused contempt, he said: "Because, my dear Clarence, I don't want to talk to myself."

"Then you have more sympathy with others." After a moment Clarence, struck by his own wit, began to laugh helplessly.

David watched him with an expression that asked the world: 'Have you ever seen a more ludicrous sight?'

Suddenly aware of the irritated tedium in the room, Guy put down the receiver, jumped up and said: "More beer?" His return to the centre of things restored the atmosphere, and David, a full glass in his hand, asked: "Well, what's been happening here since war broke out?"

Guy said: "Apart from the assassination, nothing."

Clarence suddenly shouted: "Sheppy's Fighting Force."

There was a pause. David, his tone not much interested, his glance acute, asked: "What is Sheppy's Fighting Force?"

There was another pause, then Guy, torn between the need for discretion and the desire to entertain his friend, said: "We're supposed to keep quiet about it."

"David'll be dragged in," said Clarence. "Everybody'll be dragged in, except me. I opted out. I said to him," Clarence waved his glass about, "I said: 'I'm a pacifist. I'm not prepared to take life. I'd like to know exactly what you want us to do.' 'I'm not at liberty to tell you what you're expected to do,' said Sheppy. So I said: 'I think it would save time if I told you, here and now, I'm not at liberty to do it.' "

Laughing in spite of himself, Guy agreed: "He did say that."

Clarence, revivified by the beer and his own brilliance, burst in: "I said: 'I'm seconded from the British Council. The Council does not permit its members to take part in anything but cultural activities.' And Sheppy said" – here Clarence flung a finger into air and made a drunken effort to imitate Sheppy's peremptory tone – " 'You are called here as Englishmen – young, robust, patriotic Englishmen who ought to be on active service and for one reason or another are not. You are required to perform an important mission . . . ' 'I'm not robust,' I said, 'I have a weak chest.' " Here Clarence subsided again, giggling to himself.

Harriet, sitting forgotten outside the circle, saw David smile at Guy in innocent enquiry: "Who is this fellow Sheppy?"

"He's out here to organise a sort of private army."

"What does he expect to do?"

"It's all very hush-hush."

"Have you signed the Official Secrets Act?"

"Not yet."

"Then why worry? Anyway, he can't make you do anything."

"I know that. But he's right. We ought to be on active service and if we're not, we should do what we can."

"What is he like, Sheppy?"

So much had been revealed now, that Guy clearly felt there was little point in keeping back the rest. He did not interrupt as Clarence described Sheppy marching into the room where they were gathered at the Athénée Palace, hanging a map on the wall and demanding: "What have we here?" One of the telephone engineers, stepping forward and examining it, had said, as though making a revelation: "The Danube." "Right!" Sheppy had congratulated him. "Now," Sheppy went on, "I expect from you laddies im-

plicit obedience. Two or three of my henchmen are being flown
out and you must regard them as your superior officers. You'll be
rank and file. Yours not to reason why, yours but to do and die.
Right?" He had paused for agreement and been met with silence.
He had gone on: "I'm not telling you much – security and all that
– but I can tell you this. We're forming a Striking Force to strike
the enemy where he'll feel it most. One place we'll strike him is the
belly. Nearly four hundred thousand tons of wheat went from
Rumania to Germany last year – and how did it get there? Along
the Danube. Big plans are afoot. We'll be blowing things up. One
of them's the Iron Gates. Remember, this isn't a lark: it's an adventure." He had brought his one hand down on the table and
his one eye had jerked about from face to face. "There'll be lots of
fun, and we're letting you in on it." Then he had drawn himself
upright and assuming his machine-gun rattle, had shouted: "Be
prepared. Await orders. Keep your traps shut. *Dis*-miss."

David waited until the end of Clarence's performance before
saying: "The Iron Gates? What does he imagine they are? Real
gates? Perhaps they hope to blow up the rapids and block the
navigable passage close to the right bank. The Germans would
soon clear that up." He gave a snuffling and derisory laugh. "This
is 'cloak and dagger' stuff, of course. They take on these romantic
old war-horses and say: 'If you succeed, you'll get no recognition.
If you fail, you'll take the consequences.' That makes them grit
their teeth. They love it."

At this, Harriet could keep quiet no longer. She said: "But Guy
would be hopeless at this sort of thing. If he tried to blow up the
Iron Gates, he'd be more likely to blow up himself. As for
Clarence – trust him to get out of it."

Reminded of her presence and startled by her outburst, Guy
said: "Darling, you must not repeat a word of this to anyone.
Promise."

"Who would I repeat it to?"

Clarence said slowly: "Harriet is a bitch." After some moments,
added reflectively: "I like bitches. You know where you are with
them."

Harriet made no comment but she told herself she now knew
what Clarence thought of her. The fantasy that had started on the
day of Călinescu's funeral was running its course. The situation
had its attraction. It was like being offered a second personality.

At the same time, seeing him as he lolled there, smugly smiling, she could have crossed the room and pushed him off the chair.

David, too, must have been feeling something of this, for he said: "Let's do something noteworthy."

He leant forward and smiled with reflective malice towards Clarence: "Let's de-bag him!" With a sudden, decided movement, he rose and began to advance on Clarence, stealthily, not wholly playfully. He gave a sideways glance at Harriet, knowing her an ally in this, and she jumped up at once, caught into the same impulse to ill-treat Clarence in some way.

"Come on," she said to Guy and he was drawn into the assault.

Clarence, his chair tilted back, sitting inert, with eyes closed, his head propped against the wall, seemed unaware that anything was happening until they were upon him, then, startled, he opened his eyes; his chair legs slipped and he went down, backwards, thumping his head against the floor. He gazed up at them, as though awakened from sleep, then, closing his eyes again, said dully: "What do I care?"

Although meeting with no resistance, David pinned his victim determinedly down like one dealing with a marauder. There was something vindictive in his movements. Clarence might have been an old enemy cornered at last. Harriet flung herself on him and held him down by his shoulders.

"Really!" Clarence gasped, making a feeble, almost idiotic, effort to escape. As he wrenched one hand free and tried to push Harriet away, she bit his fingers making him howl. Only Guy was treating the whole thing as a joke.

David began pulling off Clarence's trousers. Weighty and very strong, he worked with the concentrated gravity of an executioner. On his instructions, Guy pulled the trousers over Clarence's shoes. When they were off at last, David snatched at them and held them up in triumph. "What shall we do with them?"

"Put them on the balcony," said Harriet. "Make him go out and get them."

Clarence lay still, feigning unconsciousness.

As David went out on the balcony, the icy air came a moment into the room, then he returned and slammed-to the door. Sniggering, he said untruthfully: "I've thrown them into the street."

"What do I care?" Clarence mumbled again.

The force that had activated the others died as quickly as it had come. They sat around, watching Clarence as he lay in his underpants on the floor. When he did and said nothing, they started to talk among themselves and forgot about him.

After a while he began getting himself upright in stages. When in a sitting position, he shook his head and sighed, then rose slowly and went out on to the balcony. He remained out there in the snow, in the mid-winter cold, while he put on his trousers, then he returned to the room, closed the glass doors carefully, bolted them and, without a word went out to the hall. The others had stopped talking. They listened to Clarence's movements in the hall as he put on his coat. The front door shut quietly after him.

There was a silence, then Harriet said: "What is the matter with us? Why did we do that?"

"It was a joke," said Guy, though he did not sound sure of what he said.

"Really, we behaved like children," Harriet said and it occurred to her that they were not, in fact, grown-up enough for the life they were living. She asked: "What is wrong with Clarence? He told me once that he fails everyone."

With ponderous irony, David said: "Someone should dissect him and remake him nearer to the heart's desire."

Guy said: "I might be able to do it, if I had the time."

"Harriet could do it, I think." David smiled slyly at her.

Harriet grew pink, realising she had felt a pitying sympathy for Clarence as she had watched him picking himself up and taking himself so quietly, so unoffendingly, out of the flat. Both David and Guy were much younger than he and between them there was the understanding of an old friendship. Clarence could not have remained untouched by the fact the two had combined against him. She felt sorry for him, yet she disowned him, saying casually: "I don't want to remake him. Why should I?" and they went on to talk of other things.

16

THE NEXT MORNING, when alone in the flat, Harriet took out the envelope Guy had given her and opened it by rolling a pencil underneath the flap. Inside there was a print of a section through – what? An artesian well? Or, more likely, an oil well. Something else to be blown up. A blockage in the pipe was tagged with the one word: 'Detonator'. There was no written explanation of the diagram. She resealed the envelope and put it back into the drawer.

She heard no more about the Force until a few weeks later, when Guy telephoned from the University to say he would not be home for supper. He had been called to a meeting.

"Not one of Sheppy's meetings, I hope?" said Harriet.

Guy admitted it was, and added quickly that Clarence, who had refused to attend, had offered to take Harriet out to dinner. That, said Guy, would be nice for her. Clarence would take her to the new restaurant, Le Jardin, and Guy would meet them both later, in the English Bar.

Clarence called for Harriet while she was listening to the news. The Mannerheim Line had been breached but, except for the fighting on the Karelian peninsula, the war was at a standstill.

Clarence listened to such news as there was with a rather stern expression. He seemed to feel strain at being alone with Harriet, and Harriet, enjoying his embarrassment, talked vivaciously. She said that although there were people who still believed that 'something must happen soon', a good many now regarded the war as practically over. Anyway, no one gave it much thought these days. It had become like a background noise that could attract attention only by its cessation. The Jews were so confident, the black-market rate for sterling was lower than it had been before war started.

Clarence listened to all this with an occasional murmur, then picked up the book she had been reading. It was one of the D. H. Lawrence novels on which Guy was lecturing that term.

"*Kangaroo*," he read out scornfully. "These modern novelists! Why is it that not one of them is really good enough? This stuff, for instance . . ."

"I wouldn't call Lawrence a modern novelist."

"You know what I mean." Clarence flipped impatiently through the pages. "All these dark gods, this phallic stuff, this – this fascism! I can't stand it." He threw down the book and stared accusingly at her.

She took the book up. "Supposing you skip the guff, as you call it! Supposing you read what is left, simply as writing." She read aloud one of the passages Guy had marked. It was the description of the sunset over Manly Beach: 'The long green rollers of the Pacific', 'the star-white foam', 'the dusk-green sea glimmered over with smoky rose'.

Clarence groaned through it, appalled at what was being imposed on him. "*I know!*" he said, in agony, when she stopped. "All that colour stuff – it's just so many words strung together. Anyone could do it."

Harriet re-read the passage through to herself. For some reason, it did not seem so vivid and exciting as it had done before Clarence condemned it. She was inclined to blame him for that. She turned on him: "Have you ever tried to write? Do you know how difficult it is?"

Well, yes. Clarence admitted he had once wanted to be a writer. He did know it was difficult. He had given up trying because, after all, what was the point in being a second-rate writer? If one could not be a great writer – a Tolstoy, a Flaubert, a Stendhal – what was the point in being a writer at all?

Disconcerted, Harriet said lamely: "If everyone felt like that, there wouldn't be much to read."

"What is there to read, anyway? Rubbish, most of it. Myself, I read nothing but detective novels."

"I suppose you do read Tolstoy and Flaubert?"

"I did once. Years ago."

"You could read them again."

Clarence gave another moan. "Why should one bother?"

"What about Virginia Woolf?"

"I think *Orlando* almost the worst book of the century."

"Really! And *To the Lighthouse*?"

Clarence wriggled in weary exasperation. "It's all *right* – but all her writing is so diffused, so feminine, so sticky. It has such an odd smell about it. It's just like menstruation."

Startled by the originality of Clarence's criticism, Harriet looked at him with more respect. "And Somerset Maugham?" she ventured.

"Goodness me, *Harry*! He's simply the higher journalism."

No one else had ever called Harriet 'Harry' and she did not like the abbreviation. She reacted sharply, saying: "Maybe Somerset Maugham isn't very good, but the others are. So much creative effort has gone into their work – and all you can say is 'Really!' and condemn them out of hand." She rose and put on her coat and fur cap. "I think we should go," she said.

Le Jardin, recently opened in a Biedermeier mansion, was the most fashionable of Bucharest restaurants and would remain so until the first gloss passed from its decorations. Situated in a little snow-packed square at the end of the Boulevard Brăteanu, its blue neon sign shone out cold upon the cold and glittering world. The sky was a delicate grey-blue, clear except for a few tufts of cirrus cloud. The moon was rising behind the restaurant roof, on which the snow, a foot thick, gleamed like powdered glass.

The interior of Le Jardin was the same silver-blue as the out-of-doors. The house had been gutted to make one vast room, and the proprietor, breaking away from the tradition of crimson and gilt, had trimmed it in silver with hangings of powder-blue. These cool colours, more fitted for summer than winter, were made appropriate by the sultry warmth of the room. The restaurant's *décor* had been described in the press as '*lux nebun*' – a challenge to the war world in which it had opened. But there, Harriet noted on arrival, was the usual Rumanian sight of a fat official, with his hat on, packing cream cakes into his mouth.

As Harriet passed between the tables with Clarence, there was a little murmur of comment: first, that she should make this public appearance with someone other than her husband, then the common complaint that English teachers – they were all regarded as 'teachers' – could afford to come to a restaurant of this class. In Rumania a teacher was one of the lowest-paid members of the lower-middle class, earning perhaps four thousand *lei* a month. Here was proof that the English teachers were not teachers at all but, as everyone suspected, spies.

When Harriet and Clarence were settled on one of the blue

velvet banquettes, Harriet returned to the subject of Clarence's writing. For how long had he tried to write? What had he achieved? To which publisher had he sent the results? Clarence squirmed under these questions, shrugged and was evasive, then admitted he had produced very little. He had planned a novel and written six pages of synopsis, very carefully worked out, but it had got no further than that. He could not visualise scenes. He did not know how to bring his characters to life.

"So you gave up? Then what did you do?" Harriet asked, for Clarence was nearly thirty and must have some sort of career behind him.

"I joined the British Council."

"You had a good degree?"

"Quite good."

He had been sent to Warsaw. Harriet questioned him about his two years there. Where Guy's memories would have been all of the conditions of the country and its people, Clarence's memories were personal, tender and sad. His face became wistful as he talked. Harriet, realising there was about him something poignant and unfulfilled, felt in sympathy with him.

In Poland he had fallen in love for the first time. He said: "It's extraordinary to look back on the things that used to be important to one. I can remember a night in Warsaw . . . I can remember standing under a street lamp and turning a girl's face to catch the light and shadow. As I did so, it all seemed significant. I don't know why. It would mean nothing now. And I remember walking with her to the Vistula and seeing the broken ice on the water. And we went through streets where they were building new houses, with everything half finished and the pavements muddy, with planks across them. But she wouldn't have me. She turned up at the office one day and said she was engaged to someone else. I believe she'd had this other man all along. I'll never forget it."

"I'm sorry," said Harriet.

"Why be sorry? At least I was alive then. I could feel." He reflected on this, then said: "I've never had the woman I wanted. I always seem to want bitches and they always ill-treat me."

"What about your fiancée?"

He shrugged. "She's a good girl, but, really, she stirs nothing in me. With her, there's nothing to fight against. She's just a punching bag. So am I, for that matter. Anyway, who knows what will happen? The last time I wrote to her, I said: 'It may be ten years before I get home again.'"

"You think that? And Brenda is willing to wait?"

"I suppose so." Clarence sighed deeply. "But I did advise her to marry someone else."

"After Poland, where did you go?"

"Madrid. I was there when the civil war broke out. The British were being evacuated and I jumped a lorry going to Barcelona. I offered myself to the International Brigade, but I was pretty sick. I'd caught a chill on the way. I've always had this trouble with my chest. When I got better, I was put in charge of a refugee camp, where I was more use than I would have been in the lines. But I wanted to fight. Not fighting was a sort of sacrifice."

"Anyway, it let you preserve your integrity intact."

Clarence kept his head hanging for some moments, then, hurt, he said quietly: "I might have expected you to say something like that." He suddenly gave a half-laugh of satisfaction that she had fulfilled his worst expectations, then he said: "Someone had to look after the camp."

"A woman could have done the job."

He raised his brows, considered this, then drawled: "No, not really," but he did not enlarge on his denial.

"So there were no bitches there!"

"Oh yes, there was one – a magnificent bitch. An English girl looking after a crowd of evacuee children. She did exactly what she liked. She slept with anyone she wanted. Even with me. Yes, one night she pointed at me and said: 'I'll have you,' and I followed her out." Clarence sat for a while silent, smiling at the memory of it.

"Nothing came of that, I suppose?"

"What could come of it? She had a Spaniard she was mad about. One of the English fellows went on leave to Paris and she ordered him to bring her back an evening dress. When he brought the dress, he gave a party, thinking she would dance with him: but she just ignored him and danced all night with the Spaniard. I like tough women. Women of character."

"You like being pushed around."

"Not necessarily." He sat withdrawn for a while, before he said: "In Spain there was colour and heat and danger. Things were significant there. Life should be like that."

"There is danger here."

"Oh!" He shrugged his contempt of the present.

Throughout the meal Clarence pursued his memories, that were all much alike. Contemplating those worlds of delight from which he felt himself excluded, he said several times: "Life should be like that." When he had talked himself out and was waiting for the bill, Harriet asked him: "You like feeling dissatisfied with yourself. Why is that?"

Clarence stuck out his lower lip but did not reply.

"For you do like it," she insisted. "You enjoy revealing your worst aspects."

He said: "We all get corrupted. Even Guy."

"In what way is Guy corrupted?"

"Before he married he owned hardly anything. He had no room of his own, not even a cupboard. People used to put him up: they loved having him. He didn't mind where he slept. He'd sleep on the floor. Now you're surrounding him with bourgeois comforts. You're corrupting him."

"I thought he used to share a flat with you."

"Well, he did last spring, but when he first came here he had literally nothing. I've never seen a man with so few possessions."

"Now you're blaming him for having a home like everyone else."

The waiter arrived. Clarence, as he started to settle the bill, repeated obstinately: "You're corrupting him."

Harriet said: "He must have wanted to be corrupted or he would never have got himself married. A single man can go round sleeping on floors. A married couple are less welcome."

Clarence did not reply. When they left the restaurant, Harriet realised he was rather drunk. She suggested they leave the car and walk to the hotel. He replied brusquely: "I drive best like this," and shot them with a series of violent movements round the corner and across the square. They jerked to a standstill outside the Athénée Palace.

They were late, but Guy was not in the bar and Albu had seen nothing of him. Harriet and Clarence decided to wait for him. The journalists – only a handful of whom were still in Bucharest – were in the telephone boxes in the hall. Harriet, alert now for the excitement of alarm, said: "I believe something has happened."

"What could happen?" Clarence was gloomily ordering brandy.

Yakimov stood alone at the bar, holding an empty glass. Harriet was careful not to meet his gaze, but she had noticed a change in him. He was a down-at-heel, uncared-for figure very different from that she had met first in the garden restaurant. Then he had been allowed to dominate the scene, now it did not seem possible he could dominate anything. He was sallow, rheumy, crumbled – a man in defeat. When he sidled up to Harriet saying: "Dear girl, how nice to see a human face," he looked so abject that she had not the heart to turn her back on him.

Drooping against the bar, holding the empty glass out at an angle that prevented its being overlooked, he sighed and said: "Haven't been feeling too good. Bitter weather. Tells on your poor old Yaki."

Harriet asked coldly if he had seen Guy. He shook his head.

"Has anything happened?"

"Not that I know of, dear girl." He glanced over his shoulder, then, stepping nearer, confided despondently: "Just had m'head bitten off by m'old friend, Prince Hadjimoscos. He was off to some party or other. I said: 'Take me along, dear boy,' and what d'you think he said? 'You're not invited.' Not invited! I ask you! In a town like this. But I don't let it worry me. It's just anti-British feeling. It's growing, dear girl. I can feel it. Haven't been a war correspondent for nothing. They're beginning to think the Allies are too far away."

"I'm surprised they didn't think it long ago."

Albu had put two glasses of brandy on the counter. Yakimov eyed them, and Clarence, with resigned annoyance, asked him if he would take a drink.

"Wouldn't say 'No', dear boy. Whisky for me."

Having accepted his drink, he began to talk. Veering between complaint and a tolerant acceptance of suffering, he described how his friends Hadjimoscos, Horvath and Palu had all been horrid to him. There was only one explanation of it – anti-British feeling. After a while, realising that this despondent talk was not holding his audience, he made a visible attempt to pull himself together and give some entertainment in return for his drink.

"Went to see Dobson this morning," he said. "Heard most amusing story. Foxy Leverett came out of Capşa's last night, saw the German Minister's Mercedes parked by the kerb, got into his Dion-Bouton, backed down the road, then raced forward and crashed the Mercedes. Devil of a crash, I'm told. When the police came up, Foxy said: 'You can call it provoked aggression.' "

As he finished this story, the journalists began to return. Looking at the Polish girl who had entered with Galpin, he said, half to himself: "There's that dear girl!" His large eyes fixed on Wanda, he bent towards Harriet and said: "You've heard that Galpin's got her attached to some English paper?" Yakimov's tone subtly expressed derogation of the sort of paper that would employ Wanda. "Charming girl, but so irresponsible. Sends home all sorts of rumours and gossip, doesn't care where she picks up the stuff . . ." His voice faded as the two approached.

Harriet, glad to drop Yakimov, asked Galpin if there were any news.

"Uh-huh." Galpin nodded his head, his expression glum. Among the journalists now ordering at the bar, there was the excitement of a situation come to life.

"What is it?"

"Just heard Hungary's mobilising. German troops flooding in. We've been trying to get Budapest all evening but the lines are dead. It's my belief that this time we're for it."

Harriet felt the pang of fear. Now, after six months in Rumania, she reacted more sharply to news of this sort than she would have done when she first arrived. In a small voice, she said: "But aren't the passes blocked with snow?"

"Oh, that old theory! Do you think snow could keep out mechanised forces?"

"The Rumanians said they would fight."

"Don't make me laugh. Have you ever seen the Rumanian army? A bunch of half-starved peasants."

Without waiting for the order, Albu had handed Galpin a double whisky. Now, taking a gulp at it, Galpin grew flushed and stared at Harriet as though angry with her: "What do you think will happen here? Fifth column risings. This place is stiff with fifth columnists – not only those German bastards, but thousands of pro-Germans and chaps in German pay. And there's all those hangers-on of the German Legation. They're not here for their health. There're two big German establishments here – and a regular arsenal in each of them. We're all marked down. Yours truly with the rest. Make no mistake about it. We're just sitting on a time-bomb."

Harriet had grown pale. As she put her hand to the bar counter, Clarence drawled with exaggerated calm: "What are you trying to do, Galpin? Scare the wits out of her?"

Galpin now swung his angry stare on to Clarence, but he was slightly disconcerted by this reproof. He drank to give himself time, then he said: "We've got to face facts. The women oughtn't to stick around if they can't face facts. And you chaps'll have to face them, too. Everyone thinks you're agents. Don't quote me, but the chances are you'll wake up one night with a gun in your belly."

"I'll worry about that when it happens," said Clarence.

Yakimov's eyes had grown round. "Is this really true about Hungary?" he asked in shocked surprise.

"True enough for my paper."

"Meaning," said Clarence, "you and the others have just cooked it up?"

"Meaning nothing of the sort. Ask Screwby here. Hey, Screws!"

Screwby loped slowly over from the other side of the room, his smile wide and simple. Appealed to, he scratched one cheek of his large, soft, heavy face and said: "Yah, there's something to it all right. Budapest's closed down. Can't get a squeak from them. That means a 'stop' and a 'stop' can mean anything. Something'll happen tonight, and that's for sure."

Harriet said anxiously: "We must try and find Guy."

"First," said Clarence, "have another drink."

"After all," Yakimov tried to soothe her, "we can't do anything. Might as well have a couple while we're able. Doubt if we'll get much in dear old Dachau." He giggled and looked at Clarence. Clarence ordered another round. When it was drunk, Harriet would stay no longer.

As they crossed the hall, the hotel door started to revolve. Harriet watched it hopefully but it was only Gerda Hoffman, 'trying to look', Harriet thought, 'as fatal and clever as she's reputed to be'. The train of Germans that followed her appeared to be in the highest spirits; congratulating themselves, it seemed to Harriet, on the elements of victory.

"I wish we were safely out of this country," she said.

"You'll get leave in the summer," said Clarence. "Only five more months."

They drove to the Doi Trandafiri. Guy was not there. They did a round of several other bars, but could see nothing of him. Harriet was mystified by his disappearance. In the end she said she would go home. When Clarence left her at the door of Blocşul Cazacul, he said: "I expect he's up there waiting for you." This now seemed so probable that Harriet was the more disturbed to find the flat dark and silent and the bedroom empty.

She was suddenly convinced that Guy's disappearance had something to do with the scare about Hungary. Perhaps Sheppy had already taken him off on some sabotaging expedition. Perhaps he had already injured himself – or been arrested – or seized by the fifth columnists. Perhaps she would never see him again. She blamed herself that she had not gone immediately to Inchcape and asked him to interfere: now she went to the telephone and dialled his number. When he answered, she asked if Guy were with him. He had seen or heard nothing of Guy that evening.

She said: "There's a rumour that Germany has invaded Hungary. Do you think it's true?"

"It could be." Inchcape took the news lightly. "It doesn't mean they'll come here. Hungary is, strategically speaking, more important to Germany than Rumania is. It simply means the Germans are straightening out their Eastern front."

Harriet, in no mood to listen to Inchcape's theories, broke in rather wildly: "Everyone thinks they'll come here. All the journalists think so. And Guy has disappeared. I'm afraid he's gone to Ploeşti with Sheppy on one of these insane sabotage plans."

"What insane sabotage plans?" Inchcape spoke with the mild patience of one out to discover something, but Harriet did not need to be manoeuvred. She was keeping nothing to herself. All she wanted now was to seize Guy back from disaster.

She answered: "Putting detonators down the oil wells. Blowing up the Iron Gates . . ."

"*I see*! That's what he's up to, is he? Indeed! Well, don't worry, my dear child. Leave this to me, will you?"

"But where is Guy? Where is *Guy*?"

"Oh, he'll turn up." Inchcape spoke impatiently, the question of Guy's whereabouts being, in importance, a long way behind the threat to his dignity contained in Sheppy's use of his men.

As Harriet put down the receiver, she heard Guy's key in the lock. He entered singing, his face agleam with the cold. "Why, hello!" he said, surprised at seeing her standing unoccupied beside the telephone.

"Where on earth have you been?" she asked. "We were meeting you in the English Bar." She was guilty and cross with relief.

"I glanced in and there was no one there, so I walked down to the Dâmboviţa with Dubedat."

"Couldn't you have waited? Can't you wait for me even for ten minutes? Do you know that German troops are pouring into Hungary? They may invade Rumania tonight."

"I don't believe it. I bet you got this from Galpin."

"I did, but that doesn't mean it isn't true."

"These rumours are never true."

"One day one will be true. This sort of phoney war can't go on for ever. Someone's got to move some time and we'll be trapped. Galpin says the place is full of fifth columnists. He says you'll wake up one night with a gun in your belly. We'll be sent to Dachau. We'll never be free . . . we'll never go home again . . ." As he reached her, she collapsed against him crying helplessly.

"My poor darling." He put his arms round her, astonished. "I didn't realise you were getting nervous." He put her into the armchair and telephoned the Legation, where Foxy Leverett was on duty. He learnt that the rumours had derived from nothing more than a breakdown on the line to Budapest. This had now been righted. Foxy had just rung Budapest and found all quiet there.

While undressing, Guy grumbled about Galpin, Screwby "and the rest of the riff-raff we've got here calling themselves journalists. They're utterly irresponsible. A story at any price. What does it matter so long as they can startle people into buying the paper?"

Harriet, sitting up in bed, red-eyed, limp and relieved, said: "You shouldn't have gone off with Dubedat without leaving a message. You should have known I'd be worried."

"Surely you weren't worrying about me, darling? You know I'm always right."

She said: "If the fifth columnists came for you, I'd murder them, *I'd murder them.*"

"I believe you would, too," he said indulgently as he pulled his shirt over his head.

17

IT WAS A WINTER OF UNUSUAL COLD in Western Europe. The cinema newsreels showed children snowballing beneath Hadrian's Arch. Rivers were transfixed between their banks. A girl pirouetted on the Seine, her skirt circling out from her waist. The Paris roofs spilled snow in puffs, like smoke. The Parisians carried gasmasks in tin cylinders. An air-raid warning sounded and they filed down into the Métro. The streets were empty. A taxi-cab stood abandoned. Then everyone came up again, smiling as though it were all a joke. ('And perhaps it is a joke,' Yakimov thought, 'perhaps this will go down in history as the joke war.') St. Paul's appeared briefly with a feather-boa of snow. A glimpse of Chamberlain and his umbrella gave rise to a flutter of applause. At once the film was interrupted and a notice appeared on the screen to say public demonstrations of any kind were forbidden. The audience watched the rest of the film in silence.

Yakimov, in the cheapest seats, was reminded by these pictures of the fact that he would sooner or later have to return to the streets of Bucharest, where the hard ridges of frozen snow bit through his shoes and the wind slapped his face like a sheet of emery paper.

He had taken to the cinema when finally prevented from bedding down at the Athénée Palace. He had managed at first to maintain not only some sort of social life there, but a semblance of residence. Unwilling to take the long journey each afternoon back to his lodgings, he would slip upstairs when the bar closed and settle himself in any bedroom he found with a key left in the lock. If there was a bathroom attached, he would take a bath, then sleep the afternoon away. When caught, as he often was, by the room's rightful owner, he apologised for having mistaken the number. "All these rooms look alike," he would explain. "Your poor old Yaki belongs on the floor below."

But suspicions were roused; complaints were made. He was caught, and recognised, by one of the porters who knew he had no bedroom on the floor below. The manager warned him that, caught again, he would be forbidden entry to any part of the hotel. After that, he was found stretched out on one of the main room sofas. He was warned again. He then tried sleeping upright in an arm-chair, but the guests objected to his snoring and the waiters roughly awakened him.

Hounded, as he put it, from pillar to post, he went, when he could afford it, to the cinema. When he could not afford it, he walked to keep himself awake.

Morning and evening, he joined the mendicant company of Hadjimoscos, Horvath and Cici Palu, and stood with them on the edge of one or the other of the groups at the English Bar. Sometimes, ignoring insults, stares of disgust, excluding backs and shoulders, they had to stand about an hour or more before someone, out of embarrassment or pity, invited them in on a round. They expected nothing from *habitués* like Galpin and Screwby, and got nothing. They had most to hope for from the casual drinker, an English engineer from Ploeşti or a temporary American visitor elated by the black-market rate in dollars. When Galpin, seeing the three at his elbow, said "Scram", an American newspaperman said: "Oh, I guess we owe the local colour a drink."

Sometimes, to encourage patronage, one of the group would offer to buy a round, then, the order given, would discover he had come out without any money. It was surprising how often some bystander would lend, or pay, out of shame for the tactics of the group. Albu refused to pour these drinks until the money was produced, but what he thought of it all, no one knew. While the pantomime of pocket-patting and consternation was going on, he would stand motionless, his gaze on a horizon not of this world.

Something in Albu's attitude disturbed Yakimov. Not the bravest of men, he was often painfully upset by the audacity of the others, and yet he clung to them. It was not that they welcomed him – it was simply that he was not welcomed by anyone else. He, who had once been the centre of Dollie's set, was now without a friend.

He could not understand why Hadjimoscos, Horvath and Palu were 'horrid' to him; why there was always a hint of derision, even of malice, in their attitude towards him. Perhaps the fact that he had once been in the position of patron had marked him down for all time. They had once deferred to him, now they need defer no longer. And there had been the incident of Hadjimoscos's teeth. Returning drunk from a party, Hadjimoscos, sick in a privy, had spewed out his false teeth. Yakimov, in attendance, had flushed them away before he realised what had happened. At least, that had been Yakimov's story – and he had told it widely, and unwisely, round the bar. Hadjimoscos could not contradict it because the teeth were missing, and remained missing until a new set could be made. He had no memory of what had become of them. Too late, Yakimov became aware of the displeasure in Hadjimoscos's mongoloid eyes – a displeasure that gave them a truly frightening glint. He murmured: "Only a little joke, dear boy," but it was after that that Hadjimoscos refused to take him to parties, always giving the excuse that he had not been invited.

The trio also, it seemed, resented Yakimov's attempts to repay drinks with amusing talk. In front of him, Hadjimoscos said with disgust to the others: "He *will* tell his dilapidated stories! He *will* insist that he is not what he seems!"

The second accusation referred to the fact that, when asked what he was doing in Bucharest, Yakimov would reply: "I'm afraid, dear boy, I'm not at liberty to say." In reply to someone who said: "I suppose it's your own government you're working for," he mumbled in humorous indignation: "Are you trying to insult poor Yaki?"

A rumour had reached the Legation that Yakimov was working for the Germans, and Dobson, taking the matter up, had traced it back to Hadjimoscos. Dropping into the English Bar and inviting Hadjimoscos to a drink, he had remonstrated pleasantly: "This is a very dangerous story to put around."

Hadjimoscos, nervous of the power of the British Legation, protested: "But, *mon ami*, the Prince is a member of some secret service – he himself makes it evident. I could not imagine he worked for the British. They surely would not employ such an *imbécile*!"

"Why do you say he 'makes it evident'?" Dobson asked.

"Because he will take out a paper – so! – and put to it a match with fingers shaking – so! – then he will sigh and mop his brow and say: 'Thank God I have got rid of that'."

Yakimov was ordered to the Legation. When Dobson repeated his conversation with Hadjimoscos, Yakimov was tremulous with fear. He wailed pathetically: "All in fun, dear boy, all in innocent fun!"

Dobson was unusually stern with him. "People," he said, "have been thrown into prison here for less than this. The story has reached Woolley. He and the other British businessmen want you sent under open arrest to the Middle East. There you'd go straight into the ranks."

"*Dear boy!* You'd never do that to an old friend. Poor Yaki meant no harm. That old fool Woolley has no sense of humour. Yaki often plays these little japes. Once in Budapest, when flush, I got a cage of pigeons and went down a side street like this . . ." As he lifted a wire tray from Dobson's desk and moved with exaggerated stealth round the room, the sole flapped on his left shoe. "Then I put down the cage, looked around me, and let the pigeons fly away."

Dobson lent him a thousand *lei* and promised to talk Woolley round.

Had Yakimov been content to eat modestly, he could have existed from one remittance to the next, but he was not content. When his allowance arrived, he ate himself into a stupor, then, penniless again, returned, a beggar, to the English Bar. It was not that he despised simple food. He despised no food of any kind. When he could afford nothing more, he would go to the Dâmbovița and eat the peasant's staple food, a mess of maize. But food, rich food, was an obsessive longing. He needed it as other men need drink, tobacco or drugs.

Often he was so reduced he had not even the bus fare to and from his lodging. Walking back at night through streets deserted except for beggars and peasants who slept, and died of cold in their sleep, in doorways or beneath the hawkers' stalls, he often thought of his car, his Hispano-Suiza, and plotted to retrieve it. All he needed was a Yugoslav transit visa and thirty-five thousand *lei*. Surely he could find someone to lend him that! And he felt, once the car was his again, his whole status would change. It was heavy on petrol and oil, of course, but they were cheap here. He would manage. And with this dream he would trudge through the black, wolf-biting night until he found refuge in the syrupy heat of the Protopopescus' flat.

There he was comfortable enough, though things had not gone so well at first. For several nights after he settled in, he had been bitten by bugs. Awakened by the burning and stinging itch they produced, he had put on the light and seen the bugs sliding out of sight among the creases of the sheets. His tender flesh had risen in white lumps. Next morning the lumps had disappeared. When he spoke to Doamna Protopopescu, she took the matter badly.

"Here buks, you say?" she demanded. "Such is not possible. We are nice peoples. These buks have come with you."

Yakimov told her he had come straight from the Athénée Palace. Not even pretending to believe him, she shrugged and said: "If so, then you have imaginations."

Having paid his rent in advance and being without money to pay elsewhere, he had no choice but to suffer. He produced one or two dead bugs, the sight of which merely increased Doamna Protopopescu's scorn. "Where did you find such?" she demanded. "In bus or taxi or café? In all places there are buks."

Aggrieved beyond measure, he set his mind to work and, the next night, threw back the covers and gathering the bugs up rapidly, dropped them one by one into a glass of water. Next morning, smiling and pretending to click his heels, he presented the glass to his landlady. She examined it, mystified: "What have you?"

"Bugs, dear girl."

"Buks!" She peered into the glass, her face sagging further in its bewildered exasperation, then, suddenly, she was enlightened. She flew into a rage that was not, thank God, directed at him. "These," she cried, "are Hungarian buks. Ah, filthy peoples! Ah, the dirty mans!" It transpired that, in order to accommodate a lodger, the Protopopescus had bought a bed in the seedy market near the station. The salesman, an Hungarian, had sworn it was a clean bed, as good as new, and now what had been discovered! "Buks!"

Doamna Protopopescu's usual movements were indolent. Her body was soft with inertia and over-eating, but now, in her rage, she displayed the animal vigour of her peasant forebears. She turned the bed on its side and glared into the wire meshes beneath it. Yakimov, looking with her, could see no sign of bugs.

"Ha!" she menaced them, "they hide. But from me they cannot hide."

She bound rags to a poker, dipped it in paraffin and set it alight. As she swept the flames over the springs and frame of the bed, she hissed: "Now, I think no more buks. Die then, you filthy Hungarian buks. Ha, buks, this is for you, buks!"

Yakimov watched her, impressed. That night he slept in peace. The incident drew them together. It broke down the barrier of strangeness between them – a process maintained by the fact that Yakimov had to pass through the Protopopescus' bedroom to reach the bathroom.

The Protopopescus had probably imagined that, at the most, a lodger would require a bath once or twice a week. They had not allowed for his other bodily needs. When, directed by the maid, Yakimov first found his way through the bedroom, the Protopopescus were still in bed. Doamna Protopopescu lifted a bleared face from the pillow and regarded him in astonished silence. No comment was made on his intrusion then, nor at any other time. If they were in the bedroom when he passed through, the Protopopescus always behaved in the same way. On the outward journey they ignored him. As he returned, they would suddenly show awareness of him and greet him.

Often Doamna Protopopescu was alone in the room. She spent much of her day lying on her bed dressed in her kimono. Yakimov was delighted to observe that she did everything a woman of Oriental character was reputed to do. She ate Turkish delight; she drank Turkish coffee; she smoked Turkish cigarettes; and she was for ever laying out a pack of frowsy, odd-faced cards, by which she predicted events from hour to hour. He sometimes stopped to watch her, amused to note that when the cards foretold something displeasing, she would snatch them all up impatiently and, in search of a more acceptable future, set them out again.

She entered his repertoire of characters, and at the bar he told how coming out of the bathroom and anticipating recognition, he had said: "*Bonjour*, doamna and domnul lieutenant Protopopescu," only to realise too late that, although on the chair lay the familiar padded uniform and the grimy male corsets, and on the floor were an officer's spurred riding boots, the figure beside Doamna Protopopescu was that of a man much younger than her husband.

"So now," he concluded, "I merely say '*Bonjour*, doamna and domnul lieutenant', and leave it at that."

The flat, its windows sealed for the winter, smelt strongly of sweat and cooking. The smell in the Protopopescus' bedroom was overpowering, yet Yakimov came to tolerate it, indeed to associate it with the comforts of home.

One morning, when he paused to watch his landlady laying out her curious cards, he essayed a little joke. He handed her a *leu*, turned to the side imprinted with a corn cob and said: "A portrait of our great and glorious Majesty, King Carol II. You, dear girl, may not recognise the likeness, but there are many dear girls who would."

Doamna Protopopescu's immediate reaction was to display the blankness with which Rumanian middle-class women out-faced impropriety, then her peasant blood got the better of her. She spluttered, and as she handed back the coin she made an 'away with you' gesture that encouraged him to relax at the hips until he was sitting, or nearly sitting, on the bed-edge. When he did reach the point of sitting down, she gave him a swift, calcula-ting glance and said: "Tell me now some sinks about Inklant. Do I say it right: Inklant?"

A sort of friendship grew up despite the fact Yakimov was very nervous of his landlady. A few days after his arrival in the flat, he had been awakened by an uproar outside his door. Protopopescu's batman, sent to the house to do some chores, had been caught stealing a cigarette. Doamna Protopopescu was beating him with her fists while he, doubled up and shielding his head with his arms, howled like a maniac: "Don't beat me, *coăniţă*, don't beat me." Ergie the maid, standing by, caught Yakimov's startled eye and laughed. The scene was a common-place to her.

Though, after that, he often heard the howls of the batman or Ergie or Ergie's consumptive daughter, who slept in the kitchen with her, Yakimov could not get used to these rows. While closeted with Doamna Protopopescu, Yakimov would often look at her little beringed paw and reflect upon its strength.

At first, he saw the bedroom as something of a refuge from the English Bar, where he spent so many hours standing about, hungry, thirsty and often tired. In Doamna Protopopescu's room he could sit down; and, by sitting long enough, by gazing with the concen-tration of a hungry dog at everything that went into her mouth, Yakimov could obtain from her a piece of Turkish delight, a cup of coffee, a glass of *ţuică*, or even, but rarely, a meal. Doamna Protopopescu was not generous. Whatever Yakimov received, he had to earn by an hour or more of what she called 'English conversation'.

He did not object to chatting to her. What he found intolerably tedious was the fact that he was expected to pick up her errors of grammar and pronunciation, and wrestle for their correction. If these corrections were not frequent, she became suspicious. She would let him talk on indefinitely without reward.

Her pronunciation he found beyond mending. She had no ear. When she repeated a word after him, he would hear for an instant an echo of his own cultivated drawl, then, at once, she would relapse. Like many members of the Rumanian middle classes, her second language was German. Yakimov complained in the bar: "Bloke I know says English is a low German dialect. Since I've met Doamna P. I've come to believe it."

The ruthlessness with which she kept him to his task soon deprived the occasions of charm. Yakimov was driven to reflect how cruelly he was required to labour for the sustenance that was, surely, a human right.

Fortunately no more than tuition was required of him.

Doamna Protopopescu's kimono was of black artificial silk printed over with flame-coloured chrysanthemums. It was a decayed and greasy-looking garment, smelling of the body beneath. Sometimes one of her big breasts would fall out and she would bundle it back with the indifference of habit. Clearly – thank God! – she did not see Yakimov as a man at all. His comment at the bar was: "That dear girl exists only for the relaxation of the warrior."

When she talked, it was usually about herself or her husband, who was, she said, impotent. "But here," she explained, "all men are impotent at thirty. In youth, they know no restraint." She never spoke more openly of the fact that she had acquired a second bed-fellow, but frequently said: "Here it is not nice to have more than one lover at a time."

Occasionally she complained, in the usual Rumanian fashion, of the country's two despised components – the peasants and the Jews.

"Ah, these peasants!" she said one day, after a particularly furious fracas with the batman, "they are but beasts."

"So little is done for them," said Yakimov in the approved English style.

"True." Doamna Protopopescu sighed at the magnanimity of her agreement. "The priest, who should do all – he does nothing. He is the village bull. The women dare not refuse him. But were he other, would they learn? I doubt. It is the nature everywhere of the workers that they are the dregs, the sediments."

"Oh, I don't know," said Yakimov. "Some of them are rather sweet."

"*Sweet!*" Aghast at the word, she looked at him so that he feared she was about to strike him.

As for the Jews, they were, according to Doamna Protopopescu, to blame for all the ills of the world. They were particularly to blame for the war, that was causing the rise in prices, the shortage of artisans and the stagnation in French fashions.

Attempting to lighten the tone of the talk, Yakimov said: "Ah, dear girl, you should have met my dear old friend, Count Horvath. He had the finest Jew-shoot in Hungary."

She nodded. "So, in Hungary they shoot Jews! They have wisdom. Here they do not shoot them. In Rumania it is always so – the nature is too soft." As she spoke her whole face drooped with greed, inertia and discontent.

Yakimov, disconcerted, said: "They do not really shoot Jews. It was only a joke."

"A joke, heh?" In her disgust, she thrust into her mouth a piece of Turkish delight so large it left round her mouth a fur of sugar.

He had been in the house some weeks before he dared venture into the kitchen. Then, returning supperless one night to a silent flat, he opened the door and switched on the light. All about him the walls heaved as cockroaches, blackbeetles and other indigenous insects sped out of sight. He was tip-toeing towards a cupboard, when a movement startled him. He saw that Ergie and her daughter were lying on a pallet wedged between gas-stove and sink. Ergie had raised her head.

"A glass of water, dear girl," he whispered and, drawing a glass, was forced to drink the wretched stuff before going hungry to bed.

18

A FEW DAYS AFTER HARRIET HAD TOLD INCHCAPE of Sheppy's sabotage plans, the Pringles quarrelled for the first time. Guy's safe return had put all thought of Sheppy from her head. She was as surprised as Guy when one morning Inchcape entered their flat with a swagger and, stripping off his gloves and smacking them across his palm, laughed at Guy in triumph.

"Well, I've just left your friend: the mysterious Commander Sheppy." Inchcape rapped the words out in Sheppy's own style: "I think I've put him straight on a few points. I've informed him that, whosoever he may be, he has no jurisdiction over my men."

Guy said nothing, but looked at Harriet. Harriet looked out of the window.

Inchcape, enjoying himself, swung half a circle on his heel and stretched his lips in an angry smile. "Our permits to live and work here," he said, "are issued on the undertaking we do not get mixed up in any funny business. I can well understand your wanting to do something more dramatic than lecturing, but the situation does not permit. It *simply* does not permit. Whether you like it or not, you're in a reserved occupation. You're here to obey orders. *My* orders."

Guy still said nothing, but took down the *ţuică* bottle and started to look for glasses. Inchcape held up his hand: "Not for me." Guy put the bottle back.

Inchcape began fitting his gloves on again: "If you want to help out at the Legation with a bit of decoding or clerical work, no one will object. Clarence has his Poles. No objection. No objection whatsoever." His gloves on, he stood for some moments gazing in at the pleated white silk lining of his bowler hat, then added: "H.M. Government decided that our job is here. It's our duty to do it, and to stay here, doing it, as long as humanly possible. I'm willing to bet that Sheppy's outfit will be kicked out of Rumania before it's had time to turn round. Well!" He jerked his head up and his smile relaxed. "No need for you to see Sheppy again. I've dealt with him. You'll get no more notices of his meetings. And I can tell you one thing – you're well out of it." He put on his hat, tapped it, and, swinging round with grace, took himself off.

Guy gave Harriet another look. "Yes," she agreed, "I did tell him. It was that night you were out with Dubedat. I thought Sheppy had got hold of you. I was frightened."

Guy, without speaking, went to the hallway for his coat. As she began to move towards him, he opened the door. "I must hurry," he said.

Harriet was hurt by his coldness: "But aren't we going to walk in the park?"

"I won't have time. I have a students' meeting. David will be in the Doi Trandafiri at one. You can come there if you like."

When he had gone, Harriet, more desolate than at any time before her marriage, picked up a red kitten that was now her companion in the flat, and held it for comfort to her throat.

The kitten had been a stray, found wandering one night in the snow. Guy thought it might be one of the wild cats that lived in the half demolished buildings in the square, but it had been a long way from the buildings. The Pringles took it home. It became at once Harriet's cat, her baby, her totem, her *alter ego*. When anyone else picked it up, it turned into a mad little bundle of pins. Guy was frightened of it, and the kitten, sensing that it had the upper hand with him, would bite him savagely. When he was seated, forgetful of it, it would fly up the back of his chair and land, all teeth and claws, in the thickness of his hair. He would cry for Harriet to remove it.

Guy applauded Harriet, who, picking up the kitten with all the confidence in the world, was never bitten or scratched. "The thing," she said, "is not to be nervous." To the kitten she said: "You may bite other people, but I'm different. You don't bite me," and the kitten, fixing her with its curious stare, seemed to realise they met on equal terms.

Guy, though he remained nervous of it, was proud of the little creature that changed into a fury in his hands. He admired its red-gold colour and the way it would hurtle like a flying cat from one end of the flat to the other. Despina, always eager to echo admiration, said it was a most exceptional cat in every way. If the Pringles had to leave Rumania, she would take it and care for it herself.

Harriet, standing now gazing through the French-windows at

the snow-crowned palace, imagining herself abandoned by Guy,
felt for the kitten a passion of tenderness as though it were the
only love left to her. She said to it: "I love you. I love you with all
my heart." The kitten seemed to take on a look of serious enquiry.
"Because you are wild," she added, "because you are warm;
because you are living." And, of course, because Guy had turned
against her.

She reflected that he had asked Klein to try and discover what
had happened to Sasha Drucker and because of this was meeting
him with David at the Doi Trandafiri. He had never, as she felt
inclined to do, let the matter drop. He was faithful to his friends,
but (she told herself) indifferent to her. All these people – David,
Klein, the Druckers, Dubedat and a host of others – were his
faction: he bound them to himself. She had no one but her little
red cat.

Almost at once, she revolted against the situation. Putting the
cat down, she dialled Clarence's number at the Propaganda
Bureau and said to him: "Guy was taking me for a walk in the
park, but he has had to go to a meeting. Won't you take me?"

"Why, yes of course I will." Clarence sounded only too glad of
an excuse to leave his office. He came round at once for her and
drove her to the park.

It was the beginning of March. The wind was relaxing a little.
More and more people were walking abroad, and once again
nurses were bringing children to play in the open air. No new
snow had fallen for two weeks, but the old snow, blackened and
glacial, lingered on. It was lingering too long. People were tired of
it.

As Harriet walked with Clarence along the path that lay under
Inchcape's balcony, they looked up and saw the summer chairs
and flower-baskets heaped with snow. Icicles hung firm as a fringe
of swords from every edge. Yet there was a smell in the air of
coming spring. Any day now rain would fall instead of snow, and
the thaw would begin.

When they reached the dove-cotes, they stopped to watch the
apricot-coloured doves that were already perking up their bedraggled tail-feathers, dipping their heads and languishing their
soft, gold-glinting necks from side to side. The air was full of their
cooing. Behind them the snow was sliding from the branches of a
weeping willow. A false acacia, buried all winter, was appearing

again, hung over with pods that looked like old banana skins.

Under the chestnut trees by the lake some children were feeding the pigeons. A solitary salesman, with nuts and sesame cakes, stood with his hands under the arms of his short frieze jacket, and slowly raised one knee at a time in a standstill march, his feet so bound with rags he seemed to have gout in both of them. The children were bundles of fur. The little girls wore ear-rings; they had necklaces and brooches over the white fur of their coats and bracelets over the cuffs of their fleecy gloves. A little boy with a gold-topped cane struck the ground authoritatively, agitating the pigeons that fluttered up and, after flying a half-circle of protest, settled down quickly before the food could disappear. Between bites, they moaned and did a little love-making.

Suddenly excited by the coming spring, Harriet felt her quarrel with Guy was of no importance at all. As they crossed the bridge, from which they could see the dusty ice of the waterfall, she paused and leant on the rail and said: "Everything is wonderful. I want . . . I want to be . . ."

Clarence concluded smugly: "What you are not?"

"No. What I am. The 'I' that is obscured by my own feminine silliness. In some ways, I suppose I am just as absurd as Sophie or Bella."

Clarence laughed. "I suppose you are. Women are like that, and one likes them like that."

"No doubt you do. But I don't imagine I exist to enhance your sense of superiority. I exist to satisfy my own demands on myself, and they are higher than yours are likely to be. If you don't like me as I am, I don't care."

Clarence was unruffled. "You mean, you do care," he said, "that's the trouble. Women want to be liked. They can never be themselves."

"And you, my poor Clarence, can never be anything but yourself." She moved to the other side and looked to the widening lake, from which the snow had been swept. The restaurant was now no more than a cape of snow, but someone had crossed it – the footsteps were cleanly cut – and brought out the wireless set. It was playing across the ice. The music was a Russian waltz and there were half a dozen skaters pressing forward against the wind, turning and lifting feet to the waltz rhythm. This end of the lake was so overhung with trees that it seemed enclosed, like a room.

The branches, lacy with frost, glimmered an unearthly silver-white against the pewter colours of ice and sky.

Clarence crossed over to her. Staring down at the scored and riven surface of the lake, he said soberly: "There are things one can never leave behind."

"Such as?"

"One's childhood. One can never recover from that."

As they turned back on their tracks, she knew he wanted her to question him, and asked, not very willingly: "What sort of childhood had you?"

"Oh, a perfectly ordinary one – at least, it would have seemed ordinary to anyone outside it. My father was a clergyman." After a pause, he added: "And a sadist."

"You really mean that? A sadist?"

"Yes."

The wind was behind them now. Released from its stinging onslaught, they walked slowly, feeling almost warm. Harriet did not know what to say to Clarence, who looked sombre and in-drawn, possessed, it seemed, by the memory of childhood as by the memory of an old injustice. She would have chosen to say: "Don't think about it: don't talk about it," but, of course, the thing he needed was to talk. She had a pained sense that something was about to be inflicted on her.

"But worse than that – worse than my father, I mean – was life at school. My father sent me there because the headmaster was a believer in corporal punishment. He believed in it, too."

At the age of seven, Clarence had been beaten for running away from the school. Afterwards, when he lay in bed 'blubbing', he did not know what it was he had done wrong. All he had known was that he wanted to return to his mother. Harriet thought of a child of seven – a child the same age, she imagined, as the boy who had frightened the pigeons with his gold-topped stick. It was scarcely possible to imagine anyone even slapping so young a child, yet Clarence insisted he had been savagely beaten, beaten with all the fury and vigour of revenge.

After a while, he said, he had learnt to 'put up a show'. He had hidden his fears and uncertainties beneath the front he had retained until now, but the truth was that, over the years, his nerve had been broken. His home had offered him no escape from misery. His mother, a gentle creature who feared his father more than Clarence did, had been merely an object of pity, a weight on his emotions – yet, he said, she had been someone to whom he could talk. She had died when he was ten and he felt she had made her escape. She had abandoned him. His happiest times had been those Sundays when he had been permitted to cycle out on the moors with a friend.

"You got on well with the other boys?" Harriet asked.

Clarence looked sullen a moment, withdrawn from this question, then he answered it obliquely: "It's always that sort of school where boys are bullied. It had a tradition of brutality. It was transmitted by the masters."

"But you weren't actually ill-treated by the other boys?"

For reply, he shrugged his shoulders. They were walking down the main path beside the *tapis vert*. In this wind-swept area, which they had to themselves, the snow had drifted so thickly it was impossible to tell where the flower-beds ended and the paths began. Clarence kept tripping on small hedges, keeping no watch where he went, as he described those evenings when, cycling back from the moors, he had grown sick at the sight of the school gates and the sunset reddening the bricks of the school buildings. In time he had acquired a desolate resignation to his position – the inescapable position of victim. Even now, he said, even here in Bucharest, the summer Sunday light, the closed shops, the sound of the bell of the English Church, could bring back that sick hope-lessness. It filled him with a sense of failure, and that sense would haunt him all his life.

They were nearing the Calea Victoriei. Harriet could hear the squeak of motor-horns, yet, as they walked isolated on the path, she had the sense of being in a limbo with Clarence. When she thought back on the scene, it seemed to her the snow had been reddened by the desolation of those sabbath sunsets. Though his story of childhood did not relate in any way to hers, its misery seemed altogether too familiar. As she grew depressed, he began to emerge from memory and to smile. She felt that by his confi-dences he had been making a claim on her. Involuntarily, she took a step away – not only from Clarence but from the unhappy past that overhung him. He had, she felt, been marked down by fear.

He did not notice her movement. Still confiding he said: "I need a strong woman, someone who can be ruthlessly herself."

So Clarence believed her to be that sort of woman! She did not repudiate his belief but knew she was nothing like it. She was not strong, and she certainly felt no impulse to nurse a broken man. She would rather be nursed herself. At the gate, she said she was meeting Guy at the Doi Trandafiri.

Clarence frowned down at his feet and complained: "Why *does* Guy go to that place?"

"He likes people. He likes being pestered by his students."

"Incredible!" drawled Clarence, but, as Harriet went on, he kept beside her.

The café was as crowded as ever. Guy was nowhere to be seen. Harriet said: "He's always late," and Clarence grunted agreement. They had to stand for some minutes before a table was vacated.

Almost as soon as they had sat down, David and Klein entered. Guy came hurrying in behind them. Because of the estrangement, she saw him newly again: a comfortable-looking man of an un-harming largeness of body and mind. His size gave her an illusion of security – for it was, she was coming to believe, no more than an illusion. He was one of those harbours that prove to be too shallow: there was no getting into it. For him, personal relationships were incidental. His fulfilment came from the outside world.

Clarence, meanwhile, had been talking to her, continuing his story as though there had been no interval between the park and the café. As he stared at her, resentful of her inattention, she knew he was one who, given a chance, would shut her off into a private world. What was it they both wanted? Exclusive attention, no doubt: the attention each had missed in childhood. Perversely, she did not want it now it was offered. She was drawn to Guy's gregarious good humour and the open world about him.

She watched him as he came up behind David and Klein and, stepping between them, put his arms about their shoulders. Klein glanced back smiling, at once accepting this as a normal greeting, but David, though he was Guy's intimate, looked confused and, flushing slightly, began to talk away his own confusion. In a moment, Guy saw her and, leaving the others, came hurrying towards her between the crowded noisy tables through the hot and smoky air. He put out his left hand, smiled and squeezed her hand. The estrangement was forgotten.

"Who is this Klein?" Clarence asked, as though the approaching stranger brought intolerable tedium.

"A source of information," said Guy. "One of David's contacts."

When they were all seated, Clarence, doubtful and suspicious, made his usual defensive retreat into silence, but only Harriet noticed. Guy was eager to hear what Klein had discovered about the Druckers.

He had not discovered much. He said: "It seems that Sasha was taken with his father."

"You mean he was arrested?"

"One cannot say that." Klein's face creased with amusement. "This, you must remember, is a civilised country. There was no charge against the boy."

"Then what do you think has happened to him?"

"Who can say! He is not in prison. If he were, I think I would discover it. A prisoner cannot be totally hidden."

"Perhaps he is dead," said Harriet.

"A body must be disposed of. Here secrecy is not so easy. The people are given to talk. Besides, why should they kill the boy? They are not such bad people. They would not kill without reason. All I can say is, no one has seen him since his father's arrest. He has disappeared. But something I have discovered that is very interesting. Very interesting indeed!" He leant forward, grinning. "I have discovered that the Drucker money in Switzerland – a great sum – is banked in the name of Sasha Drucker. Is that not interesting? So, I think he is alive. In Switzerland the banks hold very tightly to money. Even the King could not demand it. It can be withdrawn only by the authority of this young Drucker or his legal heirs. He is an important boy."

"He is indeed!" David agreed. "Perhaps he is being held somewhere until he gives his authority."

Klein shot out his hands in delighted enquiry: "If so, where? Here we have not the Middle Ages. For our Cabinet the situation must be very difficult. Here is an innocent young man – a man so simple, young and innocent that no capital charge could be trumped against him. To hold him without a charge! That would not be civilised, not Occidental! Yet – a young man of such importance! How could they afford to let him leave the country?" Klein sat shaking with laughter at authority's predicament.

Guy frowned to himself, perplexed and concerned. "But what have they *done* with him?" he asked the table.

"Why?" Klein opened his pale eyes. "What do they matter to you, these Druckers? They have made much money – illegal money. They have lived well. Now they are not so well. Need you weep?"

"Sasha was a pupil of mine. The Druckers treated me kindly. They were my friends."

Klein smiled mockingly into Guy's face. "Tell me," he said, "how do you reconcile such friendship with your ideas on international finance?"

David snuffled and sniggered at this question, his mouth curling up under his nostrils. With his head down, he looked up in ironical enquiry at Guy, but before Guy had found a reply, Klein, relenting, said: "All things, all people – all are so interesting."

Clarence leant towards Harriet, speaking to her as though she were alone: "I must say, I think Guy squanders himself on a lot of people who aren't worth it."

"Well, you don't do that," said Harriet with some derision.

"Neither do you."

Harriet put up her hand, warding off this private controversy, so that she could listen to Klein, who had now left the Druckers and was talking of the country's internal situation.

"The King," he announced, "is granting an amnesty to the Iron Guardists."

David and Guy were astounded by this news. There had been no indication in the press, not even a rumour, that this would be possible.

"The amnesty is already signed," said Klein, speaking quietly, "but not yet announced. Wait. Tomorrow or the next day you will hear of it."

"But why should he grant an amnesty?" David asked.

"Ah, it is interesting. The war is ending in Finland. Any day now the Russians will be free to advance themselves elsewhere. And where will they advance? Here the Cabinet is very nervous. To whom can they look for help? Would the Allies defend Rumania against Russia? If so, how would it be possible? But Germany! Germany could do it, and *would* do it, at a price. Already the question has been asked: What price? What does Germany demand? And she has answered: First, grant an amnesty to the Iron Guard."

Clarence drawled crossly: "But I thought there was no Iron Guard left."

"You believed that? My friend, there are many Guardists, but they are hidden. And in Germany, too, there are many. They fled there in 1938 after Codreanu and his legionaries were shot. In Germany they were made welcome. They have been drilled. They have been trained in the concentration camps. They have become more Nazi than the Nazis. The Germans wish them to return here, for here they will be useful."

"But surely," Clarence protested, "no one wants fascism here. Rumania is still pro-British. There'd be an uproar. There might even be risings."

"Britain is loved," said Klein. "The majority would choose a liberal Government if they had nothing to lose by it. But Russia is feared too much. Great fear can cast love out. Stay here and you will see it happen."

David said: "I told the Legation a year ago that we'd lose this country if we didn't change our policy."

Clarence asked, sulkily: "What change of policy could make any difference now?"

"Now, very little. We've left it too late." David's agreement was heated. "But we need not play Germany's game for her." Taking possession of the talk, David spoke with force and feeling: "We support a hated dictatorship. We snub the peasant leaders. We condone the suppression of the extreme Left and the imprisonment of its leaders. We support some of the most ruthless exploitation of human beings to be found in Europe. We support the suppression of minorities – a suppression that must, inevitably, lead to a break-up of Greater Rumania as soon as opportunity arises."

"Perhaps the opportunity won't arise."

"Perhaps it won't. It depends on the conduct of the war. The war will have to move sometime. The deadlock can't continue and I don't believe there is a chance of a truce. If the Allies could break through the Siegfried Line and advance into Germany, then they might, without particular injury to British interests, continue their policy here indefinitely. As it is we're doing the fascists' job for them. At the first indication of a possible German victory, the whole vast anti-Communist movement here would rise against us."

"Do you expect us to support the Communists?" Clarence asked.

"Certainly not. My complaint is that, when we could, we did nothing to establish a liberal policy that could save the country from either extremity – Left or Right."

"I think you take too black a view of things," mumbled Clarence.

"You, I can see," said David, "would agree with H.E. The old duffer describes my reports as 'alarmist' and files them away and forgets about them."

"Hum!" said Clarence, hiding his annoyance under an expression of superior doubt, then he jumped up, claimed he had a luncheon appointment, and went without saying his good-byes.

David looked after him, smiling in amused pity. "Poor old Clarence," he said. "He's a bit of a half-baked intellectual, but a good fellow, really. Yes, quite a good fellow!" and he returned to his condemnation of British policy in Rumania.

PART FOUR

The Fall of Troy

19

THE IRON GUARD AMNESTY WAS ANNOUNCED as the thaw set in. The thaw, arriving late, bringing with it deluge and floods, was the more discussed. The announcement of the amnesty led, not to uproar and revolt as Clarence had predicted, but to a change in the Cabinet and the appointment among the new Ministers of the Guardist leader Horia Sima. The King assured the Allies they need have no fears. The amnesty meant nothing. A few new jokes went the rounds of the cafés. The Rumanians, it seemed, were prepared for anything now.

But the thaw was another matter. As the snow melted and ran from eaves and balconies, the whole city dripped beneath a leaden sky. Most people went about under umbrellas. When the iced surfaces on roads and pavements began to crack, people sank, without warning, deep into slush. Soon the roads were nothing but slush, ice-cold and filthy, that was sprayed by the speeding traffic on to the passers-by.

The sky grew darker and sank lower until it split beneath its own weight and the rain fell in torrents. Rivers overflowed their banks. Whole villages were drowned in a night. Conscripted peasants, having begged leave to help their families, wandered about in search of their homes, finding nothing but a waste of waters. The destitute survivors crowded into the city to replace the beggars that winter had killed.

The Finnish peace treaty was signed. Russia was free for another adventure. The citizens of Bucharest, cooped up in cafés, watching the downpour, passed round rumours of invasion. A reconnaissance 'plane was said to have sighted troops crossing the Dniester. Refugees were streaming towards the Pruth. Detailed descriptions were given of atrocities committed by Russian troops on Rumanian and German minorities. People went fearful to bed and rose to find everything much as they had left it. The rumours of yesterday were denied, but repeated the day after.

During this time there appeared in Bucharest an English teacher called Toby Lush who declared that all Bessarabia was in a ferment, the Russians being expected that very night.

It was thought at first that Lush came from the University of Jassy. Clarence and the Pringles felt much sympathy for any Englishman in a frontier town since hearing that the British Council lecturer at Ljubljana had been seized in the street one night by a German patrol car, taken over the frontier into Austria and never heard of again. However, when they started to talk to Lush, they discovered he came not from Jassy but from Cluj. He had thought that, things being as they were, he would be safer in the capital. After a fortnight, during which all the frontiers remained unviolated, he rather sheepishly said farewell to his new acquaintances, got into his car and returned to his pupils in Cluj.

One morning before Easter, when a gleam was lightening the puddles and the chestnut buds were breaking, Yakimov stood in the Calea Victoriei and stared into the window of a small restaurant. He was indifferent to the indications of spring. He was indifferent, too, to the gypsies, crowding back to their old pitch with baskets full of snow-drops, hyacinths, daffodils and mimosa, who were calling out excitedly to passers-by as though to old friends. One of them slapped Yakimov's arm, spinning him round and greeting him with fervour: "*Bună dimineață, domnule*," and he smiled, murmuring vaguely: "Dear girl," before he returned to his contemplation of the raw steaks and pork chops behind the glass.

He was without a hat, and his hair, fine, fair and in need of a cut, stirred in the cold March wind. Though the pavement snow was reduced now to a thin layer of something like wet and dirty sugar, his shoes were soaked. The hem of his coat, becoming unstitched, dipped down to his heels. He had a cold in his head; but none of this meant much compared with the fact he was tormented by a longing for food.

Guy, going home for luncheon, saw him and stopped and spoke. He drew his gaze slowly from the chops and tried to look blank. "How nice to see you, dear boy," he said. His voice was hoarse.

"Aren't you well?" Guy asked.

"Touch of *la grippe*." He tried to blow his nose without taking off a glove and the hard, wet, broken leather, prodding his inflamed nostrils, brought a tear to his eye.

Guy said: "Are you eating anywhere in particular?"

"Why, no, dear boy." At the prospect of food, Yakimov began to shake slightly and a second tear followed the first. He sniffed and said: "Not to tell a lie, I've been rather let down. Was luncheoning with my old friend Hadjimoscos, but apparently he's been called to his estate."

"Good heavens, has he an estate?"

"Heavily mortgaged, of course." Yakimov shifted hastily from the estate back to the subject of food. "Bit short of the Ready, dear boy. M'remittance held up again. Was just wondering what I'd do for a bite."

"Why not come back and eat with us?"

"Delighted." All pretences fallen in the emotion of the moment, he tripped as he turned and had to catch Guy's arm for support. Walking towards the square, Yakimov's sufferings poured from him.

"Difficult times," he said. "Your poor old Yaki's homeless. Been turned out. Thrown out, in fact. Literally thrown out by m'landlady. A terrible woman. Terrible. And she's kept all m'belongings."

"She can't do that." Guy was indignant, but on reflection added: "Unless, of course, you owe her some rent."

"Only a few *lei*. But that wasn't the main trouble, dear boy. It was a ham-bone I found lying about. Feeling a bit peckish, I picked it up – and she caught me with the bone in m'hand. You know what's on a ham-bone, dear boy! Scarcely a mouthful, but she went mad. *Mad*. She hit me, kicked me, beat me over the head, screamed like a maniac: then she opened the front door and shoved me out." He shuddered from cold or fear and glanced about as though in danger of renewed attack. "Never knew anything like it, dear boy."

"But you got your coat."

"Happened to be wearing it. It happened last night. I'd just come in." He touched the coat with love. "Did I tell you the Czar gave this coat to m'poor old dad?"

"Yes. Where are you staying now?"

"Nowhere. I just spent the night tramping the streets, dear boy. Just tramping the streets."

When Guy brought Yakimov into the flat, Harriet, who had been sitting by the electric fire, rose without a word, went into her bedroom and slammed the door. She remained so long that Guy went after her. She turned on him angrily, saying: "I've told you I will not have that man in the flat."

Guy reasoned with her: "Darling, he's ill; he's hungry; he's been turned out of his lodgings."

"I don't care. He insulted you. I won't have him here."

"When did he insult me?"

"On Christmas night. He said your limerick was in bad taste."

"Really, darling!" Guy laughed at her absurdity. "Listen! He's not well. I've never before seen him looking so thin and ill."

"I don't care. He's a scrounger and a glutton."

"Yes, you do care." Guy, holding her by the shoulders, shook her affectionately. "We must help him, not because he's a good person but because he needs help. You understand that." She let her head fall forward against his chest and, pleased by her capitulation, he gave her a final squeeze and said: "Come into the room. Be nice to him."

When Harriet entered the sitting-room, Yakimov looked apprehensively at her. He put her hand to his lips and said: "How kind of Beauty to feed her poor old Yaki."

Harriet, sufficiently recovered to be polite, was touched, in spite of herself, by Yakimov's appearance. He looked ill, aged and underfed.

He ate fiercely, saying nothing throughout the meal. When replete and revived, he looked up brightly. "Dear boy," he said to Guy, "I could put you on to a good thing. Had hoped to do the like for m'old friend Dobson, but he's been out of sight these last weeks. Keep dropping in on him but his secretary says he's busy, for some reason. Want him to get me a Yugoslav transit visa, then all I need's m'train-fare, a few thou and a C.D. number-plate. Once there I'd redeem m'poor old Hispano-Suiza and drive her back. Anyone who financed the trip would be quids in. With a C.D. number-plate, there's a packet to be made running stuff over frontiers. Take currency, for instance . . ."

"I'm sure Dobson couldn't get you a C.D. number-plate," said Harriet.

'M'sure he could, dear girl. Dobson's an old friend, deeply indebted to poor Yaki. And he'd get his whack. Now you, dear boy, if you could let Yaki have a few *lei* – thirty-five thousand, to be exact – I'd see you didn't lose by it."

Guy laughed, not taking the scheme seriously, and said he and Harriet were going to the mountains for Easter. They would need all the money they could spare for the holiday.

Yakimov sighed and swallowed down his coffee.

Guy turned to Harriet. "The flat will be empty while we're away," he said. "Couldn't we let Yaki stay here?"

She gave him a look and said coldly: "Why ask me?"

"He could look after the kitten."

"Despina will look after the kitten."

"Well, it's always a good thing to keep a place lived in."

"We're not leaving until tomorrow."

"There's the spare room."

"With no bed in it."

Yakimov broke in eagerly: "Anything will do for me, dear girl. The arm-chair, the floor, the odd mattress. Your poor old Yaki'll be thankful to have a roof over his head."

Guy looked steadily at Harriet, trying to melt her with consciousness of Yakimov's plight. She got to her feet impatiently: "Very well, but he must find somewhere to go before we get back."

She returned to the bedroom, from where she heard Guy lending Yakimov the money to pay off Doamna Protopopescu and regain his possessions.

"I suppose you wouldn't come and face her with me?" Yakimov asked.

No. Guy would do many things, but he would not do that.

After the two men had left the flat, Harriet wandered about, feeling fooled. She had refused to take in Dubedat, so this time Guy, grown cunning, had not given her the chance to refuse. He had circumvented her with her own compassion. Yakimov had been dishonestly imposed on her. She felt furious.

She went to the arm-chair where the red kitten lay sleeping, and, as though to assert the true seat of her compassion, she held it to her face, saying: "I love you." She kissed it wildly. "And I don't love anyone else," she said.

20

The thaw had reached the mountain village of Predeal just before the Pringles. The snow was wet and sliding wetly down from the rock faces above the houses. The hotels were emptying as the skiers went to the higher alps. On Easter Saturday the rain began.

Guy cared for none of this. He intended, he said, to produce a play and the choice was among *Macbeth*, *Othello* and *Troilus and Cressida*, copies of which he had brought with him. He had spoken of this intention during the winter, but Harriet had hoped nothing would come of it. Now, she realised, it had attained reality for him.

"I shall put it on at the National Theatre," he said.

She looked at *Troilus and Cressida* and saw it contained twenty-eight speaking parts. Dismayed, caught into the difficulties of such a production as into the toils of a prophetic dream, she tried to reason with him, but he simply laughed, seeing no difficulties at all.

She said: "Very few of the students are good enough to play Shakespeare."

"Oh, they'll only take minor parts. There are other people – friends, the chaps at the Legation . . ."

"Do you really think the Legation men will have time for amateur theatricals?"

Guy merely replied: "There'll be nothing amateur about my production."

"And the costumes! The expense, the work – and then, perhaps, no one will come." She spoke with an anguish which made him laugh at her.

"It will be tremendous fun," he said. "Everyone will come to it. You wait and see. It will be a great success."

His confidence reassured her, but at the same time she suffered the possibility of failure. She tried to persuade him to moderation: "Why not just do a reading in the lecture hall?"

"Oh no. We must do the thing in style. Rumanians only respond to snob appeal."

"And when are you thinking of starting it?"

"As soon as we get back."

It was late afternoon when the Pringles returned to their Bucnarest flat. Two days before they had sent Yakimov a warning telegram. When they entered the sitting-room, there was no sign of him.

"There you are!" Guy congratulated himself. "He's gone. I knew we'd have no trouble with him."

Harriet, not so sure, went into the bedroom. She was stopped as she entered by its heavy, unfamiliar smell. The curtains were pulled close. She threw them open. The windows were shut. She opened them, then, looking round at the disordered room, saw on the bed, cocooned in blankets, huddled knees to chin, head buried, Yakimov, in the depths of sleep. She went and shook him angrily.

"Wake up."

He came to consciousness slowly. She pulled the covers from his face and one eye looked at her with an injured expression.

"Didn't you get our telegram?" she asked.

He dragged himself up, trying to smile. "Dear girl, how delightful to see you back! Did you enjoy your trip? Tell Yaki all about it."

"We expected you would be gone before we returned."

"Yaki is going: going this very day, dear girl." His face, swollen and damp from sleep, the skin pink like scar tissue, turned resentfully to the open window. "Dreadfully chilly," he said.

"Then get up and dress. The bed linen will have to be changed."

Wincing at the cold, Yakimov came from under the covers, revealing pyjamas, torn and very dirty, made of flame-coloured crêpe de Chine. "Sick man," he murmured as he found, and tremulously covered himself with, a tarnished dressing-gown of gold brocade. "Better take a bath." He hurried off and shut himself in the bathroom.

Despina had appeared by now, expressing delight at the Pringles' return, but holding up her hands to warn her mistress that there had been catastrophe in her absence. The red kitten was dead.

"No!" Harriet cried, Yakimov and every other annoyance forgotten in the face of this news.

Despina, nodding in sombre sympathy, related how the kitten had died. One morning, when she was cleaning the room, it had gone on to the balcony and run along the balustrade to the balcony of the next-door flat. There the servant ("a Rumanian, of course," said Despina meaningfully) had hissed at it and flicked it back with a duster. Startled, it had lost its footing and fallen nine floors to the cobbles below. Despina went down and found it dead. It had, she was sure, died instantly.

Harriet wept. The loss seemed to her unendurable. She stood crouched together, weeping with intent bitterness, in agony, as though the foundations of her life had been taken from her. Guy watched her helplessly, amazed at so much grief.

"And the servant did it!" she burst out at last. "The beastly peasant."

Guy remonstrated: "Darling, really! The girl didn't realise what she was doing."

"That's the trouble. They have the equipment of humans and the understanding of beasts. That is what one hates." She wept again. "My kitten, my poor kitten!" After a while, she blew her nose and asked: "And where was Yakimov when it happened?"

"Ah, that one!" Despina spoke scornfully. "He was asleep."

"He would be asleep." Harriet's anger with the peasant servant was now carried over to Yakimov and Despina tried to divert her by encouraging it.

"What has he done," she asked, "but eat, eat, eat and, sleep, sleep, sleep!" She had, she said, spent all the housekeeping money the Pringles had left with her. She had managed to obtain credit at a shop where she was known to have English employers, but the credit was limited. On Easter Sunday Yakimov had invited in guests – another Prince and a Count – and had demanded a fine meal. Despina, afraid for the honour of the Pringles, was at her wits' end. She had gone to Domnul Professor Inchcape and borrowed two thousand lei.

"Did you tell him why you needed the money?" Harriet asked. Despina nodded.

"And what did he say?"

"He laughed."

"I bet he did."

Despina broke in with another grievance, speaking so rapidly that Harriet could not follow her. Guy translated in a deprecating tone: "He wanted her to wash some clothes. She refused."

"Good for her."

"A mountain of clothes," cried Despina.

"He's leaving today," Harriet promised her and sent her to make tea.

When the tea was brought in, Yakimov appeared, dressed. His demeanour was so nervous that Harriet could say nothing. Despina had bought some iced cakes for the homecoming and he ate his way through them with absentminded sadness. After tea he sat on, huddled over the fire. Harriet, longing to see the back of him, asked where he had found a room.

"Haven't found one yet, dear girl."

"You've left it very late."

"Not been fit to trudge around."

"Aren't you going now?"

He answered brokenly: "Where is poor Yaki to go?"

Despina was working in the bedroom. Harriet, half imagining Yakimov might take himself off in her absence, went to speak to her. A few minutes later Guy came in and spoke to her, quietly and urgently: "Darling, be charitable."

At the word, something turned over inside Harriet in self-accusation, yet she said: "This is my home. I can't share it with someone I despise."

"He has no money. No one will take him in unless he pays in advance. Let him stay. It doesn't cost us anything to let him sleep in the chair."

"It does. It costs me more than you could ever guess. Go and get rid of him."

"Darling, I can't. The fact is, I've already told him he can stay."

She turned her back on him and went over to the dressing-table, reflecting, in a sort of dazed wonder, on how it was that Guy, seemingly reasonable and the most gentle of men, always got his own way.

Guy, accepting her silence as agreement, said with confiding cheerfulness: "You know, darling, it would really pay us to keep Yaki here, where we have a hold on him."

"You mean you may get back some of the money he owes you?"

"No, the money's not important. It's the play. He's ideal for Pandarus. His voice is the very voice of Pandarus. He could make my production."

"Oh, that damned production!"

"If we turn him out," Guy went on happily, "he'll be found wandering and ordered out of the country. If we keep him, he'll have to behave. And I'll make him work. You wait and see."

She replied with decision: "I don't want him here," and, sweeping past Guy, she returned to the sitting-room, where she found Yakimov settled into the arm-chair with the *ţuică* bottle.

21

A FEW DAYS LATER, Guy invited his friends in to a first reading of *Troilus and Cressida*. Before they arrived, Harriet opened the French-windows on to the balcony, Outside, an azure light glinted over the cobbles and silvered the roofs. The days were growing long and warm, and the evening crowds were coming out again. The murmur of the traffic, muted for months by snow, came distinct and new through the open windows. For the first time that year, she left the doors open.

Guy was cutting an old Penguin edition of the play. It was evident, from the businesslike manner in which he answered her, that he was excited.

Harriet had been told she could read Cressida. Yakimov, for whom a camp-bed had been bought and placed in the spare room, was beginning to realise that Guy seriously intended him to take the part of Pandarus. He was expected to learn it by heart When the order had first been given him, he had dismissed it with a smile: "Can't possibly, dear boy. Always was a poor scholar. Never could remember anything."

"I'll see you learn it," Guy replied, and when Yakimov put the matter from his mind, Guy, suddenly and with an astonishing firmness, made it clear that if Yakimov wished to remain in the flat he must play Pandarus. This persuaded him to read the part. Before the night of the first rehearsal, Guy took him through it half-a-dozen times.

Guy, he realised, had complete faith in his ability as a producer. He seemed to have an equal faith in Yakimov. Yakimov himself, with no faith at all, could have wept to find Guy, usually so easy-going, turned to task-master – and no lenient task-master, either. By the evening of the reading he was beginning to remember the lines in spite of himself. He did not know whether to be relieved or sorry. Rising a little out of a nadir of depression, he did his best to greet the visitors. Finding himself treated as one who had an important part in the proceedings, his spirits rose and he began to feel rather pleased with himself.

Inchcape, when he entered, pressed a hand down on Yakimov's shoulder and said: "Good Pandarus – how now, Pandarus?"

"I have had my labour for my travail," Yakimov automatically replied, and at Inchcape's crow of amusement his old easy smile returned.

Guy had had the play typed and duplicated and was now handing out copies to each person who arrived. Soon all the men were present. Bella had been invited and was coming in after a cocktail party. The room became noisy with talk. One of the men was telling a funny story about Hitler's conduct of the war, when Guy called everyone to attention. His manner suggested that the war might be a joke, but this production was not. Rather to Harriet's surprise, the talk stopped at once. The company seated itself and looked to Guy for instructions. He said: "Cressida will read her first dialogue with Pandarus."

Calmly, Harriet moved out on to the floor, mentioning that, unlike most of the girls she had known at school, she had never been ambitious to go on the stage.

Guy frowned at the levity of this approach. Aloof and patient, he said: "Will you please begin."

Yakimov read: "Do you know a man if you see him?" to which Harriet replied with the gaiety of repartee: "Ay, if I ever saw him before, and knew him."

Harriet thought she did rather well. They both did well. Yakimov, who scarcely needed to be anything other than himself, spoke in his delicate, insinuating voice, only accentuating a little, now and then, its natural melancholy or note of comic complaint.

At the end Guy said no more than "All right," then, pointing to Dubedat, said: "Thersites."

As Dubedat ambled out, the bugle sounded from the palace yard, and Harriet began the old chant of "Come, water your horses . . ."

"Please!" Guy commanded her and, silenced, she raised an eyebrow at David, who started to snuffle. Ignoring this, Guy repeated: "Thersites," and Dubedat, his legs still scaled from the ravages of winter, came on to the floor in his new spring outfit of T-shirt and running shorts.

"Begin reading Act Two, Scene One. I'll do Ajax for the moment."

Dubedat read Thersites with a Cockney snivel that was only a slight exaggeration of his normal speech. At the end of the scene, he was applauded, but Guy, not so easily satisfied, said: "The voice will do. But the part calls for venom, not complaint."

Swallowing convulsively, Dubedat set out again, reading at a great rate, but Guy stopped him: "Enough for now. I'd like to hear Ulysses."

Inchcape, whom Harriet was certain would refuse to take a part, now got to his feet with a look of deep satisfaction. Hemming and huffing in his throat, he took a step or two into the middle of the room, and, with feet elegantly planted, shoulders back, looking even now more audience than actor, he said with a smile: "I'm an old hand with theatricals. I always produced the school play. Of course we never attempted anything as frisky as this "

"Act One, Scene Three," said Guy. "The long speech: 'What glory' etcetera."

Still smiling, matching his tone to his smile, Inchcape read with a dry and even humour that Guy accepted, anyway for the moment. "All right," he nodded and Inchcape, taking a step back, twitched up his trousers at the knees and lowered himself carefully back into his seat.

Clarence and David were not yet cast. Guy now suggested that David might attempt Agamemnon.

David's lips parted in alarm. As he came out slowly into the middle of the room, snuffling down at his feet, Harriet saw he was not only amused at the position in which he found himself: he was pleased. After some hesitation, he began to read, pitching his elderly don's voice on too high a note so that he sounded querulous.

Guy broke in on him: "Give it more voice, David. Don't forget you're the General of the Grecian forces."

"Oh, am I? So I am!" Moving his feet nervously, he pushed his glasses up his nose and started again on a deeper note.

Harriet and Yakimov, their star positions fixed in a firmament otherwise chaotic, sat together on the arm-chair, Harriet on the seat, Yakimov on the arm. They had nothing to say to each other, but she felt him relaxed as the impossible had become for him possible, and even, maybe, enjoyable.

Harriet had been feeling a painful anxiety on Guy's behalf. She would have been glad for the production to collapse first rather than last, so sure was she it must collapse sometime.

Now she was beginning to realise she might be wrong. Contrary to her belief, people were not only willing to join in, they were grateful at being included. Each seemed simply to have been awaiting the opportunity to make a stage appearance. She wondered why. Perhaps they thought themselves under-employed here, in a foreign capital, in time of war. Perhaps Guy offered them distraction, a semblance of creative effort, an object to be achieved.

Guy's attitude impressed her, though she had no intention of showing it. He had the advantage of an almost supernatural confidence in dealing with people. It seemed never to occur to him they might not do what he wanted. He had, she noted with surprise, authority.

In the past she had been irritated by the amount of mental and physical vitality he expended on others. As he flung out his charm, like radium dissipating its own brilliance, it had seemed to her indiscriminate giving for giving's sake. Now she saw his vitality functioning to some purpose. Only someone capable of giving much could demand and receive so much. She felt proud of him.

David, coming to the end of a long speech, looked uncertainly at Guy.

"Go on," said Guy. "You're doing splendidly," and David, shouldering importance like a cloak, went ahead with renewed enjoyment.

Bella, arriving in a suit of black corded silk, hung with silver foxes, was asked if she would play Helen.

"Is it a long part?" she asked.

"No."

"Thank goodness for that!" she exclaimed over-fervently.

Inchcape, bending towards her, said: "You are Helen of Troy. We ask only that you should be beautiful. Yours is the face that launched a thousand ships."

"Dear me!" said Bella. She threw off her furs and her cheeks grew pink.

She took the floor, read her exchange with Pandarus and came, flushed and serious, to sit near Harriet. She was, Harriet was beginning to realise, a woman of considerable competence. She knew nothing of acting; she never had been on a stage; her movements were stiff, yet she had done well.

"What about Troilus?" Inchcape asked. "Who can we get for him?"

Guy replied that he was hoping to cast one of the Legation staff for the part. He was waiting for the Minister's approval.

"And Achilles?" asked Inchcape. "Rather a tricky part!"

"I've one of the new students in mind, young Dimancescu, a good-looking boy and a junior fencing champion. He went to an English public-school before the war."

"Indeed! Which?"

"Marlborough."

"Excellent!" said Inchcape. "Excellent!"

Harriet burst out laughing. She said: "Most of your actors have only to play themselves."

Guy turned on her frowning. "Just try and keep quiet," he said.

His annoyance startled her into silence. Guy called the men to read in a group, himself taking the parts still uncast, and avoiding those scenes in which Cressida appeared.

Next day in the students' common-room, Guy held a meeting of those students he proposed using in his production. While he was out, Dobson telephoned to say the Minister would permit any of his staff who wished to take part in the play.

"He approves, then?" Harriet said, surprised.

"He thinks it a splendid idea," said Dobson. "Showing the flag and all that. Cocking a snook at the Boche."

So Harriet had been wrong again. She said to Guy when he returned: "This is wonderful, darling," but he was not responsive. He was, she supposed, absorbed in his production, and the fact made her feel misgiving like a child whose mother is too occupied with the outside world. Still, she was caught in a sort of wonder at the growing reality of the play.

"You are rather remarkable," she admitted. "You make it all seem so easy. You just ignore difficulties that would have brought me completely to a stop."

His only reply was: "I'll take Yaki with me tomorrow. We'll have to start rehearsing seriously."

"And me?"

"No." He was sitting on the edge of the bed tugging at his shoes, trying to get them off without undoing the laces. As he did so, he gazed out of the window with a frown of decision: "I think you'd be more useful doing the costumes."

"Do you mean instead of playing Cressida?"

"Yes."

She was, at first, merely bewildered: "But there isn't anyone else to play Cressida."

"I've already got someone."

"Who?"

"Sophie."

"You invited Sophie to play my part before you'd even told me?" She was dumbfounded. This treatment seemed to her monstrous, but she told herself she was not hurt. She did not care whether she was in the production or not. After a pause she asked: "Did you tell Sophie that I was to have played the part?"

"No, of course not."

"But someone else might have told her."

"They might, of course. What does it matter?"

"You don't think it matters if Sophie learns she has pushed me out of the play?"

"She hasn't pushed you out of the play. It had nothing to do with her. It was simply obvious to me that we couldn't work together. You would never take the production seriously." He started looking about for his slippers. "Anyway, no producer can do a proper job with his wife around."

After she had absorbed the situation she tried to explain it away. Guy, she supposed, found her presence frustrating. She had not actually ridiculed his position – but he feared she might. She made him apprehensive. Her presence spoilt the illusion of power.

After a long interval, she said: "I suppose I deserve it."

"Deserve it? What do you mean?"

"I made no attempt to understand Sophie, or to behave, so I brought out the best in her. I suppose I could have played up to her; shown sympathy or something. I didn't. I was to blame. Now you are giving her an opportunity to get her own back."

"Darling, you are absurd!" Though he laughed at her ideas, he was clearly disconcerted by them. "You can't possibly believe that!" He frowned down at her, his frown affectionate yet perplexed. He put a hand on her shoulder and gave her a slight shake as though seeking to shake her into a semblance of something more comprehensible. He said: "It was only that I had to have someone else. Sophie is suitable. You must agree. You would have done quite well, but I knew I couldn't produce you. The relationship would have got in the way."

She let the matter drop. It was only later when everyone she knew was in it that she began to feel hurt at being out of the production. More than that, she was jealous that Guy should be producing Sophie in one of the chief parts of the play. Unreasonably, she told herself. She could no longer doubt that Guy had been perfectly honest about his relationship with Sophie. Innocent and foolish as he was, the idea of marriage to Sophie had been, nevertheless, attractive as an idea rather than a reality. He was not, in fact, one to make a marriage of self-sacrifice. He was a great deal more self-protected – perhaps from necessity – than most people realised. Realising it herself, she could only wonder at the complexity of the apparently simple creature she had married.

22

THE SPRING SHOWERS WASHED AWAY the last vestiges of the snow. With each reappearance the sun grew warmer. More and more people came out at evening to stroll in the streets. Up the Chaussée, where the chestnut branches were breaking with green, the chatter of the crowd could be heard above the traffic. Despite the delights of the season, it was a disgruntled chatter.

The Cabinet had inaugurated internal retrenchment in order that exports to Germany might be increased. To save petrol, taxis were forbidden to cruise in search of fares: they could be picked up only at given points – an unheard-of inconvenience. Food prices were rising. The new French silks were appearing in the shops at an absurd price. Imported goods were growing scarce and would, it was rumoured, soon disappear altogether. In panic, people were buying many things they did not want.

Guy was not much interested when Harriet described the sense of grievance in the city. His worries were elsewhere. There was, she thought, a sumptuous aloofness about his manner these days. His preoccupation was the deeply contented preoccupation of the creator: he was not to be shaken by trivialities. Even Inchcape, coming in one breakfast time – his usual time for unexpected visits – could rouse little curiosity in Guy, although he made it evident that his news was likely to please Guy less than it pleased him.

He would not sit down, but strolled about the room laughing in high delight at what he had to tell. "Well, well," he said. "Well, *well*!"

The Pringles, knowing that, given encouragement, he would only procrastinate further, waited in silence to hear it.

At last he relented. "You've heard what's happened to your friend Sheppy?" he asked.

They shook their heads.

"Ha!" squawked Inchcape; then, coming to it at last: "He's been arrested."

"No!" said Harriet.

"*Yes*. Down by the Danube. The ass was caught with the gelignite on him."

"Trying to blow up the Iron Gates?"

"Something like that. They were caught in a river-side bar, shouting drunk, talking quite openly about bringing Danube shipping to a standstill. They imagined, because Rumania is supposed to be a British ally, the Danube bargemen would be happy to help sabotage their own livelihood. What a pack of fools! Anyway, they're all under lock and key now. 'A fair cop,' I believe the expression is."

"Who got caught with him? Anyone we know?"

"No, none of the local conscripts were there; only the top brass. This was Sheppy's first expedition – and his last." Inchcape slapped his thigh, crowing at the thought of it. "The first and last sally of Sheppy's Fighting Force."

Harriet smiled at Guy, but Guy might have been a thousand miles removed from the whole matter. She asked Inchcape: "What will become of them?"

"Oh!" Inchcape twisted his mouth down in his ironical smile. "No doubt the F.O. will get them out. They're *much* too valuable to lose."

Rumania did not want a diplomatic incident just then. Sheppy and his 'henchmen' were flown back to England. After that came official denial that he had ever existed. No saboteur, it was stated, could slip past the net spread wide by Rumania's magnificent body of security police. But the story had got around and it added to the general sense of insecurity and victimisation. The press began to write openly of the injustices being suffered by a peaceful nation in someone else's war.

Harriet could now read enough in the Rumanian papers to realise how rapidly Rumania's too distant allies were passing out of favour. No one had been reassured by Chamberlain's declaration that "Hitler has missed the bus". If it were true that England was now an impregnable fortress, then "*tant pis pour les autres*" said *L'Indépendence Romaine*. The fact that Germany, without making any move, was now receiving seventy per cent of all Rumanian exports was not, said *Timpul*, any cause for self-congratulation. Germany's demands would increase with her needs.

What she was not given she would come and take. *Universul* wrote slightingly of those who used Rumania in time of peace but in war-time not only abandoned her defenceless, but sought to sabotage her resources. When, oh when, they all wanted to know, could the great, generous-hearted Rumanian people, now left to buy off the enemy as best they might, again look forward to those summers of joyous frivolity they had known before this senseless war began?

Harriet, a member of an unfavoured nation, felt shut out from Guy's world to face the painful situation alone. With little else to do, she often dropped in at the Athénée Palace to look at the English papers. They were exceptionally dull, concerned usually with some argument about mine-laying in Norwegian waters.

The hotel was as dull as the papers. It was an inert period between seasons: a time of no news when the journalists were elsewhere. Nothing was happening in Bucharest. Nothing, it seemed, was happening anywhere in the world. And, despite all the apprehension, it was likely enough nothing would happen.

But in Bucharest, anyway, apprehension was not groundless. The political atmosphere was changing. A notice appeared under the glass of the café tables to say it was forbidden under threat of arrest to discuss politics. And arrest, it was said, might lead one to the new concentration camp being organised on the German model by Guardists trained in Dachau and Buchenwald. People said the camp was hidden somewhere in the remote Carpathians. No one could say exactly where.

One showery morning, as she came from the hotel, Harriet was struck by the appearance of a young man sheltering beneath the lime trees that over-reached the garden wall.

The rain had stopped. The young leaves flashed their green against a sky of indigo cloud. The cloud was breaking. A gleam touched the wet tarmac. The young man, although neither beggar nor peasant, remained by the wall with nothing to do apparently but stand there. He was dressed in the city grey much worn by the middle classes, but he was unlike any middle-class Rumanian Harriet had ever seen. He was hard and thin. His was a new sort of face in this town. Looking at his hollowed cheeks, meeting his unfriendly gaze, she told herself he must be one of the Guardist youths newly returned from Germany. He looked at the moment not so much dangerous as ill-at-ease. Here he was, returned to a city grown unfamiliar to him, a destroyer, perhaps, but for the moment powerless.

After she had seen this one, she began to see others like him. They stood about the streets, their pallid, bony faces sometimes scarred like the faces of German duellists. They watched the pampered crowds with the contempt, and uncertainty, of the deprived. They were waiting as though they knew their day would come.

To Guy, Harriet said sombrely: "They're a portent. The fascist infiltration."

"They're probably not even Guardists," Guy said.

"Then what are they?"

"I wouldn't know."

He was cutting down Ulysses's speeches in his copy of *Troilus and Cressida*, giving all his mind to the job, determined not to let outside things distract him.

Harriet had been comforted a little by Clarence's indignation when he found she was no longer in the cast. He left a rehearsal to telephone her, vehemently demanding: "*Harry*, what is this little bitch doing in your part? Have you walked out of the show?"

"No, I was put out."

"Why?"

"Guy said he couldn't work with me. He said I didn't take him seriously."

"Why should you? It's only a footling end-of-term show, anyway. If you're not in it, I don't want to be in it."

Harriet reacted sharply to this. It was important to her that Guy's project should succeed. "You must stay in," she insisted. "He will need everyone he can get. And it will probably be quite good."

Clarence, who had been given the sizeable part of Ajax, did not argue about this, but grumbled: "It's awful having Sophie around. She's beginning to queen it insufferably." He said he had no intention of attending all the rehearsals. Between his work for Inchcape and his work with the Poles, he was much too busy.

The truth was, as Harriet knew, he did almost nothing at the Propaganda Bureau and very few Poles remained. The camps were almost empty. Of the officers who had entertained him on several wild occasions, scarcely one remained. They had all been smuggled over the frontier to join the fighting forces in France. Clarence, who had organised these escapes, had worked himself out of work. He needed distraction. He invited Harriet to have dinner with him next evening. There was in his giving and her acceptance of this invitation a certain revolt against Guy and the importance he gave to his production.

Next morning at breakfast, when Guy announced another day of rehearsals, Harriet asked: "Must you keep at it like a maniac?"

"It's the only way to get it done."

His method revealed to her what she least expected to find in him – a neurotic intensity.

She said: "I'm going out to dinner with Clarence tonight."

"Oh, good! And now I must get Yaki up."

"When can we hope to get rid of that incubus?" Harriet crossly asked.

"I expect he'll find a room when his remittance comes. Meanwhile, he must be fed and housed and accepted, like a child."

"A pretty cunning child."

"He's harmless, anyway. If the world was composed of Yakimovs, there'd be no wars."

"There'd be no anything."

It was the morning of the 9th of April. Guy and Yakimov had just left when the telephone rang. Lifting the receiver, Harriet heard Bella crying to her: "Have you heard the news?"

"No."

"Germany has invaded Norway, Sweden and Denmark. I've just heard it on the wireless." Bella spoke excitedly, expecting excited response. When Harriet did not give it, she said: "Can't you *see*! It means they aren't coming here."

"It doesn't mean they won't come."

Harriet, though disturbed, imagining any move to be a danger signal, understood Bella's relief. The blow had fallen elsewhere. For Rumania there was, if not a reprieve, a stay of execution. Standing by the balcony door, Harriet could see the square and roofs pearl-white beneath the vast white misted sky. From different points miniature dark figures were converging on the newsboys like ants on specks of food. She could hear the mouse-squeaks of the boys calling a special edition. Wanting to share the situation with someone, she said to Bella: "Let's meet at Mavrodaphne's."

"Oh, I can't," said Bella. "Guy has called a rehearsal. I must go. Rehearsals are such fun."

Harriet went out and bought a paper. The invasion was announced in the stop press with a statement made by the Minister of Information to the effect that the news need rouse no apprehension in Rumanian hearts. Carol, the Great and Good, Father of Culture, Father of his People, had nearly completed the mighty Carol Line and soon Rumania would be surrounded by a wall of fire that would repel any invader.

People stood in groups about the paper-sellers talking loudly. Harriet could hear the agitated staccato of their voices as they called to one another: "*Alors, ça a enfin commencé, la guerre?*" "*Oui, ça commence.*" Her own fears renewed, she crossed the square and started to walk up the Chaussée. As she went, the sun that had been inching its way through the mist, broke out, suddenly resplendent, unrolling light like golden silk at her feet. All in a moment, the sky became cloudless and blue with the blue of summer. Piccolos were running out with poles to pull the blinds down over Dragomir's windows. All over the façades of buildings striped awnings were being lowered – red and yellow, blue and white, fringed, tasselled and corded – while windows and doors were opening and people were coming out on to balconies. The balcony plants could be seen now to be swelling and spreading and growing green. Already there were little bowers of tender shoots that would, by late summer, become bedraggled tangles of coarse creepers. The cement walls, blotched and grey when the sky was grey, now gleamed like marble.

Up the Chaussée, where the women, unprepared for this sudden brilliance, were holding up handbags to shield their eyes, people were distracted from the war news. The cafés were putting chairs out in gardens and on pavements. Even as the chairs were placed in position customers were sitting down on them, beginning, without delay and with a new gaiety, the outdoor life of summer.

When Harriet reached the building that was supposed to be a museum of folk art, she saw some paintings were on show. She went inside. Rumanians did not express themselves well in paint. Indeed, there were no pictures in Bucharest worth looking at except the King's El Grecos, nine in number, bought for a song before El Greco returned to fashion, and these were not on show to the public. The exhibitors at the salon were mediocre, imitating every genre of modern painting, but they were numerous. She was able to spend a long time looking at them. When she came out, she walked back across the square into the Calea Victoriei and, passing through the parrot-land of the gypsy flower-sellers, reached the British Propaganda Bureau. No one was looking at the pictures of British cruisers that curled and yellowed in the sun, but there was a crowd round the German Bureau opposite. Curiosity propelled her across the road.

The window was filled with a map of Scandinavia. Arrows, three inches wide, cut from red cardboard, pointed the direction of the German attack. In the crowd no one spoke. People stood awed by the arrogant swagger of the display. Harriet, trying to look indifferent to it, made for the University building. It was now nearly luncheon time, so she might, with reason, call for Guy.

The main door of the University building lay open but there was no porter inside. Term did not begin until the end of April. The vaulted, empty passages looked bleak and smelt of beeswax and linoleum. Harriet was guided by the distant sound of Guy's voice saying:

" 'Indeed, a tapster's arithmetic may soon bring his particulars therein to a total.' " Cressida, he went on to explain, was making fun of Troilus. A tapster's arithmetic being notoriously limited, the particulars could not be very great. "Now again," he said, beginning the speech in a bantering manner.

The words were taken up and repeated in the same manner – this time by a female voice. Sophie's voice. Harriet heard it with a pang of jealousy so acute she stopped in her tracks. She was about to retreat – but what point in retreating? Sooner or later, she had to face Sophie in this part.

She went on slowly. The door stood open at the end of the corridor. She came to it silently, expecting a crowd of players among whom she could enter unnoticed, but only Sophie, Yakimov and Guy remained.

The common-room, dark-panelled and without windows, was large and gloomy. It was lit by a central dome. The three stood under the dome. Guy had one foot on a chair and his script on his knee, the other two were performing before him. No one noticed Harriet as she took a seat by the wall.

As Sophie and Yakimov went through speech after speech, with Guy interrupting and enforcing constant repetitions, she began to realise she could not have tolerated for long the tedium of rehearsals. She might not have required to be interrupted so often or to receive so many explanations of the words she spoke – but these interruptions and explanations were no hardship to Guy. He delighted in them. In fact he probably preferred a Cressida who would be entirely of his own making.

As for the other two . . . Yakimov and Sophie? She realised that what would be tedium to her was to them self-aggrandisement.

Sophie, of course, had never lacked vanity. She had the usual Rumanian face, dark-eyed, pasty and too full in the cheeks, but her manner of seating and holding herself demanded for her the deference due to a beauty. Now that her self-importance seemed justified, there was a flaunting of this demand. All the attention must be for her. When Guy gave it to Yakimov, she wanted it back again, interrupting the rehearsal every few minutes to ask: "*Chéri,* don't you think here I might do this?" or "Here, while he is saying this, I make like so? You agree? You agree?" posturing her little backside, imbuing all her moves and *moues* with a quality of sensuous and lingering caress. She seemed to be in a state of inspired, almost ecstatic, excitement about it all. She wriggled with sex.

Although she could not refrain from flirting even with Yakimov, for Guy she kept a special look, inciting and conspiratorial, which did not, Harriet noted, appear to disconcert him. He accorded Sophie now exactly the same kindly but unemotional sympathy he had accorded her when she imagined herself neglected, injured and suicidal.

While Sophie attacked direction, Yakimov responded to it. Though he appeared to have taken on size and substance, he did exactly what Guy required him to do. Harriet could imagine Guy's satisfaction in producing from Yakimov the version of the performance he would have chosen to give himself. She could feel between the two men a warmth of mutual approval. Yakimov received the acclaim which Sophie sought, with the result that there was in her demanding interruptions a querulousness that roused Harriet's sympathy. She, too, was beginning to feel excluded.

Suddenly Guy picked up his script and said: "We'll stop now."

When they became aware of her, Harriet said: "You've heard they've invaded Norway and Denmark?"

Oh yes, everyone had heard that by now. Guy had already discounted the news. "It was to be expected," he said. "Once we started mining Norwegian waters, Germany had no choice but to invade."

"Perhaps we mined them because Germany was planning to invade."

"Perhaps!" Guy did not want to discuss the subject further.

Harriet marvelled at his ability to turn his back on the news. For herself she always faced anxieties, believing that, unfaced, they would leap upon her and devour her. Perhaps Guy would not face what he was not in a position actively to combat. She should be glad, she supposed, that he had this production as a bolt-hole.

What annoyed her was that Yakimov and Sophie, to play up to him, were echoing his unconcern. They were set apart from the implications of the invasion: they were people with more important matters in mind. Harriet felt particularly irritated with Sophie, who was, she knew, as liable to panic as any other Rumanian.

Guy said: "We'll go and have a drink." As they left the dark University hall and came out to the dazzle of day, he exclaimed: "Isn't it wonderful!"

Sophie laughed shortly: "How ridiculous the English are about the sun! In England they hold up their faces, so . . ." she goggled absurdly up at the sky, "and say..." she cooed absurdly: "'Oh, the sun, the sun!' Here, I can tell you, we get sick of the sight of it."

Harriet asked her how she was enjoying her part in the play. Her only answer was a shrug and a sulky down-droop of her full lips. Was it possible that, despite her advantage. she resented Harriet's appearance on the scene? Had she imagined that, having displaced Harriet in the part, she might displace her altogether? "Really!" thought Harriet, "the girl is ridiculous!"

As Guy made to cross the road, Sophie paused and asked where they were going. He answered: "To the Doi Trandafiri." Fretfully, she said: "I don't want to go there. It's always so crowded."

"Oh well," said Guy. "We'll see you later."

As Sophie went off, looking angry, Harriet said: "If you don't make a fuss of your poor leading lady, you'll be losing her."

"I don't think so." Guy spoke easily. "She's enjoying herself too much."

In the café, he said: "I want to hear Yakimov in a few scenes." They read three scenes and between each Guy bought Yakimov a *ţuică*.

At the end, Yakimov asked: "How was I?" and there was in the question a tremulous anxiety.

"Splendid," said Guy, his approval so whole-hearted that Yakimov's cheeks grew pink.

Gratified, Yakimov breathed: "Dear boy!" and was for a moment bemused like a child becoming aware of its own qualities.

Harriet noticed a change in him, not great, but radical. Guy had roused in him a will to excel.

"You know," said Guy, "you have the makings of a great actor."

"Have I?" Yakimov's question was modest, but not disclaiming. He fixed on Guy eyes glowing with admiring gratitude.

"But you must learn your lines."

"Oh, I will, dear boy. Don't fear, *I will*."

As Harriet watched, it seemed to her this nebula of a man, so long inert, was starting slowly to evolve.

23

A WEEK AFTER THE GERMAN INVASION of Denmark and Norway, Inchcape displayed in the British Propaganda Bureau window a map of the Scandinavian countries with the loss of the German destroyers at Narvik restrainedly marked in blue. In time came the landings of British troops at Namsos and Andalsnes.

In the window opposite, the red arrows of Germany thrust the Norwegians back and back. One day the Allies announced an advance, another the Germans announced an Allied retreat. Merely a strategic retreat, said the British News Service. The Germans, advancing up the Gudbranstal, claimed they had joined up with their Trondheim forces. The British admitted a short withdrawal.

Every morning the passers-by, lured by these first remote moves in the war, crossed the road to compare window with window; but it was the blatant menace of the giant red arrows that held the crowd. The pro-British faction of the press predicted a British counter-attack that would finish the Germans once and for all. But even while this prediction was being made, the Germans reached Andalsnes. Four thousand Norwegians had surrendered; the politicians fled; the Allies took to the sea. It was suddenly a German victory.

The map with the red arrows disappeared. The window remained empty. No one was much impressed. The move had not, after all, been the beginning of events. It seemed a step into a cul-de-sac. The audience waited for more spectacular entertainment.

At the beginning of May, Harriet had to face her task of dressing the players. Inchcape had written to the London office and obtained a small grant towards the production. Most of this money was required for the hire of the theatre and theatre staff. What remained could be expended on the costumes. Harriet had been envisaging some such gorgeous display as she had seen in London productions of Shakespeare. The money she had in hand would barely cover the cast in sack-cloth.

She found that costumes could be hired from the theatre and went with Bella to see those made for a production of *Antony and Cleopatra* some ten years before. They had been used on every possible occasion since and were threadbare and elaborately ugly.

"Filthy, too," said Bella, who had been examining them keenly. She twitched her fingers in distaste. "Can you see Helen in that pea-green plush?"

Feeling discouraged, like a child set a task beyond its years, Harriet, who had not wanted the task in the first place, tried to hand it back to Guy. Guy, adept at delegating work, simply laughed at her. "Don't make difficulties, darling. It's all quite simple. Don't have armour – actors hate it, anyway. Just suggest it. Hire a few helmets, swords and so on from the theatre. Hire the cloaks, too. Put the Greeks into skirts and corselets – quite easy to make with canvas. The Trojans, being Asiatics, could wear tights – they're the cheapest things possible."

"But the Rumanians would be bewildered."

"They'd love it. A new idea – that's all they want."

Having, with a few words, reduced the task to an absurdity, Guy swept off, leaving her with the sense that she had made a great deal of fuss about nothing.

Clarence offered to drive her wherever she wanted to go. One evening in early May they drove to a suburb where there was a factory that made theatrical tights. Harriet, when called for, found Clarence's associate Steffaneski in the car. Clarence was combining the trip to the factory with some Polish business. The two passengers greeted one another rather blankly. Neither found the other easy company and each had regarded this occasion as his own. Clarence, who had nothing to say, seemed equally displeased with both of them. It was as though the presence of each had caused a rift between himself and the other. It occurred to Harriet that Clarence was the friend of the solitary personality, and he wanted to be the only friend. He was the friend of Harriet and the friend of Steffaneski – but not of both together. Siding, as he did, with the misfits, he was troubled now by not knowing with which to side. His face was glum.

As they drove out through the long grey low-built streets that stretched towards the country, Harriet, who thought the Count the least occupied of men, broke the silence by suggesting he might take part in the play.

He turned from her in morose scorn. "I have not," he said, "time for such things. I do not make play while the war is fought."

"But you can't fight here."

Steffaneski, suspecting he was being teased, gave an exasperated twitch of the lips.

In this area of Bucharest the buildings were of all wood. These were not the shacks of the very poor, but roomy, well-built shops and houses like those in a Middle West shanty town. The wide, unmade road, under water in spring, was still a quagmire, with stretches of standing water reddened by the evening sun.

The car rocked and squelched, then came to a standstill. Clarence pressed the accelerator. The wheels turned in the mud but did not move forward.

"We're here for the night," said Clarence.

"Perhaps Count Steffaneski would get out and push," said Harriet.

The Count stared, unhearing, from the window. Clarence, unamused by Harriet's humour, was becoming acutely irritable, when, unexpectedly, the wheels caught and the car lunged forward.

They found the address Harriet had been given. She had hoped for a theatrical workroom, a sort of studio perhaps, with something of the self-contained creative life she most missed in Bucharest. What she found was a large wooden hut like a garage. Inside there was a single room where a dozen peasants, some still at the level of peasant dress, were working on knitting machines. There was not even a chair to offer the customer. The light was failing. Some oil-lamps hung from the rafters and the air was heavy from a smoking wick.

A gaunt little man, wearing peasant trousers but a jacket that was part of an old morning suit, came forward, unsmiling, and raised his brows. As he stood beside Harriet, silent and expressionless, she could not tell whether or not she were conveying her needs to him. She had written down the sets of measurements in metres and, beside each, the colour required. When she finished speaking, he nodded. She could not believe he had grasped it all so quickly. When she tried to explain further, he bent, touched his ankle and drew his hand up to his waist.

"*Da, da, precis,*" she agreed.

He nodded again and waited for her to go.

She went, doubtfully.

"All right?" Clarence asked as he started the car again.

"I don't know." She could not believe that the man had grasped so rapidly what had been conveyed in very poor Rumanian.

On the way back, Clarence turned into an alleyway, a deep rift of mud, and stopped at a warehouse, another wooden hut, its doors held with a padlock. It housed the goods sent out from England for the relief of the Poles. Harriet, when she followed the men in, gazed about in wonder at the bales of linen, the sheets, blankets and pillows, the shirts and underwear, the crates of knitted garments.

"What are you going to do with it all?" she asked.

Clarence said: "That is what we have come here to decide."

Harriet, wandering round and examining things, waited for a discussion to take place, but neither of the men said anything.

Harriet fingered a pile of shirts and suggested they could let Guy have some of them. "He only owns three," she said.

Clarence thrust out his lower lip, looking wary and important. After some reflection, he said: "I might *lend* him a few."

"Yes, do." Harriet began picking out the largest shirts.

"Just a minute." Clarence strode over to her with an air of nervous decision, obviously afraid she would get the better of him, and said: "I will lend him two."

She gave a laugh of derisive annoyance. "Really, Clarence, are you sure you can spare them?" Clarence looked the more obstinate.

Steffaneski, consciously aloof from their quarrel, said: "Is it not to be decided what we do with this stuff?"

"It might be sold to the Rumanian army," said Clarence.

The suggestion, tentative as it was, was accepted without hesitation: "Agreed. Now I wait in the car." Steffaneski strode out, leaving Harriet and Clarence to face one another, each in a state of sparking annoyance.

"What about underwear?" Harriet began turning over a pile of vests.

Clarence pushed her away: "I have to account for these things."

"Guy has almost no underwear."

The more Harriet persisted, the more obstinate Clarence became; the more she felt his obstinacy, the more she persisted. At last, Clarence said: "I'll lend him two vests and two pairs of pants."

She accepted this offer defiantly, knowing he expected her to refuse.

When they left the warehouse, Clarence locked the doors ostentatiously. Harriet, smiling with anger, carried her prizes to the car, where Steffaneski, one shoulder hunched against a window, sat biting the side of his left thumb. He stared into the distance.

Returning to the city's centre, no one had anything to say. When they reached the cross-roads and the statue of the boyar Cantacuzino, it was late twilight. The office workers were fighting their way on to the trams. In the Calea Victoriei the car was held up by the crowd round the window of the German Propaganda Bureau.

Harriet said: "There's a new map in the window." Without speaking, Clarence stopped the car and got out. Rising tall and lean above the heads of the Rumanians, he stood for some moments and gazed into the window, then turned in a business-like way and opened the car door. "Well, it's begun," he said.

"What do you mean?" Harriet asked.

"Germany has invaded the Lowlands. They've overrun Luxembourg. They're already inside Holland and Belgium. They claim they're advancing rapidly."

As he got into the car, neither Harriet nor Steffaneski spoke. Chilled with nervous excitement, she reflected that while they had been wrangling about shirts and underwear this news had been waiting like a tiger to pounce on them.

"This comes of the folly of Belgium," said Steffaneski. "They would not permit a Maginot Line to the sea. Now" – he struck his finger across his throat – "Belgium is *kaput*." He sounded more angry than anything else.

"Not yet," said Harriet.

"Wait. You know nothing. But I – I have seen the Germans advance."

"Yes, but not against British troops."

"Wait," said Steffaneski again, his face impassively grim.

Clarence hooted his way round the crowd. The windows of Inchcape's office were dark. Clarence smiled at Harriet, reconciled to her in the exhilaration that comes when outside events take over one's life. She smiled back.

"This time," he said, "it'll be a fight to a finish. Let's go and have a drink."

24

FOR YAKIMOV THESE WERE BLISSFUL DAYS. Each morning his breakfast was brought into his room. He had persuaded Guy that he could 'study' best in bed and Guy had persuaded Harriet to let him be served there. He was awakened too early, of course. The tray was slapped down angrily by Despina, who then threw up his blind, startling him out of sleep, and slammed his door as she departed. Her attitude was a pity. He could have put her to good use, cleaning and pressing his clothes: but she was not to be won. Faithfully she reflected Harriet's disapproval of him.

Harriet herself behaved as though unaware of his presence in the flat. He had always been nervous of her, but now, knowing that while Guy needed him, Guy would protect him, he no longer attempted to placate her. He merely avoided her.

Those mornings when Guy did not force him up for an early rehearsal, he would lie on after breakfast, dozing, a copy of *Troilus and Cressida* open on the counterpane. His room had two doors, one opening on to the hall, one on to the living-room. Through the delicious apathy of half-sleep, he could hear Despina complete her work in the room, and hear the front door close as Harriet left the flat. When both were out of the way, he would rouse himself and bath and dress in comfortable solitude.

Yakimov did not care to appear alone for meals in the flat. Understanding this, Guy, if too occupied with a rehearsal to break it, would send him out for sandwiches. When they returned for meals together, Yakimov would sit at the table silent in Guy's shadow. The plainness of the Pringle food was regrettable. He saw things in the shops for which he longed – a very thick, green variety of asparagus, for instance, about which he attempted a hint one day: "Am told it's excellent, dear girl; and cheap at the moment. This is the season for it," but it did not appear. As a result of this limited diet, he was constantly hungry, not for food, but for rich food. Whenever he could borrow the money he went to a restaurant to eat alone. Dobson had refused to lend him any more, but he was able to persuade an occasional 'thou' out of Fitzsimon, the good-looking third secretary who was to play Troilus, and Foxy Leverett, who was cast as Hector.

Guy had forbidden Yakimov to borrow from students, but when pestered by one of them to explain his brilliance as an actor he would take the chance to whisper rapidly: "Wonder, dear boy, could you spare a *leu* or two?" and seize what was offered and make off with the celerity that Bacon preferred to secrecy.

He could also make a little pocket-money when he dined out with the Pringles. Guy, who over-tipped in a manner Yakimov thought rather ill-bred, always left a heap of small coins on the table for the piccolo. Yakimov, insisting that Guy precede him from the table, would pocket all he could gather up as he passed.

Guy was absurdly careless with money. One noonday, when they were rehearsing alone, Yakimov saw him pull out with his handkerchief two thousand-*lei* notes. Retrieving, and borrowing, these unseen, Yakimov excused himself and went to Çina's, where he sat on the terrace eating the asparagus of which he had been deprived and heard the orchestra play in the elegant *chinois* stand over which the Canary creeper was breaking into flower.

What he experienced in these days was what he had experienced with Dollie, the consolations of security. When he did not know where his next meal was coming from, he was usually too driven by hunger to feel pity for himself. Now, as he lay in bed, contemplating his profound need for care and protection, a tear would often trickle down his cheek; a luxurious, an enjoyable tear. He had found again in Guy the figure of the provider. More than that, Guy gave him, as Dollie had failed to give, the comfortable sense that he was earning his keep. And he was not only secure in the flat, he was secure in the country. The Legation was on his side. He was doing a job for British prestige. Should his *permis de séjour* be cancelled, Foxy or Fitzsimon would see that it was renewed. Above all, he had become again what he had been in the old days – a personality.

He was modest in acceptance of praise. When Foxy Leverett said: "You're magnificent, dear fellow. How do you do it?", when the large-bosomed girl students crowded round him squealing: "You are *so* good, Prince Yakimov; tell us how you are so good," he shook his head, smiling, and said: "I really do not know," that being no less than the truth.

Since the term began, the junior students had been left to Guy's staff of English teachers; the seniors had been absorbed into the play. Only a few had speaking parts; the others, cast as soldiers and attendants, were called to all rehearsals so that they might improve their diction and their knowledge of the play. Guy frequently lectured them, elucidating its obscure passages. They formed an ever-present background to the production – and Yakimov was their hero.

His success as Pandarus surprised him less than it surprised anyone else. He had always nursed the belief that if he ever tried to exert himself the result would be remarkable. At school, where he had been the droll of the class, one of the masters had said: "Yakimov is such a fool, he must be a genius." And Dollie had often said: "There's more to Yaki than you think."

He had always supposed that success called for effort, and effort was something he particularly disliked. It was the ease of his triumph that surprised him. Guy had given him no more than a push and he had stumbled forward into achievement. He was charmed by his success, and assured. He began to believe not only in the present, but the future. Something, he was sure, would come of his performance as Pandarus. He would live off it for the rest of his life.

Had he been pressed to define what might come of it, he would have looked back no further than to the days when he had been a war correspondent. He had a hankering after the privileges and prominence of that position, and, more than anything, for an expense account that would permit him once more to revel in unlimited food and drink. Perhaps someone would invite him to become a war correspondent again!

Meanwhile, he stood unobtrusively at Guy's elbow, accepting drinks from his admirers with murmurs of gratitude. Guy was the centre of the group. Guy did the talking. Yakimov told himself: 'The dear boy likes the limelight' – this observation being no more critical than that which he had once made about Dollie: 'The dear girl likes her own way.' He did no more than speak a warning to himself: he wanted to keep his place. For this reason, quite seriously and admiringly he spoke of Guy these days as 'the impresario', flattering him with the exotic importance of the appellation.

The group usually drank in the Doi Trandafiri. For some

reason, Guy was not willing to go to the English Bar, which Yakimov much preferred. The only advantage he could see in the Doi Trandafiri was that the drinks were cheaper – and that was no advantage when one was not paying for them.

One day before the German 'take-over', having acquired a little money, he could not resist dropping into the English Bar to show himself hastily, a man much in demand elsewhere, to Hadjimoscos, Horvath and Cici Palu. The three noted his appearance with cold and narrow nods. He had just enough to buy a round of *ţuică*, thus coaxing out of them a meagre show of affability. Hadjimoscos asked: "And where, dear Prince, have you been, away from us all this time?"

"I'm taking part in a play," he replied with satisfaction.

"*A play!*" Hadjimoscos's smile grew wide with malice. "Have you then found employment in the theatre?"

"Certainly not," said Yakimov, shocked. "It is an amateur show. Several important members of the British Legation are taking part."

The others looked at one another. They pretended to hide their scorn under an air of bafflement. How very bizarre the English were! As a result, Yakimov felt it necessary to imply that the play was a cover for something more important – something to do with the secret service. Hadjimoscos raised his eyebrows. Horvath and Palu looked blank. Yakimov opened his mouth, but was saved from further folly by the entrance of Galpin, taut and jumpy with news. There was a general movement of enquiry. All present, except Yakimov, became alert with expectancy. Yakimov was bewildered to see Hadjimoscos, Horvath and Palu united with the rest.

"They're across the Meuse," Galpin announced. "The Dutch Army has just capitulated."

Yakimov did not know who was across the Meuse, but having heard rumours of their rapid advance through Holland, he supposed 'they' must be the Germans. He said: "Why so alarmed, dear boy? They're not coming our way."

No one took any notice of this remark. Yakimov felt completely outside the society of the bar, that, occupied with the movements of a far-off army, had no interest in Yakimov or his performance in a play. Discomforted, he left, with no desire to return, understanding now why Guy preferred to make his own world at the Doi Trandafiri and attend only to his production.

Rehearsals were becoming intensive. Guy had announced that the theatre was booked for the night of June 14th. That gave the players a month in which to perfect themselves. They had no time to brood on present anxieties. They lived now to pursue a war of the past. The common-room at rehearsal time was always crowded with students. Some came who had no part in the play; others were not even in the English faculty. The production had become a craze among them. Yakimov was talked about throughout the University. His arrival in the common-room would give rise to a fury of whispering. Some of the students would call out as at the entry of a hero. He would smile around, radiating good-will over his admirers, seeing no one very clearly.

The only others accorded anything like this reception by the students were Guy, Sophie and Fitzsimon. Guy was not only producer but a popular figure in his own right. Sophie was one of them. Fitzsimon was acclaimed for his extraordinary good looks and his easy, casual manner admired by the girls, whom he ogled with exaggerated eye movements whenever Sophie let his attention wander. When he announced that 'on the night' he intended to gild his hair, the girls gave little screams of shocked excitement. He took his part more seriously than anyone had hoped.

Most members of this enclosed fellowship had forgotten the war altogether, but even here reality sometimes intruded. One or other of the Legation members would throw in the bad news – there was no good news these days – with the humour of one whose duty it is to keep calm: "Just heard the bastards have taken Boulogne" or "Those blighters have got Calais now."

"*Calais!*"

Even to Yakimov this was the fall of a neighbour. Yet what could be done about it? Nothing. It was a relief for them all to turn their attention to the fall of Troy.

Before the end of May, Yakimov had memorised all his lines. Guy let him make his speeches without interruption. After the first complete run-through, Guy looked round at the thirty-seven men and women of the cast, and as they looked anxiously back at him, said: "It's shaping. Cressida is good. Helen, Agamemnon, Troilus, Ulysses, Thersites – good. Pandarus – very good. The rest of you will have to work."

One day Harriet broke in on them with the smell of outdoor anxiety still about her, startling them back to the present.

Guy, running his fingers through his hair, had been lecturing his audience on the character of Achilles, who, offered the alternative of a long life spent in peaceful obscurity and a short life of glory, chose the latter. In Homer, Guy was saying, Achilles was the ideal of the military hero: but Shakespeare, whose sympathies had been with the Trojans, had depicted him as a fascist whose feats were performed by fascist thugs. Young Dimancescu, standing hand on hip, idly playing with a foil, was smiling a wan, warped smile, satisfied by this interpretation of his part. He turned this smile, lifting his brows a little in surprise, as Harriet walked in to the middle of the room, Clarence behind her.

Guy paused, brought to a stop by something in her manner. He asked: "What is the matter?"

She said: "The British troops have left Europe. They've got away."

What she had brought was news of the Dunkirk evacuation.

"They say it was wonderful," she said. "Wonderful." Her voice broke.

Yakimov looked in a puzzled way at Guy. "What is it, dear boy?" he asked. "A victory?"

"A sort of victory," said Clarence. "We've saved our army."

But the students, crowding up against Harriet and the circle round her, glanced at one another and started to whisper among themselves. Evidently to them it was no sort of victory. The Allied armies, that existed, among other things, for the protection of Rumania, had disintegrated. The French were being routed; the English had fled to their own island: the rest had capitulated. Who was to protect Rumania now?

Harriet, in the centre of the floor, did not move until Guy put his hand to her elbow and gave her a slight push, gently impatient. "We must get on," he said.

She stood for a moment, frowning at him, seeming unable to keep him in focus, then she said: "I suppose you'll come home some time."

As she went, Clarence started to follow her, but Guy called to him: "Clarence, I want you." Clarence paused, about to excuse himself, then was caught under Guy's influence. He said: "Very well," and Harriet returned alone to the uneasy streets.

25

INCHCAPE'S SERVANT, Pauli, made a model in a sand-box of the British Expeditionary Force queueing for embarkation on the Dunkirk beaches. The little ships stood in a sea of blue wax. Inchcape put it in the window of the Propaganda Bureau. Though it was skilfully made, it was a sad-looking model. The few who bothered to give it a glance must have thought the British now had nothing to offer but a desperate courage.

In Bucharest the most startling effect of events was the change in the news films. French films ceased to arrive. Perhaps there was no one left with the heart to make them. English-speaking films were blocked by the chaos of Europe. What did come, with triumphant regularity, were the U.P.A. news films.

People sat up at them, aghast, overwhelmed by the fervour of the young men on the screen. There was nothing here of the flat realism of the English news, nothing of the bored inactivity which people had come to expect. Every camera trick was used to enhance the drama of the German machines reaping the cities as they passed. Their destructive lust was like a glimpse of the dark ages. The fires of Rotterdam shot up livid against the midnight sky. They roared from the screen. The camera backed, barely evading a shower of masonry as tall façades, every window aflame, crashed towards the audience. Bricks showered through the air. Cathedral spires, towers that had withstood a dozen other wars, great buildings that had been a wonder for centuries, all toppled into dust.

Clarence, sitting beside Harriet, said in his slow, rich voice: "I bet these films are faked."

People shifted nervously in their seats. Those nearest glanced askance at him, fearful of his temerity.

The cameras moved between the poplars of a Flemish road. On either side stood lorries, disabled or abandoned, their doors ripped open and their contents – bread, wine, clothing, medical supplies, munitions – pulled out and left contemptuously in disarray. In the main streets of towns from which the inhabitants had fled, the invaders sprawled asleep in the sunshine. These were the golden days, the spring of the year. Outside one town, among the young corn, tanks lay about, disabled. Each had its name chalked upon it: *Mimi, Fanchette, Zephyr*. One that stood lop-sided, its guns rakishly tilted, was called *Inexorable*.

On the day that news came of the bombing of Paris, a last French film reached Bucharest, like a last cry out of France. It showed refugees trudging a long, straight road; feet, the wheels of perambulators, faces furtively glancing back; children by the road-side drinking in turn from a mug; the wing of a swooping plane, a spatter of bullets, a child spread-eagled on the road. The French film cried: "Pity us"; the German film that followed derided pity.

Out of the smoke of some lost city appeared the German tanks. They followed each other in an endless stream into the sunlight, driving down from Ypres and Ostend. A signboard said: *Lille – 5 kilomètres*. There seemed to be no resistance. The Maginot Line was being skirted. The break-through had been so simple, it was like a joke.

And the fair-haired young men standing up in their tanks came unscathed and laughing from the ruins. They held their faces up to the sun. They sang: "What does it matter if we destroy the world? When it is ours, we'll build it up again."

The tanks, made monstrous by the camera's tilt, passed in thousands – or, so it seemed. The audience – an audience that still thought in terms of cavalry – sat watching, motionless, in silence. This might of armour was a new thing; a fearful and merciless thing. The golden boys changed their song. Now, as the vast procession passed, they sang:

> "*Wir wollen keine Christen sein,*
> *Weil Christus war ein Judenschwein.*
> *Und seine Mutter, welch ein Hohn,*
> *Die heisst Marie, gebor'ne Kohn.*"

Someone gasped. There was no other noise.

Harriet, alone this time, at a matinée, surrounded by women, felt they were stunned. Yet, as she left in the crowd, she heard in its appalled whispering a twitter of excitement. One woman said: "Such beautiful young men!" and another replied: "They were like the gods of war!"

It was strange to emerge into the streets and see the buildings standing firm. Harriet now had somewhere to go. She went straight to the Athénée Palace garden, that had become a meeting-place for the English since they were dispossessed of the English Bar.

The bar itself had been occupied by the Germans one morning at the end of May. The move was obviously deliberate. It was a gesture, jubilantly planned and carried out by a crowd of journalists, businessmen and members of the huge Embassy retinue. The English – only three were present at the time – let themselves be elbowed out without a struggle. The Germans had the advantage of their aggressive bad manners, the English the disadvantage of their dislike of scenes.

Galpin was the first of the three to pick up his glass and go. Before he went, he spoke his mind. "Just at the moment," he said, "I can't stomach sight, sound or stench of a Nazi." He walked out and his compatriots followed him.

There were more Germans in the vestibule. Germans were crowding through the public rooms into the dining-room. Some sort of celebratory luncheon was about to take place. Galpin, trying to escape them, marched on, drink in hand, until he found the garden – a refuge for the routed.

The next day the Germans were back again in the bar. Apparently they had come to stay. Galpin returned to the garden: anyone who wanted him was told they could find him there. Most of the people who came in search of news had not known before that the hotel garden existed.

Galpin now spent most of his day there. It was there that his agents brought him news of Allied defeats and an occasional item of Rumanian news, such as the enforced resignation of Gafencu, the pro-British Foreign Minister, whose mother had been an Englishwoman. Other people came and went. As the situation, growing worse, became their chief preoccupation, they began to sit down and wait for news; each day they stayed longer and longer. They were drawn together by the one thing they held in common – their nationality. Because of it, they shared suspense. The waiter, understanding their situation, did not trouble them much.

Clarence, Inchcape, Dubedat and David looked in between work and rehearsals, but not, of course, Guy and Yakimov. It was thought to be a sign of those strange times that the English, the most admired and privileged, the dominating influence in a cosmopolitan community, should be meeting in so unlikely a place.

The summer was established now. The city had come out of doors anticipating three months or more of unbroken fine weather. The heat would eventually force it in again, but for the moment the open air cafés were crowded all day.

Galpin had taken over as his own a large, rough, white-painted table that stood by the fountain in the centre of the garden. When Harriet arrived from her cinema matinée, she found installed there with Galpin and Screwby the three old ladies who always formed the afternoon nucleus of the group. These were retired governesses who lived by giving English lessons. They took classes for Guy in the morning and for the rest of the day had nothing to do but face disaster. They chose to face it in company. They greeted Harriet like an old friend.

As she sat down, she asked, as everyone always asked on arrival: "Any news?"

Galpin said: "There's a rumour that Churchill has made a statement. It may be relayed later."

The three old ladies had ordered tea. Harriet took some with them. She was sitting, as she usually sat, nearest to the stone boy who poured his ewer of water into a stone basin. At first she had been irritated by this monotonous tinkle, then, recognising in it a symbol of their own anxiety, she adopted it into her own mind – a vehicle of release. It had become a part of these hot, lime-scented improbable summer days in which they learnt of one defeat after another. She knew she would never forget it.

"Very nice tea," said Miss Turner, the eldest lady, who usually spoke only to mention the household of a wealthy Rumanian whose children she had educated. She mentioned it now: "We used to have tea like this in the old days. The Prince was most generous in every way. He never stinted the nursery – and that's rare, I can tell you. When I retired he gave me a pension – not a very big pension, it's true; I could not expect it. But adequate. He was a most thoughtful, perceptive man for a Rumanian. He used to say to me: 'Miss Turner, I can see that you were born a lady.'" She turned her pale, insignificant, little face towards her neighbour Miss Truslove, and nodded in satisfaction at the Prince's perception. She then gave a pitying glance at the third woman, to whom she always referred, behind her back, as 'poor Mrs. Ramsden', for she had long made it clear to everyone that the fact she had been 'born a lady' placed her in a category of human being higher than that occupied by Mrs. Ramsden, who so obviously had not.

Mrs. Ramsden whispered to Harriet: "The pension's only good here, of course. She won't have a penny if we have to skedaddle."

Having listened for a week to the conversation of these women, Harriet knew that what they dreaded most was the disintegration of their adopted world. Everything they had was here. Such relatives as remained to them in England had forgotten them. If they were driven out of Rumania, they would find themselves without friends, homes, status or money.

"I haven't got a pension," said Mrs. Ramsden, "but I've got me savings. All invested here. I'll stay here. Whatever happens, I'll take me chance." A stout woman, noted for her enormous feathered hats, she was the most lively of the three. She had come to Bucharest when widowed, after the First World War. She had never gone home again. She frequently told the table: "I'm sixty-nine. You'd never believe it, but I am."

Now she said: "When Woolley packed us all off last September, I was that home-sick, I cried my eyes out every night. Istanbul is a dirty hole. I'd never trust meself there again. Might end up in one of them hair-eems." She brought her hand down heavily on the knee of Miss Truslove and suddenly shouted: "Whoops!"

Miss Truslove was looking disturbed. In her mournful little voice, she said: "I wouldn't care to stay on here, not with a lot of Germans about."

"Oh," said Mrs. Ramsden, "you never know your luck."

Galpin had at first seemed resentful of Mrs. Ramsden and her vitality. When she first settled herself at the table, her hat shifting and shaking as though barely anchored on her head, her blouse of shot-silk creaking as though about to split, he asked discouragingly: "No private pupils this afternoon, Mrs. Ramsden?" She answered briskly: "Not one. English is out these days. Everyone's learning German."

Now he turned on her with scorn: "You don't imagine you can stay here under a German occupation, do you? Any English national fool enough to try it would find himself in Belsen double quick."

At this Miss Truslove started sniffing, but as she searched for her handkerchief, she was distracted, as was Galpin, by the appearance of the Polish girl, Wanda.

Wanda had broken with Galpin. She had lately been seen driving with Foxy Leverett in his de Dion Bouton. People, surprised at this sight, sought to explain it away. Foxy, still a frequent companion of Princess Teodorescu, had, they said, been ordered to associate with Wanda and try to persuade her to moderate the irresponsible nonsense she was sending to her paper as news. Whatever their relationship, she had been much alone since Foxy had had to give his time to the play. Now here she was, turning up in the garden, like the rest of them.

"I'll be damned!" said Galpin, his eyes staring out at Wanda so that the whole of the chocolate-brown pupil could be seen, merging at top and bottom into the bloodshot yellow of the sclerotic.

She had made something of an entry in a tight black dress and shoes with very high heels. Her bare back and arms were already burnt brown. Ignoring Galpin, she greeted Screwby. "Any news?" she asked. There was none.

The women, recognising in her the same tense consciousness of peril that united them all, moved round to make room for her. She sat, leaning forward over the table, her brow in her hand, her lank hair falling about her, and stared at Screwby. She was a silent girl, whose habit it was to fix in this way any man who interested her. She asked: "What is going to happen? What are we going to do?" as though Screwby had but to open his lips and their dilemma would be solved.

Screwby made no attempt to play the rôle allotted him. He grinned his ignorance. Galpin began to talk rather excitedly, trying to give the impression that Wanda's entry had interrupted one of his stories. He started half-way through a story Harriet had heard from him several times – how, when a newspaper-man in Albania, he had attempted to break into the summer palace and interview the Queen, who had been newly delivered of a child.

"I wasn't going to be kept out by that ridiculous little toy army round the gates," he said.

"And did you see her?" Mrs. Ramsden played up to him.

"No. They threw me out three times. Me – who'd gone round Sussex collecting two pints of mother's milk a day for the Ickleford quads."

Wanda's silent presence made Galpin's talk more aggressive

and grotesque. As he talked, he watched her, his eyes standing from his head like aniseed balls. She ignored him for an hour, then rose and went. He stared after her glumly. "Poor thing," he said. "I feel sorry for her. Really I do! She hasn't a friend in the place."

They stayed on in the garden until the evening, when the scent of lime was strongest. Galpin had his portable wireless-set and repeatedly tried to get the promised report of Churchill's speech. The bats were darting about overhead. Mrs. Ramsden bent down, frightened for her hat.

"They have to be cut out if they get in," she said, adding: "But it's not just *them*: it's what they leave behind."

The trees grew dark beneath a sky sheened like a silver plate. Unlike most other café gardens, the hotel garden was not illuminated. The only light came from the hotel windows. The possibilities of the garden had never been exploited. Grass grew in tufts from the pebbled floor. No one bothered to brush from the tables the withering lime-flowers. Except for a few clandestine Rumanian couples who sat where they would be least observed, the English usually had the place to themselves.

At last the speech began. The Rumanian couples rose out of the shadows and moved silently forward to hear Churchill promise that England would never surrender. "We shall fight on the beaches," he said. "We shall fight in the fields."

Mrs. Ramsden bowed her face down into her hands. Her hat fell off and rolled unnoticed under the table.

Each day the crowd round the German Bureau window saw the broad arrows of the German advance stretch farther into France. One crossed the Somme and veered south towards Paris. The spectators said that surely, some time soon, there must be a stop. No one could contemplate the loss of Paris.

Harriet passed the window on her way to Bella's flat. She need not have gone up the Calea Victoriei or, going that way, she could have kept to the other pavement. Instead she brushed through the crowd, giving the arrows a glance which was meant to be indifferent, and went on with her head in the air.

Bella, as Harriet entered her drawing-room, cried: "What do you think?" giving Harriet, for a second, a pang of hope, but Bella's excitement was merely a state of mind produced by her success as Helen. All she had to say was: "They've still got that portrait of Chamberlain hanging up at the club. Him and his flower Safety. I called in the servants and ordered them to take it down at once. I made them put it face to the wall in the toilet."

The dressmaker was delivering the woman's costumes, and Bella had insisted that Harriet come to see the final fitting.

The dress, made from cheap white voile from which peasant women made their blouses, was of classical simplicity. Bella had been displeased to find all the female characters were to dress alike. She wanted to have her own costume made, contemplating something rather fine in slipper satin. Now, having to put on the voile dress, she thrust out her lower lip and walked to and fro before the glass of her gigantic wardrobe, giving petulant little tugs at the bodice and skirt.

The dressmaker, on her knees, sat back on her heels and watched. She had been the cheapest Harriet could find – a tiny creature, very thin, smelling of mouldy bread. Her face, which had one cheek full and one caught-in like a deformed apple, was dark yellow and heavily moustached. She twitched nervously when Bella paused near her and, raising her hands appealingly, began to talk. Ignoring her, Bella said: "Well, all I can say is, we're going to look like a lot of vestal virgins. Of course, I've got plenty of jewellery – but the others! I don't know, I'm sure."

"Must you wear jewellery?"

"My dear, I am Helen of Troy. I am a queen." She turned sideways, drew back her head and, with a stately and reflective air, observed the line of her fine bosom and her bare, round, white arm. The dress had an elegance and perfection scarcely to be found among the best English work: "I think we need a little colour – a square of chiffon. A big hankie, perhaps. A nice blue for me, or perhaps a gold. Other colours for the other girls."

Bella's face had softened, but Harriet felt depressed. She saw her designs now as stark and insipid. She felt she had spoilt the play. The dressmaker tried to speak again. Harriet asked:

"What does she want?"

"She wants to be paid."

Harriet began getting out the money. Bella said: "She's asking a thousand *lei*. Give her eight hundred."

"But a thousand is nothing. It's barely ten shillings."

"She doesn't know that. She'll take eight hundred. A Rumanian would give her half that."

Harriet had nothing smaller than a thousand-*lei* note. The woman accepted it with a show of bashful reluctance, but as soon as it was in her hand she bolted to the door. Bella, near the door, shut it before she could reach it, then sternly demanded the two hundred *lei* change. The woman, her face drawn, whined like a professional beggar, then began to weep. Bella held out her hand, unrelenting.

Harriet said: "*Bella!* She's earned her money. We don't want a row over a couple of bob. Let her go."

Bella, startled by this appeal, moved from the door and the woman fled. They could hear her scrabbling with a lock, then, as she went, leaving the front door open, the click of her heels as she sped down the marble staircase.

"Really!" Bella grumbled in self-excuse. "You can't trust them an inch. They always take advantage of foreigners. If you'd had as much to do with them as I have, you'd be just as sick of them."

Before Harriet went, they found the dressmaker had abandoned the parcel of costumes which she was supposed to deliver to the other female players.

"There, look at that!" said Bella. "We'll have to get a man to take it to the University."

"I'll take it," said Harriet.

"No, no." Bella held it firmly. "I'll take it," she said, "I'm not ashamed to be seen carrying a parcel."

When Clarence drove her back to the knitting factory, Harriet found the tights completed and exactly as she had ordered. On the way back he called again at the Polish store and came out with an armful of shirts and underwear. He put these on her lap. "For Guy," he said.

"Why wouldn't you give me these before?"

"Because you were being so bloody-minded. Don't you realise – if you treated me properly, you could get anything in the world you wanted from me?"

That afternoon, when Harriet sat with the others in the Athénée Palace garden, the news of the Italian declaration of war on the Allies was brought out by an Italian waiter who sometimes served them. He beamed over the English faction at the table, saying several times: "You are surprise, eh? You are surprise?"

Galpin replied: "We are not surprised. We're only surprised

there aren't more of you hungry hyenas trying to get in on someone else's kill."

The waiter did not understand or, if he did, he was unaffected.
He merely said: "Now it is we, the Italians, who will go abroad to
look at picture galleries." He gave a flick of his cloth at the lime-
flowers on the table and went off singing a snatch, laughing on a
high note of triumph.

26

THE DRESS REHEARSAL of *Troilus and Cressida* was to take place after the theatre closed on the night of Thursday, the 13th of June. From then until midnight on Friday the theatre and its staff were hired by the English players. Harriet was invited to this final rehearsal, which was called for eleven p.m.

Clarence, who was taking her out to supper, called for her in the early evening. He said: "There's some sort of scare on. The police are stopping people and examining their papers."

"What are they looking for?"

"Spies, I suppose."

The crowds were out walking as usual in the streets. Police were moving among them in sky-blue knots of three or four. Police vans stood at the kerbs. No one seemed much alarmed. The situation was too desolating to cause excitement.

For Bucharest, the fall of France was the fall of civilisation. France was an ideal for all of those who struggled against their peasant origin. All culture, art and fashion, liberal opinion and concepts of freedom were believed to come from France. With France lost, there would be no stay or force against savagery. Except for a handful of natural fascists, no one really believed in the New Order. The truth was evident even to those who had invested in Germany: the victory of Nazi Germany would be the victory of darkness. Cut off from Western Europe, Rumania would be open to persecution, bigotry, cruelty, superstition and tyranny. There was no one to save her now.

An atmosphere of acute sadness overhung the city, something near despair. Indeed, it was despair. Harriet and Clarence drove up to the Chaussée in what seemed the last sunset of the world.

The *grădinăs*, that all winter had been a waste of snow, were alive now with lights and music. Here there was an attempt to believe that life was going on as usual. People were strolling beneath the chestnuts and limes that, in full leaf, were still un- blemished by the summer heat. Harriet and Clarence left the car and joined the crowd, walking as far as the Arc de Triomphe. Around them they could hear, in several languages, expression of the bewilderment they felt themselves. People were asking one another what had happened inside France. What confusion among the French forces, what failure of spirit, had enabled an enemy to make this rapid advance? "It is the new Germany," said a woman. "No one can withstand it."

Clarence laughed shortly and said: "Steffaneski's gloating a bit. He said he had to hear enough about the three weeks' war in Poland. Now we can reflect on the fact that Holland and Belgium have capitulated and the English been forced out of Europe all within eighteen days. He doesn't give France another week."

"What do you think?" Harriet asked.

"I don't know." Clarence spoke slowly, putting up a show of reflective calm. "The Germans reached the Marne in the last war. The French fought like madmen to save Paris. They went to the front in taxis; every man in Paris turned out; and the line held. It could happen again."

As they approached the Arc de Triomphe, the crowds thinned. Three little peasant girls, not yet in their teens, wearing embroidered dresses and flowers in their hair, suddenly appeared in front of them, and, dancing backwards, began chanting something at Clarence. Harriet thought they were begging, but they were not using the beggar's whine, and they occasionally gave Harriet mischievous side-glances of great liveliness.

"What do they want?" she asked.

"Why," said Clarence, "they're offering themselves, of course. They're whores."

"They can't be. They're children."

Clarence shrugged. With his chin down, his lower lip thrust out, he looked from under his brows at the girls who were dancing before him, sometimes scattering apart and sometimes bunching together and giggling at whatever they were suggesting.

"They're a lot more cheerful than most peasants," Harriet said, laughing.

Clarence grunted. "They haven't yet learnt what life is like."

"It's odd they should approach you when I'm here."

"They're inexperienced. They know no better."

Aware they were being discussed, the girls shrieked with laughter, but they had begun to look about them for more promising material. Seeing a group of men together in the distance, they suddenly ran off, squeaking among themselves like a flock of starlings.

Harriet, her mind elsewhere, said: "That was rather amusing."

"You think so!" Clarence sombrely asked.

They went to one of the smaller garden restaurants, where the dusk was clotting in the trees. It was the time of the year when the evenings were most delightful – as warm as summer but still scented and moist with vegetation. Out here, beyond the houses, the whole sweep of the sky was visible from the iris-blue of the horizon up to the zenith, that was the rich, bloomed purple of a grape. There were a few stars of great size and brilliance.

A small orchestra was playing in the garden. When it came to a stop, neighbouring orchestras could be heard wailing and sobbing in response like birds. Somewhere in the distance Florica rose to her top note. But the music soothed no one. The diners glanced from table to table, aware of themselves and those about them, all gathered helplessly here in a time of disaster. Only the lovers at secluded tables remained untouched in their private worlds outside the flow of time.

Clarence sighed and said: "I wonder what will become of us. We may never get home again. I imagine your parents are pretty worried."

"I haven't any parents," said Harriet. "At least, none to speak of. They divorced when I was very small. They both remarried and neither found it convenient to have me. My Aunt Penny brought me up. I was a nuisance to her, too, and when I was naughty she used to say: 'No wonder your mummy and daddy don't love you.' In fact, all I have is here."

She wondered what it was she had. Looking up through the leaves at the rich and lustrous sky, she felt resentment of Guy because he was not here. She told herself he was a man who could never be present when needed. This was a time they should be together. Looking at the budding canna lilies and breathing in the scent of the box, she thought she should be sharing with Guy these enchantments that gave so keen an edge to suspense.

They had ordered their food. When the wine waiter came, Clarence said: "Well, if we die tomorrow, we can at least drink well." He chose an expensive Tokay.

Harriet thought that, after all, she was not alone. She had someone. It was a pity she could feel no more for Clarence than that. It was, she thought, a charade of a relationship, given an added dimension by the uncertainty in which they existed. It had to serve for what she missed with Guy. And did Guy realise she missed anything at all?

She wondered if he had any true awareness of the realities of life. That morning Dobson had rung the flat to say that British subjects must get transit visas for all neighbouring countries against a possible sudden evacuation. Guy said: "You'll have to get them. I'm much too busy with the play." She felt his escape from reality the less excusable because it was he who, in their few pre-war days together, had been the advocate of an anti-fascist war, a war that would, he knew, come down like a knife between him and his friends in England. He had often quoted: "So I drink your health before the gun-butt raps upon the door." Well, here was the gun-butt – and where was Guy? He would be dragged off to Belsen protesting that he could not go because he was too busy.

Clarence, watching her, asked her what she was smiling at. She said: "I was thinking of Guy." After a pause, she asked him: "Did you know that Guy once thought of marrying Sophie to give her a British passport?"

"Surely not?"

"He *thought* of it. But I doubt if he would ever have done it. He might be a natural teacher but he's not taking on, on a permanent basis, the teacher-pupil relationship. No, when it came to marriage, he chose someone he thought would not make too many demands. Perhaps the trouble is, I make too few."

Clarence looked at her keenly but his only comment was to say in a tone of high complaint: "Guy picks up with the most extraordinary people. Take Yakimov, for instance. Now, there's a mollusc on the hull of life, a no-man's-land of the soul. I doubt if Guy will ever shake him off. You've got him for life now."

Harriet, refusing to be upset, said: "I think Guy saw him as a subject for improvement. He could turn him into something, even if it were only an actor. You know what Guy is like. I've heard you say he is a saint."

"He may be a sort of saint but he's also a sort of fool. You don't believe me? You'll find I'm right. He can't see through people as you can. Don't be misled by him."

Harriet said: "He's not a fool, but it's true, he can suffer fools.

That's his strength. Because of that, he'll never have a shortage of friends."

"There's a streak of the exhibitionist in Guy," said Clarence. "He likes to feel himself at the centre. He likes to have a following."

"Well, he certainly has got a following."

"A following of fools."

"That's the only sort anyone can hope to have. The discriminating are lonely. Look at me. When Guy is occupied, I have no one but you."

Clarence smiled, taking this as a compliment.

The fiddler from the orchestra was wandering round playing at each table in turn. When he reached Clarence and Harriet, he bowed with significant smiles, certain they were lovers. He struck his bow across the strings and, working himself into an immediate frenzy, produced poignant howls from his instrument. It was all over in a moment, a rapid orgasm, then he bowed again, and Clarence gave him a glass of wine. He held up the glass first to Clarence, then to Harriet, congratulating them – on what? Probably on their non-existent passion.

Clarence's beautiful, gentle mouth sank sadly as he gazed into his glass. When he had drunk enough, Harriet noted, forbearance took the place of self-criticism. He now felt love and pity for his own sufferings.

She said: "You should get married."

"One can't just marry for marrying's sake."

"There's always Brenda."

"Brenda is twelve hundred miles away," he said. "I don't know when I'll see her again, and I don't know that I want to. She isn't what I need."

Harriet did not ask him what he needed, but he was now drunk enough to tell her: "I need someone strong, fierce, intolerant and noble." He added: "Someone like you."

She laughed, rather uneasy at so direct an approach. "I don't recognise myself. I'm not strong. I suppose I'm intolerant – a bad fault. I have no patience with people. Sophie told Guy he had married a monster."

"Oh, Sophie!" Clarence spoke the name with contempt.

Harriet said: "I sometimes think I shall end up a lonely, ragged, mad old woman trailing along the gutter."

"Why should you?" Clarence tartly asked. "You've got Guy. I suppose you'll always have Guy."

"And he'll always have the rest of the world."

When they drove up the Calea Victoriei, they saw that the illuminations had been switched off in the Cişmigiu. The park, where people walked in summer until all hours, was now silent and deserted, a map of darkness in the heart of the subdued city.

Clarence said: " 'The Paris of the East' mourning her opposite number."

In contrast, the German Bureau window was brilliant with white neon, and still drew its audience. They saw, as they passed, the red arrows, open-jawed like pincers, almost encircling the site of Paris.

When they entered the theatre, they entered an atmosphere so removed from the outside tension that it might have been that of another planet. Every light was lit in the foyer. People were hurrying about, all, it seemed, so hypnotised by Guy and his production that reality had lost substance for them. They were possessed by a creative excitement, anticipating fulfilment, not defeat.

Even Clarence was caught, as he entered, into this atmosphere. He said: "I must leave you. Guy wants us dressed and ready by eleven o'clock," and he hurried off into a maze of passages to find the dressing room assigned to him.

Harriet, after standing uncertainly awhile, went in search of a familiar face, but the people she met brushed past her, too wrapped up in their players' world to recognise her. Only Yakimov, on his way to the stage in pink tights and a cloak of rose coloured velvet, stopped and said: "What's the matter, dear girl? You look worried."

"Everyone's worried," she said. "The Germans have almost reached Paris."

"Really!" He looked concerned a moment, then someone called him, his face cleared, and he left her for more important matters.

She hoped she might be needed to advise on the wearing of the costumes, but she was only the designer. The wardrobe mistress, a student, pins in her mouth, needle and cotton in hand, was surrounded by enquiries and complaints. Harriet stood beside her a while, hoping to be consulted, but the girl, with a brief shy smile, indicated that she could cope very well on her own.

Harriet had never encouraged the students. She had, indeed,

resented their possessiveness and their demands on Guy's time, so now she knew she had only herself to blame if they received her with respect rather than cordiality.

She came at length on Bella, who was sharing a dressing-room with Andromache and Cassandra. The girls were dressing unobtrusively in the background while Bella, already dressed, sat before the glass, critically yet complacently examining her face, that was richly coloured in creams, buffs, pinks and browns. Her hair, that had grown more golden since Harriet last saw it, was caught into a golden tube and hung in a tail down her back.

Harriet said: "I've brought the chiffons."

"Oh, darling!" Without taking her eyes from the glass, Bella stretched a hand in Harriet's direction and wriggled her fingers. "How sweet of you!" She threw her voice back to the girls: "*Atenţiune!* Doamna Pringle has brought us some gorgeous chiffons." Bella, it seemed, had taken on with her status of actress the elevated camaraderie of the green-room.

When Harriet had distributed the chiffons, she made her way back to the immense auditorium, with its gilt and claret-coloured plush, that was lit only by the light from the stage. She took a seat in the row behind Fitzsimon, Dobson and Foxy Leverett, who were dressed ready for the rehearsal. Dobson and Foxy were advising Fitzsimon that he must ensure his success in the leading rôle by padding out the front of his tights.

"– certainly stuffing in some cotton-wool," said Foxy, gleeful at the thought. "The girls here like to see a teapot."

On the stage Guy, dressed as Nestor, but not made up, was haranguing a line of peasants who blinked bashfully into the glare from the footlights.

Harriet whispered to Dobson: "What is going on?"

"They're the stage-hands," said Dobson. "Guy spent the afternoon explaining what was required of them and putting them through it, but just now, when he started the rehearsal, they were hopeless. They're just indifferent, of course. They think anything will do for a pack of foreigners."

Driven into one of his rare fits of anger, Guy had lined the men up before him. Some were in dark, shabby suits like indigent clerks, others in a mixture of city and peasant dress; one man, so thin that he had an appearance of fantastic height, wore on the point of his head a conical peasant cap. Some stood grinning in a sort of foggy wonder at being addressed, and forcibly addressed, by a foreigner in their own language. One or two looked dignified and pained: the rest stood in a stupor, any language, even their own, being barely comprehensible to them.

From what she could catch of his words, Harriet gathered that Guy was impressing on the men that tomorrow evening a great company of Rumanian Princes, aristocrats and statesmen, foreign diplomats and distinguished personages of every nationality and kind, was to be present. This was to be a tremendous occasion when every man must do not only his best, but more than his best. He must achieve a triumph that would stun the world with admiration. The honour of this great national theatre was at stake; the honour of Bucharest was at stake – nay, the honour of the whole of Rumania was in their hands.

As Guy's voice rose, the three Legation men stopped talking among themselves and listened.

The stage-hands shuffled and coughed a bit as the force of their responsibility was revealed to them. One, a short, stout, ragged peasant with a look of congenital idiocy, grinned, unable to take Guy seriously. Guy pointed at him. "You!" he cried. "What do you do?"

The man was a scene-shifter.

A job of supreme importance, said Guy. A job on which depended the success or failure of the whole production. Guy looked to him for his full support. The peasant grinned from side to side, but, meeting no response from his fellows, his grin faded.

"And now," said Guy, stern but satisfied that by the force of his personality he had made them attend to him: "Now . . ." and towering with his height and bulk over even the tallest of them, he began to go again through the drill of scene and lighting changes which he had worked out.

Harriet stared up at Guy, her heart melting painfully in her breast, and asked herself what it was for – this expense of energy and creative spirit. To produce an amateur play that would fill the theatre for one afternoon and one evening and be forgotten in a week. She knew she could never give herself to such an ephemeral thing. If she had her way, she would seize on Guy and canalise his zeal to make a mark on eternity. But he was a man born to expend himself like a whirlwind – and, indeed, what could one do but love him?

At midnight, while the stage-hands were still being put through their duties, Harriet went home to bed. She heard Guy and Yakimov return some time in the middle of the night. They were gone again before breakfast. That morning there was to be a final rehearsal in the theatre.

When she left the house, people seemed to be in a state of subdued confusion. They were wandering about asking each other what was happening. The red arrows had come to a stop in the window of the German Bureau. Were the German forces at a standstill? Some thought there was a lull for strategic reasons. Others said the French had pulled themselves together and were holding the line round Paris. Whatever the news might be, the Rumanian authorities, 'to avert panic', were withholding information and had cut the international lines.

Harriet went to the Athénée Palace garden. No one there had much to say. Even Galpin was silenced by the sense that they were approaching an end.

"What's going to happen to us all?" Miss Truslove asked out of the great nothingness of their thoughts.

"That," said Galpin, "is anybody's guess."

After an interval, during which the fountain's trickle was as monotonous as silence, Mrs. Ramsden said: "Well, there's the play tonight. That's something to look forward to."

"Do you think anyone will come?" asked Harriet, fearful now that there would be no audience at all.

"Of course they will," said Mrs. Ramsden. "Sir Montagu will be there. The Woolleys are going. Oh, everyone's turning up. It's *the thing*, I can tell you."

Miss Truslove said: "It's nice to have something to distract us."

The others nodded agreement. Even Galpin and Screwby had booked seats.

"Haven't been inside a theatre for months," said Galpin.

Screwby said: 'Haven't been in one for years."

"An English play," said Mrs. Ramsden. "For us here, that's quite an intellectual treat." She sighed and said: "I do like an evening at the theatre."

The morning was hot and growing hotter. The sun rose until it was poised directly over the lime trees. The English group at the table, meshed in a shifting, glimmering pattern of light and shade, was bemused with heat and half-sleep.

Harriet, lolling in her chair beside the fountain, lost sense of the garden altogether and seemed to pass into an English landscape of fields, some fallow, some furrowed, all colourless through mist. A few elms rose out of the hedges into a milky sky. The scene was so vivid, she shivered slightly in the English air, then a lime-flower dropped on to the table before her and she was returned, startled, to the sunlight. She picked up the flower and stared at it to cover the pricking in her eyes.

She remembered her arrival in Rumania, and her first long days of sunlight. That had been a difficult time, yet she thought of it nostalgically because the war had barely begun. She saw herself as she had been, nervous, suspicious and isolated among strangers; jealous of Guy's friends and of his belief that he owed his chief allegiance to the outside world. Unmarried, she had been a personality in her own right. Married, she saw herself coming in, if at all, somewhere in Guy's wake.

It occurred to her that it was only during these last weeks she had become reconciled to the place. She had faced uncertainty without Guy. Those who faced it with her had become, through the exalted concord of their common fears, old friends.

She stayed with them until early evening, then went back to her flat to dress for the evening performance.

27

ONLY STUDENTS had been admitted to the matinée performance of *Troilus and Cressida*: the seats were cheap. For the evening performance the price of seats was such that wonder had been aroused, bringing in a great many rich Rumanians and Jews who could not afford not to be seen in the audience. The profits were to be contributed towards a scheme devised by Guy and Dubedat for the housing of poor students. The fact roused more wonder than the price of the seats, for few Rumanians could believe that a group of people, even English people, would work so hard and so long at no profit to themselves.

Nikko, having formally asked Guy's permission to escort Harriet to the play, called for her at half-past seven. In his waisted dinner-jacket, with his beautifully tied bow, he looked like a dark, angry little male cat. He seemed ready to hiss. Instead he smiled brilliantly and kissed her hand.

"Harry-ott, a token of esteem!" He presented her with a rose from the King's flower-shop. "I do not often go there. I would not myself encourage a King who is not only a gangster but a common shopkeeper, but tonight, when I passed the window, I saw the rose and thought of Harry-ott."

He went on smiling, but he was on edge and, as Harriet poured him a drink, he burst out: "I am not one to speak of money. Like the English, I think it not *chic* to speak of money, but . . ." he drew up his shoulders and spread his hands like fins. "For weeks I am grass widow. I have no wife – and now what do they say? 'Domnul Niculescu, please pay five thousand *lei* to see Doamna Niculescu walk upon a stage.'" He gave a gulp of disgusted laughter and tried to look amused. "It is funny, is it not?"

Harriet said: "There were no free seats. The proceeds are for charity."

"The poor students, you mean? Ah, Harry-ott, cast half an eye around. There are too many poor students. Every son of a peasant-born priest or schoolmaster must go to the University. All seek to be lawyers. Believe me, there are already too many lawyers. There is not the work for them. What we need are artisans." Here he interrupted himself: "But this is no time for solemn talk. I take a beautiful lady to a great occasion. It is rather a time for levity. Come, the taxi awaits."

In the taxi, he asked: "You have heard the news?"

"No. Is there news?"

"Madame has demanded a speed-up of the Drucker trial. She is afraid the German influence may squash it. A trial could be embarrassing to Germany."

"So the German influence may save Drucker?"

"Indeed not. Nothing can save Drucker. For him, if it is not Bistriţa, then it will be Dachau. He is no use now to Germany or anyone else."

"Then I do not understand – what is Madame afraid of?"

"Without a trial, his oil holdings cannot be seized by the State. They would remain the property of Doamna Drucker."

Harriet was thankful to see the theatre foyer full. "A brilliant audience," said Nikko as they took their seats. He rose frequently to bow from the waist in this direction and that, his bared teeth white beneath the black bar of his moustache. Between bows, he indicated to Harriet the titles about them. Among these were a great many princes and princesses. "Of great family," whispered Nikko, "but almost all on their uppers. I wonder who paid for their seats!" Among them was Princess Teodorescu with her Baron.

"Ah, Harry-ott," said Nikko, "you can be proud. And reflect also, Harry-ott, we are even now the ally of England. We come to show sympathy."

Every seat was taken before the curtain rose. Harriet smiled about her in relief at the sight. She even smiled at Woolley, who, sitting with his arms folded high on his chest, turned his chin on to his shoulder and accorded her a brief nod.

Sir Montagu and his party appeared in the royal box. The audience rose while 'God Save the King' was played as a dirge. This was followed by the Rumanian national anthem, after which the orchestra slid into a waltz that faded with the fading of the lights. The crimson curtains glowed. Between them appeared a student, wrapped to the chin in a black cloak, who spoke the Prologue. He had been well rehearsed. As he backed out of sight, members of the audience whispered congratulations to the parents. The father half-rose to bow his acknowledgments. Harriet watched this interruption anxiously. Fortunately the rise of the curtain brought it to a stop – and there, standing languidly, hand on hip, was Fitzsimon in white and gold, padded out as Foxy Leverett had advised, his looks enhanced with a golden wig.

The audience gasped. Heads went together. A twitter of excitement passed like a breeze over the stalls. The impression was such that some of the women began to applaud before they realised what they were applauding. Fitzsimon stood with a fine air of disconsolate virility, waiting for silence. His eyes moved slowly over the women in the front rows. When satisfied by the expectant hush, he fixed his gaze on Princess Teodorescu, sighed and said:

"Call here my varlet; I'll unarm again;
Why should I war without the walls of Troy,
That find such cruel battle here within?"

No one noticed Yakimov until he asked: "Will this gear ne'er be mended?" conveying in his light, epicene voice a world of bawdy insinuation while moving towards the footlights with a gentle confidingness that was bewilderingly innocent.

The audience stirred, not knowing how to take it until Sir Montagu gave a guff of appreciation and the Rumanians relaxed. Once reassured, they took wholeheartedly to Yakimov. He, for his part, had given himself at once, never for a moment doubting their response. In little more than a moment, they loved him. After his first speeches, they were scarcely breathing for fear of missing a nuance of impropriety. The women enjoyed themselves under cover of darkness while the male laughter burst out repeatedly without restraint.

Harriet watched him intently, drawn in in spite of herself. This was 'your poor old Yaki' – the same that had entranced the dinner-table that first night in Bucharest. 'Your poor old Yaki,' she thought. 'My poor old Yaki. Anyone's poor old Yaki, providing they're doing the paying,' yet that was not wholly just, for now it was Yakimov who was making repayment. Guy had befriended him and Guy was being rewarded. Yakimov had learnt his part; he was giving himself without stint. He was helping to make Guy's production, and Harriet was thankful to him.

His exit led to a tumult of applause and comment that held up the action for several moments. Harriet remained tense, watching Fitzsimon, who accepted the delay good-humouredly. When at last he held up a hand and, smiling, said: "Peace, you ungracious clamours! peace, rude sounds!" the laugh accorded him left no doubt but that the audience was on the side of the players. Harriet felt about her the willingness to be pleased. Unless something went badly wrong there was nothing to fear.

She relaxed gradually as the scenes passed, not only without mishap, but with gathering pace. The show was succeeding with its own success and she was warmed to all those who were doing so well: Dubedat, Inchcape, David – and the men from the Legation whom she had supposed would treat the whole thing as a joke.

As for Sophie! Sophie's performance was beyond expectations. As she sauntered and swayed with little meaningful looks and gestures, letting her pink chiffon drift, like a symbol of her own sexual fragrance, about Troilus or her manservant or, indeed, any male who happened to be near, Harriet realised the girl was a born Cressida, a 'daughter of the game'. Even in her scenes with Pandarus she was not overshadowed. The two enhanced and complemented each other, a scheming partnership of niece and uncle set to devour the guileless and romantic Troilus.

Nikko turned excitedly in his seat, trying to read her name on the programme. "Who is she?" he asked. "Is it Sophie Oresanu?"

"Yes."

"But she is *charming*!"

The interval came after Pandarus had conducted the lovers to 'a chamber with a bed'.

In the bar, where Nikko had to struggle for drinks, Harriet, wedged into the crowd, listened to the comment about her. She heard mention of Clarence ("You would not think, to see him in the street, that Mr. Lawson could be so comic") and Dubedat, who, with his snivel schooled to virulence, was declared to be "*très fort*".

"And that young Dimancescu!" exclaimed a woman. "Such a beautiful English! And in manner the English aristocrat, no?" recalling Dimancescu's throw-away indifference and the wearily drooping eyelids that had been lifted once, in rapid rage, when Patroclus had missed his cue.

"And Menelaus!"

"Ah ha, Menelaus!" A titter passed among the men, for Dobson, unable in his Greek dress of skirted corselet to emulate the effect created by Foxy Leverett and Fitzsimon, had managed to suggest that, even had his dress permitted, his part called for no such display. He conveyed, with rueful and apologetic smiles that appealed to the Rumanian sense of humour, his unenviable position.

When Nikko returned to Harriet with two glasses of whisky, he was congratulated on Bella's performance. Her appearance had caused no small sensation.

One of the men said: "She looked like Venus herself." She had indeed, Harriet thought, looked like a Venus of a debased period; a great showy flower without scent.

The student who had played Paris, not very well, had been completely dwarfed by his impressive paramour as she swept to the centre of the stage, keeping her profile well in view. Yakimov, who had excelled in this scene, had carried the weight of Bella's playfulness, glossing the exchange with the ebullience of wit.

Someone in the audience, having consulted his programme, had whispered in amazement: "Is it possible this lady is a Rumanian?"

"Yes, yes," another whisper answered him and Nikko had been scarcely able to contain his pride.

Now, as he received congratulations, his face was so contracted with bliss that he seemed about to weep.

The congratulations were carried over to Harriet as those in their circle reflected on Guy's playing of the not very rewarding part of Nestor. Someone praised him with the words: "You would have thought him truly ancient," while Nikko said in wonder: "But, Harry-ott, your husband knows how to act!"

Pressed for expert opinions on this performance and that, Harriet found she could not sort out her impressions. She had been too fearful of failure and now, grateful for success, she said only: "They were all good."

There was general agreement.

"A production of genius," Nikko concluded. "We are having, I may say, our money's worth."

In the second half, as Inchcape gave himself with the full force of his histrionic irony to his exchange with Achilles, the vice-consul sniggered in the row behind Harriet and said: "By Jove, Ulysses is just old Inchcape to the life."

And there, Harriet thought, lay the strength of the production. Except for Yakimov and Guy, no one was called upon to act very much. Each player was playing himself. She had, she remembered, criticised this method of casting, yet, with the material in hand, what else would have been possible? And the audience accepted it: indeed seemed to find this heightened behaviour more impressive than acting. When the final curtain fell, the actors who received most applause were those who had been most themselves. For Yakimov there was an almost hysterical acclaim. The curtain rose and fell a dozen times, and there could be no end until Guy came forward and thanked everyone – the audience, the actors and, above all, the theatre staff, that had 'co-operated so magnificently'. When he retired, the audience began to file out.

"By Jove," said the vice-consul again, "never knew Shakespeare wrote such jolly stuff. That play had quite a story to it."

On the wave of great good humour, laughing, calling to one another, the members of the audience made their way to the street. They must have looked to the passers-by like maniacs.

Abject faces stared into the lighted foyer. Someone spoke into the happy crowd that was emerging: "Paris has fallen."

Those in front fell silent. As the news was passed back, the silence followed it. Before most people had reached the pavement, despondency had hold of them.

The vice-consul was now ahead of Harriet. His companion, a Jewess, turned to him and, making boxing movements with her little fist, she sadly asked: "Why is it you Allies cannot fight more good?"

Harriet said: "I'd forgotten Paris."

"I, too," said Nikko.

They had all forgotten Paris. Chastened, they emerged into the summer night and met reality, avoiding each others' eyes, guilty because they had escaped the last calamitous hours.

28

INCHCAPE WAS GIVING a party in his flat for the English players and those of the students who had speaking parts. Harriet and Nikko, the first to arrive at his flat, were welcomed by Pauli, who, if he had heard the news, appeared unaffected by it.

The room, with its many gold-shaded lamps and displays of tuberoses, was hot and pungent. There was nothing to drink but *ţuică* and Rumanian vermouth. The food comprised some triangles of toast spread with caviare. Harriet asked Pauli to make her an Amalfi. As he was shaking up the mixture, he told the visitors that Domnul Professor Inchcape had given him a ticket for the matinée. Although he had not understood much of the play, he had thought it all wonderful, wonderful, wonderful. He began strutting around, taking off one actor after another – the professor, and Domnul Boyd, and Domnul Pringle. He gave the impression of being a big man like Guy or David, a general in a general's cloak. He went on for a long time, entertaining Inchcape's guests in Inchcape's absence.

Harriet laughed and applauded, but her mind was on the fall of Paris. She had a sense of remoteness from the members of the cast when they arrived in jubilant mood, still caught up in the excitement that had carried them through the evening.

Nikko ran at once to his wife and caught both her hands. "*Dragă*," he cried, "but you were magnificent. Everyone was saying to me: 'How beautiful, your Bella! How rightly named!' "

There was something febrile about the laughter with which Bella accepted this praise. She turned to Harriet, ready to accept more, and Harriet said: "You have heard the news?"

"Oh, my dear, yes. Isn't it terrible!" She spoke on a high note and swept away, leaving Harriet with the certainty she had said the wrong thing.

Guy, in the midst of his company, had the vague benevolence that came of contentment and physical exhaustion. When Harriet went to him, she slid her arms round him and squeezed his waist in love and thankfulness that the play was over and his companionship would be restored to her.

She said: "The show was a tremendous success. The audience forgot all about France."

"It wasn't too bad," he agreed, his modesty that of a man well satisfied with his achievement. He went on to criticise the production. It had, he thought, been full of minor faults, but one must learn from experience. "When I do another : . ." he began.

"Oh, surely not another?"

Bewildered by her demur, he said: "But I thought you enjoyed it," and turned aside in search of more encouraging praise. He found it at once. It was being given on all sides. Harriet did her best to join in, but she was outside their union that resulted from weeks of contiguity – besides, she was in the real world, they were not. She could not emulate their high spirits.

She looked around for Nikko, but he was in attendance on his wife, growing drunk on the overflow of congratulations. She retreated to the terrace doorway and stood there, half in the room, half out, watching the clamour within.

Yakimov was wandering round, his face vacant and happy, holding out his glass to be refilled, receiving congratulations with "Dear girl, how kind," "Dear boy, what nice things you say!" but not bestowing them. He looked a little anaesthetised by his success; and so, for that matter, did the others. They were like travellers unwillingly returned from brilliant realms, not yet adjusted to their return.

The room was dividing into two groups, one centred upon Sophie, the other upon Bella. Bella had seated herself on an armchair, with Nikko on one of the arms. She plucked at Yakimov and he let himself be pulled down to her other side. Having organised the students into a semi-circle at her feet, she appeared to be holding court again, but it was really Yakimov who was the heart and centre of attention. The students gazed at him, waiting for him to speak, and when Dubedat, chewing glumly at the caviare, asked disgustedly: "What's this stuff?" and Yakimov replied: "Fish jam, dear boy," they rolled about in their delight. Encouraged, he began to rouse himself and talk. Harriet could not hear what he was saying, but she saw Bella break in on the acclaim by slapping him and saying with mock severity: "Behave yourself."

Sophie, who had changed into a black velvet evening dress but was still wearing stage make-up, was attended by all the men from the Legation and, Harriet noted rather jealously, Clarence.

Guy, David and Inchcape stood together between these groups. When Inchcape noticed Harriet alone, he crossed to her and said: "Let us go out to the terrace."

Outside, a breeze came cool and moist from the trees, and there was a scent of geraniums. The park was still in mourning, a cloudy darkness starred at the heart with the lights of the lake restaurant.

When they reached the rail and looked over it, Harriet realised that the path below was a-rustle with people walking in silence in the darkness. She began to speak of them, but Inchcape showed no inclination to listen.

"The situation's serious, of course," he said, "but we haven't much to worry about. The Germans are too busy to bother us. I think we're lucky to be here," and before Harriet could contest this optimism, he went on to ask her opinion of each performance in the play.

When Yakimov, Sophie, Guy, David, Dimancescu had been given their due, Inchcape remained expectant.

"And Dubedat was good," said Harriet.

"Remarkable!" Inchcape agreed. "He certainly knows how to exploit his natural unpleasantness."

Inchcape still waited, and Harriet, suddenly realising what was amiss, said: "And your Ulysses, of course, was tremendous – that slightly sour manner edged with wit: the tolerance of experience. People were very impressed."

"Were they, now!" Inchcape smiled down at his small, neat feet. "Of course, I hadn't much time for rehearsals."

Pauli came out on the terrace, eagerly summoning his master. Sir Montagu had arrived. Inchcape snorted and gave Harriet a wry smile that could not hide his satisfaction: "So the old charmer's turned up after all!"

He hurried inside and Harriet followed him. Sir Montagu was standing in the middle of the room, leaning on his stick. His face, dark, handsome and witty, with thick folds of skin on either side of a heavy mouth, was like the face of some distinguished old actor. He was smiling round at the girls.

Fitzsimon, on the sofa, holding Sophie in a casual clinch that she tried to make look like an embrace, suddenly saw his chief and sprang to his feet. Sophie slid to the ground. She looked furious until she saw who was the cause of her fall, then she began to rub her buttocks with rueful humour.

" 'Evening, sir," said Fitzsimon. "Good of you to patronise the show, sir."

"I must say, I enjoyed myself." Sir Montagu looked at Sophie then smiled at Fitzsimon. "Very nice," he said. "Nice, plump little partridges. Very fond of 'em m'self. Sorry to be late. I had to offer our condolences to the French."

"And how were the French, sir?" Dobson asked.

"Apologetic. The Rumanians have sent us their condolences. They think the war's over. I told them it's only just begun. No more demmed allies round our necks. Now the real fighting can begin."

During the laughter and applause that followed, Inchcape approached the Minister, who held out his hand. "Congratulations, Inchcape. Fine show. Clever fellows you've got on your staff; very clever fellows! And I must say" – he gave a long look first at Fitzsimon, then at Foxy Leverett – "I admired the mixed grill put up by the Legation."

"All my own, sir," said Fitzsimon with a smirk.

"Indeed!" Sir Montagu smiled in bland disbelief. "Very enviable, if I may say so."

Inchcape had gone to a corner cupboard. After some clinking of hidden bottles, he came back with half a tumblerful of whisky, which Sir Montagu, watched respectfully by the whole room, drained in two gulps. After that he excused himself, nodded his good-nights and limped out.

"See you to your car, sir." Dobson followed at his heels.

"Oh," screamed Sophie while the Minister was still within earshot, "*what* a sweetie-pie!"

Now, with his chief safely come and gone, Fitzsimon became animated. He went to the pianoforte and started to thump out the tune of the 'Lambeth Walk'.

Guy and David were standing playing chess on the piano-top with some valuable ivory chess-men while Inchcape hovered about them, apparently afraid something might get broken.

Clarence, his expression gentle and bemused, saw Harriet and came over to her. He was, she realised, rather drunk. He put a hand to her waist and led her out to the terrace away from the growing uproar of the room.

The students were on their feet now and dancing while Dubedat, loudly and tunelessly, bawled a München version of the 'Lambeth Walk'.

> "Adolf we say, that's easy.
>   Do as you darn well please-ee.
>   Why don't you make your way there,
>   Go there, stay there?
>
>   When the bombs begin to fall,
>   Behind our blast-proof, gas-proof wall,
>   You'll find us all,
>   Having a peace-time talk.
>
>   If you walk down Downing Street,
>   Where the Big Four always meet,
>   You'll find us all,
>   Having a peace-time talk."

Peering down over the rail at the end of the terrace, Harriet said: "Do you realise there are people still walking in the park? They don't know what's going to happen now. They're afraid to go home."

Clarence looked down on the moving darkness and said: "This is a bad time to be alone," adding, after a pause: "I need someone. I need you. You could save me."

She did not feel like discussing Clarence's personal problems just then. She said: "What do you think will happen to us? I wish we had diplomatic protection like the Legation people."

Clarence said: "According to my contract, the Council's bound to get me back to England somehow or other."

"You're fortunate," she said.

"You could come with me."

The din from the room was growing. The ferment of the party, that had been precariously balanced, tilting for moments over the verge of depression, had now righted itself. A new abandon had set in. Some of the students were stamping out a *horă* while others were clapping in time and shouting to encourage them. Fitzsimon was still at the pianoforte attempting to produce *horă* music while Sophie, beside him, sang shrill and sharp in imitation of Florica.

Harriet said: "Let's go and watch." She tried to move, but Clarence caught her elbow, determined to retain her attention. He kept repeating: "You could save me."

She laughed impatiently: "Save yourself, Clarence. You said that Guy is a fool. There may be ways in which that sort of fool is superior to you. You show your wisdom by believing in nothing. The truth is, you have nothing to offer but a wilderness."

Clarence stared at her with sombre satisfaction. "You may be right. I've said that Guy was a sort of saint. The world has not been able to tempt him. He may be something – but I'll never be able to change now."

"You're like Yakimov," said Harriet. "You belong to the past."

He shrugged. "What does it matter? We're all down the drain, anyway. Where are we going if we lose England?"

"Home. And we won't lose England."

"We won't get home. Here we are, stuck on the wrong side of Europe. Pretty soon the cash'll run out. We'll be paupers. No one will start a relief fund for us. We'll . . ."

As Clarence's voice dropped with despondency, the noise from the room was such that Harriet could scarcely hear what he was saying. Suddenly both Clarence and the music were interrupted by a Rumanian voice that screamed above everything else with a rage that was near hysteria: "*Linişte! Linişte!*"

Startled, Clarence released Harriet. As she escaped, she heard him complaining behind her: "I think you've treated me pretty badly."

When she reached the room, she saw a little ball of a woman, wearing a dressing-gown, her hair in curlers, who had entered and was storming at Inchcape's astonished guests:

"What is it you make here, you English? You have lost the war, you have lost your Empire, you have lost all – yet, like a first-class Power, you keep the house awake!"

For a moment the English were stunned by this attack, then they surged forward calling out: "We've lost nothing yet." "And we're not going to lose." "We shall win the war, you wait and see."

Bella's voice, indignant but still lady-like, rose from the back of the room. "The English have never lost a battle," she cried.

David amended this with an amused reasonableness: "That's not quite true. We lose battles, but we do not lose wars."

This authoritative statement was taken up by the others. "We never lose wars," they shouted, "we never lose wars."

The woman, unnerved, took a step backwards, then retreated rapidly, as Rumanians tended to retreat before assault. When she reached the hall door, she bolted through it and Pauli, laughing, slammed it after her.

"Rule Britannia," commanded Fitzsimon as he re-seated himself at the pianoforte.

There were no more interruptions. The party went on until daybreak. By that time the park was deserted and silence had come down over Inchcape's room. A number of guests had left. The rest, encouraged by Inchcape, prepared to follow them. Yakimov had slipped off his arm-chair and was lying unconscious on the floor. Inchcape agreed to let him stay there until he waked, so the Pringles left with David.

As they reached the street, the dawn was whitening the roofs. Wide-eyed and wakeful from lack of sleep, Harriet suggested they stroll up to the German Bureau and see what had been done to the map of France. When they reached the window, they saw the dot of Paris hidden by a swastika that squatted like a spider, black on the heart of the country.

They stood staring at it a while. Soberly, Guy asked: "What do you think will happen here? What are our chances?"

David pursed his mouth, preparing to talk, then he gave his snuffling laugh. "As Klein says, it will be very interesting! The Rumanians had hoped to do what they did last time – keep a foot in both camps. But the Germans have put the lid on that. What they're organising here is one gigantic fifth column. The King hoped to rally popular support for the defence of the country, but too late. He's lost the trust of everyone. The régime cannot last."

"You think there'll be a revolution?"

"Something of the sort. But, worse than that, the country itself will fall apart. Rumania cannot preserve her great fortune. She has been too foolish and too weak. As for our chances . . ." He laughed again. "They depend on knowing when to get away."

Guy took Harriet's arm. "We'll get away all right."

She said: "We'll get away because we must. The great fortune is life. We must preserve it."

They turned from the map of France with the swastika at its centre and walked home through the empty streets.

A Selected List of Mandarin Classics

While every effort is made to keep prices low, it is sometimes necessary to increase prices at short notice. Mandarin Paperbacks reserves the right to show new retail prices on covers which may differ from those previously advertised in the text or elsewhere.

The prices shown below were correct at the time of going to press.

☐	7493 1392 7	**The Good Companions**	J. B. Priestley £6.99
☐	7493 1391 9	**Angel Pavement**	J. B. Priestley £6.99
☐	7493 1393 5	**Lost Empires**	J. B. Priestley £5.99
☐	7493 0658 0	**A Question of Upbringing**	Anthony Powell £3.99
☐	7493 0656 4	**A Buyer's Market**	Anthony Powell £3.99
☐	7493 1200 9	**What's Become of Waring?**	Anthony Powell £5.99
☐	7493 0343 3	**The Moon and Sixpence**	Somerset Maugham £4.99
☐	7493 0422 7	**Cakes and Ale**	Somerset Maugham £3.99
☐	7493 0344 1	**Of Human Bondage**	Somerset Maugham £5.99
☐	7493 0134 1	**To Kill a Mockingbird**	Harper Lee £4.99
☐	7493 9054 9	**Goodbye to Berlin**	Christopher Isherwood £4.99
☐	7493 9900 7	**Single Man**	Christopher Isherwood £4.99
☐	7493 0461 8	**The Balkan Trilogy**	Olivia Manning £9.99
☐	7493 0562 2	**School for Love**	Olivia Manning £4.50
☐	7493 1198 3	**The Doves of Venus**	Olivia Manning £4.99
☐	7493 1199 1	**A Romantic Hero**	Olivia Manning £4.99

All these books are available at your bookshop or newsagent, or can be ordered direct from the address below. Just tick the titles you want and fill in the form below.

Cash Sales Department, PO Box 5, Rushden, Northants NN10 6YX.
Fax: 0933 410321 : Phone 0933 410511.

Please send cheque, payable to 'Reed Book Services Ltd.', or postal order for purchase price quoted and allow the following for postage and packing:

£1.00 for the first book, 50p for the second; **FREE POSTAGE AND PACKING FOR THREE BOOKS OR MORE PER ORDER.**

NAME (Block letters) ....

ADDRESS ....

....

☐ I enclose my remittance for ....

☐ I wish to pay by Access/Visa Card Number

Expiry Date

Signature ....

Please quote our reference: MAND